Gillian Slovo w.................................e has spent all of her adult life. She lives in London with her partner and her daughter. She has written eight novels and a family memoir, *Every Secret Thing*.

Also by Gillian Slovo

Morbid Symptoms
Death By Analysis
Death Comes Staccato
Ties of Blood
Façade
Catnap
Close Call
Every Secret Thing
The Betrayal

red dust

GILLIAN SLOVO

VIRAGO

A *Virago* Book

First published by Virago Press 2000

This edition published by Virago Press 2002

Copyright © Gillian Slovo 2000

The moral right of the author has been asserted

A CIP catalogue record for this book
is available from the British Library

ISBN 1 86049 915 5

Typeset in Berkeley by M Rules
Printed and bound in Great Britain by
Clays Ltd, St Ives plc

Virago Press
An imprint of
Time Warner Books
Brettenham House
Lancaster Place
London WC2E 7EN

www.virago.co.uk

Is not the truth the truth?

Henry IV part I, ii.4

1

SARAH GLANCED DOWN, watching as her black suede ankle boots clipped up the subway stairs. She was smiling. No matter how often she sat in her prosecutor's seat waiting for a jury to deliver its verdict she would always find herself gripped by tension. Now the case was over, she felt almost light-hearted with relief. Coming out of the subway at 79th Street, her smile broadened. Not only had her victory buoyed her up, but on days like this she would experience anew the joy of being in New York.

She turned right on Broadway. As she moved out of the protection of the Apthorp, the wind cut into her. She didn't mind. This was one of those dry February days she relished, the sky a clear ice blue, the air crisp and sharp, highlighting

the city's hard outlines. She walked briskly, thinking of the
malt she would pour herself when she got home. Broadway
was so wide, she thought, and so solid with its for once
smooth gliding traffic, its stores summoning passers-by into
glutted end-of-season sales and its markets with their laid-out
wares. She stopped outside one and looked over the polished,
perfect fruit and glistening vegetables, clean and healthy
under the light, all varieties despite the season. It was all so
luxurious and so different from that bleak, dry place where
she'd been born.

That thought took her aback. It had been such a long time
since she had used that other place as a reference point.
Nowadays the sharp, clean outlines of this city felt so natural
that, on the rare occasions when memories of her home town
occurred, it was almost as if they conjured up a world that
had lost all meaning. Taking a basket, she chose a dark green
bunch of arugula, a couple of huge, shining, beef tomatoes
and some Chinese cabbage.

She was outside her apartment door, juggling keys and bags,
when she heard the phone ringing. She didn't bother hurrying. She always needed a moment of solitary reflection after
a case finished and she knew that whoever it was trying to
contact her would either leave a message or call back later.
She slipped the key into the lock and pushed open the door,
dropping her bags, unwinding her scarf and kicking off her
boots, as the warmth of the place reached out to envelop her.
She hung up her coat and walked into her open-plan living
room.

It was the first place she had ever owned and gradually she
had turned it into something that was truly hers. She loved its
solitude and its uncluttered elegance, the two plush, brick-red
sofas standing stark against the pure white wall, the expanse
of gleaming, wooden floor and the huge windows that faced

out on to the seventh floor of the apartment block opposite. This was home.

The phone kept ringing. She walked over to the kitchen and put down the paper bag on one of the slate-grey surfaces. There was a click: the answerphone switching on.

'Sarah.'

She froze. There was no mistaking that voice. There was something biblical, and something unique, in the way Ben Hoffman said her name. There always had been.

'This is my third call,' he said. He sounded irritated.

Stubborn old man, she thought, smiling as she hurried towards the phone. She could just picture him, sitting in the solitude of his overdecorated study in that little town on the edge of the desert and picking up the phone to summon her, outraged to discover that she wasn't waiting for him at the other end.

The tape kept turning, recording his injunction: 'I want you back.'

She hesitated, her hand hovering in the air. Back? she thought. There is no going back. Not after all this time.

'Please,' his testy old man's voice continued, 'ring me as soon as you get this message. I have need . . .'

And yet, how could she ignore him?

She couldn't. Picking up the phone, she cut him off: 'Ben?'

2

THE ROOM WAS dark and, save for the sound of Marie's breathing, as quiet as it should be in the dead of night. But something, some alien noise, had visited Pieter Muller in his dreaming and pulled him out of it. Getting up quietly so as not to wake Marie, he swapped his striped pyjamas for a pair of khaki trousers and a short-sleeved shirt before padding across the worn green carpet.

A thickset man with a big square face, unblinking narrow eyes and heavy jowls that dragged his puffy flesh into a fading ginger beard above his bullish neck, Pieter always, even in his own bedroom, moved with purpose. Ham hands, their freckled skin dusted by downy ginger hair, swung by his side as he walked to the door. It creaked when he went through. He made a mental note to have it oiled. Then down the long, dark corridor he went past the games room with its full-size pool table, turning right at the corridor's end and going into the kitchen, an ungainly utilitarian space with an oversized deep freeze, ill-fitting metal-lined wall cabinets, scratched melamine counters and a long, central pine table which years of scrubbing had bleached almost white. A kitchen without the nonsense of current city fashion, Pieter thought proudly, as he passed the range where a cast-iron kettle and a pot of pre-cooked pap stood on the hot plate.

His three dogs had heard him stirring and they were waiting for him outside, their thin tails beating the hot, still air. They were good, well-trained dogs, who followed when he moved to the middle of the gravel driveway and who stood quietly as he looked beyond the row of pine trees that bordered his land.

The land was almost completely dark, lit only by the softest moonlight: the first pale rays of the day had not even begun blanching at the edges of the mountain. Nothing here that could have disturbed him.

He moved down the driveway and over the wire fence, making his way up the slope and towards the south-west field, walking with purpose as his torch picked out a twisted grove of aloes and the jagged edges of a thorn tree. And all the while his dogs, grey shadows dancing in the dark, stayed close enough for him to hear their watery panting syncopated with the sound of his heavy work boots crunching down on the desiccated land. There were no other noises, nothing out of place.

He crested the hill, then stopped and stood drinking in the quietness of the night. Above him, the stars flickered pinpoint-bright in the domed sky as he listened to the gradual easing of his own breath and to the scratching of a rodent through the undergrowth. The night was so intense it

shrouded definition: lowering his gaze he saw the land
stretching out as if it were one long unbroken whole. The
stark rim of mountains that in the daytime dominated the
countryside was indicated now only by a vague increase in
the intensity of darkness. Standing, breathing in the solitude,
Pieter knew that there had been no intruder. There could not
have been. Which meant that the dulled sound that had
awakened him – like the thud of a spade thumping into hardened ground – must have been just part of a dream.

His youngest dog whimpered. He reached down and
stroked her silken head, gentling her into calm. He could feel
the heat rising off the parched earth, filling the air with the
oily fragrance of eucalyptus. He turned and looked away from
the mountains to the place where, ten kilometres away, the
town of Smitsrivier cast up its vague yellow glow.

He thought then about his encounter with James Sizela.
Sizela the headmaster. On crossing paths with Pieter, Sizela
had stopped and, saying nothing, had stood and stared, his
brown eyes burning into Pieter's face.

Of course. Now Pieter knew why he'd awakened so suddenly. It was this damned Truth Commission that was
heading into town, stirring it all up, stoking Sizela's rage.

3

IT WAS EIGHT hours since Sarah's plane had landed in Port Elizabeth and three since she'd driven into town. Now freshly showered and wearing the lightest of her summer dresses, she stepped out of the Smitsrivier Retreat. And stopped abruptly – bowled over by the sight that met her eyes.

For fourteen years the glass and steel forests of New York, with its chrome and marble atriums and deep polluted colours smeared across the downtown sky at dusk, had been the sights and shapes that were burned on her retina. Now she'd journeyed to this town in South Africa that was New York's polar opposite – a town where men walked slow and where the road to the east ran out into the desert, straight and true for close on fifteen miles until it hit the rim of burned-out mountain cores. This petrified sea of mountain tops rolled around the town in a 360-degree arc, shimmering maroon under the weight of the vast blue sky, the joining of these two solidities so seamless that it was hard to imagine that anything else would have the temerity to exist beyond them.

From Smitsrivier to New York. A stunning dislocation. A continental shift for which there could be no mental bridge. And yet, as Sarah's gaze moved down Smitsrivier's Main Street to its distant end, she realised how familiar it was. Even its climate felt right: although the thermometer was pushing forty, the day was dry and sharp and clean like a day should be.

She set off down Main Street, taking long lazy strides, zigzagging under the patchwork shade of a line of jacaranda trees which, heavy with purple blossom in early spring, had since sunk back into dusty-brown indifference. From the urban jungle to the deep frontier. The settlers who'd created the town of Smitsrivier hadn't tried to compete with the immense vista that surrounded them. Instead, they'd built small houses with shade, aspiring to two-storey in a good year, and fashioned neat verandas out of tin sheets and cast-iron balustrades on which they could sit and look out at the mountains. That and those wide, tarred avenues that never completely kept the red dust at bay were as much permanence as they could muster.

The character of the town had been indelibly forged by those early settlers. They were tough people who'd trekked with ox-wagons through semi-desert and then, having decided to put down roots, had created their town with the same methodical determination that they later applied to every other aspect of their lives. Deeply religious, their first project had been the Dutch Reform church which they'd placed dead centre on Main Street. With its jagged white spire thrusting up into the sky and its gleaming white stucco building and three high arched entrances, the church could afford to stand back behind a fenced-in courtyard and still be seen from every point in town. Having settled with their God, the settlers had turned their attention to the state, siting their town hall with its scrolled leaves and thatched roof at the far end of Main Street and a scaled-down version, which served as police station and courthouse, near the church. The church, the state and then commerce: a series of banks – the New Standard, the Eerste Nasionale, the Volkskas, the Boland – were interspersed by garages where bakkies refilled and people queued for paraffin.

Until this moment Sarah had been so struck by the familiarity of the place that she hadn't taken in any of its changes. Now she noticed how much more crowded Smitsrivier was and, even more radically, as she passed the municipal garden stocked with strangely twisted aloes, she saw three black men sprawled out on a wooden bench that had once been reserved for whites only. They were passing a bottle of cheap Golden Mustang between them – an act of defiance that in the old days would have brought police sjamboks raining down.

She moved on, crossing the road and, just as she reached the other side, a kombi van, part of the local township's informal mass transit system, cut in front of her. Its left wheel partially mounted up the pavement as its back door opened to disgorge passengers. Skirting round the van she was assailed by the rhythmic blasting of its sound system, deep men's voices thumping out that strange lyrical fusion of pop and revolutionary metaphor that was unique to South Africa. And then the kombi moved off while three young black men, newly disembarked, joined a fourth who'd been waiting on the pavement. Seeing their exchange of greetings and the slapping of their hands, Sarah re-experienced the liveliness of her mother country. It's good to be back, she thought: to hear the laughter in those once familiar voices and to be surrounded by all those different loud South African accents.

Except of course that this was still South Africa. When one of the men saw her looking, his eyes flicked sideways. It was an almost imperceptible movement which his companions nevertheless instantly understood. Their laughter was abruptly stanched as was their conversation and they moved together, cutting her out, their expressions mutating from animated to morose, reminding her of such encounters endlessly repeated during her childhood. Fourteen years had gone by since she'd last been witness to any, but the feelings this one evoked came flooding back – that horrible composite of shame and fear.

But wait a minute, it was different now. It had to be. She was no longer just another white Smitsrivier girl, embarrassed and awkward in the face of a black man. Looking the stranger in the face, she smiled pleasantly and walked by, continuing down Main Street.

The spotless sidewalks of before, once a testimony to a combination of Calvinist order and cheap labour, were chaotic, overgrown with improvised stalls, wooden crates on which were laid wrinkled oranges in groups of four or five, spotted pawpaws, piles of green prickly pears and cobs of roasted corn. She took in all those old familiarities as she kept walking until a combination of curiosity and hunger drove her into an old convenience store.

Pushing open its glass door, she was sucked once again into that other, earlier time. The storekeeper, the only other occupant of the place, was a wrinkled old woman in a faded lavender-print frock. She was perched on a high stool under a huge buzzard of a fan that was turgidly moving hot air from one section of the ceiling to another. She didn't bother greeting Sarah but continued to sit motionless, conserving her energy as she presided over a collection of counter goods – some packs of Chiclets chewing gum, two jars of gobstoppers and a few long strings of liquorice – that might have sprung straight out of Sarah's childhood. The smells that wafted over were the powdery sweetness of icing sugar, the stink of flies sizzling now on infra-red tubes wired into the wall rather than the old blue flypaper, and the tangy aroma of strips of biltong, streaked by globules of yellow fat, that hung down from ceiling hooks. A price list stuck up crooked beside the biltong told her she could also buy half a loaf of oversweetened white bread, if she wanted, or a single cigarette, or a scoop of frozen peas.

There was nothing here that Sarah felt like eating. She nodded at the woman, who once again failed to acknowledge her, and left the shop.

The sun blazed down as she made her way towards the town's central shopping area, weaving along pavements even more packed with makeshift stalls selling cheap clothes. She was still jet-lagged and her concentration wandered, so when eventually she found herself opposite a once familiar row of shops, she was taken by surprise. She stopped and stared in amazement at the low-slung buildings whose striped awnings still hung above each entrance and whose green corrugated-iron roofs still shimmered in the brightness. They were so distinctive and so much a part of her childhood, she could have closed her eyes and conjured up the sequence of their colours: sky blue, lemon yellow dulled by time, olive green and then back to blue again.

Her father's shop had been the one with the green awning. Shielding her eyes from the glare of the sun she stared across at it and saw that although her parents had been gone ten years her father's sign – Barcant's Optics – was still hanging from the metal bar, caught by a sudden, hot gust of wind to swing backwards and forwards once in sync with the sign for Venter's Supermeat, the one for Sue Anne's Unisex Salon and finally, Lou's Pharmacy.

It was completely still again. The sun was too harsh: her

vision bleared. She turned away and looked up Main Street, to the end of town where its flatness was engulfed by semi-desert. The colours she saw were the colours of the land: the browns and reds of the distant horizon and the olive green of the scrub-covered hills that took off from the roadside. Then she was transfixed by a sight: a huge crucifix anchored at its four points by high-tension wire to the top of the hill. That she could have forgotten how this symbol of white rule, and the church that backed it, so dominated the town, was a mark of how far she had travelled. Then again, perhaps not: as a teenager she had spent time on the hill caught up in gloomy contemplation of the deficiencies of her life, oblivious to the significance of the cross.

A loud bang – a pickup truck backfiring – jolted her into the present. Just in time. She didn't know what she was doing standing there, caught in reverie. That was the pact she'd made with herself when she'd agreed to answer Ben's summons, that she would not allow herself to be dragged into a contemplation of her past. Leaving small-town Smitsrivier had been her childhood goal and she had managed it as completely as she could ever have wished. She was here to do a job of work because Ben had asked her to come and because she owed him too much to contemplate refusal. That's all.

She crossed the road and walked past the arched street lights to the optician's glass door, stopping then to peer through one of the grimy top panes. Another step back in time. She saw three men standing in front of the scratched wooden counter examining a pair of off-the-shelf reading glasses. Their callused, brown, farm-labourer's hands caressed the wire frames as each in turn lifted the spectacles to his eyes to stare at the newspaper she knew they must have bought especially for the occasion. When she pushed the door open, hearing the brass bell's familiar strangled cry, the three customers turned. They were dressed almost identically in snowy-white open-necked shirts and brown trousers, neatly pressed but with cuffs frayed by age and stained by too much contact with Smitsrivier's red soil. Two of them touched the brims of their hats in greeting, while the third nodded gravely.

The men were standing in front of the counter blocking Sarah's view. For a moment she imagined that, just as they and the shop's signpost and the landscape and the feel of the place were the same, nothing else had changed either and that when they moved aside she'd see her father, soft and white and malleable, with his kind face, his weak blue eyes and his limp smiling mouth.

One of the men moved aside to reveal, not her father, but another optician thirty years younger than her father and much thinner, a stranger who spoke in the accented English of an Afrikaner: 'Can I help you, miss?'

She didn't answer. She stood there in that tawdry space thinking how much her father had loved this place. It had been the fulfilment of his ambition – a shop of his own. She smiled. He must have wondered often how it was that he, a mild-mannered man content with his business, his town and his introverted wife, had such a wild, uncontrolled, uncontrollable daughter. She, with her grandiose ambitions and her determination to cross the mountain range, must have seemed like a cuckoo to her parents, much more the sort of child that the exotic Hoffmans – Ben and Anna – rather than the ordinary Barcants would have produced.

The optician spoke, insistently, into her silence: 'Do you need help?' He was staring hard.

She shook her head and smiled again: 'I was only looking,' she said, and left the shop.

Outside, a line of blue-overalled men was passing beer barrels from a pickup truck into a liquor store. Watching the easy swing of their arms, slick in the heat, she wondered vaguely whether life suited her parents now that they were resettled in

Perth. They wrote, of course, and there had even been an exchange of visits, but they were not expressive people and she had no idea whether her mother was happier away from the uncertainties of South Africa or how her father kept his anxious flapping hands busy in retirement.

A voice shouted out abrasively: '*Kwela. Kwela*,' and she watched the last of the beer offloaded and the men hefting themselves up into the lorry's back. When it drove away, she moved too, continuing her pilgrimage down Main Street.

4

BEN HOFFMAN HEARD footsteps outside his study and then the creak of the door opening. He knew it couldn't be Sarah — he would have spotted her coming up the drive. Which meant it must be his wife Anna, checking to see if he was asleep. He quickly shut his eyes. Why should he give Anna any further cause for worry? She wanted him to rest . . . well, then, she would find him doing so.

After a while the door closed, taking with it Anna's fragrant mix of jasmine and soft-risen dough. Still Ben continued to lie motionless and only when he was certain that she really had gone away, did he vacate the sofa for his desk. His gold fob watch was lying on the polished wood where he'd left it. He glanced at it. Three o'clock. Was this possible? Time seemed to be moving very slowly. Putting down the watch, he looked out through the casement window, past the lush green of Anna's garden and into the distance where the blazing sunlight had bleached out all but the edges of the distant mountain rims. His watch must be right. It was too bright to be much later than three.

He dropped his gaze and the photograph of James Sizela's son, which James had laid down carefully on the blotter, caught his eyes. Picking it up, he peered at it though his half-rimmed glasses. There was, he thought, no mistaking Steve Sizela's paternity. He had the same cinnamon-bark skin as his father and the same gently slanting eyes, high cheekbones and high forehead. Father and son: in fact, Ben thought, the only apparent difference between the two lay in their ages and in the way that, in the photograph at least, the youth displayed none of the formality that was the old man's defining characteristic. While James Sizela was a man who never seemed to unbend, this image of his smiling son was so vibrant and so alive that it was almost impossible what Ben knew to be the truth: that Steve was long dead.

Putting down the photograph Ben remembered James's recent visit. He had sat over there on the sofa, tall, gaunt and grey-haired and, in that slow, stiff manner of his, had described to Ben how he had come across Pieter Muller on Main Street.

'I looked into Muller's heart,' James had said.

Oh yes. Even now, a week after James had been and gone, Ben could still visualise the encounter. Those two men, locked in eye-to-eye contact on the flat expanse of a dust-strewn Main Street. The stern headmaster facing down the solid, determined ex-policeman, Muller, both of them so much products of the old South Africa.

'I know now for certain,' James had continued, 'that Pieter Muller killed my son.'

As James's words had died away, Ben had sat thinking that for James to pin the blame for Steve's death on Muller wasn't entirely unexpected. Muller's culpability was a theory that had being doing the rounds of Smitsrivier for more than thirteen years, ever since Steve had been arrested on Pieter Muller's orders and then had disappeared. Although they had no concrete proof of this, most people in town – certainly most black people – believed that Steve was dead and that Muller was responsible. But in all the years that Ben had known James, James had never said as much.

Now, however, Ben had heard a new resolve and urgency in James's voice. Ben knew why. It was the coming of the Truth Commission – James's last chance to find his son's body.

Ben looked down, impatiently, at his watch. Ten past three. Time was moving far too slowly. Turning away from the window, he cast round the study to the rich weave of his beloved Persian carpet, the deep muted purples of his tasselled lampshades and the burnished wooden surfaces of his desk. He was alone but he didn't feel alone. The spectre of James seemed to be in the room with him, reminding him in turn of that unending line of other Africans who had, over the years, come here to ask for his help as a lawyer. Never James. For him to make the trip from the township into Smitsrivier, to come and knock, unannounced, on Ben's door, showed how determined he was.

Not, Ben thought, that James had displayed even the slightest impatience. That was not his way. He had continued to sit almost motionless, saying in that slow stiff manner that was his defining characteristic: 'I am a realist, I know Muller will never stand trial for Steve's murder. I can accept that.'

James had paused then, leaving Ben to wonder: could a man as righteous as James Sizela really dam up his need for justice, for revenge, even? Perhaps. There was a part of Ben that hoped so. If the present was not to be sucked down into the swamp of the past, then many fathers like James must do as James professed to do – must say enough is enough.

'The time has come,' James had eventually continued. 'We must find Steve.'

Noting James's use of the collective pronoun, Ben had thought how, until that moment, he had never turned a client away. Or at least not one that mattered. There had been no qualified black lawyers within fifty kilometres and Ben had been the only white lawyer prepared to take on a 'political' case when political meant almost anything that happened to any black person. He had thus been kept very busy. Not that he had minded. True, in the old days the odds had been so stacked against him that he'd ended up losing far more cases than he had ever won, but it had nevertheless been a life well lived. A good life, a rewarding life. A part of a life that was now over. Ben had officially retired – everybody in Smitsrivier knew that. He had promised himself that he would turn a deaf ear to the siren calls of his own enthusiasms and live out what remained to him in peace with his Anna. South Africa had changed: his work was over.

And thus when James finished speaking, Ben had done his best to head him off. He had told James that he need only to wait until Muller applied for amnesty from the Truth Commission. When Muller did that, Ben told James, he would be forced by the amnesty rules to disclose what he knew of Steve's whereabouts.

But James shook his head and said that Muller had been overheard boasting that he would never apply.

Ben knew better than to doubt it. Although some ex-policemen had queued up voluntarily for their amnesties, most of those who had applied had done so in order to free themselves from jail. As to the ones who had never been taken to task for their past actions: they saw themselves as loyal, law-abiding functionaries who had only done what duty demanded and who did not, therefore, see why they should abase themselves in front of any commission. Muller was that kind of man.

'I have accepted the truth,' James had said. 'My son is gone. All I want now, all we both want, is to be allowed to lay his body to rest.'

Feeling the strings of obligation being tightened, Ben had shifted uncomfortably.

'Please, Ben,' James had reached out and had taken hold of Ben's pale, liver-spotted hand.

At that moment, Anna had passed by and, looking in, saw them holding hands in that South African way. In her expression Ben could tell what she was really seeing. Two old men. One living out the last days of his life, the other labouring under the weight of death that he often must have wished had been his own. She had stood, still, and Ben had known what she was thinking when eventually she shook her head and walked away. He knew that had he asked her what he should do, she wouldn't have bothered replying. She wouldn't have needed to: he knew that what she wanted was that he turn his back on work. But he couldn't give her that. The parameters were too clear: James was a stubborn man and a determined one, as set on finding out the truth as Pieter Muller was in withholding it and there was nothing Ben, or anybody else, could do to stop the two colliding. And if Ben couldn't stop James then he must help him.

He could read Anna's thoughts; he told her as much. He knew she was right. He was the first to admit that a sense of obligation was not his only motivator. There was also that anticipation of a battle to be joined: that fusion of intellect and morality. The chase. He had felt the first glimmers of that old excitement as he suggested to James that, if Muller would not apply for amnesty, they could sue him in a civil court.

'Sue him?' The notion jogged James's expression out of its characteristic control. 'But I thought the Truth Commission precluded the possibility of resorting to the law?'

'It does,' Ben had replied. 'But only for those who actually apply to the Commission.' The more Ben thought about it, the more sense it made. If Muller applied for amnesty, he would be automatically protected from a civil suit. But since he refused to apply they could turn his defiance against him. They would make his repudiation of the new rules of the game too uncomfortable to resist. By suing him, they would use the law to frighten him into making an amnesty application and that way tell them what he had done with Steve's body.

The timing was perfect. The Truth Commission was heading into town, bringing with it an ex-colleague of Muller's – the jailed policeman, Dirk Hendricks.

'Dirk Hendricks is applying for amnesty for the torture of Alex Mpondo,' Ben had told James. 'We could use Alex to twist Hendricks's arm. Do you know who Alex's lawyer is?'

James pursed his lips in disapproval as he always did on mention of Alex Mpondo. 'He doesn't have a lawyer,' he said. 'He has let it be known that he won't come to the hearing. Maybe he thinks this is all beneath him now that he's an MP.'

Ben blinked. 'That's no good. You know how it works: without Alex to oppose him, Dirk Hendricks's hearing will be mere formality. Alex is our lever. We need him in Smitsrivier, opposing Hendricks.' Ben looked keenly at James. 'Can you persuade him to change his mind?'

For a moment James had sat, calculating, and then he had said: 'I will ask someone to approach Mpondo,' and had looked away.

That was all Ben needed. They were set. It was a simple

plan. The best plans always were. They would use Alex Mpondo's presence at the hearing to threaten Hendricks that unless he revealed what he knew of Muller's complicity, he might not get his amnesty. That way Muller would be caught in a pincer movement: on the one hand, his fear of what Hendricks might say, and on the other, the threat of a civil suit.

A simple plan requiring, now that Ben's energy was so low, one other person: Sarah Barcant.

Sarah. Here at last was the excuse he needed. 'If you get Alex to come to the hearing,' he told James Sizela, 'I'll phone my ex-pupil, Sarah Barcant. She has all the experience we need. I'll tell her we need her.'

And that was it. The trap was set.

Ben looked at the watch again. Only half an hour had elapsed. He frowned and impatiently pushed a strand of grey hair back from his face.

5

DUST. IT SATURATED the space and kept on coming: clouds of red dust puffing through the gaps in the kombi's back door. Not that Dirk minded it. On the contrary. In his Pretoria jail cell that nauseous concoction of stale sweat, acrid bleach and glutinous floor polish was a continual reminder of his incarceration, but now as he sat staring at the windowless walls of the kombi, the feel of the particles, gritty against his skin, and their smell helped him imagine the endless stretching of a landscape that lay beyond the confines of the vehicle.

He glanced at his watch to confirm what he already knew: they'd soon be in Smitsrivier. Despite the fact that he had trained himself to remain always calm, he felt his spirits lifting.

At that moment the kombi jolted, pitching him off the short steel bench and against one of the metallic sides. As he hauled himself back there was a second jagged lurch. This time he was ready and braced his feet to stop being slammed against the side again. Another wayward lurching. Jesus, surely nobody, certainly no trained policeman, could drive this badly? He heard the engine revving madly. The bastard's doing it deliberately, he thought, even an imbecile would find it difficult to make such heavy weather of the long, straight, evenly tarred road into Smitsrivier.

The only possible explanation suddenly occurred to him. They must have come off the road.

The kombi shuddered, its engine straining. Listening to the roar of its over-pumped accelerator, Dirk could also feel the wheels spinning. Sand. If the moronic driver wasn't careful he'd use the wheels to dig a hole so deep, he'd need a tractor to dislodge the vehicle.

Suddenly the kombi jolted forwards, breaking out of its burrow and continuing along the uneven surface. But where were they? Not on their way to Smitsrivier: there was only one road into town and one road out and that was smooth tar. Any track this bumpy led away from town, up into the mountains to that parched, unforgiving country where a rare farmhouse was the only sign of human habitation.

A change of route?

And a change of plan? The driver's instructions, barked out for all to hear, had been clear. He was to take Dirk from Port Elizabeth airport, where his plane from Pretoria had landed, and deliver him to the Smitsrivier police station where he would be held for the duration of the Truth Commission hearing. The time of Dirk's plane landing, the names of his escorts along with their service numbers and their dates of birth, the route the kombi was instructed to take, had all been duly written down. It couldn't be an

ambush: to entrap him deliberately in this situation would be
madness.

The kombi stopped – so suddenly that Dirk was thrown
forward. Concentrating on righting himself he missed the
sound of boots hitting the earth. The wrenching open of the
door took him by surprise. He was half down, half up, blinking like an animal. The glaring light of the day flooded into
his darkness, so that all he could make out was the dark
shape of a man, rearing up, leaning in, reaching across and
unlocking the chain that bound Dirk's manacles to the floor.
An almost magical manifestation of a man, who then stepped
away and seemed to vanish.

Silence. Dirk had forgotten just how quiet the semi-desert
could be and how intense the light. All he could see out there
beyond the kombi's back door was a bleached landscape
shimmering in the heat haze, a vast, brown, ill-defined stretch
of scrub and earth. A once familiar sight. It wasn't the farm,
was it?

The very idea made him hold in his breath. If they'd
brought him to the farm then no good could come of it. No,
of course. He felt the tension flowing from him. It wasn't the
farm. This landscape was much wilder and more unkempt.
He breathed out and sat, waiting.

And then it dawned on him that he must make a perfect
target, sitting passively like this against the light. As soon as
that thought occurred he was on the move, springing into
motion, pushing himself forward and out. He landed,
crouching in the dust, and straightened up, scanning his surrounds. The sun blared, its brilliance reducing everything to
monotone but, by the absence of any building or fencing, he
knew for sure that they were not at the farm but somewhere
else in the midst of the vast, undistinguished, uncultivated
wasteland that surrounded Smitsrivier. He looked to the left.
There was a dried-up tree, one of its half-severed limbs ashen

against the horizon and beside it the silhouette of a man, one of the guards whose dark glasses were glinting, his shotgun resting on his hip. Looking away and to the right, he saw how the second of his guards had placed himself symmetrically on the other side and was also standing armed and motionless against the backdrop of an immense, unwavering blue sky.

There just beyond this second man, tucked to one side off the rutted track, was an ancient, well-preserved, polished Mercedes. Dirk knew it well. It was Pieter's car. One glance at its familiar sludge-green exterior was enough to make its signature aroma – that strange mix of fresh varnish and stale chicken shit – come flooding back.

And there: the man himself, Dirk's old friend Pieter Muller. Pieter's distinctive ginger beard, ginger turning to grey. His thickset easy frame as he stirred himself into motion. His mighty head, nodding at the nearest guard and at the same time stretching out a hand. As Dirk watched, the two men's palms glanced against each other. It was expertly done, the exchange swiftly accomplished and then the guard said, 'One minute. That's all,' and walked away.

Any other man would have come up to Dirk and shaken his hand or clapped him on the back. But Pieter was not any man. Always controlled, always in charge, he merely walked a little closer before stopping to say: 'Dirk.'

Dirk dipped his head. 'Pieter.'

Any other man might now have made reference to the circumstances in which they found themselves – Pieter a businessman and Dirk a jailbird – or expressed pleasure at seeing Dirk or told him that he looked like shit. Pieter stood there saying nothing.

Silence. It had once been their familiar. A silence that had sprung first from Dirk's nervousness of the older man and then gradually from a growing understanding that had bound

them eventually in friendship. A silence as well that was
steeped in days of blood, an escape from all those words
shouted out in fury. A silence that was no longer possible
because, in the shifting sands of the new, even if words were
hard, the unspoken things that lurked beneath the surface
were much more dangerous.

Dirk broke the silence: 'How's Marie?'

'You know Marie.' Pieter shrugged. 'She doesn't complain.'

Yes, Dirk did know. He stood there, thinking about the
way Marie's illness must have affected Pieter's career, limiting
his room for manoeuvre, keeping him close to home. Was
that the source, Dirk thought, of that rage that he suspected
lingered inside that apparently calm frame?

'And Katie?' Pieter said.

'Gone.'

Pieter accepted this information as if it wasn't really news
to him. 'Is there anything I can get you? Cigarettes? Money?'

'No,' Dirk said. 'Thank you. I have everything I need.'

'Anything else?'

Dirk smiled and said, 'No. But thanks,' thinking that few
of his old compatriots would have gone to so much trouble
to offer support. In fact, he thought, his smile fading, those
who in the old days had been the first to brag about their
bravery in defence of their republic, were also the first to
react to Dirk's ill fortune by melting away into the new South
Africa.

'If there is something,' Pieter said, 'then you tell one of
those two,' inclining his head in the direction in which the
guards had disappeared. 'They'll pass it on to me.'

As if in answer to some secret signal, both guards reap-
peared. 'Time,' one said. They were intent: nervous.
Understandably so. Their time of departure from the airport
was on record: if their journey to Smitsrivier was further pro-
longed, questions would inevitably be asked.

Pieter nodded. To the guards he said, 'I'll wait until you've gone,' but to Dirk he said nothing, he only held out his hand. In that moment, looking into Pieter's eyes, Dirk saw something he didn't altogether understand. Was it a question?

No – much more than a question.

He knows what I did, Dirk thought.

And then Pieter's hand touched Dirk's and the moment passed and Dirk was left thinking he was imagining things. What was done was in the past. Over. Long gone. All that mattered now was the present and in this present he could see Pieter smiling and feel Pieter's hand in his.

Strange how what turned out to be most important was the simplest thing. To experience the touch of another's hand – not a lawyer's perfunctory businesslike shake, nor the flaccid offering of a Truth Commission investigator – but an exchange between friends. Between equals.

'Come,' the guard said, leading Dirk to the kombi.

When he climbed into the back he found a package on the bench. A carton of Camels. A present from Pieter. Dirk moved the carton aside and sat down, waiting for one of the guards to chain him down but instead of doing so, they merely closed the door, sealing him in the half-light. Was that Pieter's doing as well?

'There's a car down there on the road,' he heard a voice saying. 'We leave as soon as it has gone.'

Dirk sat back, waiting as the engine sparked into life. A door slammed and the kombi jerked forward. He sat, holding the metal bench. One thing he had learned: too much introspection could drive a man to the brink of madness. To think of Pieter, even if only in passing, was to invite in other thoughts that were better filed away. He leaned his back against the wall of the kombi, stretching out his feet, closing his eyes. Soon, he told himself, he would face Alex Mpondo and then it would be almost over.

Not long now, he thought, as the kombi jolted down the track.

6

ALEX MPONDO'S OLD powder-blue Corolla had no air-conditioning and he'd been hot so long that his sweat had worked
channels down his skin and was now sliding unfettered down
from his forehead on to his already soaking T-shirt. In normal
circumstances the prospect of an ice-cold Castle beer would
have had him flattening his foot on the accelerator, but these
were not normal circumstances. The closer he got to
Smitsrivier, the slower he drove. A road sign told him he was
a mere five kilometres from town and, in response, he lifted
his foot further off the accelerator. More dominant than the
prospect of any cold Castle was his reluctance to reach
Smitsrivier. The thought that something terrible would
happen there persisted, even though rationally he knew this

wasn't likely. Nothing was going to happen. Nothing. It had
happened long ago.

He looked through the window, concentrating his attention
on the monotony of a landscape that seemed to stretch without end. He was driving through the arid expanse of land
that, bounded by the line of the Sneeuberg Mountains, lay
between the Great Fish River and the Great Kei. Centuries
before, the white settlers had advanced here, driving the vanquished Xhosa ahead of them. It was an exacting land, its
unending scrub and stunted trees bleached brown and beige
and grey in the dazzling light of the midday sun, silent witness to all that butchery.

How long since he was last here? A long time: more than a
decade. He noticed how the light affected everything it
touched, turning the hide of that ordinary cow over there to
a sensual rich red-brown velvet. It was 1985, during the emergency. Thirteen years ago, nearly fourteen, pre-history, a
history that was gone.

He had no family left in Smitsrivier and yet here he was
heading into town, exhausted by the same repetitive thought
that had become his constant companion. One thought, a
question really: 'Why did that bastard have to apply for
amnesty?'

That bastard. Dirk Hendricks. It had taken years for Alex to
recover, even partially, from what Hendricks had done to him.
Years in which he'd wake up after two hours and know there
was no more sleeping that night, when the smell of a Lux
soap bar or a particular brand of cheap cologne or a floor
polish would be enough to annihilate everything but that
moment, frozen in its agony, when only death offered relief.

And now, because of Hendricks's bloody-minded stupidity
and the pressure that James Sizela's friends had indirectly
applied, it was all seeping back. His past was being slowly
excavated and there was nothing he could do to shut it out.

Soon he must do what he had vowed never to do again: he must come face to face with Dirk Hendricks.

No good could come from it, not for Alex. There was nothing in it for him.

And not for Dirk Hendricks either, who was so proud of his own pathetic intellect that he'd ended up outsmarting himself. Alex could guess at the logic that must have filtered through that twisted brain. Hendricks must have thought that if he didn't apply for amnesty for torturing Alex, then Alex would somehow turn up like the ghost at the feast at Hendricks's other amnesty hearing and use the full disclosure clause to stop him going free.

Hendricks couldn't have been further off-target. The truth was that Alex wanted nothing to do with him. If he hadn't volunteered the information that he had once been Alex's torturer, Alex certainly would not have made it public. He didn't want Hendricks exposed. Or humiliated. Or forgiven. He didn't want compensation and he certainly didn't want to have to sit and listen to Hendricks saying that he was sorry. Alex had come to terms with what happened. All he asked was he be left in peace.

And yet now he had no option. Hendricks had applied for amnesty for torturing Alex: Alex must oppose him. Not for his own sake, oh no, but for James's sake. Like a series of trip-wires radiating out: Pieter Muller would only fall if Hendricks fingered him, Hendricks would only finger Muller if Alex was there to apply the pressure and Alex would only oppose Hendricks because that's what James wanted.

Ahead the road curved to the left. Beyond it, he knew, lay the small bridge and the outskirts of Smitsrivier. He lifted his foot off the accelerator and the car slowed down some more.

7

By way of sloughing off her jet-lag lethargy, Sarah had gone on a running tour of Smitsrivier. She ran with ease, pounding her way through those once familiar streets much faster than she ever could as a child, conscious that her progress was being tracked from behind a succession of curtains. She knew the spectacle of a white woman running in shorts and sneakers would be the talk of white Smitsrivier for weeks to come, but there was little she could do to deflect attention from herself. In New York there might be a myriad bizarre people for her to scrutinise, but here in Smitsrivier she, with her modish clothes and her city ways, was the outlandish one.

The run had done its job, kick-starting her metabolism, but it had also made her very late. By the time she'd showered and changed into a simple linen shift, a blue mist floating in on a band of deeper purple was already creeping down the distant mountain flanks. Ben would be waiting for her: leaving the hotel she walked quickly, turning off Main Street, on automatic as she made her way to his house.

His street was deserted. She could hear her heels clicking against the pavement. Glancing down she saw that a sheen of dust was working its way into the soft green suede of her high-heeled sandals. They would soon be ruined. She must have been either seriously distracted or deranged when she'd done her packing, she thought: despite a collection of footwear that her friends had laughingly declared the rival of Imelda Marcos, she had arrived in this dusty town with an array of completely inappropriate shoes. If she wasn't careful she'd end up having to borrow a pair of espadrilles from Anna – not, of course, that Anna's wardrobe would include anything even as fashionable as an espadrille.

Francis Avenue was one of a series of tree-lined roads that, radiating out from Main Street, were home to most of Smitsrivier's white population. Never to the Barcants – Sarah's father had not made enough money to move his family off Main Street – so as a child she had always thought of Francis Avenue as the height of unattainable riches. Now, as she walked past its line-up of modest bungalows, low concrete walls and orderly front gardens, it seemed very much reduced.

It was, however, still picturesque, teeming as it was with colour, with lush mimosa, dusty pink and purple bougainvilleas, broad trees heavy with leaves and, oddly for a town surrounded by desert, roses.

Number 43 was no exception. Trailing strands of pastel-white and pale-pink wild dog roses wound through a luxuriant creeper and spilled over its wall. Brushing past the foliage, Sarah pushed open the gate and walked up the short brick path. The squat brick house that lay at the head of the path might be devoid of style but it had the power to charm her. The sheer exuberance of its garden had something to do with this, as did the patterns on the lace curtains, the polished brass door knocker, the wind chimes hanging off the mimosa tree and the score of other details that were a tribute to Anna's brilliance as a homemaker. But Sarah knew that the real reason she loved this house had less to do with the decor than with Ben.

They had met when he was middle-aged and she was fourteen. To her parents it must have seemed an odd alliance – the irascible, theatrical, childless Ben twinned with their feisty misfit – but it had stuck fast. More than that. To Sarah, the friendship proved a turning point. By opening up for her a world that she had only vaguely suspected might exist, Ben changed her life. Unlike all the other white inhabitants of Smitsrivier, his interests lay far beyond the confines of town. Everything excited him: politics, art, the law, history. When he offered her this world she reached out to it with both hands and was soon spending more time on Francis Avenue than she ever did on Main Street. It was no surprise therefore that, on going to university, she chose to follow in Ben's footsteps and study law, and no surprise either that when she got into trouble, it was to Ben that she had turned and Ben who had rescued her.

The memory made her smile. After all the cases she had prosecuted, her own now seemed so trivial. And it was trivial – she had been caught in an illegal shebeen, that's all. And yet at the time it had felt momentous. In hindsight she knew that the police who'd threatened to prosecute her under the Immorality Act were merely trying to humiliate this white girl who'd broken all the taboos by daring to hang out in a black bar; at the time she'd taken their threats seriously. She had sat in a cell, scared half to death by what they might do to her, envisaging not only her reputation, but also the career she hadn't yet begun, disappearing. And then she had heard Ben's authoritative voice demanding her release and within minutes he had achieved it.

They never spoke of it. He didn't ask why she'd taken such a stupid risk merely for rebellion's sake. Perhaps he had understood that the discomfort of the experience had started long before her arrest, when she had realised, by the way she'd been treated in the shebeen, that she didn't fit in that world either. No wonder then that when, soon afterwards, an offer of a place at Harvard had arrived, she hadn't hesitated.

Fourteen years ago. She was overtaken suddenly by an unfamiliar fit of shyness. The closer she got to the front door, the more her feet dragged.

She was within a few yards of the study window when she noticed Ben. He was sitting by his desk, concentrated on peering down through his half-moon glasses. He didn't seem to sense her presence. She was glad of that. She stopped and stood quite still, watching.

He stretched out and clicked on a tasselled lamp and she saw him caught in a shaft of artificial light – his pale face, his curly hair completely white. The sight took her aback. She'd thought she'd prepared herself – she knew he would have aged – but now what she saw was not just ageing but something much more dramatic. He looked old, she thought, really old and framed by the casement window, a frail shell of the flamboyant showman she'd once known. The suspicion that had visited her in New York when she first heard his voice, returned: was he ill?

He glanced up then, and saw her. He seemed startled. He took of his spectacles. But then, after looking through the window as if he couldn't quite believe his eyes, he pushed it open and said: 'Sarah,' his voice full of pleasure, 'you made it,' smiling and turning to the door, calling out: 'Anna. Come. Sarah's here.'

When Ben asked Sarah about her parents, she smiled.

'They like Perth,' she said, 'especially my mother,' and, looking across the polished dining-room table she smiled again.

When she smiled like that her whole face lit up, and Ben saw how beautiful she was. She'd changed, he thought, and for the better. Her dark brown eyes were still as alive, as deep, as ever, but she had learned to tame her shock of black hair and to soften it, pulling it off her face so as to emphasise its contrast with her fine pale skin. She must make many conquests, he thought.

'She's taken up synchronised swimming.' Grinning, Sarah took a sip of water. 'Brenda Barcant in a Busby Berkeley routine. It defies imagination, don't you think?'

'Your mother always did have more to her than she let show,' Ben said, returning her smile.

His magnanimity to the woman who had never shown him much grace warmed Sarah. She was at ease now, no longer affected by Ben's apparent frailty. It didn't matter how he looked, she thought: he was still the same generous, impossible Ben she had known.

'How else could your mother have produced a child like you?' he said.

'And I always thought I was a genetic throwback,' she answered just as the door from the kitchen was pushed open and, looking across, she saw the hefty figure of Anna framed against the fluorescent kitchen light.

Anna dipped her ladle into the silver tureen. 'More dumplings?'

'No thanks,' Sarah said, 'although it was delicious.'

She put her hands behind her neck, arching backwards to reinforce the fact that she was quite finished. She was glad of it. The thick meat stew with its dark piquant sauce and chunky home-made dumplings was delicious – but it had also reminded her of just how sleepy Anna's rich fare had always made her, especially when the weather was as hot as this. And now she had an added difficulty. She no longer shared the passion for red meat that was common to all Smitsrivier.

Not of course that the rest of Smitsrivier ate the same food as the Hoffmans. Anna with her moon face, milky complexion and soft folds of fat might seem ordinary. But by the very things she chose to cook, she set herself apart from every other white woman in town. And Anna's singularity didn't stop in the kitchen. Her dining room was furnished with a splendid polished mahogany table, rich woven carpets and embroidered lamp shades – so much more reminiscent of middle Europe than a New World settler town.

'Perhaps for you, Ben?' Anna glanced hopefully over at her husband's plate where the small portion she'd served him was lying there almost entirely untouched.

'No.' Picking up his cutlery, Ben said, 'No more, thank you, Anna.' Cutting off a sliver of meat he raised it to his mouth but there was little conviction in his gesture and before the fork could reach its target, the argument he'd started as soon as the food was served now reasserted itself. He waved the fork, meat and all, in Sarah's direction, and said, 'Well?'

She grinned. This was Ben all over. She might be his darling girl, back after many years, but that didn't mean he was going to give her an easy ride.

He said, loudly, 'What exactly would you have done in their situation?'

'I would have waited to see if the balance of forces . . .'

'Oh, come on, Sarah.' He cut right through her. 'Never

mind "the balance of forces". You forget that in 1990 there were two opposing sides. Call them what you will: the torturer and the freedom fighter, or the law-abiding policeman and the terrorist. They were at war with each other and they need to negotiate a peace. That's how the Truth Commission came about.' He scowled at her, ferociously, daring her to contradict him.

There was a time when such a forceful look might have been enough to silence her. Not any longer. After years of independence, she was game for any of his dares. 'So, are you now telling me that this is all your Truth Commission is – a compromise? Because if you are . . .'

'No, of course not. It's much, much more than that. This country, *your* country, Sarah, must be given the chance to heal itself. Don't you understand that? Or have you become so much the prosecutor that you can no longer see beyond the law?'

She'd been expecting that: she'd always known how much he disapproved of her joining the DA's office. She wouldn't, however, let him distract her: 'Come on, Ben,' she said. 'Even the name's a give-away. The Truth and Reconciliation Commission! Whose truth exactly? In your words: the torturer's or the freedom fighter's? The policeman's or the terrorist's?'

Ben let his silver knife and fork drop clattering on to his plate. 'Your point?'

'My point,' Sarah said, as Anna padded over to pick up Ben's plate, 'is that truth is not neutral. And before you point out the obvious, I'm not trying to say that the law is neutral. I know it works unevenly. But at least the law provides some standards for inequalities to be judged.'

Taking Sarah's plate as well, Anna went through the door that led into the kitchen.

'You value the law above the truth, do you?' Ben pushed

back his chair so roughly it scraped loudly against the wooden floor. Letting out a loud 'pah' of disgust, he got up stiffly and began to walk away. Like old times: Ben had always liked to walk and argue. Now he limped over to the wall as he said: 'So you would prefer the full force of the law to be brought to bear?' He was back by the table. In a well-remembered gesture, he leaned over his chair to stare her in the face. There was something in his expression – as if he were weighing her up – and when he said: 'Tell me this, Sarah. What must a man like James Sizela do?' He was no longer drawing on his rhetorical power to back her into a corner. 'All James wants is to bury his son,' he said. 'Such a human desire.'

She felt herself soften. 'And you think this Truth Commission of yours will make this possible?'

'Yes. If Pieter Muller applies for amnesty, he'll have to say where Steve is buried.'

She shrugged. 'And there lies your problem: there are too many ifs involved. *If* Muller applies and *if* he tells the truth. And what about this one: what happens *if* Muller applies and tells the truth and the body is uncovered but James finds this isn't enough – that he wants more.'

'More? Like what?'

'Oh, I don't know. Revenge? Justice? Both also perfectly understandable human desires. At least the law, however imperfect, tries to deliver the latter.'

'But the law can only come into play when there is evidence,' Ben said. 'There is none in this case: in all likelihood Muller himself destroyed it.'

'Sure,' she said. 'Now that is an argument for the Commission I might concede: that it's better than nothing. Fine. But please let's not pretend it's anything else. Let's put a stop to the grandiose claims the Commission keep making for their project.'

'You're wrong, Sarah,' Ben said. And she knew he would
have proceeded to detail precisely where she had gone wrong
if Anna hadn't come back into the dining room carrying an
apple strudel and a silver cruet of thick cream, and with one
gentle look summoned Ben to table.

Standing by the kitchen door, Sarah watched Anna filling the
dishwasher. As soon as supper was over, Ben had stumped off
and Sarah was beginning to think that if he didn't come back
soon, she might as well go back to her hotel. In the meantime,
she was flagging. She could really have done with a drink, but
she knew that there was no point in asking for one.
Cosmopolitan though the Hoffmans had once seemed to her,
they had never been drinkers.

She looked around. Although the kitchen was the plainest
room in the house it was still, for Smitsrivier, almost baroque
with its elaborate line-up of wood-faced wall cabinets, its
lavish dresser display of Dresden china and its wooden table,
around which were positioned four padded, floral chairs.
Everything was in place, its perfect order maintained by Anna
who would not countenance any help.

'Is Ben unwell?' Sarah asked of Anna's back.

Anna shrugged. From where she was standing Sarah could
see the other woman's broad figure bending a little further forward before Anna said: 'He's old. That's all.' She straightened
up and then turned to look at Sarah. 'And he missed you. He's
pleased you're back.'

But *she* isn't, Sarah thought, wondering why it had never
before occurred to her how difficult it must have been for
Anna to see her house invaded by Sarah's brash, argumen-
tative younger self. It was one thing for Ben, who had
relished the challenge of channelling Sarah's rebelliousness
into intellectual rigour, but what must Anna have felt like,
when the two of them had sat at her table immersed in

some argument with only the occasional careless comment in her direction? And now? Dinner had been like old times. Did Anna resent the fact that Sarah was back to disrupt her calm?

'He'll be in his study,' Anna said, 'waiting for you. Go on. Go to him.'

She found Ben sitting in the far corner of his study, on a straight-backed chair. He was leaning forward. The rest of the room was in darkness but his corner was illuminated by a powerful spotlight shining directly over his shoulder. He didn't seem to hear Sarah come in, and only when she stopped inches away from him did he look up and acknowledge her presence.

The sight of him wearing a peaked green visor, his unruly hair flying out from under it, made her laugh out loud.

He grimaced. 'I need the strong light to see, but if I don't wear the visor the light blinds me,' and then nodding to draw her attention to the grand inlaid tray in front of him, said: 'It's Bonnard. *The Open Window*. I only just started. I've managed the cat and the vase.'

She was amazed. Ben with a jigsaw! It seemed unimaginable. She stared down at the many-sided fragments that were lying around the tray. And yet, she thought, pulling up a chair and sitting down beside him, now she considered it properly, Ben with a jigsaw, especially one as complicated as this, made a lot of sense. After all, the putting together of disparate fragments to build a picture – that had been his lawyer's speciality.

Ben handed her the empty box. She looked at the picture on its top cover that was vivid with textured colour and this view of a place and a time so different from Smitsrivier.

'Don't you think it would make it easier if you first put the window in place?' she said.

'Ah.' He pounced on a piece and slotted it triumphantly into the wall of mottled orange that he was building. 'But why assume I want to make it easier?'

Why indeed? She gazed down at the individual fragments until finally selecting one; she held it out to him.

He spared it only a cursory glance. 'Too dark,' he said. 'That goes above the cat.'

Above the cat, she repeated to herself, and transferred the piece to the outline of an almost perfect cartoon black cat. Yes. He was right: it fitted snugly. She reached for another piece. And so they sat, side by side, in the quietness of his study, each picking up pieces of the jigsaw and slotting them into place or rejecting them.

How different this was from the way she had imagined it. In New York, her thoughts of Ben would conjure up his flamboyant courtroom tricks, or his leading a jury round to an understanding of a complicated point of law, or his sarcastic destruction of a lying witness – all of these based on the quickness of his tongue. Now, as they sat in silence, she remembered how silence had also once been a part of their time together. Like the evenings when he would sit at his desk studying a brief, while she sat on the sofa and did her homework. Or when they would escape to the porch, Ben in his rocking chair while she settled herself down on the deck, both of them silent at the sight of the myriad stars in that immense sky. I've missed him, she thought.

He spoke suddenly, in a low serious voice: 'Can't you see how your emphasis on the law is a prosecutor's obsession that would lead to the most terrible injustice?'

She slotted a jigsaw piece into the mass of his, joining up two sections into one. 'Justice is not about this person or that person,' she said, 'it's about all of us. And the fact remains: the Truth Commission amnesty seems to be a way of saying that the guilty can go free.'

'Which,' he said, quickly adding another piece before shooting her a triumphant look, 'never happens in your precious United States?'

'Why precious?' she said, sitting back. 'Is that because you think I deserted South Africa?'

But instead of answering her, Ben changed the subject. 'We're wasting time,' he said. 'We must get down to work.'

She opened her mouth to protest but he was already pushing on his chair arms, winching himself up. Stubborn old man, she thought, watching him, knowing that he'd refuse her help if she offered it, and thinking, fondly, how it must have been when he decided to involve her in this latest project. She could just picture him sitting here in this study and picking up the phone to summon her. Despite their long separation, and his criticism of it, he still thought of her as his starry-eyed protégée ready to snap to his every command.

Except she thought, smiling wryly to herself, he'd been right, hadn't he? One phone call and she had sloughed off her caseload on to her reluctant colleagues and come running.

'Come,' he said, glaring at her. 'We must prepare. Tomorrow we will meet Alex Mpondo and the Sizelas. Let's see now if you're still capable of crossing the divide from prosecutor into people's champion.'

8

It was still dark when, having unlocked the gates and then locked them behind him, James Sizela walked up the path and towards the school.

It didn't take him long to reach the central quadrangle and when he had, he stopped and stood and took in the sight of it. The buildings, four of them arranged around him, were just long, low breeze-block constructions with square windows whose glass was fractured here and there. But there were small victories, visible by moonlight, that gave him quiet satisfaction. The courtyard was litter-free and the harsh veld grasses had not yet encroached on the flagstones since the last day of weeding. The array of desks in the classroom, which he could vaguely detect through the cracked glass of the window, were neatly laid out in those long lines that experience had taught him created the optimum conditions for learning. Nodding to himself, he went over to the entrance, unlocked both the metal grill and the door that lay beyond it and went in.

There was nobody around – of course not, it was far too early. James felt his way down the deserted corridor. He could have turned on the lights but what for? He was able to negotiate his way through the school no matter how dark it was. It was his life, this place: or what remained of his life after Steve had been killed. He knew it intimately, each corner of it, each floor stone, each crack in the wall and what they meant, each worrying symptom of decay and each improvement he had hard won over many years arguing with the authorities.

Yet this morning it was different. For once the school seemed a strange, abstract thing. After all, how could any school compete with the possibility that with Ben's – and now this woman, Sarah Barcant's – help, he might finally lay his son to rest?

It wasn't often James allowed himself to dwell on Steve's fate. He had always been a realist. While his wife had kept her spirits up by waiting out the return of the exiled ANC, hoping against hope that their son would be among their number, James had been unable to find comfort in self-deception. When, in 1985, months passed without a word from Steve, he had faced the truth. Their boy was dead.

In silence James had trained himself to accept this. It was the way he was. Just as he had helped successive generations of pupils understand that some things could not be changed, so had he acknowledged that Steve's death was one of these. A fact. Unalterable.

And yet occasionally questions would insinuate themselves into his mind. Questions he did not want to address. Like:

How much had his boy suffered? Had he cried out? Had he been brave? Questions that should not even be asked.

And now with the Truth Commission about to start these questions might not only be asked but also answered. They came at him, breaking into consciousness, throwing him off stride. Today they had even visited him in sleep, waking him up, driving him from bed. Driving him to school. For what? He wasn't entirely sure. There was no task waiting for his attention or at least no task he could complete before he was due to meet with the lawyers and James made it a point of principle never to start anything he couldn't finish.

He settled, therefore, for a quick inspection. Using touch to select one from a huge cluster of keys, he unlocked the door of a classroom and went in. He saw four rows of individual desks, each one scratched and scrawled on, lined up symmetrically in front of a blackboard. Weaving his way past the desks, he went over to the window. The words he could just make out on the blackboard were of fjords and ravines and crevasses. Turning away he occupied himself by running his finger along the window edge. He didn't need light to tell him just how much dust was picked up in that one motion, he could feel the particles clinging to his skin. That didn't mean the cleaners had been neglectful – there was so much dirt in the township and so little greenery to keep it down. Nevertheless, James made a mental note to speak with them about it. He knew he had to do it. Anarchy was all too ready to assert itself in this country of theirs. If he let the cleaners off the hook the wrong message would soon spread through the school, closely followed by all manner of disobediences. James could not risk that: his job was not to save the one but to safeguard the whole. His life path was not for the faint-hearted or the impatient. He was a headmaster, not a politician whose business was the making and the breaking of promises. Governments and their different systems might come and go but he stayed in place, working at the painstaking business of helping the next generation make something of itself. He couldn't afford easy solutions – he had to take the long view.

He sighed and, deciding to go home, walked back down the corridor heading for the exit.

It was only when he had nearly reached the door, that a thought occurred to him – so suddenly that it caught him unawares. Did this kind of issue also weigh on Pieter Muller's conscience? Was Muller driven out of bed by the things that he had done and the things that he must do?

James was shocked to catch the thought. Muller. Again. But Muller was nothing to James. A vehicle, that's all. A way of doing what James must do – find Steve after all these many years and give him a decent burial. If the Truth Commission was useful in this, then James would use it too.

All James wanted was his son. His son to bury before he himself grew too old to do so.

He turned the handle of the door, harder than he intended and, wincing at the noise it made, went out.

9

SITTING AT ONE end of a plastic-covered sofa, Sarah could hear James Sizela's voice thumping down the narrow corridor: 'Why did you do it?' James demanded.

Ben, who was sitting at other end of the sofa, seemed unperturbed either by James's anger or by the long delay. In fact, with his eyes closed and his head lolling back, he looked asleep. Lucky him. She glanced at her watch. Two o'clock: they'd already been there an hour.

'I'm waiting for an answer,' she heard.

Leaning forward, she looked past the open door and down the narrow corridor and could just make out the sight of James Sizela. Dressed in a formal pinstripe suit whose wide lapels and generously cut trousers said country not town and

1950s not 1990s, he was standing by a schoolboy who was perched on a high, tubular, steel chair.

'I am still waiting,' James Sizela said.

The boy's scrawny legs, dangling out of his long grey shorts, swung back and forth as he mumbled a reply Sarah couldn't quite catch. It was hot in the house and hotter in the kitchen: the boy was probably sticking to the cracked red plastic covering of his stool.

'Ah – so you were hungry.' Stepping back, James Sizela seemed to be surveying the boy. 'Tell me: did you eat the desk?'

A shake of the boy's head – no.

'Did you sell it for food?'

Another shake.

'If you didn't eat it and you didn't sell it, what did you do with it?'

The boy sat motionless.

'I will tell you what you did,' James Sizela said. 'You chopped it up for firewood and had yourself a braai. Is that correct?'

This time Sarah could see the boy nodding.

'And tell me,' James Sizela said, 'do you have the desk now?'

'No, sir.' The boy's words were delivered soft and high and in a voice that was yet to break.

James Sizela's bass righteousness bulldozed through this tentativeness. 'Of course you don't have it. You've reduced it to ashes. Tomorrow when you feel hungry you will not have the desk. You will not have it tomorrow, nor the next day, nor the one after that either. On each succeeding day you will rise hungry and you will have nothing on which to cook. The difference is that when you get to school you will also have nothing on which to write.' He leaned in, his face almost touching the boy's, his skin dull in comparison to the boy's high reddish-brown. 'And neither will the other pupils,' his voice was pounding out evangelistically. 'That is the consequence of your action.'

Sarah leaned back again.

'Do you think that is the way our President behaves?' she heard.

She glanced again in Ben's direction. He looked peaceable and gentle in repose. He'd been so testy since she'd come back, she'd almost forgotten that he was also a warm, generous man who had once given her so much. Now, watching the rise and fall of his breath, she felt like reaching out and stroking his hand.

But she didn't want to disturb him. She sat thinking that in all her years before, and even in all rebelliousness, she'd never been invited into a black home nor thought to beg an invitation for herself. The divide was so complete then, she thought, no wonder I left. She let her gaze wander idly round the room.

It was an uninspired orderly lounge in a small, square concrete township house, and it was furnished with two plastic-covered armchairs to match the sofa, a long low-sided table and a set of metal bookshelves on which resided a polished hi-fi along with the complete works of Shakespeare. Although there were only dirt roads outside, with no greenery to pin down the earth, inside the room there was not a speck of dust. The room even smelled new, as if it and its contents had been picked out of a warehouse and deposited here, five kilometres from the centre of Smitsrivier, and never used again save for the hanging of the framed photographs that lined the wall to the left of the bookshelf.

'Does Nelson Mandela steal desks?' she heard James Sizela asking.

Getting up, she approached the photographs, scanning each one in turn. They were chronologically arranged and featured a single subject: a fresh-faced Steve Sizela. At first, Steve was just a boy posed awkwardly against a sky-blue background and dressed in the same grey shorts and gleaming white shirt as the child in the kitchen. Then, as Sarah's gaze shifted down the chain, he grew taller and more confident until he was finally captured by a news photographer as he stood on a platform with clenched fist raised high.

From the kitchen Sarah could hear the sound of James Sizela in full rhetorical flight: 'Does our President break windows he cannot afford to fix?'

Looking at the picture of James's dead son, Sarah thought that if Steve had lived he would have now been thirty-six – the same age as her. She stretched out a hand.

'That is the last picture of him ever taken,' she heard.

Startled, she turned to find that Ben was already on his feet and standing by the door, holding it open for Mrs Sizela who was bringing in a large tea tray.

'It was taken the week before his arrest,' Mrs Sizela said, putting down the tray and then, swaying from her broad hips, leaning heavily on her left leg, favouring the right, walked over to stand by Sarah. A short, stout, solid woman, she tilted her head back to gaze at the photograph of her son. Her broad flat face, its brown skin mottled by dark patches which were almost black under her eyes, was strangely expressionless as she reached out and, as if in imitation of what Sarah had felt an impulse to do, touched the image. Her face softened and she smiled as she sketched her son's outline with her finger. 'This is the way I like to remember him,' she said. 'It's the moment I keep.' Her hand dropped down.

Watching, Sarah saw a shadow passing over Mrs Sizela's face, and when she spoke again her voice was expressionless. 'That picture helps drive out my last sight of him,' she said, 'the sight of my son lying on the ground as they kicked him.'

Sarah winced. 'They did that in front of you?'

'They always used to beat him when they came to get him.' Mrs Sizela's voice was flat, as if she were talking about some routine matter like a credit-card check or a chicken being double-wrapped. 'It was part of the softening-up process. They came in the middle of the night: they always did that as well. They hauled Steve out of bed and handcuffed him. I could see the metal cutting into his flesh and the blood beginning to run as they dragged him out of the house. When he fell down they kicked him and then they hauled him up and threw him into the back of the van. They drove off with the door open. I could see them hitting Steve with a sjambok.'

'Was Pieter Muller wielding the sjambok?'

Mrs Sizela looked at Sarah, puzzled, as if she didn't quite understand the question and then she said, 'Pieter Muller wouldn't have gone with him. The van, a mellow yellow, was for Africans.'

Of course – and Pieter Muller was white. Stupid of me, Sarah thought, I've been gone so long I've forgotten the way that everything, from waiting-room seats to police wagons, was always colour-coded.

Dragging her bad leg to an armchair, Mrs Sizela lowered herself down. 'Pieter Muller followed in his car,' she said. 'Him and another white warrant officer. The other policemen, the Africans, beat Steve in the mellow yellow but they didn't kill him. A comrade was booked in at the same time – he saw Steve alive. And Steve was alive three days later on the nineteenth when they brought him to Alex's cell.' She blinked, her gaze moving off Sarah. At first, her eyes focused on a point in the distance, but then she sighed and refocused her gaze, returning herself to the confines of her living room and to the repetition of what had happened.

'When I went to collect Steve's dirty washing that next week,' she said, 'as I had always done when he was in detention, they told me he'd been released.' She leaned forward suddenly and dropped her head down into her hands and began rocking backwards and forwards, rocking smoothly, making no sound. When finally she stopped and raised her head, Sarah saw that her eyes were dry. Perhaps her words were all the more powerful for that: 'A mother should not outlive her son,' she said. 'He was my flesh and blood. I would have gladly given my life for his. Now, all I ask is that you help us find Steve so that we may bury him.'

Sarah swallowed and looked down, blinking, willing away her tears and when that didn't work, closing her eyes. I hate this place, she thought, I hate what it does to me, her throat constricting as she forced herself to swallow down her feelings, as she sat remembering scenes from her childhood: a woman of Mrs Sizela's age waiting in vain for the police to come and attend to her after an attack; the voice of a white baas raised in anger; a black man's look, eyes lowered, in sullen resistance; Smitsrivier in all its ugliness, in all its inequality. And it hasn't changed, she thought.

Or had it? A voice followed her into darkness. A cheerful man's voice saying: '*Molo*, mama,' and then: 'Ben my bro.'

She opened her eyes to find the atmosphere transformed. Mrs Sizela was smiling broadly at a man who must be Alex Mpondo and who was already moving on to Ben. Ben was also beaming, obviously pleased, not minding that Mpondo was over forty minutes late for his date with them. Leaning back and watching the two men embrace, seeing Alex Mpondo's strong hands almost covering Ben's frail old man's back, Sarah thought how this stranger's energy had transformed the lounge from an arid waiting room into a place of warmth, uniting each of its occupants by the simple act of acknowledging their presence.

Her turn had come. Charming, at ease, casual in blue jeans and a white T-shirt that hung beautifully from his boxer's shoulders, he came up close to where she was sitting, gripped her hand and said, 'You must be Sarah,' as if they were already friends, adding, 'thank you for coming to help us,' as if this was his home and Steve his relation. She felt his hand warm and dry against hers and was taken aback by her reluctance to let go. She withdrew it quickly.

Alex's attention had already moved back to Mrs Sizela: 'Is that Jacob's son I saw in the kitchen?'

'It's Jacob's nephew.' Mrs Sizela leaned forward and began pouring out tea. 'Sipho – the youngest brother's son. The parents live out on a farm near Sagiesdorp. It's too far to travel so the boy stays on his own in the township during the week. He ran out of money for paraffin: he burned one of the school desks.'

'And thus will be scrubbing school floors for months to come, if I know anything about the old man,' Alex said.

'Well, it appears then that you do not know me.' James Sizela must have tiptoed down the corridor. He was standing in the doorway, using that stiff, stern voice of his to say: 'My intention is to expel the boy.'

It was startling for Sarah to see how fast Alex Mpondo's expression could change. It wasn't just in his lips which closed and tightened, but in his eyes as well which hardened as he said abruptly: 'The boy was hungry.'

'They are all hungry.'

'Come on, comrade . . .' Alex was in control again, the picture of conciliation as he walked towards James Sizela, reaching out a hand as if to reach out with his reason.

He was never given the chance. James Sizela said, angrily, 'I am speaking to you not as a comrade, Alex, but as a headmaster. This is the fourth time Sipho has destroyed school property. If I am lenient with him, how many desks do you think I will have left next Monday?'

'But . . .'

Once again the older man overrode his junior. 'No, Alex,' firm, unbending, 'there can be no more buts. Apartheid made victims of us but apartheid has been abolished. This is our country now. We are in charge: we must use what we have to improve ourselves. You too, Alex, use the education I gave you not to raise your fist and shout *Amandla* and call a boycott because of one thieving boy but to help all my pupils. We've put you in Parliament so you will give up the slogans and find us more desks, Alex, more books, more teachers.'

Something – the repetition of the name, *Alex*, or James Sizela's condescending tone, or the expression of rage only partially suppressed on Alex's face, made Sarah know that the real issue between these two men was not the fate of one boy or even one country but something else, unspoken.

'Granted, the community is important,' Alex said firmly, 'but so is the fate of individuals.'

Sarah knew that this argument, once joined, could go on for a long time. She cleared her throat, saying loudly and in the face of Ben's glared disapproval: 'The hearing begins tomorrow. If you don't mind, I think we should start.'

'No,' Alex Mpondo was smiling again. 'I don't mind,' he said, his handsome face untroubled as if his argument with James Sizela was a trifle, easily discarded. 'It's a good idea: let's make a start.'

10

SARAH WIPED HER forehead with the back of her hand. The kitchen was very hot, its tin roof trapping the sun's heat and that of a huge cast-iron pot whose contents were bubbling on the stove. She looked across the table to where Alex was sitting next to Ben. Seeing her eyes on him, Alex smiled. His face lit up then, his brown-red skin crinkling around his eyes.

'Let's go back to the morning when they brought Steve to your cell,' she said. 'Why did they do that?'

At that his face stiffened and he said, dully, 'It was part of their interrogation technique.'

She added the words, *interrogation technique*, to her notes, the sum of which told her what she already knew – that she was getting nowhere. No matter what she tried, the pattern remained stubbornly the same: Alex was the model of co-operation until she led him anywhere near the pivotal event, his last sighting of Steve Sizela, and then he would seize up on her. She put down her pen. She needed to take a moment and figure out why. She looked past him and out through the open door, looking down the track that fell away from the house.

At first, what she saw were those same plain, squat, brick township dwellings that could be found all over South Africa. But gradually as the track sloped further downhill, the build-ings grew smaller and frailer until they were no longer houses but makeshift shacks knocked together from a patchwork of materials – plastic, hardboard, sheet metal, recycled glass – awkward, crooked constructions that could never have kept the elements at bay.

It was the kind of place where Alex had grown up: that, at least, she'd learned so far. It was difficult to believe – he had so much of the city about him. She frowned. A lone gum tree stood at the very edge of the hill, its shredded skin hanging loose, its roots littered by ribbons of plastic, burned-out tin cans and filthy bundles of balled-up paper. A young boy passed by the tree, licking a stick against the rubber of an old car tyre, whipping it up, setting it rolling furiously as, whoop-ing, he chased it.

She heard Ben clearing his throat, summoning her back to the kitchen's thickened silence.

She pulled in her gaze. She needed to cut through and quickly. Exaggerating the twist of her head so as to make it clear she was directing what she had to say exclusively at Alex, she said, 'Listen to me, Alex. I'm trying to prepare you for court. To do this I have to know everything that hap-pened. In the last hour that we've been talking all we've done is skirt round the issue. I think you and I both understand why: I think we both know that you're withholding some-thing.' She held up a hand to stop either of the men breaking in. 'Don't misunderstand me: this is not a moral judgement. I'm sure you have your reasons. But unless you can find a way of trusting me long enough to tell me the truth, I can't risk calling you to the stand.'

'I do trust you.' Alex grinned.

His grin was so infectious it was an effort to keep on target. 'If that's true,' she insisted, 'why do you look to Ben before you answer me?'

'Perhaps that's to do with the manner of your asking,' Ben shot in.

Damn Ben. He had kept doing this, interrupting; under-cutting her. She couldn't understand why. Why haul her all the way from New York so he could dump this case on her and then do his utmost to undermine any rapport she might possibly have reached with Alex? 'This is hopeless,' she said, her gaze shifting from one to the other and then back again. 'If Alex has to pass everything through a censor, I might as well not be here.'

Alex's voice: 'I'm sorry,' offered an opening. 'These are hard memories. I'll try to be more forthcoming.'

She edged in her chair closer to the table: 'OK.' Getting down to business: 'Let's start from where we left off: the moment when they brought Steve to your cell. You said he stood there. What happened after that?'

Alex swallowed. 'Steve pointed . . .'

Steve pointed, she wrote.

'. . . at me.'

She wrote that down as well – *at me* – and looked up. 'Why did he point?'

'It was a trick.'

'A trick?'

He dropped his gaze, staring down at the oil cloth as if the answer might be found there among its dark green swirls.

'Alex,' she said.

Alex said: 'Steve had agreed to turn state witness,' speaking softly and at the same time swallowing down his words so that she only fully understood the sentence after his voice had died away.

In her surprise, she leaned in too far to exclaim: 'Steve was going to give evidence against you?' speaking so loudly that even to herself she sounded as if she were shouting.

Not that Alex seemed to care. As he said 'Yes', and as he nodded to reinforce this confirmation, all the life seemed to drain from him. 'Hendricks told me that Steve had agreed to identify me as an MK operative who had buried some RPGs in the dried-up river bed outside town,' he said.

She steadied herself. 'And was this true?'

He looked at her.

'Was it true?'

'Does it matter?'

She asked it a third time. 'Was it true?'

'Sarah . . . please . . .' This from Ben.

She raised her voice. 'Answer the question, Alex. Were you an operative of the ANC army?'

Alex's wiry frame stiffened

'Did you bury a box of rocket-propelled grenades by the river?'

The sinewy muscles on his upper arms tightened.

She sighed. 'Did Steve betray you?'

'I will not answer,' he shouted, at the same time slamming his hand down so hard against the table that the clap of the impact resounded through the small concrete room.

She acted instinctually. She turned round; she didn't know why – perhaps to escape Alex's fury. She was in time to see the living-room door opening and James Sizela appearing. The gaunt, stern figure of James Sizela standing and staring. She looked away. Sounds came to her: the soft bubbling of the stove, the rustle of something blown along the dust-strewn track, the rhythmic thwack of the stick against rubber, the deep breaths Alex was taking.

She looked again. The doorway was empty now.

She turned her gaze back into the kitchen. Alex was sitting quietly. He seemed very calm now and very still. 'Listen to me, Alex: Soon after the Hendricks hearing begins, we will serve Pieter Muller with a writ. If Muller's got any brains, and I gather he has, he will immediately hire himself a lawyer. This lawyer is bound to ask you all these questions. If you have so much difficulty answering me here, with Ben at your side, imagine what it will be like in court. You're a crucial witness, our only witness: if doubt is cast on what you say, the Sizelas' case will be seriously weakened. Do you understand?'

A nod.

'Good. Now I'm going to ask you again. Is it true that you were working for the ANC military?'

'Yes.' He swallowed.

'And did you in fact hide weapons for the ANC?'

It came again. 'Yes.'

'Did Steve Sizela know this?'

A long silence. Too long.

'Yes,' Alex said. 'Steve knew.'

She wrote it in her pad: *Yes, Steve knew.*

'But don't you see? It didn't matter what Steve knew. His turning traitor was a bullshit line. They didn't need a witness: the way the law was, they could have kept me in jail for as long as they wanted without ever charging me.'

They came to her again, the doubts that kept on dogging her: 'So why was he at your cell door?'

'Because they thought the sight would break me. Yes, he was standing in the doorway, but he wasn't really standing. They were holding him up. His face was swollen. His eyes were puffed up, the colours you never think a skin can turn.

He didn't know what he was doing. He would have danced a fucking Highland fling if they'd told him to. We all would have.' He swallowed, again. Hard, bitterly. 'And yes. Steve pointed. But what did it matter? He didn't even know I was there. They told him to lift his hand and he lifted it. That's all. Then they took him away.'

'They?' she said, trying to push away from her mind's eye the image of Mrs Sizela's finger gently stroking the image of her son.

'Two African warrant officers. I don't know who they were.'

'And this was the last time you saw Steve?'

'No.' Alex's voice was dull, but when he said 'There was one other time', there was some undercurrent riding there. A warning?

She was immediately alerted. 'When was that?'

He shook his head. 'I can't remember.'

'A day later?'

Silence.

'Two days?'

'I don't know.' Soft again, so soft she had to lean in to hear him. 'I can't remember.'

'A week?'

'I'm sorry.' He did sound genuinely sorry. 'I can't remember,' and also genuinely as if he could not remember.

Time to move on. 'Was this second sighting like the first? Did they bring him to your cell?'

'No. I was outside my cell then. Steve was at the other end of the corridor. They were carrying him out.' A beat. 'He was dying.' Another beat. 'Or he was already dead.'

'What makes you say that?'

'The way they were carrying him, like a dead weight. I was looking down the corridor. No conscious being could have stayed as still as he did when they hit him against the bars of the gate.'

Her hand moved rapidly across the page, taking down what he said but all the while she kept on frowning. There was still something not quite right. She looked up. 'Was Pieter Muller there?'

A nod.

'Please, Alex, say the words out loud. Was Pieter Muller present?'

'Muller supervised the taking-out of Steve. He was in charge. When one of Steve's arms got stuck in the bars, Pieter Muller laughed and wrenched it out.'

Strange how the plainest of descriptions could also be the most evocative. That lack of inflexion in Alex's voice conjured up for Sarah the sight of that arm – that live arm that once had been raised so proudly now a piece of flesh hitting metal.

'And Dirk Hendricks?' she said. 'Was he also there?'

'No.' Alex shook his head. 'Not Hendricks.'

Something out of place. But what? 'What were you doing outside your cell?'

'They were taking me for interrogation. That's why Hendricks wasn't there. He was already waiting in the inter-rogation room. He liked to do that: he liked to jump on me as I came in.'

The way he spat out those acrid words, *jump on me*, startled her. She looked at him. He met her gaze full on. He was unblinking. And it came to her suddenly: why what he was saying couldn't be right. Unhooking her bag from the back of the chair, she took out a piece of paper and laid it, face down, on the table.

'Let me see if I've understood the sequence correctly,' she said. 'You were leaving your cell to go to the room where Dirk Hendricks was waiting? Is that right?'

'Yes, that's right.'

'At that moment you saw Steve being carried out? You looked down the corridor and saw him?'

'Yes.'

'He was by the exit? They were taking him outside?'

'Yes.'

She turned the paper over, swivelling it and pushing it across the table so it was facing Alex. 'This is a plan of the police station,' she said. 'The layout is as it was fifteen years ago. If you wouldn't mind, please point to your cell.'

While Ben leaned in closer, Alex stared down at the line drawing. For a moment all three sat in silent contemplation of a square structure whose front half consisted of a reception area off the street, a door which led to a series of interview rooms and, beyond that, the back half of the building made up of a narrow corridor from which ran a series of small cells.

She broke the silence. 'Where was your cell?'

Alex's finger touched a line – the last cell door on the left.

'Now please indicate the door that leads to the interrogation rooms.'

Once again his finger stabbed the paper – this time on a point directly opposite his cell.

It was as she'd thought. 'That's the only exit, isn't it?'

He didn't answer. He didn't need to.

'Which means that what you described to me could not have happened. If they were carrying Steve out, if they bumped him up against the railings of the gate then they would have had to have been here,' she pointed at the place Alex's finger had just vacated, 'opposite your cell. But that doesn't tally with what you said before. You said,' she flicked back through her notes, 'you said, and I quote: *Steve was at the other end of the corridor. They were carrying him out.* And later you said: *I was looking down the corridor . . . they hit him against the bars of the gate.* But it couldn't have happened like that, could it?' She traced her finger to the end of the corridor to where an unbroken line indicated a solid wall: 'There's no exit there.'

She looked at him.

He looked away.

'What did you really see?'

He was busy staring at the floor.

'Did you see anything?' She had him: she had skewered him. Any moment now . . .

'Sarah.'

No, Ben, she thought, not now. She said, loudly, to override Ben, 'Answer me, Alex. What did you really see?'

'That's enough.' Ben hauled himself to his feet, 'I'm sorry, Alex,' pulling at Sarah's collar as if she were his stubborn puppy. 'Come on, Sarah. We're leaving.'

11

BEN'S TAXI, A dilapidated township car with an exhaust pipe trailing in the dirt, was waiting with its back door open. He didn't get in. He stood instead on the dusty track that ran outside the Sizelas' house glaring at Sarah.

She didn't understand why *he* was so angry. She looked away.

His voice summoned her back. 'What the hell did you think you were doing?' He was almost shouting.

She turned, and said calmly, 'I was taking a preliminary statement – as we agreed I would.'

Ben's pale face flushed a deep dark red. 'That was no statement taking.' He was really shouting now. 'It was a crucifixion. You were acting like a prosecutor bent on cross-examining a hostile witness in court.'

If it hadn't been so absurd, and Ben so serious, she would have laughed out loud. 'I'd never have asked such open-ended questions in court. It's because we weren't in court and because, according to you, we soon will be that I tried to find out what Alex knew.'

'Alex is on our side,' Ben said, more softly now. 'And he's a friend.'

Since when had Ben ever used friendship to justify a legal argument? 'He's also a witness. He might be our only witness. Some witness! He doesn't seem to remember what he saw.'

'He was badly tortured.'

'And so? You're not trying to suggest, surely, that because Alex was tortured we should help him fabricate his evidence?'

'How dare you?' Two bright red spots, one on each cheek, was all that remained of Ben's colour. 'Is that what you think of me?'

She sighed. 'I don't know what to think, Ben. Yesterday you agreed that without some kind of evidence against Muller our case would be a non-starter. You assured me that Alex would supply this evidence. You also said that, to put my mind at rest, I could be in charge of the interview. And then look what happened: as soon as I started pressing him on the obvious discrepancies in his story, you pulled the plug. Now tell me: what exactly am I missing here?'

'What you're missing,' Ben's voice was undercut with derision, 'is a basic grasp of human nature. After the way Alex was treated it wouldn't be surprising if there were gaps in his memory – especially when you subject him to such intense pressure.'

'I didn't really pressurise him.' She was now the one who was struggling to stay calm. 'I asked him simple, factual questions which he either couldn't, or wouldn't, answer.'

'Couldn't? Wouldn't? Why bother supplying both options? It's obvious which one you've chosen.'

How dare he? She raised her voice. 'Oh, come on, Ben. You know as well as I do that Alex Mpondo is hiding something. If we're serious about proceeding, we have to find out what.'

'You're wrong.' Ben's weak blue eyes were watery with agitation. 'You've been gone too long. This isn't fast-talking New York, Sarah, it's Smitsrivier. People are slower here, they're much less direct. If Alex was oblique then that's because it's his way, his people's way. You've forgotten how this world works.'

'OK. Suppose for the sake of argument that you're right: suppose I did jump too fast. Isn't this why you brought me all the way from New York: because you needed my objective eye?'

'Objective!' His soft voice was bleeding scorn. 'You're not objective, Sarah, you're a hunter. Why else did you think to bring that map in your handbag?'

That astonished her. 'I brought it because that's what I would always do,' she said. 'It's called preparation. I was taught to do it properly. By an expert. By you.'

'Don't implicate me in your behaviour.' Ben narrowed his eyes. 'Yes, it's true: I was once your teacher. But you're no longer the person I knew or the lawyer I trained. You think like a prosecutor and you act like one even among friends. It's inappropriate.' He turned away.

Did he think he could insult her and then leave? If he did, he was wrong. 'Why don't you look to your own behaviour, Ben?' she spat at his retreating back.

He stopped and in that moment of his hesitation, she saw him anew. He was so thin and stooped and frail. I should have left it, she thought, I should have refused the bait.

But when he turned, his face was set in an ugly frown, and when he said, quietly, 'Go on,' his words were delivered on a current of such ominous warning that they drove away any notion of her lowering the animosity. She went on. 'You've always been in the right, Ben,' she said. 'That's your great strength. But times have changed. Things are no longer so clear-cut.'

Ben was no longer frowning. He wasn't doing anything much. His face was almost blank, so blank, in fact, that she even wondered whether he knew who she was. The thought frightened her. She wanted to reach out and take back what she'd just said. His skin was stretched so tight, she saw, it was almost translucent. Suddenly the truth came to her. He wasn't just ill, he was dying. Dying. The pain of this certainty engulfed her. She took a step towards him. 'I'm sorry . . .'

His anger cut down her apology. 'Is this what New York has done to you? Did it turn you into such an unfeeling monster?' Without waiting for her reply, he hobbled over to the taxi, climbed in and, banging his door shut, stared straight ahead as he instructed the driver to get him out of there.

There was nothing for her to do save stand and watch as his car moved off.

She wondered whether she should follow, calm him down, show him how much he meant to her. But even as this thought occurred, she knew it wouldn't do. Ben might be slow to rouse, but once roused, he was also impossible to placate. If she went to him now, he would only rebuff her. Stubborn as he was and convinced of his own righteousness, he would never change his mind.

Maybe I should go back into the Sizelas' instead and speak to Alex she thought, find out what he's hiding. But no. That would not do either. Ben was most likely correct. She had probably jumped in too fast. Alex needed time. She would wait for him to come to her – always the best strategy.

12

Dirk woke up flailing, shouting out, his cries bouncing off the concrete walls. A dream, he told himself, it was only a dream. He clamped his lips together and lay still, and as the images receded, the sound of his horror also faded. Now other thoughts took its place: like where the hell was he? He looked round. He couldn't tell whether it was day or night and he didn't recognise this place. He leaned over, half hanging off his bed, retching.

The floor – dark flagstones – was his first clue. The coarse grey regulation blanket that he must have kicked off sometime during the night was the second. He looked up. A light bulb encased by metal was burning harshly. Of course. He knew now where he was. In a cell, but not in Pretoria. In a cell in Smitsrivier. A prisoner where once he had been master.

A prisoner who would soon be free. Today was his new beginning. Despite the fact that it must still be very early, he might as well prepare himself for what lay ahead. He got off the bunk, lowered himself down on to the cold stone floor and began his sequence of push-ups.

The view from the front of the Smitsrivier Retreat as Sarah finished her run was at its most extravagant, the last remnants of a late dawn tinting the land a rich shade of crimson. From the window of her room on the first floor, however, the sight that greeted her was a dilapidated backyard, with a tumbledown outbuilding and a jumbled washing line, surrounded by a high picket-fence crowned by razor wire. She didn't let the tawdriness of the spectacle bring her down. She was feeling great, her limbs loose and easy, the toxins and the jet lag burned out by the intensity of her run. Moving away from the window, she peeled off her soaking T-shirt and went over to the shower.

She turned both taps on hard and stepped back. From somewhere deep inside the building came the sound of pipes clanking before a spurt of scalding water, rust orange and then turning a deeper, darker red, the colour of the land, erupted from the shower head. No problem. She stood at the edge of the encrusted tiles waiting until the water flow increased, its colour cleared and its temperature reverted to its standard tepid, before she stepped in.

She was just finishing when the phone rang. Perfect timing. Wrapping a towel round her, she went over to the narrow bed, sitting down on its sky-blue candlewick bedspread and picking up the receiver to say a cheery 'Hello'.

Anna's voice sounded faintly. 'Here is Ben for you.'

Of course: Sarah remembered how Anna always had acted

as telephonist for Ben. In court he was quite capable of cutting through the most obscure of scientific evidence, but out of it he was such a technical klutz that he somehow, on the rare occasions when he tried, always dialled the wrong number.

He also always spoke too loudly on the phone. Now, as if yesterday's argument had never occurred, he boomed out 'Sarah' so loudly that she wrenched the receiver from her ear.

As usual he didn't go in for small chat. He delivered down the line a sequence of staccato sentences that brooked no interruption. 'I won't be at the hearing. Press on the Sizela case as agreed. Ring Alex. Coordinate with him. His mobile number is in the file,' and then, without waiting for her to reply, he hung up.

He left her sitting, astounded, on the bed.

It took a moment to come to her senses. When that happened she let the receiver drop. Bloody Ben. He always had been unpredictable but this was going to extremes. The gall of it. Not only was he acting as if no cross words had passed between them, but now he was sending her to a hearing to represent one reluctant client, Alex Mpondo, who Ben had stopped her questioning, so that she could raise the concerns of another, James Sizela, who was almost a complete stranger!

And yet she couldn't quite stoke up her indignation. Maybe it was the running. Or maybe it was just that surge of adrenaline that always hit her at the beginning of every case, especially one as challenging as this. Thousands of miles from her New York home she was feeling those old familiarities: that tingle at her fingertips, the performance about to begin. Move on, she told herself, move on. Time was running out. She got up briskly. She knew what she must do. She must get dressed, ring and speak to Alex Mpondo before the hearing began and, finally, decide which of her collection of shoes she should ruin that day.

Anna reached to take the phone. 'How did she react?'

Lying in bed, propped up by a high mound of pillows, Ben responded: 'She'll manage,' he said. 'She always does.'

Which was true, Anna thought: Sarah had always risen to the challenges Ben set her; it was one of the many character-istics they shared. Oh, well. Taking up the bowl of porridge, Anna proffered it to Ben.

He shook his head: 'Thank you, Anna. Later perhaps,' and closed his eyes.

She knew there was no point in arguing. He wasn't hungry, he hadn't been for days. So she stood for the moment by his bedside, looking down. He'd had a bad night and he was very pale. Never a large man, his shock of hair (in her opin-ion far too anarchic for a grown man), was splayed out wildly on the pillows, making his face look even more shrunken than usual. Nevertheless, the sight brought a smile to Anna's lips. Sick as he was, she knew he was nowhere near surren-der. And she didn't believe the excuse he'd used on her – that he was too weak to go to the hearing. It was just a manoeuvre, something to do with his continual challenging of Sarah.

Ben and his agendas, Anna thought, taking the bowl of porridge to the door. No, that wasn't quite accurate. Rather, it was Ben and his passions.

Anna had always known that her husband was the most ardent and the most unusual of men. Not for him that common striving for status at work, or that urge to secure his family's future, or even to perfect his skill at sport: instead, what he had opted for was a lifetime spent battling the injus-tices he saw everywhere around him. A laudable aspiration, Anna thought, and yet with drawbacks.

For a start it meant that his work was never over. But then he was his work; Anna knew that. Maybe, she thought, if they'd had children, it might have been different. But somehow she doubted it. From early in their marriage she'd had to learn to weigh his obsession with putting the world to rights alongside the love he felt for her. Only rarely (like now, for example) would she catch herself yearning for a husband who would set his sights on ordinary goals. To be with her, in solitude and calm; to enjoy the world without at the same time trying to change it.

He spoke suddenly from bed. 'Sarah will do fine without me.'

Sarah, Anna thought, why is it always Sarah? And she left the room.

As soon as Alex's hand brushed against the tiled edge of the pool he pushed his legs out, using them to flip himself round, and started swimming back. He'd been doing this for almost half an hour and was quite relaxed, settled into an easy crawl. His arms arched up, each in turn, elegantly into the air and then tucked down, propelling him smoothly forward. He felt very peaceful. Here, in this deserted place, he could hear none of the ugly reverberations that would bounce off the walls of his Cape Town gym: here, all was calm and so quiet, the only sound his legs' hushed flip as they moved through water and even that was filtered distantly through ear plugs.

And he was completely alone – just as he had wanted to be. The pool, a new municipal facility located in the sports ground outside Smitsrivier, only opened at 9 a.m. and to get in he'd had to scale the high brick wall that encircled it. Discarding his clothes by the poolside he had begun swimming as he liked to do each early morning, alternating ten lengths of crawl with two of backstroke, and all while the sun climbed higher in the clear blue sky.

His fingers touched base again. This time he turned on to his back and as he did this, he heard a sound. Ringing. It was coming from his mobile in his trouser pocket. This was the third call in the last twenty minutes: somebody was trying, persistently, to get hold of him. He knew the call would not be about constituency business or either of the parliamentary committees of which he was a member: he'd made sure to switch all that over to an answering service. Someone else then.

He didn't try and guess who: he didn't much care. He did what he had done the last time and the time before that: he ignored the ringing. Stretching his arms back and kicking his legs he propelled himself across the pool, turning on to his front when he reached the end.

There. The ringing stopped. Good. As he continued ploughing through the water, his thoughts wandered aimlessly. He thought how ironical it was that this pool was one of the first things the new South Africa had delivered to the desert town: perhaps someone on the ANC-dominated council, remembering the scores of young black men who had been drowned trying to move arms across southern Africa's river borders, had resolved to remedy the situation in case of an uncertain future. He curved round again and this time thought, vaguely, about the discussion that must have gone into the siting of this pool, neither in the township, where the water supply was still too uncertain, nor, because of the message this might entail, in the white-dominated town, but here, in this no-man's-land between the two. And he thought about Smitsrivier: how it must be waking up, men coming out sleepily from their square brick houses, their cars starting up and moving slowly along those straight tarred roads, and in the midst of all that rigid order, the police station.

And in the police station – Dirk Hendricks.

No. He kicked down hard.

The sun was climbing higher. He could see its rays glancing off the water's edge. Soon it would be very hot. What a good idea to come here, he thought, and rid his muscles of the tension that had built up all night.

He had slept, hadn't he? Come to think of it, he didn't really know. He wasn't aware of having lain awake for long in that tiny concrete township room and yet, if he had slept, he must have descended into that shallow unconsciousness that brought with it little rest. He hit the poolside and turned again.

At that moment shards of a distant dream returned. A face. A woman's face. Sarah Barcant? The face looming close, too close, asking questions he couldn't, wouldn't answer. A voice calling his name. Two faces. Two hands. Or was it one? One hand laid upon the other. Two faces that seemed like one. Not a woman any longer: two men. Dirk Hendricks. Alex Mpondo.

No. His legs slapped down. He would not think of it. Not now. He would not. Windmilling his arms into the water he hauled himself forward, kicking down wildly, until he seemed almost to be flying across the surface of the turbulent water.

13

STANDING IN THE wings of the town-hall stage, Dirk flicked his hand down his pressed blue jeans, brushing away a fleck of barely visible dust. That done, he straightened up and breathed in and out, in and out, nice and regular, nice and calm.

At last. The moment for which he had been waiting was almost upon him.

Beside him, his lawyer, Hannie Bester, coughed. He knew Hannie was annoyed. He wasn't used to waiting, not like Dirk. Now Hannie craned his neck, trying to see why Dirk's guards wouldn't let them go on stage.

There was nothing to see. Dirk kept still. The guards were checking, that's all, as they should, and, in contrast to Hannie,

Dirk was grateful for the delay. It gave him time to stand and to look and acclimatise himself to this place.

From where he was standing he could hear the buzz of the arriving crowd and, beyond the stage, could see sections of them flurrying about the place, trying to pick out the best seats. These were going rapidly, but Dirk didn't flatter himself into thinking that he was an extra special attraction. He knew Smitsrivier too well for that. Even the most insignificant of public occasions could draw a huge crowd of people intent on breaking the monotony of their small-town lives. As if anybody who wasn't in jail truly understood monotony!

Not that he was feeling sorry for himself. His ordeal was over. Almost over. He was sure of that.

He looked across at the wall opposite. Nelson Mandela's portrait was hanging in the place from which other presidents had once looked down. Not that Dirk objected. Mandela was President and therefore due the respect of his office. Fair enough. And anyway, even though Dirk's police career had been spent trying to keep the likes of Mandela in jail, Mandela could hardly turn out worse than the men who had gone before him – Dirk's one-time bosses, who'd spent the years since the election safeguarding their own skins by insisting they'd never known what their juniors like Dirk had got up to.

Hadn't known! Dirk's blue eyes clouded over in fury. It was a joke. No: it was beyond a joke. If they hadn't known, then why had they gone to the killers' training farm at Vlakplaas to celebrate the most daring of the missions with braais and beers? Or invited these same killers into their offices in Pretoria to pin the Police Star for Outstanding Services on their chests? Or . . .

Ag. He must not, he would not, think of it. That kind of stuff could eat you up. He drew his gaze in, concentrating on what was happening on stage. He saw his guards busy moving

chairs, making sure that their seats were where they wanted.
They weren't trying to guard against his escape – after all,
where could he go? – but rather against a prospective attack
from somewhere in the audience. Good for them; not that
Dirk thought such an attack would come, but it was good that
they took the right precautions.

A new appearance. A man, emerging from the opposite
wing and walking slowly, deliberately, over to a table. Not
just any man: Alex Mpondo. Alex, who was smart in a black
suit and a flash yellow shirt that looked like it might have
been sewn from silk. Christ, how different he looked. So different, in fact, that if Dirk hadn't known he would be there, he
wouldn't have recognised him. The changes covered every
aspect of the man. He seemed taller, more confident, more at
ease and even slightly fatter, but none of that was what was
really different. On the contrary, the dramatic change lay
entirely in Mpondo's face, in his expression. The jagged lines,
that ugliness, that battered visage . . . all of those were gone.
Well, of course. Dirk shook himself. Prison must be making
him stupid. What else had he expected? Mpondo was no
longer a prisoner. He was an MP. No wonder he looked different.

Mpondo was looking across the stage now, to a stylish
woman who was crossing over towards him. Smiling, hand
outstretched, Mpondo welcomed her. Of course: Dirk had
always suspected that, given the opportunity, Mpondo would
turn out to be a ladies' man.

'At last,' Hannie muttered.

The policemen were almost ready, one of them walking
round the stage, heading for them. Hannie shouldn't be so
impatient. They were well trained. Dirk respected that. He
had never forgotten how his own carelessness had nearly got
him shot on his first day in uniform. Not that he regretted
that. It had taught him a crucial lesson. Never again. Never

would he walk into any situation without first guarding his own back, a lesson he had never forgotten.

'On we go,' Hannie said.

What was the phrase that actors used? It came to Dirk as he stepped forward.

Showtime.

14

To Pieter it seemed as if the whole township had pitched up to gawk. Not literally, of course – the township would never have fitted into the auditorium – but still it was fortunate, he thought, that so many of the youth had chosen to toyi-toyi outside, rather than coming in and competing for seats.

He stood at the back of the auditorium looking at the small, raised stage with its scratched parquet flooring, dingy grey backdrop and musty green curtains – fully parted now to make space for the extended range of furniture that a hearing like this apparently demanded. His gaze drifted down and along the hall, from the knot of pressmen in its front, past rows of sludge-brown chairs that were bolted to each other and to the floor. More seats had been similarly packed into

the wooden gallery that hung suspended over the back half of
the auditorium, the audience there almost within touching
distance of fans that drooped down from the ceiling like pre-
historic insects.

There was a vacant seat towards the rear, but on the other
side. Rather than squeeze through he walked the full length of
both aisles, and even so he was conscious of the buzz of whispered comment that followed him. As he lowered his
substantial frame, his neighbours shifted restively away. He
took no notice. He simply sat down and looked over the sea
of napped heads.

On the stage, Dirk, accompanied by two heavily armed
policemen, walked from the wings. Once a brash, boisterous
man, Dirk now looked thin and pale and insecure with that
convict's way of cutting out peripheral vision by always
looking down. The thing that had once distinguished him
from other men – that unpredictable wildness that had
driven him to climb the steepest hill and there at the top to
reel off every stanza of his favourite pop song, or to drag
Pieter out on a midnight drinking spree, or to arrive for
lunch with a car teeming with carnations for Marie – all of
that was gone.

It made Pieter sick to his gut.

But what if it had happened to him? If he had to face the
prospect of never being able to walk the open veld again or of
never watching his Marie at peace in sleep or of never seeing
the bantam he'd bred through generations make Breed
Champion . . . Was it possible, he thought, remembering the
night when he had awakened so abruptly . . . No. He was
being fanciful. Dirk's priority, the focus of his concentration,
was his own predicament not Pieter's.

A voice spoke from the stage: 'Please rise.'

Silence while the three-man committee of judges filed on
stage.

Despite the fact that Truth Commission officials kept repeating that these hearings were neither contests nor exercises in revenge, the set-up looked undeniably confrontational to Pieter. The judges' table, elevated slightly above the participants and sited centre stage, faced the audience. As to the combatants: three separate tables had been assigned for their use. One on the right for Dirk and his advocate (with Dirk's guards close behind), and two on the left: the first for the Commission lawyer and the second for Alex Mpondo and his team.

Pieter craned forward in surprise. Who was that sitting next to Mpondo?

Well, well. Sarah Barcant. Although she wouldn't have known him, Pieter could never have mistaken her. He remembered her from two occasions: that first time on the road and the second when he'd viewed her through a peephole. He couldn't quite remember why that was. Oh yes, it came back to him, she'd been arrested in a black area and some of the uniformed branch had amused themselves by threatening to charge her under the Immorality Act. He remembered how she looked sitting there, a mere slip of a girl isolated in a cell, patently frightened but putting on a brave face. Just as her drinking with blacks had infuriated his colleagues, her childish defiance, once in their care, had enraged them further. Pieter's reaction had been different. She'd intrigued him – Marie might even say she'd taken his fancy – and, from a distance, he'd followed the progress of her astonishing academic achievements and inevitable emigration. Her mentor, Ben Hoffman, must have hoped she would return to take over his practice but Pieter never thought so. Her exit from Smitsrivier had not surprised him for a moment – she was far too big a character for small-town life. She was the kind who felt little loyalty for their country and who, on fleeing, so completely remade themselves that they could never come back.

So why then was she here? – this woman who, with her pale skin, flowing black hair and provocative manner, had seemed once a wild, flower child, but who now looked so composed, so chic, so alien as she put on her earphones when the middle member of the judges' panel, a thin, old, grey-haired bearded wisp of a man, said: 'If we could begin.'

The judge nodded at Dirk's lawyer, who adjusted his microphone as slowly and deliberately as lawyers who were paid by the hour did everything.

'Mr Chairman.' It was the participants' right to speak in Shona or Zulu or Xhosa or any one of the other official languages currently turning the country into the Tower of Babel. Dirk's lawyer chose Afrikaans: 'I am Advocate Bester,' he said, slowly so as to give the interpreters in their glass-walled booth time to relay his words in English or Xhosa to an audience all of whom, Pieter knew, were bound to be fluent in Afrikaans, 'and I appear for the applicant Dirk Hendricks.'

Then it was musical chairs. Sarah Barcant used English to say: 'Mr Chairman, I am Sarah Barcant, here to represent the victim Alex Mpondo who also reserves the right to cross-examine Mr Hendricks himself.' At this, a wave of muttered approval wafted through the audience – which presumably, Pieter Muller thought, was why she had wasted time by laying claim to a right that everybody knew was Mpondo's anyway. If Mpondo was so clever, Pieter thought, then why bother having a lawyer at all? – never mind one fetched all the way from New York.

A third grey-suited man, yet another English speaker, announced, 'I am Advocate Kelly and I'll be leading evidence for the committee.'

And that, counting the committee of judges, made six. Six highly paid lawyers for this one insignificant case! No wonder the South African legal profession kept slathering over the workings of the Commission – it would be their bread and butter for years to come. And not just here in Smitsrivier. Amnesty panels like this were meeting all over the country. The whole circus must be costing the country a fortune.

Up on stage, Dirk got to his feet and raised his right hand just as he had done so many times before.

'Mr Hendricks,' the chairman of the judges said, 'do you swear to tell the truth . . .'

The truth, Pieter heard, and he saw Dirk confident and at ease, the old Dirk sprung back to life, no longer a beaten prisoner but the man he once was, a policeman giving evidence as he had so many times before, while the judge clipped his way through the oath.

'. . . the whole truth and nothing but the truth so help you God?'

'I do,' Dirk said, hitting the same efficient note as he always had when giving evidence in court. Pieter felt his spirits lifting.

'*I do*,' Sarah heard as she sat beside an eerily still Alex Mpondo. She felt her interest rising. That dusty, dead-end Smitsrivier should be witness to the likes of this! This dance of the past, this baroque blending of court ceremonial, street party and revivalist meeting. That a white policeman should have to come and explain his actions was astonishing enough, yet what felt really incredible was that the faces out there in that sea of an audience were mostly black: here in this town hall where blacks had only ever been allowed to sweep up after the white audience had long gone home. Every rule by which all Smitsrivier had once lived out its life seemed to have been vanquished. She found herself leaning forward, entranced.

Dirk's lawyer had also leaned forward. Advocate Bester was a short, thickset man, who looked more like a farmer than a lawyer, with his grey trousers, bow tie and braces poking out from under his grey jacket, as if what he would have preferred to do was take off the jacket, roll up his sleeves and pitch in. 'My client Dirk Hendricks is applying for amnesty in connection with an assault on Mr Alex Mpondo that took place in 1985,' he said, talking in English.

The chairman nodded. 'Proceed, Advocate.'

The lawyer turned to his client. 'Mr Hendricks, before we proceed to the main section of your evidence, would you confirm that you understand that section of the Promotion of National Unity and Reconciliation Act that allows this committee to grant amnesty only if they are satisfied that the act you committed was for a political purpose and that there has been full disclosure of all relevant facts?'

'I do, Mr Chairman,' the prisoner said, also in English, his voice imbued by the lifelessness that was a familiar part of the courtroom game of point and counterpoint taught to every new police recruit. Some policemen never got it right no matter how hard they practised. Not this one.

'You understand this means you must tell the truth?'

'That is correct, Mr Chairman.' Like every good witness, Hendricks took care to direct his answers where they really mattered – at the judges.

'Thank you, Mr Hendricks. Is it true that you are currently serving fifteen years in jail for your part in the death of one Mr Desmond Ngoepe?'

'Yes, it is true.'

'Your part in Mr Ngoepe's death is the subject of a separate amnesty application to be dealt with at a separate hearing?'

'Yes, Mr Chairman. That is correct.'

'So tell me, Mr Hendricks: why did you choose to put in this application for amnesty?'

Dirk Hendricks frowned. 'I beg your pardon?'

'Let me explain,' the lawyer said, patiently as if this whole manoeuvre hadn't already been thoroughly rehearsed. 'You have not been convicted for anything in relation to your stewardship of Mr Mpondo. Is that correct?'

'Yes, sir, it is correct.'

'And Mr Mpondo has never threatened to charge you? Is that also correct?'

It came again. 'Yes, it is correct,' accompanied by a tacked on 'Mr Chairman.'

'So why then did you decide to put in this particular amnesty application?'

'Because this is the Truth Commission.' For the first time Dirk Hendricks sounded like an idiot. 'I have to tell the truth.'

His lawyer raised his voice above the laughter that had rippled through the audience. 'You have to tell the truth, merely because a commission says you must?'

Clever, Sarah thought, as Hendricks said: 'No, Mr Chairman,' and this time when he faced the judges he seemed less a controlled policeman than a man ill at ease in a foreign language as he stuttered out: 'Not only that. I am doing it so I may help clear up on the past. It is the time for me, for everyone, to make a clean breast of things.'

'Thank you, Mr Hendricks,' the lawyer said, softly so as to underline his client's plea and then, after silence had fallen, he turned over a page of his notes. 'And now, if you don't mind,' he was all businesslike efficiency, 'I will take you back to that same past. Is it correct that you were a police officer for twenty years. From 1973, in fact, until your imprisonment in 1993?'

'That is correct.'

'And in your amnesty application you have detailed your career in the police force?'

'That is correct, Mr Chairman.'

That is correct, Sarah heard, and she wondered whether the prisoner was ever going to say anything else.

'On page five of that application you describe how, having

come top in your sergeant's exam, you were invited to apply to the security branch of the police?'

'Yes.' Dirk Hendricks remained blank in his confirmation of a summons to join the police's most elite corps that would once have been the highest aspiration of every South African cop. 'That is correct.'

Pieter settled his broad frame into the rickety velveteen seat. Dirk was in good hands.

'In 1984 . . .' the lawyer said.

1984: it was the year that Dirk had come to Smitsrivier. Pieter remembered it clearly. It had been vintage Dirk: as he drew up outside the police station, his old Peugeot 304 had backfired so loudly that the desk officer had thought they were under attack and had sounded the alarm.

'. . . you were seconded to Smitsrivier?'

'That is correct.' Dirk's voice drifted over.

'And the year after that – 1985 – was the Emergency?'

'That is correct.'

1985: when the insurrection took hold. Caught on the hop by the ferocity of the uprising, the authorities had found themselves battling to regain control. No place was immune, not even Smitsrivier.

'This Emergency having been declared by the government after the ANC had ordered its supporters to render the country ungovernable?'

'That is correct,' Dirk said.

Was Dirk remembering that time as well? Pieter wondered, detecting a change in Dirk's tone. Opening his eyes, Pieter looked at the stage. He was in time to catch Dirk's head turning, his piercing blue gaze raking the audience as if he were searching out Pieter. But no, that wasn't right: alighting on Pieter's face, Dirk's gaze didn't falter, it kept on moving past the place where Pieter was and in an arc back again.

'Could you tell the Commission what was happening in the country at that time?'

Surprise flashed across Dirk's impassive face, and when he said, '*Jirra*,' his voice loud, lilting, 'it was absolute chaos, man,' a blast of laughter belted its way across the auditorium.

Dirk's lawyer was smart, Pieter thought. The upheavals of the mid-eighties had been so frenzied that, no matter what side of the barricade you'd been on, the chaos of that time would remain burned in memory.

'And in this explosive situation, what was your brief?'

Dirk was back on track. In monotone: 'I oversaw local detentions in terms of the security legislation.'

'It was in this capacity that you first encountered Mr Mpondo?'

'That is correct.'

'You were put in charge of his interrogation?'

'That . . .' Dirk stopped abruptly and jerked his head as if something had startled him.

'Mr Hendricks?'

'. . . is correct.'

That momentary hesitation alerted Pieter. He knew Dirk too well to think that the equivocation might be accidental. And anyway, Dirk's voice was no longer blank – it was strained as if he were heading into deep water.

Pieter looked down at his own right hand. It was flexing involuntarily. Dirk's forced tone, the things he'd left unsaid yesterday, the way his gaze had just moved past Pieter, made Pieter think that Dirk was ashamed to look him in the face. Pieter thought he knew why. He conjured up a single explanation: a chain. The Sizelas were angry at the loss of their son. They wanted a scapegoat. They pressurised Dirk and Dirk, desparate to get out of jail pointed the finger at Pieter.

As if in confirmation there was a movement on stage. Stage right. Sarah Barcant's unamplified voice calling out: 'Mr Chairman.'

'Is that your signature at the end of the statement?' Dirk's advocate said, riding through the interruption as if he hadn't heard it.

Dirk looked straight ahead. 'That is correct,' his voice sounding over the wave of unrest that had begun spreading into the audience.

That call again. 'Mr Chairman.'

Once again Dirk's lawyer used his microphone's power to override the noise of an audience trying to draw the panel's attention to the disruption. 'And do you also confirm the accuracy of your statement?'

'I do,' Dirk said.

'Mr Chairman.' Now that Sarah Barcant had found her microphone switch there was no avoiding her.

Although Dirk's advocate did try. He began: 'By the time you came across Mr Mpondo in the interrogation room . . .'

She called again: 'Mr Chairman.'

'. . . was he already well known to the security branch?'

'Advocate Bester . . .' The chairman was at the edge of his chair, frowning.

Dirk looked at his lawyer, who nodded at him to reply.

'Mr Mpondo was an activist,' Dirk said, 'who'd been arrested on many different occasions . . .'

'Advocate Bester, Mr Hendricks . . . if you wouldn't mind,' the chairman said, at the same time tapping his microphone and setting up a feedback hum loud enough to have people wrenching off their headsets. Into the silence that descended the judge glowered down on the crowd. 'Mr Hendricks is entitled to a hearing without intimidation or interference,' he said. 'If these interruptions continue I will have no option but to order the hall cleared.' Sitting back, he addressed himself to the left of the stage: 'You were trying to catch my attention, I believe, Miss Barcant.'

'Thank you, Mr Chairman,' Sarah Barcant said. 'I would like to draw the committee's attention to the fact that although I am acting for Mr Mpondo in this matter, I also act for Mr and Mrs Sizela in the matter of their son's disappearance.'

So Pieter was right. It was a set up.

'Given that Mr Hendricks's last statement covers the period during which Steve Sizela was last seen,' Sarah Barcant continued, 'I hereby give notice of my intention to cross-examine him on the matter of Steve Sizela's murder.'

Pieter must be right: Dirk Hendricks's lawyer had been expecting this. He leaned forward, almost languidly, to click his microphone on, and to say: 'Mr Chairman, I must protest.'

The grey-bearded judge also leaned forward. 'Already, Mr Bester? But we have only just begun.' He sighed. Deeply. Theatrically.

Hannie Bester looked across the stage. 'May I remind my colleague,' – staring with his hard brown eyes at Sarah Barcant – 'that this hearing has been called to determine whether my client, Dirk Hendricks, qualifies for amnesty for his stewardship of Mr Mpondo. Since my client's application makes no mention of Mr Sizela, I cannot see the relevance of Miss Barcant's intervention.'

'Miss Barcant?'

The judge looked at Sarah Barcant who was deep in whispered conversation with Mpondo. Some client/attorney understanding, Pieter thought, watching the display. Their body language – Mpondo bending urgently into her physical space, she appearing to want to back away – said it all: Mpondo was trying to stop her proceeding any further down this line.

'Miss Barcant, is there some problem between you and your client?'

On stage the vehemence of Alex Mpondo's shaking head

abated and he subsided back into his chair, simultaneously waving his hand dismissively at his so-called lawyer. Just as Pieter would have predicted: no matter what their private beliefs, men like Mpondo had, as their most important priority, to present a united front. 'No, Your Honour,' Sarah Barcant said. 'There is no problem.'

'Then, if you have quite finished, perhaps you would reply to Mr Bester's objection: briefly, if possible, even though you are a lawyer.'

Smiling to acknowledge the crack, (it was all one big joke to them, Pieter thought), Sarah Barcant said: 'Steve Sizela was a friend and close colleague of Mr Mpondo's, who was also held by the Smitsrivier police during that same time period. Mr Mpondo was naturally not at liberty to wander the police station but Mr Hendricks was. He would have been ideally placed to know what happened to Steve Sizela. With the panel's permission, I would therefore like to ask Mr Hendricks what he knows of Steve's whereabouts.'

'To what end, Miss Barcant?' Hannie Bester shot in.

'To the end, as you put it, of helping Steve's ageing parents find their son's body so that they may bury him in peace.'

'An admirable goal,' Hannie Bester said. 'And I'm sure all of us would like to join with you, Miss Barcant, in extending our sympathy to Mr and Mrs Sizela for the terrible uncertainty under which they have been forced to live. However,' his broad face hardened as did his voice, 'I would be remiss in my duty to my client if I did not remind the panel that Truth Commission investigators have already interviewed my client about this matter and have been satisfied that he had nothing to do with either the interrogation or the eventual fate of Mr Steve Sizela, whatever that might have been.'

'Miss Barcant?' the chairman said.

'Your Honour,' Sarah Barcant said, 'as my learned friend has

pointed out, amnesty can only be granted if the applicant com-
plies with the criteria laid down by the Act, central to which is
the requirement of full disclosure. Mr Mpondo and Mr Sizela
were comrades. They were arrested within days of each other.'

'What has that to do with this case?' Hannie Bester again
shot in.

'Your Honour,' Sarah Barcant said calmly, 'I would submit
that even if Mr Hendricks did not interrogate Mr Sizela, he
would have worked closely with whoever it was that did.'
She raised her voice, cutting across Hannie Bester's attempt to
get the judge's attention. 'And in anticipation of my learned
colleague's repeated objection, I would further submit that
what Mr Hendricks knows about Mr Sizela is relevant to this
application precisely because it goes to the heart of his application. To question him on this matter is simultaneously to
examine the credibility of his intention and thus the credibility of his whole application.'

'Mr Chairman,' – Hannie Bester's voice was carefully
pitched to include a measure of ridicule – 'if we follow Miss
Barcant's logic, we will end up creating a precedent that will
have long lines of lawyers queuing outside every hearing to
ask applicants what they know about every single arrest,
shooting, disappearance or death that has happened in this
country since 1948 – and when anybody questions the relevance of this, any Tom, Dick or Harry can insist that it goes to
this same issue of credibility. The hearings will stretch on for
ever and degenerate into farce.'

'Unlike this one,' the chairman of the panel said dryly,
before adding quickly, 'If you would be kind enough to give
us a moment?' Punching down on his microphone, he bent
his head, talking softly to his colleagues. They moved closer
and for a while there was almost total silence in the hall as the
three whispered together.

Then at last, with the other two staring straight ahead, the chairman said, 'We will take this matter under advisement. Until we have made our final decision, we will disallow all questions which do not relate directly to the application in hand. Interested parties should submit written argument by tomorrow morning at 8 a.m.' He looked ferociously from one lawyer to the next. 'We are not after a thesis here, people: just a summary of the argument with precedent if necessary. To give counsel time to prepare this, we will continue with the hearing until the short break and then adjourn for the day.' His gaze fell on Dirk Hendricks's table. 'Mr Bester,' he said, his voice showing that the matter was now closed, 'please continue leading your client.'

15

ALL THAT HOT air, Pieter thought, as he walked down Main Street. As if doing that would change anything for anybody. While the townships danced to the Commission's music, men like Dirk were being brought from jail and made to sit in countless other town halls like this one and take their punishment. Their role was clear. They were the designated freaks at the centre of the Truth Commission circus, their job to make everybody else look and feel good. It was justice, rainbow-nation style: the new stereotyping where black had become white and white, black.

As if the other side hadn't also played their part. Take, for example, Mpondo, Dirk's so-called victim. Mpondo was no angel. He was once a gun-runner and a would-be bomber, whom only luck and his own ineptitude with explosives had stopped from murdering innocent bystanders. And yet despite his past – no, it was worse than that, *because* of his past – Mpondo was now an MP, a VIP who held Dirk's fate in his hand.

It was all so bloody hypocritical, Pieter thought. He for one would have nothing to do with it.

And he wouldn't have to. He wasn't worried any longer. Although he was in no doubt that James Sizela had somehow put Dirk under pressure, he was also sure that this was as far as it would go. Dirk was Pieter's friend. He'd never let him down in the past and he would not now. Even if the judges gave Sarah Barcant the right to cross-examine him about Steve Sizela, Dirk would never finger Pieter.

'Pieter.'

Glancing up, Pieter saw the heavy figure of Kobus de Wit hailing him from across the road. Pieter stopped and waited while Kobus's huge flat feet propelled him forward.

'Kobus. What can I do for you?'

Kobus didn't need asking twice: he never did. He pulled a piece of paper from a trouser pocket. 'This is a list of hopefuls for some casual work I need doing on the farm. If you wouldn't mind, Pieter: could you check them out for me?'

'Sure. No problem,' Pieter took the paper from Kobus's outstretched hand. 'Ring me later.'

'Thanks, Pieter.' Kobus grinned. 'Give my regards to Marie, hey?' And with that he swung round and moved back across the road.

Two hundred yards more and Pieter turned off Main Street, going into an alleyway and down its length to a two-storey breeze-block building. His offices were through the main door on the ground floor and to the right. He went down the corridor, pausing by the advertising plaque promising instant armed response for anyone within a radius of ten kilometres before punching numbers on the keypad and then, when the door swung open, going in.

The outer office was clean and quiet and functional and cool exactly as he liked it to be, with his secretary Kristal behind her desk. Seeing him, she put the phone down and brought her long red nails to rest on a spotless blotter as she said, smiling, 'Môre, Pieter. Mr and Mrs Parker were early. I showed them into your room.'

'You gave them coffee?' he said, knowing that she would have, and going over to the side table to pour some of the thick over-percolated brew into the oversized mug that she had given him as a present last Christmas. 'What kind of night was it?'

She flipped open her pad. 'Three false alarms: that Smit kid again playing silly buggers with the panic button; a dassie tripping an infra-red; and a woman thinking she saw someone in her garden, but it turned out to be a cactus. Two break-ins. In one, the owners left the house without activating their alarm, so by the time they found out what had happened and called us, the burglars had long vamoosed. In the other, our guys were on site within seven minutes and the offenders in custody within fifteen.' She flipped the pad closed and looked up, all pert blonde hair and smiling sweetness. 'A quiet night.' Her voice fell. 'Except . . .' a dramatic pause and then: 'Sizwe was drunk again.'

Which, Pieter thought, made the third night running. Bloody Sizwe. When was he ever going to learn?

'You want I should hand him his papers?'

'No.' By dropping two tabs of Sweetex into his coffee and stirring vigorously, Pieter avoided the reproach he knew would be visible in Kristal's eyes. She was a good girl but she was still too young to understand the consequences that sacking Sizwe would have on his whole extended family. 'Tell him

I want to see him first thing tomorrow morning. Sober and washed.' He looked up sharply, daring her to comment. 'Anything else?'

Kristal blinked. 'Your wife phoned. She said to tell you the silkie hatched and its toes are perfect.'

Now that was good news. For the first time since he'd heard that Dirk was coming back to town, Pieter felt his spirits lifting. Maybe this time, he thought. His chances of winning Champion Breed had always before been dashed by inbreeding problems that showed themselves in crooked toes, but no longer. Now he was in a position to give the other breeders a run for their money and he had a feeling it would be better than that. He was home free. He was going to win.

Maybe life isn't so bad, he thought, smiling and taking his coffee, and putting down the piece of paper that Kobus had given him on Kristal's desk. 'Check these guys out with the police, will you?' he said, going into his inner office.

Kristal was a good girl and Pieter's visitors were comfortably seated in front of his desk. 'Mr and Mrs Parker?' He shook hands with each in turn before going to sit down opposite. 'I'm sorry if I kept you waiting. I'm Pieter Muller – the boss of this outfit. Welcome to Smitsrivier. Can Kristal bring you some more coffee?'

They shook their heads. He took a sip of his and, grimacing, put down the cup. 'I don't blame you: Kristal makes coffee strong enough to fuel a car halfway to Jo'burg.'

Mr Parker was thin and dapper and in his late sixties, with that clipped English accent of someone who'd spent his working life in the British army and who had no time for pleasantries. 'Do you have many employees?'

Well and good: Pieter also disliked wasting time. 'I have twenty full-time staff on the books plus a reservoir of trusted part-timers,' he said. 'We run a tight ship here. Constant armed surveillance of our clients' properties.'

'Is that really necessary?' In contrast to her husband's vigour, Mrs Parker had the faded appearance and nervous voice of a woman who'd been relocated too many times. 'We left the city because we couldn't take the crime. We thought we'd be safe in Smitsrivier.'

'And so you will be,' Pieter said, hearing, even through the closed door, how Kristal was arguing with someone. Sizwe, he thought. 'Our town is one of the most crime-free in the country.'

'So why do we need you?' Mr Parker asked.

Kristal's voice rose another notch. Pieter hoped she wasn't trying to take issue with Sizwe, because if Sizwe was still drunk there was no telling what he might do. To the Parkers Pieter said: 'You might decide you don't need us: that's entirely up to you. Ours is a tight-knit community, we practise the dying art of good neighbourliness. What you would add to this if you were to sign a contract with Muller Security would be complete peace of mind.'

'No,' he heard Kristal saying, 'you can't.'

He raised his voice. 'We are not like the police. We are in the business of crime prevention. Our job is to anticipate trouble before it occurs.'

'No.' There was no mistaking the agitation in Kristal's voice. 'You can't do that.' Frowning, Pieter said, 'You bought the old Schroder property on Trevor Street, I believe? A lovely house: it looks over the veld.'

'The veld,' Mr Parker said. 'Precisely.'

The shouting had stopped. Kristal must have Sizwe under control. Pieter was glad of it. If he had been called on to intervene, he would have ended up having to sack the man.

'That's the worry,' Mr Parker was saying, 'anyone could climb the fence and obtain access to our garden and then our . . .'

The voices had escalated again and this time were accompanied by the unmistakable sound of scuffling, loud enough to silence Mr Parker. If that's Sizwe, Pieter thought, I'll have to do more than sack him. 'If you'd excuse me a moment,' he said, getting up and striding over to the door and opening it to snap out: 'What's going on here?'

He didn't need an answer. It was his old friend Johan, who was trying to get at the door while Kristal was using her body to stop him. I see, Pieter thought; and said, 'Thank you Kristal.'

When Kristal moved away, Johan stepped forward. Pieter held up a hand to stop him. 'You think it's clever to assault a woman?'

'I'm sorry,' Johan's angular face was red with embarrassment. 'I brought you this,' he said, thrusting out a paper.

Pieter didn't have to look to know what it was. It was a writ, a demand that he attend court to answer the case for damages against the Sizelas. A gift from Ben Hoffman sent through his handmaiden Sarah Barcant. Pieter had been expecting something like it. Because he had refused to apply for amnesty, they were going to sue him in a real courtroom.

'Later,' he said, 'I'm busy,' moving to close the door.

In his many years of service to the town hall, Johan had often delivered writs. Now, stepping forward he thrust both hand and paper into the narrowing gap. He was fast, but he was also stupid – he didn't have the sense to use his foot. Anyway, Pieter had always been much faster than Johan. He pushed at the door, trapping Johan's lily-white clerk's hand between the door jamb and the closing wood.

Johan cried out.

Pieter had the advantage: if he were to go on applying pressure he knew he'd end up breaking Johan's hand. For what he had done, Johan deserved a broken hand, he thought.

'Pieter.'

Pieter didn't have the heart for this. He lifted his weight from the door.

'I'm sorry, Pieter,' Johan said, stepping back, massaging his sore hand. 'I have to do this,' and thrust out the paper again.

This time Pieter took it. It wasn't heavy. Writs never were. He looked down at the paper and then up again at Johan. 'I saw you at the town hall only ten minutes ago. Why didn't you serve this on me then?'

'I'm sorry, Pieter,' Johan mumbled. 'I have to make a living.'

And your new bosses told you to make sure you served me with this poison in my office, Pieter thought, preferably when I'm with clients. And you did it, he thought, staring at his old friend, thinking about the favours he had once done Johan.

Johan couldn't hold Pieter's gaze. He dropped his head, concentrating it on his polished brown shoes.

Ag, what was the use, Pieter thought. Times had changed. The past was gone. Pieter closed the door and turned back to face his visitors.

They were staring slack-mouthed. He'd lost them: he knew that. Nevertheless, he could only smile as he went back to sit and say: 'I apologise for the interruption. Now. About your fence . . .'

16

WHAT SARAH WANTED more than anything was a drink. She pushed open the door of the bar. Walking down the lobby she'd been conscious of the rumble of voices and the clinking of glass emanating from inside but now silence fell as men's heads swivelled round to look her up and down. Once it would have been inconceivable to find blacks and whites drinking in the same place, but now only she was out of place. She saw herself reflected back in their hardened stares: tendrils of black hair still damp from her recent shower, her long moss-green skirt with its high side slit, her sleek short-sleeved top, her manicured nails, the only woman in an all-male crowd.

She took another step and the barman supplied the only

matching movement. A fleshy, pasty, unhealthy-looking man he pulled up his wooden bar counter and, wiping his hands down the sides of his khaki trousers, ambled over. 'Can I help you?'

She said, 'I'd like a drink,' her voice sounding very loud.

'You wouldn't feel more comfortable in the ladies' bar?'

The silence was so total that she might have said yes, if she hadn't already treated herself to a preview of the ladies' bar. It was a small windowless space with dingy flock wallpaper and plastic flowers on each of its three rickety wooden tables, and it was empty. She said, 'I'd rather be here.' And smiled. 'That's not a problem, is it?'

'Yes. No. No problem.' The barman shrugged. 'I just thought you would prefer the quiet.' He walked away.

She followed. He led her to a table in the furthest, deepest, darkest reach of the bar. Pulling out the dishcloth that had served to shroud his paunch, he swiped it over the table's scuffed skin. She sat down.

'What can I get you?'

'Malt whisky please.' She didn't specify a brand: she assumed there would only be one malt. If she was lucky.

The barman nodded and made his way ponderously back behind his counter. As he did so a handful of disparate conversations started up again, freeing her to look around. It was a large bar, wood-panelled up to eye level, with a dirty mud-brown carpet, a scattering of tables, an alcove which contained a pool table under spotlights, and a long bar counter. Apart from herself, all the other occupants were either men or dead animals. The men – Africans and whites in approximately equal numbers but grouped separate from each other – sat by tables, or leaned against the bar, or stood by the pool table watching out the progress of a game. The animals were on the walls – a line of grotesques that included an ugly wildebeest whose straggling grey beard had been sprayed with so much preservative it stood out like wire, an elegant kudu head hung next to the head of a kudu bull complete with trademark jagged horns and, to make up the complement, a sad, ragged, moth-eaten lion's face; all these mounted on polished wood. Their glazed eyes stared sightlessly forward, while the guns that shot them were also there, locked up behind glass.

The barman put a coaster on her table and a tumbler on the coaster. 'Glenfiddich,' he said.

Glenfiddich. She was impressed. 'Thank you.'

'I thought it would suit your taste.'

She picked up the glass.

'But if you'd rather have a Glenmorangie? Or a Black Label?'

'No. Thanks. This is great.' She shot him a brief, dismissing smile.

'No ice?'

She wished he'd go away. She shook her head, no.

'And no water either?'

'No,' she said. 'Thanks. No ice. No water.'

'So nothing's changed then?'

What was that supposed to mean? She looked up. Did she know him?

He was staring, his pale moon-face set in that blank, unsmiling, Smitsrivier style that could either mean he wasn't pleased to see her or alternatively that there was just nothing in his life to be pleased about. She said, tentatively, 'Andre?'

He nodded. 'The same.'

Of course. Andre. She should have recognised him before. They'd gone to the school together from aged seven until matric and although he was a little older and a lot fatter, he was otherwise unchanged. She said, overenthusiastically to make up for her rudeness, 'How are you?'

His reply, accompanied by a shrug and the same two words:

'The same,' confirmed that he really was the same. A fanatical rugby player from an early age, Andre never had been much interested in words.

'Still a flank forward?' she said.

He shook his head. 'Ag, no, man, I don't have the time,' and walked away.

She wasn't offended. He was like most white Smitsrivierans, not interested in anything that happened beyond the confines of their immediate environment. Small-town life, she thought, sipping her drink, rolling the taste appreciatively over her tongue and thinking about her day.

Oh, well, she thought, at least it's almost over.

An hour later she was on her way out. When she got to the door, however, she registered a change of atmosphere. There was an edge to the place that had nothing to do with her and a pace that had been missing when she had first come in. She turned round, her gaze drawn to the alcove where groups of men had now galvanised round the pool table. Curious, she changed course.

Smoke drifted in dense streams above the crowd that had congregated around the pool table. As she moved in closer she could hear the clack of a game being played out and see, by the tension on each face, black and white now mixed, that most of them had something at stake in it. She pushed through the fringes of the circle.

A voice sounded from deep inside. 'You think I can't do it again?' A familiar voice – Alex Mpondo's.

Going in deeper she saw two young black men weaving through the mêlée. As they moved, money and slips of paper were being passed into their hands: strange to see this in Smitsrivier where gambling would once have been counted a sin as ugly as adultery.

'Get him another Castle, quick,' someone muttered.

'Don't count on it,' came the reply. 'This one plays better when he's juiced.'

She edged in, until she had secured herself an uninterrupted view of what was going on.

Alex Mpondo – chameleon, she thought. At the hearing she'd been witness to three of his about-turns: first his charm as he had greeted her, then his fury when she had raised the subject of Steve and finally his breathtaking ability to cut her from his consciousness so successfully it seemed that when the hearing ended he had left without even saying goodbye.

And now he'd undergone another, different metamorphosis, this one into hard-drinking pool player. He'd propped his cue against the table and was crouched low, his eyes narrowed, ostentatiously figuring out the angles. His opponent, a scrawny, badly dressed white man in his twenties, was leaning against the wall, unsuccessfully feigning nonchalance.

Alex was the consummate showman. He straightened up, waiting for the conversation to die away and the last bet to change hands, and then he moved. He had the fluidity of a sportsman intercut with the blurred clumsiness of a drunk: reaching for his cue he misjudged his distance from the edge of the table and stretched too far, tilting and almost falling over. A collective intake of breath agitated the waiting crowd. More money changed hands. But was this all part of the act? Sarah wondered, as Alex righted himself, leaned over the table, angled his cue and then smoothly pucked it forward, perfectly placing his shot. An exchange of high-fives and muttered curses. The game was nearly over. Only one more ball to go.

'Aha the Ice Woman Cometh,' Alex said.

He had been moving round the table, checking out the angles, but now she saw that he had stopped and was looking straight at her. 'Welcome to the No-Chance Saloon.' He executed a formal half bow. 'And you, I assume, are our own private Hickey, come to peddle the truth,' bending his knee then, angling his cue, moving so fast that even as someone muttered, 'For Christ's sake, Alex, you'll never hit it from that angle,' he thrust the cue forward, sending the white ball surging off, hitting the cushions, once, twice, three times and potting the last striped ball. There was an escalation of sound, swearing and jubilation as the rush of money intensified.

Alex, who was slowly straightening up, seemed oblivious to the furore. His eyes were still on Sarah. He said, 'What's the matter, Sarah Barcant? Didn't expect a small-town kaffir to know his Eugene O'Neill?' He leaned his cue against the table and bowed, theatrically this time, one hand on his stomach, the other sweeping backwards. 'I was well taught. By old man Sizela. Literature is his life.' He cocked his head, listening for a moment to some whispered words from one of the young men Sarah had noticed before, and then he said, more loudly, to Sarah, 'Another set of lines springs to mind. Perhaps you know them? If you do, excuse any misquoting.' Standing straight, his eyes on her as if they were alone in the bar, he projected out his voice: '"Hath not I eyes? Hath not I hands, organs, dimensions, senses, affections."' Tottering forward suddenly and throwing out a hand to steady himself, he frowned and repeated the last three words: '"Dimensions, senses, affections . . ."'

'Come on, professor,' someone said.

'". . . dimensions, senses, affections . . ."' He looked round wildly.

Someone sniggered.

'". . . senses,"' he said, stuttering, 'affections . . ."'

'"Passions,"' Sarah said.

'Yes. "Passions." Thank you.' He bowed and then straightened up, continuing so fluently that the memory lapse must have been just another part of the act. '"Dimensions, senses, affections, passions, fed with the same food, hurt with the same weapons, subject to the same diseases, healed by the same means, warmed and cooled by the same winter and summer. If you prick me, do I not bleed? If you tickle me, do I not laugh? If you poison me, shall I not die?"' He stopped suddenly, looking at her, lowering his voice. 'And if you torture me,' he said, speaking so softly she had to strain to hear his words, '. . . if you torture me . . . What then, Sarah Barcant. What then?'

What then? What could there be then? She turned on her heels and walked out.

She was still up when he came knocking. She knew it was him. She left the desk where she'd been reading through transcripts of previous hearings, and opened the door a crack.

He was leaning casually against the door jamb. 'I've come to apologise.'

She nodded. 'Did you make a lot of money?'

He raised a puzzled eyebrow.

'Don't tell me you didn't bet on yourself?'

His face relaxed. 'I made a little. The others made more. Don't worry: it's official ANC policy. The redistribution of wealth from town to township.' He smiled, his face once more transformed, opening up, including her. 'Can I come in?'

'What for?' She kept a hold on the door. 'So you can play me for a sucker like you played the crowd?'

He grinned lopsidedly. 'I don't know what you mean.'

'Let me see.' She held up her other hand and used her fingers to count off the points. 'One: the slow build-up. Two: the feigned drunkenness. Three: the brothers in the crowd stirring up the tension. Four: the impossible angle of the shot and the voice doubting you could do it. Five: a quick dose of *The Merchant of Venice*, complete with prompting from me, to ease the pain of the collection. Did I miss anything?'

'OK.' He held up both hands, high in the air, a gesture of

defeat – and almost overbalanced. Perhaps his drunkenness was only partially feigned, she thought. 'I admit we helped the odds along a little. Does that bother you?'

She shrugged.

He moved in closer with that sinewy ease of his. He no longer sounded drunk. 'Oh, I get it,' he sounded angry. 'It's Andre. The fat barman. You went to school with him, didn't you?'

He would know that. Of course he would. Nothing stayed private, not in Smitsrivier.

'What's the matter? You don't like us running a scam on poor Andre?'

She wanted to be rid of him. She pushed the door.

His foot shot out. 'What next? Planning to break my foot?'

'I'd do it.'

'Well,' he said, 'before you do, let me tell you something about your friend Andre.'

She lifted her weight off the door.

'You have to know that Andre is a rugby fanatic,' he said.

She nodded.

'Did you also know that Andre knew Dirk Hendricks well in the 1980s? Yes the same Hendricks. Those two were drinking buddies, Andre and Dirk. But you just try talking to Andre about those days. He's like the rest of them in this god-forsaken town. He says nobody was tortured. Or if they were, he says, he certainly didn't know about it. He stands behind the bar and offers me a drink for my troubles, while trying to get me drunk so I'll play badly, and never once . . . never once . . .' his dark eyes glistened dangerously, 'never once does he admit that what was done in this country was done in his name and in the name of all those other Andre clones who welcomed men like Dirk Hendricks into their lives.'

She stood there, looking as his eyes welled with tears. Roughly, he wiped the tears away. 'Shit.' He blinked. 'I'm sorry.

I hate maudlin drunks. And I really did come to apologise. I was drunk. And perhaps you're right: I was using you for distraction. I'm sorry.'

She smiled. 'Apology accepted. See you tomorrow.' She moved to close the door.

'So?' he said, looking at her.

She looked back at him repeating that one word: 'So?'

He raised an eyebrow.

She shook her head.

He shrugged. 'I thought . . .' his voice tailing off.

'That white guilt would do it?' she said, thinking that when she was young it might have.

Alex seemed to sense what she was thinking. His face broke into an open smile. 'Nothing wrong with a bit of white guilt,' he said, 'not at the right moment,' and then tipping his hand up above his head, raising a hat he wasn't wearing, he said, 'Good night, Sarah Barcant,' and turning, sauntered off down the corridor.

17

PIETER MULLER CAME to instantly and without changing the rhythm of his breathing. A dream again, he thought, but it wasn't a dream, not this time. Something else then. He lay still, trying to work out what.

The bedroom was dark and, save for the ticking of the grandfather clock outside, completely quiet. And yet something had awakened him. Carefully he let his hand play over the nylon sheet, moving it along the topmost edge of his bed and then sliding it under his pillow to where he kept his Glock. He stopped and listened some more and when nothing happened, he manoeuvred the gun round, gripped it by the butt, pulled it out and waited again. Still nothing. He undid the safety catch.

Outside, a lone cicada sounded but inside all stayed dark and quiet. There was no intruder in the bedroom, Pieter was sure of that. But if that was true, why was he awake? Marie, he thought, she must be having a bad night. He turned to look at her. Which is when he saw that Marie's bed was empty. It's impossible, he thought, she never gets up at night.

There was only one explanation: someone had taken her.

As the thought occurred, Pieter was up and at the bedroom door. Steadying the wooden frame with his foot he turned the knob and, inching his foot away, slowly opened the door and moved out into the corridor. The ticking of the clock was louder now. With his gun hanging easy by his side, Pieter moved down the passageway.

And stopped abruptly seeing the light filtering out from under the study door. This wasn't right. He'd toured the house before going to bed, just like he did every night, checking catches and switching the rooms into darkness. He specifically remembered closing the safe, turning the combination, clicking off the study's lights.

The safe, he thought. The study housed the safe and in it his collection of guns. And now a stranger had Marie in there.

He went up to the study door, placing himself to its left and leaning across, resting one ear against the wood, listening. He could hear a noise. There was someone in there all right. A kind of creaking. Listening carefully, he conjured up a mental picture of the room, concentrating on the source and the rhythm of the sound.

Marie, he thought. He put his gun in his pyjama pocket and opened the door.

The sight that met his eyes was almost exactly as he had pictured it. The large room was in darkness save for the Anglepoise on the mantelpiece. Its narrow yellow beam illuminated Marie, dressed in her long cream nightdress, and sitting on the rocking chair by the empty fireplace, her eyes closed as she rocked gently to and fro.

'Marie,' he said.

She opened her eyes. She didn't seem the slightest bit alarmed. 'Pieter. I'm sorry if I disturbed you.'

He shrugged – it didn't matter. 'Did Bessy come into the house to help you up?'

She shook her head and when she said, 'I managed on my own,' she sounded almost boastful. He could understand that. It was a feat for her these days merely to get out of bed unassisted.

Nevertheless, he thought, it was also foolish: she could have fallen and hurt herself. 'You should have woken me.'

She shivered and her pale cheeks coloured slightly, but all she said in reply was a mild: 'You were fast asleep.'

He went over to the rocking chair, intent on sitting with her a while but coming closer he saw something in her lap. It was the jacket of his Sunday suit, the one he'd ripped on a boundary fence on his way back from church. He was standing by her now, close enough to see that a needle was threaded through one of the sleeves. She's been darning, he thought, thinking fondly that this was just like Marie – she had the daintiest and the most skilful hands in the Eastern Cape.

But no, that version of his wife existed only in the past. Now, when he looked down at those same hands, all he could see was how arthritis had twisted her fingers out of shape. He said, gruffly, 'You must ask Bessy to do that.'

'I wanted to do it myself.' She spoke softly but even so there was no mistaking the determination in her voice. She's unnecessarily stubborn, he thought. He should be angry. But how could he be? If she'd got out of bed voluntarily and on her own, this was going to be one of her rare good days.

'You'll need the suit for court,' she said.

Oh, so that's what this was about. She knew. One of their neighbours must have come bustling over to break the news as soon as the writ was served. He couldn't imagine how she had taken the news. This was not part of their communication. Never once in all the years of their marriage had she ever asked him about his work. She didn't need to. He knew how proud she was of him, how happy at his standing in their community. And she trusted him, of course she had, there was no need to speak any further. And now? How would she have taken the knowledge that he, the upholder of the law, had actually been subpoenaed? He stood, his face in neutral, waiting to hear what she had to say.

She kept on rocking, backwards and forwards, her gaze focused on the dark green carpet.

She was right: there was nothing to say. 'I'll make some rooibos,' he said, turning away.

He was almost out the door when he heard her speak again.

'Pieter.' She was calling him back.

He turned.

'Rooibos would be nice.'

Long after Marie had gone back to bed, and after her breathing had grown softer and more even, Pieter lay awake. He knew he'd never get to sleep again but lay quite still, checking that Marie was not pretending for his sake to be asleep and that if he left he would be leaving her at ease. Eventually, satisfied, he got up and took his clothes from the chair where he had laid them and left the room.

It was quiet inside the hatchery. A good omen: it meant that the chicks were comfortable, and their positions, grouped together near the light but not too near, showed the same thing. He checked the water fount: his workers had remembered to put in marbles to stop the chicks from drowning. Satisfied, he went to the place where his favourite, Silkie, was sitting by her chicks. She was a beautiful bird, a blue partridge of the bearded variety, who was as friendly as any bantam he'd ever had and as soft as a Persian cat. She looked up in greeting, her eyes large and bright, and when he laid his hand on her, she let him stroke her downy hair. He pushed it back, checking her deep black-purple pigmented skin for lice, shifting back the muff that covered her turquoise-blue ear lobes and looking for any sign of Marek's. She was in perfect health – the only one of the thirty chicks of her batch he hadn't culled. She was the one, he thought; she had it in her to raise a brood that would be the envy of the local bantam fanciers. He nudged her, and she obligingly moved away. He picked up a chick, the last one of the batch. What Marie had spotted in her was right: this one was a real beauty, with all the characteristics of a potential champion – a smooth black skin, a fine wrinkle-free face, large bright eyes, a small circular walnut comb and, most important of all, five short stout toes, well set apart.

The hen was growing anxious, butting against Pieter's hand with her head. Putting down her chick on the mealie-meal bedding, he ruffled the hen's feathers. She was a born mother: when she didn't have a brood of her own, she was always trying to steal some other bantam's chicks and raise them for her own. Now she was so fluffy with pride it was hard to believe that she was the same bird who would spit and fly out aggressively if any different breed of bantam had the temerity to poke his comb inside her living quarters. She never did this if the interloper was another Silkie, which meant that she was somehow able to distinguish between her own breed and others.

'What I don't understand,' he said out loud to her, 'is how you can tell the others are different from you? How do you even know what you look like?'

She ignored him, fluffing out her feathers and sitting down by her chick.

It's enough, Pieter thought, time for me to go. He walked to the door, stopping for a moment to check the thermometer. The temperature, he saw, was already climbing. Overheating was always a worry at this time of year: even with the ventilation system full on, it could get hot enough in the hatchery to kill a whole batch of newborns. Oh well, if that happened, that was fate, he thought, fixing the safety grill into place and going out.

It was still quite dark as his boots crunched against the gravel. He moved briskly now, going over to the concrete dwelling that stood behind the house, rapping gently on the door and, when Bessy called out a sleep-thickened 'Yes', he said, softly, 'I'm leaving now.'

After a light clicked on, he could hear the creaking of Bessy's mattress and her heavy tread, then she opened the door a crack and poked out her sleep-sozzled head.

'Madam had a bad night,' he said. 'Let her lie a while.'

Bessy nodded and when she yawned he got a whiff of her breath, sour from last night's beer.

'Tell them to put electrolytes in the chicks' water,' he said. 'They must read the instructions and use the exact amount – not less and not more either. It's not some rich man's medicine that works better if you increase the dose.'

'Yes, baas.'

'They must also keep a watch on the temperature and move the ventilation grills as the sun rises. I'll be back later in the afternoon.'

As his feet crunched across the gravel path he heard the click of her door. Getting into his car, he turned the key, and when the engine came purring to life he switched his headlights on full beam and drove off.

18

WHEN ANNA CAME into the bedroom Ben was slumped back against a slew of pillows. He looks so frail, she thought, like a broken doll. She felt suddenly enraged: how could Sarah have been so stupid as to detain him the other day in that dirty, dusty place, arguing with him as the sun blazed down on his unprotected head?

He opened his eyes. 'What did she say?'

She – Sarah. 'I couldn't get hold of her,' Anna said. 'I left a message.' Going over to the bed she lowered her ample body.

He shifted to give her room. There was no need. In the fifty years they'd shared a bed, he'd never taken more than half unless invited to. She reached over for his hand, feeling his lizard skin against hers.

'You know what I was thinking before you came in?' His voice was dreamy.

She stroked his hand.

'I was thinking how lucky I am that I will die at home, in bed, with you at my side. Not like Steve Sizela.' He opened his eyes suddenly. 'For me, this is a privilege.'

She nodded. She didn't trust herself to speak.

'It's not so easy for you,' he said, and let his words hang, as if he were waiting for her to rebut them.

She wanted to oblige but could find neither the energy nor the will. She was still considering what the doctor had said last night – that Ben's heart was gradually failing him and that there was nothing to be done. This wasn't new. But somehow having seen Ben's pallor when he got back from the Sizelas', she had stared at the reality.

Why her? Why should she be the survivor? Why should he go first?

She focused her gaze on the primrose yellow wall.

'Was Sarah right?' Ben said. 'Am I always tilting at windmills?'

That he should need to ask her that? Smiling, Anna looked at him.

He didn't look so ill now that he was also smiling. 'Of course, I know that the path I chose demanded a kind of quixotic endurance.' His smile was already draining away. 'But you should have heard her, Anna. She all but accused me of becoming so used to losing cases that I no longer know how to win.' He was glaring now, thunderous, outraged. 'That she could say that of me. Of me! Ben Hoffman!'

The way he spat out his own name made Anna wonder: was his acceptance of his dwindling health also a deception? Was he also railing in secret against his end?

In that manner he'd perfected in the courtroom, he made one of his abrupt emotional shifts, this one from outrage to calm contemplation. 'Maybe she has a point,' he said. 'The odds were so stacked against us: winning was rarely an option. The most we could expect was that our eloquence might win some vital concession: twenty years rather than forty, life rather than death. Perhaps in the process I did get so caught up in the politics that lay behind the courts, that I forgot my first love: the law.' Another transformation: his voice hardening. 'But at least I have not taken to persecuting torture victims.'

He didn't say more. He didn't need to. Anna knew what he was thinking, that he had never stopped hoping that Sarah eventually would come home. Not that he would ever say as much to Anna. He had shared his life with her, outside of his work.

'Do you think I did the right thing?' he said suddenly. He was talking, of course, of Sarah. Sarah his constant preoccupation. 'Was I wrong to bring her back?'

'I don't know, Ben.' She sighed. 'And I also don't know why having sent for her you won't tell her, or let me tell her, that you're ill.'

He shook his head. 'I didn't bring her back to Smitsrivier because I'm ill. I did it because she should never have left.'

How many times had they been over this same ground? 'It's what she wanted.'

'No. She was young. She relied on me and I failed her. I encouraged her to go and I didn't make sure that she came back. And now she no longer belongs here. Or anywhere perhaps.'

'You don't know that, Ben.' She squeezed his hand. 'She has so much going for her. She's beautiful, she's intelligent, she has friends, a good standard of living, she's a good lawyer.'

He pulled his hand away. 'Look at her, Anna.' His eyes were unnaturally bright. 'She accuses me of being too much the idealist. But what's happened to her is worse. She has hardened. She has the soul of a prosecutor. She thinks not of what should be, but only of what is possible. Can such a person be happy?'

There were many thing that Anna could have said to that. Like they both knew Ben's standards were impossibly high, that Sarah still had the capacity to change, that she was probably disoriented by coming back . . . that . . . But Anna discarded all of these. Ben was right: Sarah didn't look particularly happy. Sighing, Anna said, 'Come on now. Rest a little before Sarah gets here.'

Walking up the path Sarah heard the long, pure, melancholy notes of a tenor sax issuing from out the back of the house. Turning away from the front door, she followed the sound to where it was coming from – their bedroom. It puzzled her that anybody would still be in there: Ben and Anna had always been such early risers.

But not this time apparently. Although it was gone eight o'clock when she looked through the open French doors she saw that Ben was still in bed while Anna was in her dressing gown, uncharacteristically indolent for Anna, sitting on a high backed chair near to the bed. They were both motion less, apparently absorbed in the music, as a breeze from the electric fan caught the edge of the white sheet puffing it up in counterpoint to the cascade of notes.

As Sarah stood watching, Anna leaned down and took a washcloth from the basin on the floor, wringing it until it was almost dry and then straightening up and wiping the cloth across Ben's forehead. Her movements were so gentle, like a mother tending her sick child, except that when Ben opened his eyes and they looked at each other, what Sarah saw was no longer mother and child but two lovers enveloped in each other.

Definitely the wrong time to be visiting. She turned. But she had mistimed her move: the music ended and the sound that dominated was her foot snapping against a twig, closely followed by Anna's: 'Sarah. I'm glad you got my message.'

By the time Sarah turned back, Anna was already up and moving towards the internal door, pausing when Ben said something that Sarah couldn't quite catch, then changing course and going over to the dresser to rewind the tape. The same sweet notes filled the air. 'I'll make fresh tea,' Anna said, and left the room.

Ben, who had raised his head when Anna first spoke out, smiled. He looked exhausted, Sarah thought.

As she walked in through the French doors, he sank back down and closed his eyes. She chose a chair, not the one Anna had vacated but a wicker armchair by the wall which she moved halfway to the bed before sitting down. Ben continued to lie motionless, his lips slack and slightly parted. Like a corpse, Sarah thought.

Although it was still early, the room was already heating up. Sarah shifted her chair into the path of the fan's flurry and then, feeling self-conscious about staring, also closed her eyes. She was enveloped by sound, by Ben's laboured breaths running under the lilting tension of the saxophone's mellow control and her own breathing synchronising with his as she let the music wash over her.

'You don't know what love is.'

What? Her eyes snapped open.

'That's the title of this ballad.'

Deep breath. 'I didn't know you were a Coltrane fan.'

'There's a lot you don't know about me,' he said. There was something in his tone, something both snappish and restrained, that alerted her. Was he trying to tell her something?

She hoped that he was. Ever since his voice had sounded out in her New York apartment she'd been waiting for an explanation of why he had rung. What she wanted was a real explanation, not some cover story involving Truth Commission hearings and his need of her to conduct this particular prosecution. Sure, she knew she was good at her job and, sure, she also knew that most indigenous prosecutors would be too implicated by the past either to be interested in the case or to do it justice. But even so, the country was teeming with lawyers many of whom would have been happy, and more than competent, to take on the case.

He was looking at her. His blue eyes seemed very pale.

'Are you feeling unwell?' she said.

He shrugged. 'I had a bad night. Anna fusses so. She has forbidden me to get out of bed. You'll have to attend the hearing on your own again.'

She nodded. 'Fine.' Then she leaned forward and said, 'Ben . . .'

He got in first, his agenda overriding hers. 'The judges will almost certainly rule against your submission to question Dirk Hendricks about Steve. Your next step is to ask Dirk Hendricks's attorney . . . what's his name?'

'Hannie Bester . . .'

'That's right . . . ask him if his client will agree to talk to us privately. Hendricks is vulnerable. He's so keen to get out of jail he might decide it's in his interest to show willing by telling us what he knows about Muller and Steve Sizela. But first ask Bester's permission . . .'

She gave another nod. 'Will do.' And said again, 'Ben . . .'

'The news of the Muller subpoena will have spread through town like wildfire,' Ben said. 'With all the changes in this country, the white community is less protective of its sinners than it used to be. I expect developments on that score.'

She nodded.

'That's all for the moment,' he said, and closed his eyes.

He seemed to be drifting off. 'Ben . . .' she said, and then, when he opened his eyes, added quickly, 'I'm sorry about yesterday.'

He waved one hand dismissively in the air.

She wouldn't, couldn't, be so easily dismissed. 'I said some things I shouldn't have.'

He shrugged. 'We both spoke out of turn.' He shrugged again. 'It's not important. The things we say in the heat of the moment are never that important. And you were right. We don't have enough evidence to take Muller to court. Not yet . . .' he sighed, and his voice faded, his eyelids closing on the release of his breath.

She sat watching the rise and fall of his chest as he lay there, frail in his old man's striped pyjamas. For years she had thought that what she and Ben had together would never change. Now, sitting next to him she thought: there is no going back.

The silence had stretched so long that she thought he had fallen asleep, but suddenly his eyes flickered open.

'Don't you see.' His voice was hectoring as if they were still deep in argument. 'I had to act. What the Sizelas want is such a simple thing – to be allowed to bury their son in the place where their forefathers are buried, to know that they will also one day lie by his side. If the Truth Commission and the courts can't give them that, I, we, must. We have no other choice. We . . .' His eyes closed.

She looked out of the window, aimlessly, at the hot day rising. When Ben didn't continue, she kept on looking, her thoughts drifting until gradually she realised that the interval between each of his breaths had lengthened. She glanced across. This time she could see he really was asleep. Getting up carefully, she tiptoed from the room.

19

ALEX WALKED TOWARDS their table. He nodded briskly at Sarah and sat down. He smelled sweet and damp, as if he'd only just got out of the shower.

'Before we begin,' the head judge said. Despite his quiet, grey looks he was quite a showman. He leaned back, surveying the audience, taking his time, scanning each row methodically so that when eventually he bestirred himself to speak again the silence had a strained quality broken only by the creak of the slowly orbiting fans. 'Before we begin,' he repeated. He paused again and then rapped out those same words: 'Before we begin,' and went on: 'it has been brought to my attention that certain members of this audience were jostled and intimidated as they were queuing for a seat to this morning's hearing.'

Down in the audience, heads turned to the figure of Pieter Muller who was seated near the back. He was difficult to miss. One of the very few white faces present and certainly the only redhead, he was also distinguished by the fact that in this packed hall, he was alone in a long line of empty seats.

The judge, his grey face set in a grim frown, raised his voice, pulling the audience's attention back on stage. 'We take the most serious view of any attempt to interfere with witnesses or participants in this hearing and that includes spectators,' he said. 'Any repetition of this behaviour will be reported to the relevant authorities, who will take prompt action to deal with it.' He pursed his lips, giving time for what he'd said to sink in and then punctuated the point by putting on a pair of half-rimmed gold glasses and looking down at a set of notes.

His voice was softer now and much more neutral: 'The question is whether we should allow Miss Barcant to cross-examine Mr Hendricks about the disappearance of Mr Steve Sizela. This committee has taken into account the fact that the last known sighting of Mr Sizela was at the Smitsrivier police station where Mr Hendricks was based. We agree with Miss Barcant that it would be reasonable to assume that Mr Hendricks might have been in a position to observe what happened to Mr Sizela, but . . .'

Ben was right: they were going to refuse.

'. . . but we use the world "might" advisedly since Miss Barcant has supplied neither evidence nor argument to link Mr Hendricks to Mr Sizela's disappearance. We have therefore ruled that Miss Barcant will not be allowed to cross-examine Mr Hendricks on the question of Steve Sizela's whereabouts.' The judge turned to address Dirk Hendricks directly. 'We would, however, suggest to you, Mr Hendricks, that you might decide to meet with the legal representatives of Mr and Mrs Sizela with a view to helping these parents find the answers for which they have been seeking.' And then, punctuating the judgement, with a brisk 'Thank you', he addressed himself to Dirk Hendricks's table again: 'Mr Bester, please continue leading your client.'

Alex sat looking straight ahead as Dirk Hendricks's voice seeped into him.

'I handcuffed the prisoner . . .'

It was different from the voice Alex had once known. That had been harsh, boisterous, bullying, not this dull monotone, the words issuing out so softly that Alex had to strain to pluck them from the air.

'And then I suspended the prisoner between two tables,' the voice dropped even further, 'with a broomstick inserted below the knees and above the forearms. That's why we called it . . .'

'Mr Hendricks,' the judge boomed, 'I must ask you again. Speak up. We know this is difficult for you . . .'

Difficult for him?

'. . . but our interpreters, who are doing a valiant job of translating for the benefit of those who do not speak Afrikaans, cannot hear what you are saying. Please . . . try.' The judge leaned back.

'Yes, Mr Chairman,' Dirk Hendricks said. Much more loudly. That strident, taunting voice. Hendricks looked across the stage, as if by accident, at Alex. Then, dropping his gaze, he picked up his train of thought. 'We called it the helicopter,' he said. 'The prisoner was flying.'

'Thank you,' the judge said, settling back in his chair. 'That is much better. Please go on.'

'When we had thus immobilised the prisoner . . .'

The prisoner, Alex thought; even after all this time, he can't say my name.

'. . . we would strike him with a sjambok.'

Except, of course, then he called me kaffir, not prisoner.

'Our aim was to get the information before the terrorists . . . I mean, the enemy forces, Mr Chairman,' backtracking and trying it again. 'We needed to get the information from the prisoner before the enemy forces had time to regroup. We were in a hurry. We knew the detainees had been instructed to hold out for three days.'

Three days.

'. . . which is how long it took them . . .'

Seventy-two hours. Four thousand, three hundred and twenty minutes.

'. . . to reorganise their networks.'

Two hundred and fifty-nine thousand, two hundred seconds.

'Once the prisoner was in *situ*,' Dirk Hendricks said, 'we used a sjambok and sometimes water . . .'

On the rare occasions when they left him alone, and when he was conscious, Alex used to count as well.

'And if that was not productive,' Dirk Hendricks's gaze was directed down, 'I also used the wet bag method,' he said. 'The prisoner would be made to lie on his stomach, with his hands tied behind his back.'

That was enough. Alex did what he had learned to do in jail. He cut Hendricks's voice from consciousness.

He looked at Steve's parents; Steve's mother sitting as stoically as always, the rock that bound that family together and, in contrast, Steve's father, uncharacteristically agitated, his face contorted in a grimace.

'I put the bag over his head . . .' Dirk Hendricks's voice broke through.

He looked at Sarah Barcant. She was listening intently through headphones, frowning in concentration and simultaneously making notes. He thought about her as she had been that night before at her bedroom door. So bold for a local woman, and so at ease in her polite rejection of him. He wondered whether she'd always been this confident or whether New York had made her that way.

'Are you married?'

Married? What kind of question was that? Alex refocused on his torturer.

'For the record please, Dirk,' Dirk Hendricks's lawyer said.

'Yes, Mr Chairman. I am married.'

So he went back to his wife at night.

'And you have two children?'

Dirk Hendricks nodded at the floor.

'How old are your children?'

A smile played across Dirk Hendricks's face. 'Jannie is in sub B, Mr Chairman, he's just six,' and then his face reverted so quickly to its familiar blankness that the smile seemed more like a passing facial tick as he added, 'My daughter, Elsie, is two.'

What had this to do with anything?

'And where are your children now?' the lawyer asked.

'I don't know where they are, Mr Chairman,' Dirk Hendricks said. 'My wife took them overseas.'

Overseas . . . Hendricks had used that word on him: '*Your friends overseas*,' that's what he'd called them as he'd taunted: '*they can't help you, can they?*', spitting out the sentence, his phlegm hitting Alex's face, no hands to wipe it away. Dirk Hendricks's face so close, the stench of his body, his arms . . . moving . . . his . . .

'Will your family be soon back in the country?' Hendricks's lawyer said.

'I don't know, Mr Chairman. I received a letter from her only this week, asking . . .'

Wash yourself.

You're filthy – speaking to Alex as if he was a child.

You want another hiding?

You stink.

You disgust me – and himself: he disgusted himself as well. *Wash yourself.*

'. . . for a divorce,' Dirk Hendricks said.

'And will you agree to give her one?'

'Yes, Mr Chairman. I will,' sitting there, stolid, offering up his broken marriage as sacrifice.

The bastard.

'It's better they start a new life separate from me,' Dirk Hendricks said.

'Because of your imprisonment?'

The torturer as victim. That's what was going on.

'That is correct, Mr Chairman, because I am imprisoned. But not only that. My wife's problems started before I was ever charged. It was not easy for her to live with the consequences of my work.'

Sitting back, Alex watched the rehearsed play.

'The consequences?' the lawyer said. Interested. Intrigued. 'You mean the long hours? The danger?'

'Those as well,' the prisoner answered. 'But what really bothered my wife was the fear. I was a member of the security branch in this small town of Smitsrivier: everybody knew us. We had to take precautions or else we became targets. My son was guarded when he went to school, he couldn't play out in the open, he had to spend the breaks in the headmaster's office. At home we always kept a wet blanket handy . . .'

'*I can treat you like a man or I can treat you like an animal,*' that's what he used to say. '*It's your choice.*'

'We soaked the blanket in the bath in case of hand-grenade attacks. We taught the children how to use it in the event of an attack.'

Alex was pulled back into the past while in the present Dirk Hendricks's lawyer kept droning on: 'Was it this threat to your family's security that your wife found so intolerable?'

'That and . . . that . . .'

The lawyer cut through his client's mumbling, saying loudly, 'Please, Dirk. I know this is painful for you but the committee needs to hear what you are saying.'

'During the worst times,' Dirk Hendricks said, 'I was not so easy to live with. I had nightmares.' He gulped, his Adam's apple undulating. 'I love my wife but one night I even woke up to find my hands around her neck. Her eyes were bulging. I was choking her so badly she could barely cry out.' He looked down, helplessly, at those huge hands. 'It happened also on another occasion when I was awake. I was not angry with my wife,' he said. 'I didn't understand how that could happen.'

He left me nothing, Alex thought. Not even my anger.

'And now do you understand why you changed in that manner?' the lawyer asked.

'The psychologist who came to see me explained that this is a result of how my job damaged me inside.'

'He told you that you were suffering from post-traumatic stress disorder?'

Alex raised his head. Looking at his torturer.

Who did not look back, but only said, dully, 'That is correct,' reverting to that policeman's habit of addressing the judge: 'Mr Chairman.'

'For the record,' – the lawyer handed a sheaf of documents to his assistant who began distributing them – 'I am submitting as evidence this same psychologist's report.'

A copy landed on the table in front of Alex.

'. . . the psychologist's finding is that my client suffers from post-traumatic stress disorder. Page three, second paragraph,' the lawyer said, turning the page, his action echoed by all the others on stage.

'This paragraph, as you can see, lists the symptoms of hyper-arousal that are characteristic of PTSD, referring specifically to the occurrence of nightmares, memory loss and sudden bouts of inexplicable anger . . .'

He left me nothing. Not even anger. Alex's revulsion was physical. He could taste the nausea rising in his throat.

'. . . the psychologist states that in his opinion these symptoms are not the results of a personality disorder, which would include the anti-social personality disorder also known as psychopathic, but rather the direct result of the strain of his position.'

Shoving back his chair, Alex left.

20

DIRK HENDRICKS'S VOICE followed Alex down the aisle. 'I was a
loyal policeman. We were taught that the enemy was all
around, that we must fight communism and its terrorists with
all our might. This is what I did. I did not benefit financially
from my actions – apart from drawing my police salary, that
is. I did it for the good of South Africa.'

The good of South Africa!

'Or that's what I believed I was doing then,' Dirk Hendricks
said. 'We were in a war situation. People do all kinds of terrible things in wartime.'

'But in hindsight?' the lawyer prompted.

Alex lunged for the exit, reaching out for the door handle,
wrenching it open.

'Ja,' Dirk Hendricks said. 'In hindsight: it was wrong. I am truly sorry for the hurt I caused . . .'

Alex was out, striding away, as the door swing shut on Dirk Hendricks's plaintiveness.

I am truly sorry.

Sorry? Alex thought. That man? That Dirk Hendricks was an impostor.

Alex knew all about Hendricks: he was a man empty of conscience and unashamed to find himself putting forward a series of ritualised lies to a commission that had been set up to hear the truth.

I'm sorry. How many times had Alex heard those words? Such a familiar South African litany, recited endlessly in their past. *I'm sorry, baas,* offered up nervously to a white man not out of real regret but out of fear. And now again: *I'm sorry,* those same words adopted by those same people who'd inspired the fear in the first place, but who now saw nothing wrong in using this practised apology for the purpose of getting themselves off the hook. And for Dirk Hendricks to precede this hypocrisy with an account of a stress disorder! He had no shame.

The self-pity that had sifted through his torturer's voice took hold of Alex. A sharp, puncture stab at his guts.

He couldn't stay on the steps. He must get out of there, go and hide, before the hearing adjourned. He moved out, searching in chaotic circles for his car, so that by the time he found it a few blocks away, he was bathed in sweat.

The car was as hot as hell: his own stupidity for parking it in the sun. When his hand touched the steering wheel it was scorching. Tearing a page from that morning's newspaper, he used it to protect his hand while he released the handbrake. The car rolled forward into the dappled shade of a jacaranda tree. Then at last, having laid down newspaper on the driver's seat, he shut the door and drove off.

It was still sweltering hot. His hands were stiff; they didn't seem to be working properly. He drove foolishly. Carelessly. Coming to an intersection he turned the steering wheel too far so that, as the car rounded the corner, it also mounted the pavement. If I go on like this, he thought, I'll end up having an accident. Even killing somebody.

He passed a school, saw children spilling out, turned the corner, heard their excitable voices. It was too hot in the car. He was suffocating. He was ill. He was going to be sick. He slammed his foot down on the brake and got the door open and the handbrake up even while the car was still moving forward. He jumped out. He had stopped the car by a fenced-in stretch of unoccupied veld. He could hear the voices heading closer. He headed for a break in the wire fence, walking through, taking a few steps . . . and . . .

His breakfast came spewing out of his mouth. It slithered down, hitting the ground in one slimy stinking stream of regurgitated pap. He felt his guts convulsing and he gagged again, his hands pawing at his stomach as he bent double. His mouth opened, spewing out a mucus liquid that no longer bore resemblance to any solid food. He tried to swallow it back but the taste was so revolting that his swallowing only provoked a renewal of the gagging that had him bending down lower to the ground.

And all the time the memory was just as he must always have feared it would be, without knowing that this is what he feared. This was why, he now realised, he hadn't wanted to attend the hearing – to revisit Smitsrivier – because he hadn't wanted to remember. The memory was being delivered, not in an ordered, structured form that might have been easier to assimilate, but in jagged splinters. Images – Steve's pointing, the dirt under Dirk Hendricks's nails. Sounds – those screams building up, battering his ears, the terror gripping him so tightly that it was all he could do to stand and shout, then screaming himself until they came and held him down.

And Steve's lifeless body. Always that. Steve's death: his fault?

Alex didn't know. Those fragments kept intruding. The things he had said; his voice, craven, pleading for mercy. The things he did, battering his own head against the wall in a bid to end his misery. And before as well. That time before. A muffled distant time.

The way they used to talk, not only him and Steve, but all the comrades, about what would happen if they were ever caught. If! When the police clamped down, almost every single one of them was picked up and none of them was properly prepared. They were all so young and so innocent. They'd no idea of the lengths to which those bastards were ready to go. They had sheltered each other from reality, substituting for their parents' warnings fairy tales which they passed between them. Stories of their strength, their invincibility, the power of their collective. As if any of that mattered once you were the target. And when they punished you, they punished you alone.

Alone. No one else there to take the pain for you, to tell you it would soon be over, or to share the memory. And when it was all over there was no one to listen either, really listen, because not one of them had wanted to hear. To really hear. In the face of this, what choice did Alex have? What choice but the path he took? What choice but, afterwards, to forget?

The irony of it. Having survived what Dirk Hendricks had done to him by deliberately forgetting it, he now found that he could no longer choose to remember. All the questions that Sarah had asked in the Sizela kitchen – the layout of the police station, his last sight of Steve, his limp arm banging against a metal door that shouldn't have been there, Steve carried through an entrance that did not exist – kept churning, an assortment of pieces that would not fit together.

Another wave of nausea moving up Alex's gullet: there was no resisting it. Standing there, in the middle of waste ground, he dropped his head, powerless to do anything but let out this distant echo of his betrayal.

21

WHAT AN EMBARRASSMENT, Sarah thought: a client who will neither talk to me nor even stay in the hearing. She pushed through the doors of the Smitsrivier Retreat and immediately spotted Alex. He was sitting on a moth-eaten brown sofa, slumped down at one end near a plastic aspidistra, his face partly obscured by an unrealistically lurid green leaf.

Was he waiting for her? It was hard to tell. As she began walking down the lobby, he looked up but, seeing her, quickly looked away. Mr Communication, she thought.

He must have been waiting for her. As soon as she sat down next to him, he said, 'Did they go on without me?'

'No.' She thought how it had been, herself on stage waiting for Alex, and trying to explain why he wasn't there.

'I'm sorry.'

Another apology: this was getting to be a habit.

'I couldn't come back,' he said.

Couldn't? She looked at him more closely. Although he still refused to meet her gaze, even from side on she could see how sad he seemed. She gentled up her voice. 'No harm done. They adjourned until tomorrow at eleven.'

He shrugged as if he didn't care.

'Dirk Hendricks has agreed to meet privately with me. He's going to tell me what he knows about Steve.'

Another shrug.

So that's how he was going to play it? Just when they were getting somewhere he would clam up? She sighed, saying without much expectation: 'Anything I should ask him?'

She had expected indifference. What she got instead was a loud 'No', accompanied by a violent shake of his head. He said it again then. 'No', following through with 'I don't want to know anything from him', so loudly that a man on his way to the bar stopped abruptly to look in their direction before moving off again, while Sarah sat wondering whether Alex's denial was so intense precisely because there was something he wanted to know from Hendricks. She kept her counsel. If this really was the case, she thought, how unbearable: to need something from your former torturer. She looked across at him. He was slumped, the picture of dejection, and for the first time she saw him not as the showman in control but just a man caught in a situation he couldn't escape.

'Let me help you, Alex,' she said, putting her hand on his arm.

She felt his warmth and, she was sure of it, his longing, before he pulled away. 'I don't know if I can be helped,' he said, fast, as if the words had issued involuntarily from his lips, this confirmed by the silence that followed.

'I'm struggling here, Alex,' she said. 'I know I'm good at my job, but I also know that this isn't New York and it isn't like any case I've ever had. Now his lawyer has finished with him, I should cross-examine Dirk Hendricks. I can't – not unless you help me – I don't know what to ask him.'

Alex sat unmoving. His face was so blank that she wasn't sure he'd even been listening.

She tried again. 'I could start somewhere else,' she said. 'Are there, for example, any witnesses you'd like me to call?'

No answer.

'Anybody that could talk about Dirk Hendricks and the things he did to you?'

He broke the silence, suddenly. 'Thulo.'

She waited for more.

'Jackson Thulo. He was a junior policeman, Dirk Hendricks's black helper. He's doing what they all do these days – trying to put as much distance between himself and his former masters as he can.'

'And you'd have him as a witness?'

A shrug. 'Why not?'

'We'll have to move fast. Do you know how to contact him?'

'Somebody will know. He lives in the township.'

'Can I get a statement from him then?'

He didn't answer. He sat, quietly, as if he had used up his quota of words.

'Alex,' she said, as gently as she could. 'I know you're not ready to talk to me. Which means you're not ready to give evidence yourself. It's probably too late to get Thulo for tomorrow but, given the adjournment, I have some time to prepare. I could use the basis of what Dirk Hendricks has already said to do him some damage in cross. But I can't go on too long – not without your briefing me. Which means we need a standby. Thulo could be it, but I can't risk questioning him in public without having a good idea of the kind of thing he might say. I need to meet him, or at least get a statement from him.'

He was looking at her, blankly.

'I'll get one,' he said.

'One?'

'A statement.'

When? She nearly said it, but she didn't. There was something in Alex's expression that told her not to push it. 'Can I buy you a drink?'

'No.' He got up abruptly. 'Thanks, but I have to go,' then, turning away from her, he almost immediately turned back, as if something had just occurred to him. 'Sarah?'

'Yes?'

'Be careful with Dirk Hendricks,' he said. 'He's much more dangerous than he seems.'

22

SARAH AND DIRK Hendricks met at the police station in a tiny
cream-painted interview room. When the door opened to
admit Hendricks the space seemed to shrink even further. He
was followed in by one of his guards who'd come down from
Pretoria – a huge, gym-built figure of a man with crew-cut
blond hair and clear blue eyes. Seeing the two men framed in
the doorway Sarah was surprised to note that Hendricks was
both a few inches taller and a good deal broader than his
jailer. It was odd, she thought, getting up to greet him, that
she hadn't realised how big he was.

His hands were big as well. Huge and smooth with square-
cut nails, impeccably clean. She saw all this when he offered
his hand and when she felt the pressure of his skin against

hers she found herself thinking that for a big man – and an admitted torturer – he had great reserves of control.

'Ms Barcant,' he said.

Hiding her surprise at the *Ms*, she said, 'Mr Hendricks,' nodding to indicate the chair opposite hers. 'Thanks for agreeing to see me.'

'No problem.' He waited for her to sit down before pulling out his chair and swinging himself into it. Given what she'd heard of the cramped conditions in his Pretoria jail, she was surprised at the ease of his movements. He must also be a man of great determination, she thought.

'I'll do anything I can to help,' he said, tilting his head, directing his gaze downwards, drooping as he had held it throughout the hearing. And when he did that, the huge, confident man became the withdrawn petitioner, the transformation so complete that Sarah found herself wondering if the stoop of his shoulders was deliberate.

'You'll be all right, miss?' his guard said, and, seeing her nod, went out.

She took out a pack of Camels, opened it and offered one to Hendricks.

'You don't, do you?' he said.

'No. I don't. But it's fine by me if you want to.'

'That's good of you, but if you don't, then I won't smoke either.'

Feeling awkward as if some unsubtle power play of hers (rookie prosecutor visiting con for information offers cigarette) had been exposed, she put the pack down, cleared her throat and opened her notebook.

'We've met before you know,' he said.

What? She looked up. 'We have? When?'

'Your father was the optician?'

'Yes. That's right.' Surely she couldn't have forgotten meeting him?

'It was 1984,' he said. 'On the road outside Smitsrivier. You were barefoot.'

Of course. It came to her then. She'd just turned twenty-two and, as Dirk Hendricks said, she was barefoot. It was almost dusk and she'd been limping towards town. She'd started out in high heels, but after one broke off she'd discarded them and staggered on, leaving a trail of blood after a stone had sliced into her heel. The righteous indignation that had driven her out of a boyfriend's car had long since worn off and the town seemed no closer. The shadows had started to lengthen with the sinking sun. It would soon be dark. Usually so fearless, she kept remembering her mother's predictions of disaster that would befall her if she wasn't more careful.

'I gave you a lift,' Dirk Hendricks said.

Just as she'd been on the verge of despair, a bakkie had come trundling down the road and stopped, and a man – Dirk Hendricks? – had leaned out of the window and, smilingly, offered her a ride. 'Weren't there two of you?'

'That's right. Pieter was driving.'

The second man was Pieter Muller! Her stomach contracted.

'We never did figure out what you were doing on your own in the Karoo,' Dirk Hendricks said. 'You wouldn't tell us.'

Well, how could she have told them that she'd gone slamming out of her boyfriend's car just because he'd annoyed her?

'You were such a pretty girl,' Dirk Hendricks said. 'And so plucky – out there in the middle of nowhere.'

And he was such a flirtatious man. Both of them were in fact. They'd teased her all the way into town, not threateningly but gently, making her laugh. I enjoyed their company, she thought, remembering how she'd sat between them, flattered by their attention. They'd both been kitted out in blue jeans and short-sleeved shirts, two tanned, strong men who picked her up and joked and flirted with her all the way into town, not minding that she wouldn't tell them what she had been doing alone on the road with no shoes on. If she thought about them at all afterwards, it was with vague affection for their casual acceptance of her. She certainly could never have guessed that they were policemen. And not any policemen but members of the elite security police that in 1984 was busy launching itself into its last, most brutal phase.

Now she wondered – where had they just been when they came across her? What had they been doing?

'We reckoned you must have had a fight with your boyfriend,' Dirk Hendricks said.

She said, 'Let's get on with the business in hand, shall we?'

'I'm sorry.' He smiled. 'I've spent too long in jail, I talk too much when I get the chance. Please – ask me what it is you want to know.' His smile broadened into an open grin.

'Let's start with Steve Sizela's arrest. What can you tell me about it?'

'Nothing.' He pulled an apologetic face. 'I wasn't the arresting officer. I was dealing with only one prisoner at the time with Mr Mpondo. I don't even think I was there that day. I was working between Port Elizabeth and Smitsrivier. I was frequently away.'

'But you heard that Mr Sizela had been picked up?'

'Not so much heard as knew it was about to happen. We had Mr Mpondo in custody and he wasn't being cooperative, so when one of our informants told us that the two had often been sighted together, we decided to pick Mr Sizela up under Emergency Regulation 10 – the prohibition or publication or dissemination of subversive statements – and see if we could squeeze anything out of him.'

'Squeeze?'

He looked across at her. 'It was the way we talked,' looking at her straight. 'It was the way we acted. I can't pretend anything else.'

She couldn't help liking him for his honesty. 'Steve's mother says Pieter Muller was one of her son's arresting officers, that he came to the house,' she said.

'If Mrs Sizela says so, then I'm sure that this is how it happened.'

'Would that make Muller Steve's interrogator?'

'Not necessarily,' he said. 'You have to remember – those days were chaotic. If you were a policeman you had to be a jack of all trades. One day you'd be patrolling a primary school and the next picking up a high-profile activist. Pieter could easily have been in on Sizela's arrest and then never had anything more to do with him.'

'But you don't know?'

He shook his head. 'Have you tried looking at the arrest record? It should give the name of his interrogator.'

'No.' She shook her head. 'All the records, save for one signing-in book that covers the day Steve was brought in, have gone missing.'

'Ja.' He knew that already. 'I remember now, I heard that happened.' He sighed.

'If not you or Muller – who else could have interrogated Steve?'

He shrugged. 'I'm sorry, ma'am. I just don't know. I was a newcomer to Smitsrivier and, as I said, I wasn't there all the time.'

She was suddenly alerted. It was the *ma'am* that did it, reminding her that he was a policeman playing out the game as all policemen are taught to play it. 'Mr Hendricks, newcomer or not, you and Pieter Muller were both members of the security branch.'

'Yes, ma'am, that is true.'

'And you were known to be good friends.'

'We spent time together outside – yes.'

'And intelligence was your stock-in-trade. I cannot believe you didn't know what each other was doing.'

He looked at her. 'I am not responsible for what you believe,' he said, and paused a moment, his face set in disapproval. 'I can only tell you what I know.'

'But you had connected Steve and Alex Mpondo; is that not true?'

'Yes, ma'am, it is correct.'

'And given that you were Alex Mpondo's interrogator, you would surely have been interested in what Steve Sizela had to say?'

'I would. And I would surely have been told if Sizela had said anything of relevance.'

'But you weren't?'

'I can't remember.'

'You can't remember?' She didn't try and keep the disbelief out of her voice; if anything she reinforced it.

He acted as if he hadn't noticed. 'I'm sorry.' He sounded almost innocent. 'There are many things I don't remember.'

I don't remember: it was the most frustrating of responses. If they'd been in court at least she could have poured scorn on the notion that a policeman could not remember the lead-up to a death in such a small place as Smitsrivier. But they were not in court and might never be. She was here on sufferance: by Dirk Hendricks's consent. 'Alex Mpondo says that while he was in your custody, two warrant officers brought Steve Sizela to his cell.'

'It's possible,' Dirk Hendricks's expression was bland. 'I don't remember it. Does he say I was present when that happened?'

She shook her head. 'No – he doesn't say that.'

He shrugged and said again, 'It's possible.'

'He also says that he saw Steve one more time after that. Steve was being carried out of this police station.'

'No. That's impossible. It wasn't . . .' Dirk Hendricks shook his head, frowning as if he were genuinely confused. 'It wasn't . . .' He stopped again, tongue-tied, and then continued. 'That's not possible. Alex Mpondo would never have been let out into the corridor at the same time as a prisoner he knew. We would never do that in case the two communicated.'

'I see.'

'I'm sorry, Ms Barcant,' he said. 'It's just not possible. I'm not saying that Mr Mpondo is a liar: I'm sure he believes that's what he saw, but it cannot be. It wouldn't have happened like that. Not here.'

In her years as prosecutor, Sarah had met many proficient liars. Some of them had suckered her and those were the ones that had taught her never to take anything, not even her own instinctual reactions, at face value. And yet, against all odds and all knowledge of the wrongs that he had committed, Dirk Hendricks sounded genuine. The fact that Alex's story had made no geographical sense only added weight to this. She said: 'You know I'm acting for Steve Sizela's parents?'

He nodded.

'And do you understand why they want to know what happened to their son?'

He nodded again. Vigorously. 'Of course I understand.' He looked across, his bleak grey eyes hardening. 'Christ,' he said, 'if my son disappeared, if I thought somebody had killed him, I would be just like them. Worse. I'd want to strangle whoever did it with my own hands.'

'Then, Mr Hendricks,' she raised her voice, 'if you really

understand what the Sizelas are going through, then you will forgive me if I am brutally honest with you.'

'Please, Ms Barcant. Be . . .'

She interrupted him. 'I've walked through this police station; I know you have as well. I have seen how small it is. When your warder left we could both clearly hear his retreating footsteps. But you're trying to persuade me that while you interrogated Alex Mpondo, some other, unnamed, person interrogated Steve Sizela, and yet you never knew who that person was – and neither, I assume, did you hear that other interrogation as it proceeded. Can you see why I'm having trouble believing you?'

'Yes. I see. Of course I do. But . . . but . . . I don't how to say this . . .' He seemed to be struggling for words and for breath as well. He looked helpless: how had he become a torturer?

'Would it bother you if I stood up?' he said.

'No. Go ahead.'

He stood up, abruptly, as if something was propelling him there. Standing, he was huge.

He must have sensed how big and threatening he seemed, towering over her like that, because he backed away until he had backed himself against the furthest wall. He took a deep breath. 'To be a good interrogator,' – he was staring at his feet – 'you must focus on your prisoner. You must get to know him. To understand not just his strengths or his weaknesses, but also the things he likes, the music that moves him, the smells that have special meaning for him, the people he cares about, the enemies he's made. If you do your job properly he must become like your child.' He looked up then, straight at her. 'Or your lover.' His grey eyes seemed to fill with tears then, but she couldn't be sure of that because he blinked rapidly. 'You must think only of him,' he said. 'You must get inside his head. And when that happens, I mean when it really happens, you are concentrating so hard that even if the My Lai massacre was going on next door you wouldn't hear it.'

23

'Why My Lai?' Ben was lying in bed, propped up on a mound of pillows.

She hadn't thought about it. She shrugged. 'Because I live in the States?'

Ben shook his head – no. 'From him I would have expected a South African example – the Jameson Raid, perhaps, or the Sharpeville shootings or, even better, the ANC Church Street bombing – not a massacre in Vietnam. And yet he chose My Lai. Why?'

He was right; now she thought about it, there was something peculiar in Hendricks's example. 'My Lai conjures up ordinary GIs gone mad,' she said, 'and eye witnesses who kept insisting that nothing had happened. Do you think Hendricks shares this same association?'

'It's possible.'

'So you think he was trying to tell me that he knows who killed Steve Sizela?'

'You mean you actually believe he doesn't know?'

'He must have known.'

Ill as he was, Ben's sharp intelligence was still in evidence. 'And yet?' he prompted.

He was right. 'And yet,' she said. 'Yes, I guess I did half believe him. Or at least I believed he might have chosen not to know.' She thought about the suffering on Dirk Hendricks's face as he had stood there against the wall. 'I certainly believed him when he talked about his relationship with Alex. I was looking at Alex during the hearing. I saw something between those two, something intimate.'

'And that surprised you?'

'I don't know.' She sighed. 'Yes, I guess it did. They seem so very different.'

'They are,' Ben said. 'But nevertheless there is a bond that links Alex to Dirk Hendricks.'

She was surprised by the reproach in Ben's voice. She shot him a questioning look.

He was staring straight ahead. 'It's the same bond that binds this country to its past. None of us are free of it. Not me. Not Anna,' he said, pausing a moment before adding, 'Not even you, Sarah.'

There it was again in the way he pronounced her name, *Sarah*, as if he disapproved. 'Ben . . .' she said.

But he was looking at the ceiling now, cutting her out. It was an old trick of his and one that he used to play on those occasions when she'd either disappointed or offended him. Seeing the thin closed line of his lips, she wondered what she'd done wrong this time. She knew better than to ask. She sat, waiting for him to speak.

When, eventually, he did, it was in that didactic manner he

used to adopt when he was at his most angry. 'Two days ago,' he said, 'you accused me of selecting the truth to suit myself.'

So that's what this was all about: despite his earlier disavowal, she had hurt him.

'But you must see,' he said, 'that nothing is as simple as you would have it. If you were to take the trouble to understand, to really understand, those guns-for-hire like Hendricks, then you would also understand why this country is still so violent. We are all interconnected here. You cannot pay attention only to the one side as if it stands separate from the other. If you look at the pass system, the township necklace makes sense: look into the fear in ordinary white eyes and you will understand black hatred.' He focused his eyes, suddenly, on her. 'Alex and Dirk Hendricks have something very basic in common. They are both, in their own way, patriots.' He paused a moment and then added, 'As is Pieter Muller.'

Muller as well? That took her by surprise. It wasn't like Ben to go soft on his opponents.

'What Hendricks and Muller did, they did for their country,' Ben said.

'Are you defending Muller now?'

'No.' He shook his head wearily. 'I'm not defending him.' He shut his mouth, shutting her out.

This is hopeless, she thought. She looked away, looking through the French doors watching a mist spreading down the mountain flanks.

'The person I'd really like to defend,' she heard, 'is you.'

'I beg your pardon?'

He was looking at her now, meeting her gaze, calmly but without much expression.

She tried to make a joke of it. 'What's the charge?'

He didn't return her smile. He was staring, as if he were searching something out. Something, she thought, in her mind? Her heart? Her soul?

She looked at the tight cast of his lips and remembered how he had used to do this in court as well, using silence to intimidate an obdurate witness. Is that what she was to him now?

'I'm sorry you never decided to come back,' he said.

Oh. So it was as simple as that. 'I know,' she said, nodding. 'I should have, if only for a visit. But in the beginning I was so busy settling in, and after that . . .'

'I'm not talking about a visit. You should have come back permanently.'

Should she? Was he right? She didn't know. That she, who had fitted into neither black nor white society here, had to leave was indisputable even to Ben.

'Without Smitsrivier,' Ben said, 'without South Africa, you will always be less than you could have been.'

He was so sure of himself and so arrogant. She looked at him, her eyes hurt. 'We weren't all born heroic like you, you know, Ben.'

He didn't seem to be listening. All he said was: 'I'm tired,' and closed his eyes.

Just like that, shutting her out. 'Ben!' she said.

No reply.

She was furious now. She wanted to reach out and pull at him, shaking him until he explained.

It was no good. He wasn't going to volunteer anything more and she didn't have the heart to force it out of him. His bones were sticking out visibly through his striped pyjamas; he looked so frail. She leaned over and touched him gently on the shoulder. He did not respond. She sat. He didn't say anything; he didn't even give a sign that he knew she was still there. Getting up, she tiptoed to the door.

She had almost reached it, when he mumbled something. She turned. 'Did you say something?'

His eyes were closed.

She stood, framed in the doorway, looking at him. He was on his back, his mouth open, his face unmoving. It's like a death mask, she thought, although she could still hear his laboured breathing. She waited for a long time for him to speak again but he did not. He had been tired; he really was asleep. Going through the doors she shut them quietly behind her.

Outside, she stood for a moment, watching the mist moving closer and bathing Anna's brilliant garden in an uncharacteristically muted light. As the colour leached from the flowers, she thought: this is death's most malicious feat, that at the same moment it ends everything, it also leaves everything unfinished. She started moving slowly through the garden, breathing in its fragrance.

'Sarah!'

Turning, she saw Anna hurrying over the lush lawn. 'Will you stay for supper?'

'Thanks.' She shook her head. 'Not tonight.'

'Another time then,' Anna said. 'Come, let me walk you to the gate.'

They went together, across the grass and round to the front of the house. They didn't speak. Just like of old – she and Anna had never had much to say to each other – but coming upon one of the most extravagant of her rose beds, Anna took out a small pair of secateurs from her apron pocket, snipped the buds, collected a small bunch and made a posy that she wrapped in a piece of tinfoil she must have brought especially for this purpose. She presented the posy to Sarah. 'To make your hotel more like home.'

'Thanks.' Touched, Sarah smiled at Anna.

But Anna did not return her smile. It was always this way for us, Sarah thought: we always missed each other in the past as well. She was overcome suddenly by a sense of exhausted resignation. Wacky Smitsrivier, she thought, the only place in the world where I can find myself feeling more empathy for a torturer like Dirk Hendricks than for the loving wife of my dying mentor. 'Are you cross with me, Anna?' she said, and as the words emerged she felt like kicking herself for sounding so childish.

But Anna didn't seem to mind. 'Cross?' She frowned as if she were thinking about it. 'No. I'm not cross.'

In for a penny, Sarah thought. 'Is Ben?'

Anna repeated the word again. 'Cross?', vaguely this time, lost in thought, adding it seemingly as much for her own benefit as for Sarah's: 'No, the person that Ben is really angry with is himself.'

24

As SARAH MADE her way back to the hotel the mist came sweeping into town. At first she didn't notice. she was too busy
thinking about what she still had to do. Without Alex to
brief her, she must spend most of the night trawling through
her notes and through the records of previous Commission
hearings and that way develop some design for cross-examining Dirk Hendricks. It wasn't ideal, but it might just hold
the hearing long enough for her to get some sense out of
Alex.

She came to suddenly. Either the mist had arrived simultaneously with the dusk or else it had created a depth of
darkness all on its own; whichever it was, the night was now
so intense she could barely see two feet ahead. The street

lights were no help, their auras visible without penetrating
the gloom. She walked slowly, feeling out the route more
from memory than any visual clue. As she went, jagged
sounds – a warning shout, dicordant music, glass cracking –
blared out and were then almost immediately cut off.
Something was happening, somewhere, out in the darkness.
She speeded up. She heard another sound: footsteps coming
up behind her.

She stopped. So did the footsteps. She started again, walking even faster. There it was again: that soft flap of a stranger's
shoes against the paving stones keeping pace with her.
Anxiety fluttered like moths wings but she knew she must
not run. She stopped and turned: 'Who's there?'

No answer.

She called again: 'Who's there?'

Nothing. She stood her ground, breathing in, holding her
breath. Still nothing. She must be imagining things: there was
no stalker. It's only the cloying mist, she thought, and turned
again and this time kept on walking, neither fast nor slow,
ignoring the footfalls that continued to pursue her.

The sidewalk dipped. Wait a minute – that didn't seem
right. She stopped and, peering into the darkness, could
just make out the fat outline of a white milkwood on the
other side of the road. She knew that tree and she knew it
stood one block beyond the hotel. Which meant that she
must have been so caught up in thought, she'd managed to
pass the Smitsrivier Retreat.

She turned. A shadow, the wisp of a man, flitted briefly
before merging with the darkness. There had been somebody
there and he had been following her. Her heart thudding, she
retraced her steps.

The hotel was shrouded by the night: that's why she'd
missed it. Either there was a power cut or else somebody had
secured each curtain, blind and shutter so tightly that not a

chink of light escaped. She felt her way past the stone pillars and up the stairs, feeling for the door. Finding it, she turned the handle. The door didn't budge. It must be locked. Strange: it was never usually even shut. She rapped her knuckles against the door but the fog absorbed the sound. She knocked again, much louder.

A voice called out. 'Yes?' An aggressive voice. 'Who's there?'

She stopped knocking. 'It's Sarah Barcant.'

A moment's hesitation and then she heard keys turning and metal sliding – the door was not only locked, it was double-bolted – before Andre, the barman, revealed himself. He wouldn't let her in – not right away. He used his ample figure to block the entrance, checking that she was who she had said she was, and only when he was satisfied did he step out of the way. Even so, he kept hold of the door so that, to get in, she had to squeeze past him. He closed the door behind her.

There was no power cut but the hall was gloomier than usual, with all its lights, save for a distant one, off. Confused, she turned to look at Andre. He was busy sliding the last bolt back into place. She did a double take: he was carrying a shotgun.

Fat Andre with a gun. 'Who exactly were you planning to shoot?' she said.

'Nobody.' He winked. 'If they're lucky.'

Uh-huh, she thought seeing his belly bulging over his off-white T-shirt and hearing the strained wheezing of his breath.

'There's a gang of tsotsis rampaging around town,' Andre said.

She frowned. That didn't sound like Smitsrivier. And yet somebody had been following her.

'They tossed a rock through the bar window: that's why I closed.'

'But why?'

'Don't ask me,' Andre shrugged. 'I have no idea why these people do half the things they do.'

Now that sentence, with its all-encompassing 'these people' to categorise an entire population, was reminiscent of the old days.

'It's this Truth Commission business,' Andre spat out the name as if it was a curse. 'It's got everybody worked up.'

'But the gun?'

Andre shrugged and changed the subject. 'Something came for you,' he said, and walked away, going behind the reception desk before emerging with an envelope. 'Here.'

She took it and opened it and found a single typed page inside. Pulling this out she read the heading: *Statement by Mr Jackson M. Thulo, formerly warrant officer.* Amazing. Alex had come through. She glanced up idly.

Andre was staring hard, but when her eyes met his all he said was: 'Can I fetch you anything?'

She was hungry. Very hungry. She couldn't remember when she'd last eaten. 'Is the kitchen still open?'

'No.' He shook his head. 'The staff have all gone home.'

Definitely not my day, she thought, yawning and stretching. 'I better go find myself a restaurant. Would you mind reopening the door?'

'You shouldn't do that,' Andre said.

It sounded like a warning. She threw him a questioning look.

'It's not safe out tonight,' he said. 'Not if you're on your own. I'll tell you what. I was making myself a bite to eat. You can have some if you like.'

It was like old times: the two of them sitting at a scratched, wobbly, wooden table reminiscent of the one that had stood in Andre's childhood kitchen. And yet there were differences: she and Andre no longer knew each other like they used to, and that old kitchen had been homely and full of burnished copper pots and pans Andre's mother loved to collect, while this one was inhospitable – big and difficult to use, designed for a legion of cheap domestic labourers.

The food, however, was the same: a huge platter of boerewors, accompanied by boiled potatoes and over-sugared carrots. Red meat that Sarah no longer ate. When Andre brought the sausages in from the yard where he had braaied them, her stomach turned. So as not to offend him, she took one from the platter and bit into it gingerly. As that combination of meat juice and fat spurted out, its once familiar thick, pungent, spicy taste brought back to her those childhood days spent ranging wild. She cut off another piece. She was actually enjoying it. This she hadn't expected: that Smitsrivier would turn her back into a carnivore. She made short shrift of what Andre had given her.

'Have some more.' He offered up the platter.

'Thanks, I couldn't. They were delicious though.' She laid down her knife and fork. 'I never figured you for a cook.'

He shrugged. 'Cheryl taught me.'

'Cheryl?' The name conjured up a strong, stout, plain girl with a pair of thick mouse-brown plaits and an apron bib she always wore over calico dresses. 'The two of you got married?'

Andre nodded.

'Who would have guessed it?' she said, remembering how Andre and Cheryl used to fight. 'Weren't you always pulling at her plaits and making her cry?'

'Well, if I was, she got her revenge. She ran off with the cutlery rep.'

'Oh dear.' She bit back a smile. 'I'm sorry.'

'Ag, don't be.' Andre stretched out his legs. 'We were no good for each other. This way is better. She remarried and got the nice house and the nice garden she always wanted and I have the hotel and a set of fancy silverware I never paid for.' He grabbed a can of Castle beer from the table and tipping it up, took a long slow slug. 'What about you? Ever meet Mr Right?'

She shook her head: no.

'Well, you never were the marrying kind,' he said, adding in that Smitsrivier way that assumed there was only one or the other, 'You were more of career girl.'

Maybe he was right, she thought.

'You know what I most remember?' he said. 'Your temper. You kicked me in the shins once – you must have been all of six years old – and then you told me in no uncertain terms that you were going to get a job and leave Smitsrivier. *Jirra*, you had a harsh kick in those days.'

'If we're remembering the same incident, Andre,' she said smiling, 'I kicked you because you looked up my skirt.'

He was also smiling. 'Never,' he said, 'I would never . . .'

He broke off then. He didn't have to say why: she heard it also – tapping. Not a sporadic but a rhythmic sound, like a code, issuing from outside the yard. Someone rapping out a message on the high yard gate and repeating it. Once. Twice. Three times. Andre didn't respond, not at first. He sat frowning in concentration and only when the third sequence was completed did he get up. 'Excuse me.' Taking up his huge bunch of keys from the table and his gun from where he'd laid it against the wall, he went out into the yard, calling out softly, 'I'm coming,' as he moved towards the back.

She shifted until she had an unobstructed view of the gate. She saw him reaching it, undoing its giant padlock and opening up, just a fraction. She couldn't see much more: she could only hear the low murmuring of a man's voice.

Andre didn't add much to the stream of his visitor's verbiage: he merely interposed the occasional 'Ja' until eventually the conversation ended as abruptly as it had begun when Andre pulled the gate to, locking it and striding back.

He was a man on a mission. He passed her by: 'I'm sorry. I have to go out,' and walked quickly out of the kitchen.

Intrigued she followed, catching up with him just as he was pulling up the counter that led to his back office. 'Don't worry,' he said, seeing her. 'You'll be safe. This place is a fortress and anyway I'll get the others to check up on you occasionally.' He dropped the counter and went through the door labelled *private* that stood at the back of the reception area.

She kept on going, lifting the counter and following him through, going into the office. She found him standing in front of the open door of a wall safe. He was removing something from the safe and dropping it into the pocket of his baggy brown trousers. Something small that jingled – bullets. 'What's happening, Andre?' she said.

He spun round, shotgun raised.

She jumped back. 'It's only me,' she held up both hands. 'Don't shoot.'

'Jesus – Sarah.' He lowered the gun. 'Don't you know not to creep up on a man with a firearm?'

She nodded, feeling the jagged pounding of her heart.

'There's nothing for you to worry about.' He turned back to the safe and stuffed more bullets into his pocket.

'Are you doing this for Pieter Muller?'

'For Muller?' Andre snorted. 'Ag, no: Muller's nothing. He's on his own now.' He closed the safe and spun the combination. 'They're running amok out there so a few of us are going to see what we can do.'

She remembered how scared she had been outside. And yet she had not been hurt. 'What can you do?' she said.

'Stop them.' Andre turned round.

'Like a lynch mob?'

He was walking towards her. 'No. Not like a lynch mob. Like the good neighbours we are. If you lived here, a woman on your own, you'd be grateful.'

'No. I wouldn't. I'd call the police.'

He laughed. 'The police! That's a joke. They're all related to each other and they're all in league.' He was by her side.

'Andre. You can't just go out there with a gun like nothing's changed.'

He stopped. His eyes were angry slits. 'You're telling me what I can and can't do in my town?'

Piggy eyes, she thought, that's what we used to call him.

'You haven't changed, have you, Sarah? You and your varsity education and your fancy ideas,' spitting out his words. 'You're so sure of yourself, aren't you? Well, let me tell you,' he said, reaching up and taking her by the shoulder and turning her, 'Smitsrivier is no longer your town.' His voice in her ear as he marched her to the door. 'You left. Remember?' Reaching out and opening the door. 'You weren't here during the hard times and if you think you can now swan back into town and tell us what to do, you and your *blerry* subpoenas, you've got another thought coming. And now if you wouldn't mind,' he nudged her over the threshold, 'this is a private area. No guests allowed.'

25

PIETER WAS HALFWAY between the hen house and the kitchen door when he heard the phone ringing. He didn't take much notice. Marie was there: she would answer. He kept walking slowly towards the house, listening to the crunch of his work boots against the gravel drive and the contented clucking of his bantams.

It was a pleasant night, not too hot; the mist that had floated off the mountains to envelop the farm had also cooled it down. It had been a strange mist, he thought, first suddenly covering the land and then, just as unexpectedly, lifting off and moving away into town. Now that it was gone, countless pinpoint lights pricked the jet sky. A good night for sitting out on the porch to watch the shooting stars, he thought.

The phone was still ringing. Marie must have been in the dining room when it started up. He could picture her levering herself out of her chair and walking slowly, agonisingly, down the corridor. He resisted the impulse to quicken his pace: she always found it annoying if he got anywhere before her.

If only she'd let Bessy answer, but of course she wouldn't: it would have been one more surrender to her accelerating illness. It was understandable, he thought, pushing open the mesh door: she could do less and less these days.

Bessy was by the sink and, as Pieter moved towards her, he heard the ringing of the phone stop, to be replaced by Marie's soft-spoken hello.

'If you wouldn't mind, Bessy.'

She knew what he wanted and she moved away from the sink. He took her place in front of its basin of hot soapy water. The temperature was just right. He immersed both hands in the water, leaving them to soak a while before taking up the scrubbing brush and cleaning them thoroughly, paying special attention to the area under the nails. That done, he held up both hands for inspection, turning them like hams on a spit. They were as clean as he always liked them to be, but he couldn't help noticing that the ginger hair on their backs was glinting almost blond in the harsh kitchen light. I'm getting old, he thought: it wasn't really blond, it was grey.

Turning away from the sink, he grabbed a dishcloth and dried his hands. Bessy was still busy clearing the last of the supper things off the kitchen table, picking up two plates from the large steel serving tray, one of them still filled with half-congealed food.

'She didn't eat anything?'

'A little lettuce,' Bessy said, 'that's all.'

He pictured Marie as she had been at the dinner table.

She had toyed busily with her food at the same time as encouraging him to leave. 'You always were a faster eater than me, Pieter,' she'd said, 'don't lose the light.' Now he knew why: she'd been trying to hide her lack of appetite from him.

Tossing the dishcloth on the table, he said, 'Lock the kitchen door on your way out, will you?'

When Bessy answered, 'Yes, baas,' she also threw him a querying look: he never usually asked her to lock up.

'And you better lock your room as well,' he said and left the kitchen.

As he turned into the corridor, Marie was finishing her conversation. Standing there by the telephone table with her back to him she said a soft goodbye, put down the receiver and reached for the walking stick she'd propped up against the table.

'Who was it on the phone?'

She took fright and dropped the stick. It fell, clattering to the floor.

She started the long slow process of bending to retrieve it. He strode over and picked it up for her. It was a heavy, carved, knobbed walking stick that had once been his: he had used it as extra ballast to climb on his longest walks. Now the stick was Marie's and it helped her hobble round the house. He handed it to her.

'Thank you, Pieter.' Her hands were so distorted she could barely hold it. Looking into her eyes he saw how worn by pain they were.

'Here,' he said, offering her his arm and leading her slowly towards the study where she liked to sit during the evenings.

She didn't say anything until she was on the rocking chair and he by the desk. Then she said, casually as if making everyday conversation, 'That was Dora.'

He nodded.

'She rang to let us know that there's been trouble in town. A lot of windows smashed. She was checking to see that we were all right.'

'Neighbourly of her.'

'It was.' Marie nodded. 'Dora's a good woman.' She frowned. He hated that, he hated to see how deep the lines were etched into her forehead. 'But why, if the trouble's in town, was Dora asking after us?'

This was not like Marie: she didn't ask questions, she waited for him to tell her what he thought she needed to know. He kept his expression open. Easy. He said, 'You know what Dora's like. She worries about everything.'

'I see,' Marie said, as if she didn't see, and then: 'I think I'll go to bed.'

Bed already – she must be feeling bad. 'I'll help you,' he said.

'No, Pieter – you have the accounts to do. Just help me out of this chair and then you must send Bessy to me.'

Two hours later when he looked in on her she was lying in bed. She was on her back staring up at the ceiling. Her book was on her bedside table: it didn't look as if she had even picked it up. She was lying very still and if she heard him coming in she gave no sign of it.

He went to stand beside her. 'Is there anything I can get you, Marie?'

She shook her head and smiled. 'Thank you, Pieter. I'm about ready for sleep.'

'Should I switch off the lamp then?'

'Thank you,' she said again.

He clicked it off and leaned down, touched her cool lips with his and said, 'Good night, Marie,' as he straightened up.

'Good night, Pieter.'

He left her and walked over to the door. But then, instead

of walking through it, he stopped and turned and called her name 'Marie?' into the darkness.

'Yes, Pieter?' she said promptly.

'If anything happened to me . . .'

'Why would anything happen to you?'

'No reason,' he said. 'But if it did, I want to be sure you know that my insurance policy and all other documentation is kept in the safe.'

'Thank you, Pieter. I know now.' He heard her sighing, not sadly, but as if in resignation, almost as if she were letting go of her day.

'Good night then,' he said, and stepping out into the corridor, closed the door and made his way slowly towards the kitchen to check that Bessy had remembered to lock up.

26

As Alex drove north along the ribbon of tarmac that stretched out to the petrified sea of mountains, dawn swept across the land like a wall of flame, shadows of magenta and crimson flaring up before gradually fading away. Not that Alex noticed it: he was too busy concentrating on his tally of electricity poles that had been planted along the roadside. Fifty . . . fifty-one – there: the next was it. He stopped the car on the gritted edge.

Getting out, he stood a moment, breathing in the solitude of this, the first light of day. It was very sheltered in this part of the valley and the wind that was rocking Smitsrivier was no longer evident. And then gradually, as the sun climbed higher, the landscape reverted to that normal, undifferentiated stretching-out of browns, tawny yellows and dappled beiges. Business as usual, he thought, climbing over the fence.

Except it wasn't business as usual. He hadn't been here in over fourteen years and he'd never been here by day. He knew the way only by instinct and by Steve's instructions that were, even after all these years, still ingrained in memory. He pulled them to the forefront of his consciousness, walking by number like he used to, crossing a barren field and then going down a short incline to the dried-up river bed. When he reached the twisted tree skeleton some fifteen yards away, he started counting again, crossing the river bed and walking downstream, all the time counting. One hundred and eighty-three, eighty-four, eighty-five. The sun blazed down. He stopped to wipe his forehead and to catch his breath. It was so quiet here and so arid. The space where once a river had flowed was now a narrow winding of dust and stones and crumbling flanks that stretched out ahead. Here and there a rodent, a dassie maybe, skittered across the barren surface, soon disappearing into the thorny bushes on either side.

Picking up the count, Alex got moving. Two hundred and thirty-five. Thirty-six. Thirty-seven. Two hundred and thirty-eight: the magic number.

It looked no different from any other section of the river bed. Two moth-eaten olive-green bushes were still gripping on to the crumbling bank and beside them lay the usual scattering of stones that flash floods and earth slides had once deposited all along the river side. You had to know what you were looking for and still look carefully (in the old days, when he visited at night, Alex would by now have clicked on his torch) before you'd see how some of the stones had been arranged in a rough circle with a line leading away from it. This was the place. Three hands span from the last stone was where it used to be – the dead letter box in which Alex and Steve would, in an emergency, leave messages for each other.

Not on the surface, of course – that would be easy bait for any passer-by – but buried below.

There won't be anything here, Alex thought. He told himself he was convinced of it. Still he dropped down to the ground, placing himself to one side of the line of stones and twisting back to turn his hand, once, twice, three times. There. That's where it used to be.

He had brought nothing: no shovel, no spade. He hadn't thought to bring anything. In fact, he hadn't thought at all. He'd just got up off the floor of some stranger's house where he must have fallen into a drunken sleep, reclaimed his car and started driving, aimlessly, he thought, until he found himself driving down the tarmac, counting pylons. Now he stretched out to pick up a jagged stone and began to dig.

It was years since anyone had been here and in their absence the sun had hard-baked the earth. What Alex was doing was heavy going, not so much digging as chipping away at the surface, shaving off the top layer of dust, before sweeping it to one side and chipping at the surface again. A waste of time: he didn't know why he was doing it. The tin would be gone. It, and its location, must have been one of the first things Steve gave up to them.

Nevertheless, he continued to dig and as he did so he found himself thinking about Steve. He hadn't done this in a long time, not really, not since then: that was one of the ways he'd saved himself. He had put Steve out of his mind, buried him as surely as Steve himself had been buried. And now, even though he was in the place that Steve had found, Alex found it almost impossible to summon up Steve's image. Steve on a platform – yes – with fist raised. And yet, was this real memory or was it merely created by the fact that Alex had seen that photo hanging in his mother's house?

Steve had been a friend, not just a fellow activist. But trying to summon up a different image of his friend, all Alex ended up doing was scrolling through frozen portraits of the other dead. So many of them: so hard to mourn them all.

Sometimes looking around Parliament at the other survivors of those terrible years, Alex thought that what they had in common was not just their shared suffering but the manner in which they had all been forced to keep their humanity by generalising it. To each of them in different ways, the collective had become more important than the individual – not just because this made political sense but because it was one way of surviving all that pain. What was that slogan they used to chant at funerals? Don't mourn, mobilise. A necessary slogan then, but now a way of life. Only the close relatives, parents like Steve's, managed to hold on to a normal, human grief. You could spot them at every Truth Commission hearing, sitting in the front row, staring numbly at their children's killers as if that way they could understand what had happened and that way could accept that the result would not be justice but the truth.

The truth: had any of them uncovered it? And if they had – had it made them better? Sometimes, Alex doubted it. Take James Sizela. He said he accepted that his son was dead, that he only wanted Steve's body. Alex wasn't so sure. He knew James well enough to know the reserves of anger that lurked there far below the surface. If the truth, the whole truth, came out, would James accept it?

Alex came to with a start. He looked down. His mind might have wandered but his hands had stuck to their task: digging out a hole. It was still quite small but it was big enough.

Inserting a hand, he felt around the hard packed dust. It was as he had anticipated: only earth. The DLB *was* empty: they had taken the tin away. He let out his breath, a release of the tension he hadn't even realised he was holding. For good measure, he made one last stab of the stone into the earth.

He heard it then. A slap – a noise that was not just earth and stone. No. It couldn't be. Steve must have told them about the DLB, and they would have dug it up.

Alex was overtaken, suddenly, by the strong urge to get up, to get away from this place. He looked at his watch. Half past seven. If he wasn't careful he'd be late for the hearing. He needed to go back, to shower and change.

But he didn't go. No matter how much he wanted to, he knew he couldn't. Once again he picked up the stone and used it. There was no mistaking either its dull ringing or the rigidity of the surface that it hit. Putting the stone down, he brushed away the dirt.

It was there. The tin in its shallow grave. Waiting for Alex to come and dig it out. For Alex and not for them. He felt strangely detached as he watched his hands moving. They looked odd, he thought, as if they belonged to some stranger, those long fingers scrabbling at the earth, those nails tearing as they cleared the space around the tin. He could see its metallic facing.

He got it out, pulling it from the earth. It was the same as it had always been: an old tobacco tin, its markings long worn away. He held it in the palm of his hand, feeling its weight. It wasn't heavy but then it never had been: it was only meant for messages. Transferring it from the right hand to the left, he prised his fingers around its lip, wrenching at the lid. It will be empty, he thought, it has to be.

The lid came off so suddenly that his hand jerked it away. The lid dropped. He left it there. He looked at the base. It was quite corroded. Sometime during the last fourteen years water had penetrated, eating away at the metal in one corner and smearing an orange sludge over the contents. Because there were contents. There was something there just as there always had been. A piece of paper, once carefully folded, now almost a mush. A sheet torn from out of one of the exercise books at Steve's father's school: Alex could see the vague outline of its light blue feint. But he could see more than that. Some words had survived the years and the weathering. Not just words but also a name written by him. A name of one of their comrades. Of a man who was never picked up by the police.

Alex's most dominant memory of Steve – Steve pointing his finger at Alex – came flooding back. The previous day when Sarah was harassing him, Alex had insisted that Steve hadn't known what he was doing when he stood, pointing, in Alex's cell. But even as Alex had heard himself saying this, he hadn't believed it. Back then, when Steve had been brought to his cell, and for all the time that had elapsed since, Alex was convinced that his old friend Steve had broken, had betrayed not only him but also all their hiding places.

Now he wondered. If Steve had broken, he would have needed information to show he was telling them all he knew. Which meant he would have had no choice: he would have told them about the dead letter box.

But if they knew about that they would have picked up the comrade who was implicated here. Doubt surged through Alex's mind. Had it been as he had told Sarah? Was their bringing Steve into his cell a trick they had played on him so he would turn against Steve? Or was it instead possible that Steve had never talked?

He didn't want to think about it. He scooped out the paper. The rest was too far gone, it disintegrated in his hand. Looking down at it, rusted orange in his fingers, he groaned.

A single thought: Steve, what did I do to you?

27

SOMETIME DURING THE night a wind blew into town, blowing off the mist, and when Sarah stepped out of the Smitsrivier Retreat she was met by a wild and dazzling day. Past the town, there towards the distant horizon, thin, white clouds skittered across the high sky before streaking off into the expanse of blue. The wind was still fierce. Shading her eyes against the dust storm, she began walking across the road, heading for her car.

Halfway there, a fresh blast of wind swept down Main Street, this one so strong that it almost knocked her off her feet. As she struggled for balance a dayglo-orange plastic bag ran into her, a modern-day desert thistle threading itself around her ankles. When she kicked it, it whirled away in its own dust eddy, fast and furious enough it seemed almost to propel it down Main Street, past the town hall and all the way to the jagged outline of the mountain tops. Another blast of wind. She closed her eyes and stood quite still, waiting for it to pass.

When she opened her eyes again, the turbulence had temporarily subsided and now, instead of feverish agitation, what she saw – in the moment before the wind started up again – was Alex. Alex, standing there across the road, doing nothing, just standing. Thank God, she thought, he's come to brief me.

It had only been a brief respite. The wind started up again sending up a curtain of dirt that enveloped her, obscuring vision, forcing her to close her eyes again. When next she opened them, Alex had gone. She looked up and down the road. He seemed to have vanished.

Either vanished down a side road, she thought, hurrying to her car, or else he was never there. She was very tired: she'd been up most of the night. She got into the car and turned the key. As the engine revved into life, the wind started up again. Ignoring it, she followed the route of the plastic bag – down Main Street towards the town hall.

The road and the pavements on either side were uncharacteristically deserted – the town sleeping off a night that had been punctuated by the sound of breaking glass, shouting voices and revving engines. Now all that remained was its desultory mopping-up operation. Everywhere she looked African women were sweeping glass into the gutter or tapping the last jagged shards from window frames, while at the end of Main Street four men manoeuvred a huge pre-cut pane of glass off the side of their van.

Turning right at the town hall, Sarah headed out of town. On the outskirts she passed a group of low buildings that stood slightly back from the road – the district's central police headquarters. She watched the retreating complex in her rear-view mirror, seeing its ugly brown-brick guardhouse out front, its flag whipped up by the wind, and its series of brown-brick buildings laid out in a quadrangle and slapped into the middle of an enclosure. The surrounds seemed like an advertisement for the many different kinds of security wires – barbed, razor, Gothic and with added glass – that were currently on sale throughout the country. Andre was wrong, she thought: the police inaction was much more likely the result of fear than a refusal to side with whites.

Thinking about that brought back Andre's shame-faced morning greeting. He'd been scrupulously polite throughout, as if his night-time tirade had never occurred, but when she asked how his patrol had gone, he acted as if he hadn't heard the question.

She put it to one side. She had other matters to preoccupy her mind: like what she was going to do if Alex failed to turn up, and how she was going to question Dirk Hendricks without knowing what Alex wanted. She had a plan, or at least half a plan, but it was the kind of plan that might easily go awry. She yawned and decided to stop worrying about it, dismissing it from her mind.

She had soon reached the township that lay not far out of town – or at least not far in distance. In terms of its surroundings, she might have crossed the frontier into a foreign land. Even the air felt different. Coming off the tar road, she drove over thick-clad dirt, which the wind kept swirling up so that the blue clarity of the day was clouded by a floating brown film. That huge variety of trees and those splendid displays of contrasting flower beds that were the pride of Smitsrivier had given way to ditches piled with old cans and crumpled newspapers, bloated plastic containers and bits of wire.

She turned off the dirt road and steered the car down a

rutted path which dipped and bent. At least she didn't have far to go: the path ended abruptly in a patch of dirt. She braked. Looking through a high iron fence she could see another set of brown-brick bungalow buildings – reminiscent of the police complex. A typical piece of apartheid logic, she thought, to model a school on a police station.

She switched off the engine and stepped out into the blaring, blowing heat, walking through a set of steel-mesh gates that half hung off their hinges, down a short path to a central courtyard where a set of buildings was grouped together in an ugly rectangle. The ground of the courtyard enclosure was hard-packed dirt and cracked paving stones, and the buildings all had double doors. Despite the wind, the windows were all wide open so that she could hear the chanting of a times table, the crack of a ruler against a blackboard and, dominating those, a hesitant boy's unbroken voice saying: 'Me . . . me . . . meeth . . .' interrupted by a sudden, impatient man's voice: 'No. No. Sit down . . .'

Following the voice with her eyes, she looked across the courtyard to where James Sizela was standing at the head of the furthest classroom. Above the wind, she could hear his stern voice saying: 'Like this,' as, standing thin and tall and strict, holding out a book at arms length, he took over: '"Methought the souls of all that I had murdered,"'

Richard III, Sarah thought, remembering that Alex had also quoted from Shakespeare.

'"Came to my tent; and every one did threat / Tomorrow's vengeance on the head of Richard."'

A voice that was not his but the tyrant king's on the eve of Bosworth Field, the words ringing out into that desolate space, an unaccustomed cry of shame for what he'd done, a man about to meet his fate:

'"And every tale condemns me for a villain. / Perjury, perjury . . ."'

'". . . in the highest degree,"' Sarah said to herself, caught up in the power of the moment, saying the words so as to accompany Sizela's. Except she realised that she wasn't. His voice had been abruptly cut off and he had turned and was looking at her, holding her gaze for an impatient beat before he said to his class: 'Read the speech quietly to yourselves,' and walked away, disappearing from sight.

He soon emerged, his jacket flapping in the wind as he strode over, straight and stern in his old-fashioned pinstripe suit, stopping abruptly within a few feet of her. 'I wasn't aware we had an appointment.'

'I'm sorry, Mr Sizela. I tried to catch you at home but your wife said that you had already left. If I could have a few minutes of your time?'

James Sizela shook his head as if he were about to refuse, but before the words were out something drew his gaze back to the windows of his classroom where his students had congregated and that seemed to change his mind because he snapped out an abrupt 'Follow me'. He walked back the way he'd come, except that once inside the building he turned in the opposite direction, leading Sarah down a dingy corridor to a door which bore the legend 'Headmaster'. Taking a clump of keys from his trouser pocket, he used two to unlock first the iron gate and then the wooden door, pulling them open so they clanged against the brick, then switching on a fluorescent light. 'You may go in,' he said, then he turned away, walking back down the corridor.

Going in, Sarah found herself in a dingy windowless room, not much bigger than a stationery cupboard and much less well equipped. It contained only two pieces of furniture – a large steel desk and a low plastic chair behind it. The desk held a neat pile of feint-lined exercise books, two red marking pens, a coin-sized brass pedestal with a mast on which was flying a tiny South African flag, and a battered telephone.

'Here.' James Sizela was back, carrying a chair which he put down in front of the desk and then, going behind it, said: 'One of my students is now standing,' and sat looking impatiently across at Sarah.

Lowering herself down – much lower than he was – Sarah instantly became a supplicant. James Sizela's students must feel like this, she thought, as he barked out a harsh: 'What was so important that you needed to pull me from class?'

'I apologise for that,' she said. 'I didn't know you'd be teaching.'

'We don't have enough staff.' James Sizela raised his voice against a blast of wind that rattled the tin roof. 'I am both headmaster and English teacher. Please, Miss Barcant, get to the point.'

She leaned forward. 'I assume you heard what happened in town last night?'

He nodded.

'To summarise – a gang of youths smashed the windows of a number of white-owned businesses. In response, a posse of the businessmen went out looking for the window-breakers. Luckily for all concerned the two groups never came face to face.'

'So I have been told. But what has it to do with me?'

'According to Truth Commission officials who contacted me this morning,' she said, 'the window-breaking was a way of warning the white community not to shield Pieter Muller.'

Sitting very straight, James Sizela said, 'That may be so.' He put his hands, clasped tight, on the desk in front of him. 'But I ask you again: what has it to do with me?'

'Those same officials asked me to talk to you. They wanted you to know that if people start taking the law into their own hands, the whole thing might blow up in all our faces.'

'I see.' James Sizela dropped his gaze, looking down at his hands.

In the silence she could hear the wind battering at the tin roof, some voices raised in song, someone shouting out.

James Sizela raised his head. 'You want me to call off my dogs.'

'In a manner of speaking.'

'I cannot do that, Miss Barcant,' he said. 'Not in any manner. For one simple reason: those are not my dogs.' He unclasped his hands and leaned back, gripping her with his brown eyes. 'I have been teaching in this area for almost forty years and in that time I have dedicated myself to producing law-abiding, productive adults. I have never encouraged anybody, no matter what the circumstances, to break the law. What happened last night was not at my instruction. I see no reason why you have come to me.' He was glaring.

Meeting his glare, she said, calmly, 'They wanted to ask if you'd be willing to speak at a meeting. The idea is that if you, Steve's father, were to appeal for calm, this would have impact. They will also ask Alex Mpondo to speak.'

At the mention of Alex's name, the intimation of a smile that contained no humour crossed James Sizela's thin face.

'Between the two of you,' she said, 'you could calm the community.'

'No.' James Sizela said, blankly, without moving.

That refusal, so fast and so determined, was the last thing she had expected. She leaned forward. 'Mr Sizela. I understand . . .'

'No, Miss Barcant, you do not understand,' James Sizela said. 'You cannot understand. You can't know what it is like to lose, literally to lose, your son.' He got up suddenly, turning away so that he was facing the blank wall, staring out of a window that didn't exist, his voice sounding from a distant place so that Sarah had to strain to hear him. 'You don't know what it is to wait for your son's return, to see him in the street and call out and see a stranger turning.' He reached up, straightening a black-and-white photo of himself shaking hands with a white man. 'You cannot know how it feels to see the way grief has diminished your wife, or what it is not to want to face the fact that your son is dead because that would seem like betrayal, to think of him every day, every waking minute and at night as well and then finally to know that he is dead and yet not to be allowed to mourn him.'

He turned so suddenly that the photo juddered and settled back again at a crazy angle. He took no notice. 'You cannot understand,' he said. 'You cannot. I am no savage. Nor am I a vigilante: I have no desire to "get" Pieter Muller. As far as I'm concerned, what he chooses to do is between him and his conscience. All I want is to find my son's bones so that I may finally lay Steve to rest. And now if you will excuse me,' – he picked up his chair – 'my students are waiting.' Then, only when he was already out in the corridor, did he turn and say: 'Please, Miss Barcant. Find my son.'

28

THE JUDGE SWITCHED on his microphone. 'I'm afraid we can't wait any longer, Miss Barcant. You had better proceed without your client.'

Plan B then, Sarah thought, and leaned forward, reluctantly, about to switch on her mike when the door at the other end of the auditorium opened and she saw Alex pushing through. Such a narrow escape. She watched him from her high vantage point. He had on the same clothes, beige cotton trousers and a white shirt, as the previous day – more crumpled now and slightly grimy. He seemed oblivious to the whispered comments and to the whirring of camera motors that punctuated his progress down the aisle. Nearing the stage, his gaze alighted on Sarah and stayed there, but seemingly without recognition. She could see the effort of his breathing and the quivering of his chest, and when he hesitated at the top of the stairs there was something in the way his face sharpened that made her wonder whether he was going to turn round and go back the way he'd come. But the moment passed and he moved forward, not hurrying, but determinedly coming to sit beside her. She was surprised at how conscious she was of the way his brushing against her acted on her like an electric charge.

'Glad you could make it, Mr Mpondo,' the judge said, and then, more sharply, 'Carry on, Miss Barcant.'

Only a moment's grace. She stretched out again, aiming for the microphone but once again, she never reached it, because this time Alex beat her to it, clicking down the switch and moving his mouth close so he could say in a loud, clear, sure voice: 'I would like to ask the questions myself.'

She was so taken aback that her hand was still hovering in mid-air.

'Any objections, Miss Barcant?'

Object? She shook her head. 'No, Your Honour. No objections.'

'Very well.' The judge leaned back again. 'Carry on, Mr Mpondo.'

It was time. Alex raised his head to look straight at his torturer. 'Tell me again why you made this application for amnesty,' he said.

Dirk Hendricks's head, already bent, dropped lower.

'Mr Hendricks?'

Dirk Hendricks looked up – dully – to say: 'My application?' before lowering his gaze again, folding in on himself.

So far to plan, Alex thought, and said, patiently, 'Yes, the one that brought you here. Why did you apply?'

Dirk Hendricks was staring, dumbly, at his nails. 'You know why.'

'Yes, I think I do know. But I'm asking you to tell the committee.'

Nothing. No reply.

'Too obtuse for you?' Alex said. 'Well, let me ask the question more directly: did you put in this application because you thought that if you didn't, I might turn up at your next amnesty hearing and prevent you from going free?'

Dirk Hendricks nodded.

Looking across the space that separated them, Alex found himself looking at a stranger. This man who sat opposite him was not the torturer who had haunted his life: he was just an ordinary man brought down by history and by the compulsion to grab history's second chance and cross the line from instigator to applicant, from perpetrator to reconciled.

A pathetic man. A liar.

Well, no matter: Alex would expose the reality. 'You nodded, Mr Hendricks,' he said. 'Was that the reason?'

'Yes,' Dirk Hendricks said. 'You know that's why.'

'I see. So does your application only include the minimum you thought you'd get away with?'

Dirk Hendricks shook his head. 'I wouldn't say that.'

The man Alex had known, the real Dirk Hendricks, had never spoken with such unrelenting monotony. 'What would you say then?' Alex asked, pitching his voice to provoke the other.

Without result. 'I was in jail when I filled out the form,' this tamed, unfamiliar Dirk Hendricks insisted. 'Nobody told me how to do it. I was trained as a policeman only to write down the basic points and that's what I did here. I wrote what I thought was needed. If it wasn't enough, I'm sorry.' Repeating it, that meaningless utterance, 'I'm sorry,' this time accompanying it by the briefest of smiles and a renewed lowering of the head, a continuation of his courtroom artifice, a construction for the purpose of getting amnesty which his satisfied lawyer punctuated by reaching across and clicking off the microphone.

It's all an act, Alex thought.

And yet, if it was just an act, it was also a consummate one. That different Dirk Hendricks, the man whom Alex had known, seemed to have vanished. Dirk Hendricks's grey eyes, for example: surely they weren't grey like that before? His mown blond hair – was it so short then, and was it really blond? His huge, plump body-builder's shoulders – weren't they rather gristle and sharp bone?

That was the worst of it – how well Alex had known his enemy, knowing him not only by his appearance but also more intimately. Even now he could summon it back, the corrosive sweetness of the other's sweat, the tobacco-menthol fusion of his breath, the pressure of those blunt fingertips, strangely soft, his rasped demanding voice.

Alex swallowed. He knew what he had to do. He must challenge this ersatz version and draw out the other.

In the silence that stretched between the two men and then expanded outwards, enclosing the audience, Sarah knew one thing for sure. There was something going on between the two that had not yet surfaced into words – a different kind of question and answer that showed itself in every gesture. When Alex swallowed she looked across the stage: she was just in time to catch an answering sign of satisfaction flickering over Dirk Hendricks's face. These two, who had stood on opposite sides of the race divide that had rent South Africa open, were joined together now. They knew each other not like enemies or strangers, but like intimates. Almost brothers. And they're stalking each other, she thought, and doing so as if no one else – neither the committee nor the interpreters, nor the lawyers, nor the audience, nor her – mattered.

Ben was right: they were bound to each other, these two enemies, Alex Mpondo and Dirk Hendricks. Sitting on the edge of her chair, she could feel the fear of it.

Small though it had been, Alex caught sight of Dirk Hendricks's triumphant smile and he also saw the smile knowingly cut off before it could be generally witnessed. Good: let Hendricks grow in confidence. He thought he was so clever, he always had, and as long as he continued think-ing this, he would take no notice of changed circumstances, of the fact that Alex was no longer his prisoner.

'Tell me,' Alex said, looking straight into the other's grey eyes, 'did you ever use the wet blanket?'

Hendricks wasn't expecting that. His mouth opened: no answer came.

'Did you?' Alex said. Patiently, as if he were talking to a child.

The stranger opposite shook his head and, leaning for-ward, stuttered something that was lost because he'd neglected to switch the microphone on. He seemed too dulled to work out why his voice could not be heard. He repeated the words loudly at the same moment that his lawyer switched on the mike so that the applicant's voice boomed out: 'I'm sorry?'

That voice. That was more like the voice Alex had known. Involuntarily, he recoiled from it. Breathe, he told himself, breathe. This was the man he wanted to bring out: this Dirk Hendricks. The real one. 'There's no need to be sorry,' he said. 'What I want to know is whether you ever used the wet blanket.'

He was too late: the old had gone. The new, unfamiliar, broad forehead was creased in concentration as that uncertain, bewildered head moved from side to side and Hendricks – the one Alex did not know – said, 'It was a bag.' Speaking slowly as if Alex might well be stupid, he added, 'A bag, not a blanket. I used the wet bag method.'

'No, Mr Hendricks,' Alex said. 'I'm not asking you about your favourite means of torture. My question centres on the blanket that you yourself introduced into evidence. You told us about it yesterday. Remember? You told us that you kept a blanket in the bath and that you taught your children what to do with it should the need arise. My question is – did the need ever arise?'

An Adam's apple convulsed. 'No,' Dirk Hendricks said, 'it did not,' adding lamely, at the end, 'Mr Chairman.'

'Why not?'

'There was no need to use it.' Dirk Hendricks, the apologetic, beaten one, looked down.

'What? No grenade attacks?' Alex said, pitching ridicule into his voice, coaxing out his torturer. 'No firebombs?'

But the new Dirk Hendricks was still too firmly ensconced to let loose the other. The new one shook his bowed head.

'So all those tales of woe you told us about your family,' Alex said, 'about the strain your work imposed on your marriage, was that just talk?'

Dirk Hendricks looked away, looking towards the committee of judges. 'I wouldn't say that, Mr Chairman.'

'Perhaps you wouldn't say it,' Alex said. 'But it's true, isn't it? None of you were ever under threat, were you? Neither you, nor the wife that left you . . .'

There, that did it – the mention of the wife: in the flashing of the stranger's grey eyes was a glimmer of the other.

'. . . nor the children you can no longer see . . .' Alex said.

There. Another flash.

No wonder Alex had not recognised this Dirk Hendricks. In that moment of anger, those eyes changed, so that when they caught the light they were no longer grey but colourless. Like ice. Like they had been in the past. Those once familiar, unfeeling eyes. Alex turned the ratchet. 'Your family was never really under threat, was it?'

Once again Alex had taken too long and the old had slipped away. The colour was already flooding back into Dirk Hendricks's eyes. 'The fact that we were, happily, not attacked, Mr Chairman,' Dirk Hendricks the prisoner said, looking to the head of the stage, avoiding Alex's gaze, 'does not mean that we were not under threat.'

The other had hidden himself.

A game of hide-and-seek, Sarah thought, and without really intending to she summoned up a dark cupboard and a memory of herself nestling in her mother's long unused winter coats. She could almost smell that sour mixture of mothballs and frayed fur, and hear the laughter that had filtered through the door while she had lain, not caring that the game was almost certainly over and everyone found but herself, half swooning in the claustrophobic heat but too lazy, too comfortable, to move. But then, she remembered, everything had suddenly changed. The door was wrenched open and, blinking into the artificially bright light, she saw a shadow. A shadow of a silent figure who struck terror, provoking a scream at the same time as the figure moved and she saw it was just a neighbour come to get his jacket, and the threat evaporated.'

Hide-and-seek, she thought: that's what Alex is playing now. A dangerous game.

Fixing Dirk Hendricks in his sights, Alex changed tack. 'Yesterday you told the committee that the first three days of any interrogation were the most important.'

'That is correct, Mr Chairman. We needed to get hold of all

the information before the terrorist networks had time to reorganise.'

'I see. And how many days did you keep me in jail?'

Dirk Hendricks shook his head: 'I disremember the exact number.'

'I'll remind you then,' Alex said. 'It was thirty-one days.'

No reply.

'A month,' Alex said. 'I know that for sure, because you told me so a few hours before you released me. You made a joke about a calendar month without a calendar. Don't you remember?'

'No.' Another shake of that farm boy's head. 'I don't remember.'

'Never mind, Mr Hendricks. It wasn't a very good joke. But do you remember how you continued to torture me way beyond the first three days?'

It came again. 'I don't remember.' Those eyes focused on those blunt-cut nails.

'You don't remember?' Mocking, calling up the other.

The other would not respond. Instead, this new man, this prisoner, looked up, his grey pupils swimming in a bulging lens of liquid. 'There are many things I don't remember.'

'Would you disagree then, if I told you that after the first week you continued to torture me every fourth day for twenty-one days?'

Dirk Hendricks's face was blank. 'I never made a note of it.'

'But you'll take my word for it?' Alex said. He waited a minute, then said, 'I see you're nodding. Let's take that as a given then. Your three days were over – did you continue to torture me because you enjoyed it?'

A flaring of resistance in the other's face, which died down as this new Hendricks said, 'No, Mr Chairman. I never enjoyed it.'

'And yet you did it?'

'Yes, Mr Chairman.' That voice dull again.

I must keep moving, Alex thought. 'Tell me about the bag,' he said. 'The wet bag you used on me. Where did you get it?'

'It was standard issue, available at all police stations. It was a property bag for putting in prisoners' effects.'

A property bag.

That dank, foetid stink – the unfolding of his fear.

'I submerged it in water before I used it,' Dirk Hendricks said.

Now that Alex had called up the bag there was no escaping it. He felt the tug of it, its heavy fabric closing in, filling his mouth, his nostrils, smothering him. He shivered. Dark. Too dark. He lowered his head. He could feel the silence, building up around him, bringing with it dread. He looked round wildly.

'Alex?' He heard someone whispering his name. Someone: Sarah.

No. He shifted away.

She would not let him go. She shifted with him, whispering again, urgently in his ear: 'Alex?' first as a question and then an injunction. 'Alex!' as the judge leaned forward and . . .

She was right. He had started. He must finish. 'Did you blindfold me before you put the bag over my head?' he said, clumsily blundering his way somehow into the question that he'd told himself to ask.

Dirk Hendricks was quite calm. 'That is correct,' he said. 'And I lay you down on the floor with your hands tied behind your back.'

'And then?' Alex heard the quaking of his voice. 'What happened then?'

'Happened?' The other had grown in strength. 'I tightened the bag, pulling your head back,' – that same confident voice, soothing, calming, quietening down Alex's moaning – 'cutting off your air supply.'

It came again: his own putrid fear filling the void. He forced himself to speak. 'And then?'

That's all it took. When Alex said those two words: *And then?*, everything was changed.

Dirk Hendricks's tongue flicked out, a snake's lick, before it hurriedly withdrew, a lustful, greedy, anticipating move. Watching, Sarah saw another man breaking free of the prisoner's chrysalis. She saw the narrowing of his eyes and the draining away of their colour. His lips tightened: no longer the Cupid's bow. His head lifted, his back straightened: he looked somehow more substantial and also much more dangerous. The shift was extraordinary. This was no longer the man who'd sat compliant on the stage ever since the onset of the hearing, nor the man that had charmed her yesterday with his tales of roadside meetings. That one was gone – replaced by some other being that Alex had conjured up – a dangerous being. The transformation both fascinated and repelled Sarah almost in equal measure.

And then? Sarah heard, and willed Alex to pull back.

But of course Alex could not read her thoughts. And if he had, Alex would not have listened to them.

Dirk Hendricks was composed, sitting straight as he had not done throughout the hearing. It was Alex who was now diminished. Alex, Sarah thought, wanting to reach out and take over, knowing she could not: Alex, I hope you know what you're doing.

'And then?' Alex said. 'What did I do?'

Dirk Hendricks, not the courteous man Sarah had met but the other one, narrowed his glacial eyes. 'You know what you did.' He paused for effect and then added, loudly: 'You told me where the weaponry was stored. Just like I knew you would.'

There. Finally. It was out in the open.

His betrayal.

He hadn't been expecting it. Not now; not yet. He had expected Hendricks to answer the question by describing how he had cried out, and often blacked out as well. But he should have known that what he had done instead was unleash his own disgrace. He could feel Sarah stiffening and he could also feel the way the audience absorbed the information. The collective was united: like a wounded animal it gave up a soft burrowing hum that hovered above the hall until very gradually it died away. Nothing now – only silence – as the crowd let sink in what Alex, their hero, had done.

They didn't yet know the half of it. They didn't know that he hadn't just told Dirk Hendricks where to find the guns, but had offered up the information as a gift, accompanied by other words . . . *please* . . . *I'll tell you anything* . . . surfacing in that moment, a verbal purging, at the same time as he could smell the rankness of his own terror and its physical manifestations – his soiled trousers, the urine trickling down his leg, his foul breath as the bag was pulled away.

He remembered it like yesterday. He remembered Dirk Hendricks's triumphant smiling face. Dirk Hendricks, victorious not because Alex had told him what he wanted to know – Steve, of course, had already led them to the arms cache – but because Alex had wanted to tell him. Had wanted to please his torturer. That moment, that feeling was burned into his heart. The way Dirk Hendricks's expression had changed – from elation to a visible sense of relief – Alex had known was mirrored in his own face. At that moment Alex would have done anything for Dirk Hendricks.

Anything. All these years he thought he had forgotten it. What stupidity. He had not forgotten, he had only pretended to. Now it came flooding back, his taking the hand that Hendricks offered to him, taking it eagerly, the pupil wanting to please his master, allowing Dirk Hendricks to pull him gently up, to smooth his hair, to say softly: *go wash now*, as he patted Alex's shoulder. Like a father – and Alex his compliant son.

'It was better between us after that,' said the Dirk Hendricks opposite, joined now to the one that Alex had known. 'Remember? You needed fresh air so I took you for a drive.'

How could Alex have done this? Sarah thought. It was an exercise in masochism. Alex summoning up his torturer!

Who now smiled, almost kindly, at Alex and said, gently, 'You were hungry. Remember? I stopped and brought you Kentucky Fried Chicken. You said it was the tastiest food you ever had.' And again: 'Remember?' using the repetition like a whip, flicking it across the stage, lashing Alex with it, forcing him to yield, to bow down lower after each assault.

'We talked about our feeling for the countryside,' Dirk Hendricks said. 'We agreed we both felt at home in wide spaces. Remember?'

Sarah could feel Alex nodding. He was nothing now, a plaything of his enemy. She felt her own agitation spreading out, mirrored by the audience.

Dirk Hendricks could feel it too. He turned up the ratchet of their fascination.

'Remember?' he said. 'We stopped at the foot of the mountain. You got out and you ran about, *jirra*; like a child you were, you were so enjoying yourself.'

'Remember?' Dirk Hendricks said, while the man whom Dirk Hendricks had created sat numbly in his seat, conscious only of those bloodless eyes, those soft, sympathetic, sadistic eyes, pulling him into the intimacy that had never been breached.

He had no choice. He closed his eyes and he remembered. As Dirk Hendricks continued to describe the trip, Alex saw it re-enacted as a series of closing doors. His cell door, clicking shut. That door to the outside, followed by another – the car door, opening to welcome him, closing, sealing him in. All that time, all the distance that he had put between himself and Dirk Hendricks no longer existed. Nothing existed but this man; no words, no deeds, nothing. He sat.

Dirk Hendricks was relishing the moment. 'Remember?' Smiling eagerly. 'A man and his wife, they were taken by the sight, they stopped their car nearby and took a picture of you.'

Snap. Another sound. The shutter of a camera clicking.

'You were so happy. Remember?'

And suddenly, Alex did remember. But what he remembered didn't make sense . . .

'We chatted with them,' Dirk Hendricks said.

. . . Because what Alex had heard resounding in memory was a single domestic click. That first door that had closed behind him. It didn't echo like a cell door should have. He closed his eyes again, trying to visualise what happened next.

'We asked them to send a copy of the photograph.'

The door that had opened. The light so dazzling that he was blinded. Dirk's hand – he had thought of the man as Dirk then – his hand on Alex's shoulder, gently steadying him. The shadow taking shape – a dead thorn tree, its misshapen branches, sprawled out.

A thorn-tree – but not in Smitsrivier.

'I bought you a Coke,' Dirk Hendricks's gleeful voice was saying. 'We joked about how you were going to pay me back.'

Of course. Alex's memory of Steve's body being carried out – no wonder it was wrong. He'd tried to fit it to the map that Sarah had produced, and he had failed not because the map was wrong but because the location was.

'Remember?' Dirk Hendricks said.

Alex nodded, straightening up, and said, 'Yes,' and nodded again. 'Now I do remember. Tell me, Mr Hendricks, where were we when you tortured me?'

'. . . where were we when you tortured me?' Dirk Hendricks heard the question coming at him so unexpectedly that he dropped his guard, doing what he had told himself he shouldn't ever do, turning his head and looking to the back of the hall, searching out Pieter. But Pieter was no longer seated. He always did have better reflexes than Dirk: Dirk was just in time to spot him on his feet, pushing through the row of empty chairs, heading for the exit.

And as usual Pieter was right. Dirk should have known it would come to this. No matter how much it was that he and Pieter had shared, no matter how strong their friendship, that time was gone. The past was over – definitively over – it was every man for himself.

Alex Mpondo was resolute: he'd scented blood. 'Where were we?'

Turning his head, Dirk looked to the left, at his lawyer who looked away, while the judge switched on his microphone.

'Mr Hendricks.' Calling to Dirk as if Dirk was some tiresome youngster. 'Perhaps nobody informed you that when you are being cross-examined you cannot communicate with your legal counsel unless you do so through us?'

As if he had to be told: he – Dirk Hendricks – who'd been

a policeman for Christ's sake, had given evidence in court on countless occasions!

Peering over his half-moon glasses, the judge continued. 'Are you in fact in need of legal advice?'

Dirk shook his head. No: he didn't need legal advice.

'Well, then, answer the question please.'

Dirk looked at Alex.

'Where were we when you tortured me?' Alex repeated.

It was over, Dirk thought, really over. He answered the question. 'At the farm,' he said, gripping Mpondo with his eyes, seeing Mpondo shivering, and at the same time hearing his own words repeated tinnily and in Afrikaans through Hannie Bester's earpiece. How many nights had he spent thinking what he would do if this moment ever came? How many long, sleepless nights wondering how he would respond if Mpondo figured out that they'd moved him from the police station?

More than he could count. And yet now that the moment was upon him, what surprised Dirk was his relief. A curative relief that moved through him like a wave of light, lifting the pressure from his shoulders, from his tongue.

'The farm?' the judge said.

'That is correct, Mr Chairman.' Even his voice sounded stronger.

'Well, why didn't you say so before?'

Dirk shrugged. How could he answer that? By lying and saying that he had forgotten? No. He would not get away with that.

By telling the truth then: that he didn't mention the farm because he thought it would complicate things?

No, not that either. The judge would not accept it, because, like all judges, he thought that what he wanted he would get, and that what he got he would understand. Dirk knew differently. He knew that the courts were a closed system whose facts must be carefully selected to prevent overload and that a good witness must learn to winnow the truth. It was all part of the rules of the game, the system. Sometimes the state benefited from it – sometimes the prisoner did – that was how it worked.

And yet, Dirk thought, remembering the sensation of his relief, it was better this way. Better to tell as much of the truth as could be tolerated.

Or better, at least, for Dirk. Across the stage he could see Alex Mpondo swallowing, once, twice, compulsively, as if he were having trouble swallowing down Dirk's answer. Dirk the prisoner took a good look at the man who had once been his prisoner. He saw Mpondo's gaze drawn downwards, like Dirk's had been. It came flooding back to Dirk, the memory of Mpondo's thick, lustrous eyelashes veiling Mpondo's expression. How those eyelashes used to irritate Dirk – he even considered cutting them off one day.

He heard the judge's voice. 'Carry on, Mr Mpondo.'

A long beat before Mpondo said, dully, 'What farm?'

Funny how quickly and how completely the tables had turned. While Mpondo seemed to have been drained by the truth – Dirk felt himself enlivened by it. 'It wasn't really a farm – it was long abandoned. We only used the building – the old farmhouse.'

'A farm in Smitsrivier?' Mpondo sounded perplexed.

As if there could be a farm in the middle of town! 'No, not in town,' Dirk said. 'About ten kilometres outside to the east, off a dirt track.'

'But you never told me,' Mpondo said.

Dirk bit his tongue, biting back the natural retort, that of course Dirk hadn't told him: it wasn't Dirk's job to tell Mpondo anything. Surely even somebody as slow as Mpondo could work out for himself that the whole point had been to disorient his prisoner so thoroughly that he wouldn't even notice he'd been moved.

'You never told me,' Mpondo said again.

That was just like Alex Mpondo – always railing against reality, unable to understand that his bloody-mindedness had consequences. He was a dreamer who wanted it both ways: who wanted his fantasy and at the same time wanted logic to be applied in every situation. Even war.

'And you also neglected to mention any farm in your application,' the judge said.

Christ, what an old woman this judge was – harping on like this. Didn't he realise that there were many other details – like the time that Dirk had been witness to a township neck-lacing, powerless to intervene because he was alone, watching a tyre shoved around the neck of some passing stranger who'd been fingered as an informer by an uncontrolled mob – which Dirk had also 'neglected to mention'?

'Mr Hendricks?'

'I apologise, Mr Chairman,' Dirk, the cooperative prisoner, said.

The judge nodded a curt acknowledgement of this formal obeisance, while Dirk continued to sit stranded on the stage, far away from everybody who had ever cared about him, thinking about the many, many happenings like the neck-lacing, equally true and equally as relevant to the case in hand, which he had left out of his application because he knew they would not have been believed. But Dirk did not draw this to the attention of the judge. One thing he knew for sure: the new history of their country could no longer fit the old truths. Nobody would be interested in listening to him trying to describe how it had been to have to close his eyes (because what else could he do?) but not his ears, which would not be closed, while the tyre was lit and the poor bas-tard burned to death, and the sound of his screaming followed Dirk long after the mob had dispersed, following him home and into sleep. And nobody was interested in that night when he had woken up with his strong fingers pressing into his wife's throat, because in his sleep he had imagined he was squeezing at those black faces with their laughter and their red underlips exposed as they gaped in wonder at black skin and molten black rubber fused together, producing a stench that he could not remove from his nostrils no matter how he tried, until the blood ran . . .

'Your base was the small police station on Main Street?' the judge asked.

Dirk blinked. 'That is correct, Mr Chairman.'

'There is also a larger police complex on the outskirts of town?'

'That is correct.'

'Why did you therefore need to take suspects to a farm?'

Why had they needed the farm? Dirk shrugged. What could he say? That everything they had done in those days was a product of the strike and counter-strike and decisions, albeit imperfect (Dirk would never deny that), taken under fire? If he were to try and explain this, the truth, as it had really been, with all its complexities, the people here would think he was lying, just as Mpondo had made Dirk look like he'd been lying about the wet blanket that his family had kept in the bath.

Dirk had not been lying. The necklacing, the blanket, the pain: all of it was true.

They all thought they were better than him. They looked back and they judged him. Hindsight was a fine thing: it made judges out of sociologists and journalists. And yet Dirk knew that no matter how intricate and how clever the theories, the so-called experts could never really know what it had been like to be caught up in the centre of that whirlwind, caught by history in the making and at the same time making history and watching it unmade, and all the time having to take decisions like where to put the overflow of prisoners, or how to get the information before more lives were staked, or how to explain to your kids why you turned up from work unable to look them in the eye.

'Mr Hendricks?' The judge was glaring. 'Why did you use the farm?'

It never did any good to keep a judge waiting. From the morass of different reasons floating through his mind, Dirk extracted one. 'We needed to isolate the prisoners, one from the other,' he said. 'To hold them in peace and quiet, away from the endless traipsing in-and-out of relatives . . .' his voice tailing off as his eyes alighted on those two old people in the front row, sitting there patiently, like all those other relatives used to sit . . .

Shit. This South Africa that they had all created. It made Dirk Hendricks sick.

He heard a voice then, summoning him back.

'Mr Mpondo.'

No, not summoning him, but Alex. Alex, who, sitting opposite, was visibly affected. His rich brown skin, which could look almost like molasses when the sun shone on it, had turned ashen in the artificial light and it was slick with droplets of sweat.

The judge called his name again: 'Mr Mpondo,' leaning forward: 'Are you unwell?'

Dirk felt for Alex. He would never be as foolish as to say so out loud but it was true. He had a fellow feeling for this man. Dirk wasn't afraid of that. No matter how much Alex Mpondo might deny his connection to Dirk, Dirk knew better. Out of the most terrible of circumstances he and Alex had forged a link. It was inevitable. Whatever Alex might think of Dirk (and Dirk could understand Mpondo's resentment), in the deepest recesses of his heart, of his memory, Alex must know that they were bonded together. These were bonds that could not be easily severed. Even now, when Alex was the man who might stand between Dirk and his freedom, Dirk still felt an impulse to reach out to Alex, to gentle him into calm just the way he had once done.

He alone, of all the people in the hall had heard and understood Alex's question: 'How did you take me to this farm?'

Dirk answered the question, saying quickly, 'In the boot of my Peugeot,' so that Alex would not be asked to repeat his question; so that he could sit, quietly, as his lawyer stretched out and switched off the microphone before overlaying her hand on Alex's, at the same time speaking intently into her client's ear.

Even somebody with half a brain could see Alex's agitation. The judge rose. 'I think this is an appropriate time for us to adjourn for twenty minutes,' he said, gathering up his colleagues to lead them backstage, while Dirk's guards nudged at him to get up. Dirk got up and turned back to see that all that time Sarah Barcant continued to hold down Alex's quaking hand.

29

IN ONE TIME frame Alex was sitting on a stage in a hall where every seat was occupied: in the next, only he and Sarah remained. He looked down at the table. She was holding on to him. Together their hands formed an alien shape, his brown against her white, his jittering against her solidity.

'I have to go,' he said, and got up. He was grateful that she didn't try to hold him back, and grateful also, as he walked across the stage, that she did not pursue him.

He pushed through the curtains and into the wings. Backstage was a dismal, crowded place. He scrabbled past old props and broken furniture, through the door and found himself in some kind of dark place. Just ahead was a fire door; to the side a set of narrow stairs. He could hear the murmur of voices issuing through the door. The back stairs, he thought: nobody uses them.

He went up the stairs, two at a time. At first, he was entirely alone but then, after he had reached the first landing and was starting up the next, a township clever came bounding down and stopped just in front of him.

'Alex my *bra*.'

On automatic, Alex moved his palm against the other's, this way and that: once, twice, three times.

'Don't listen to that *Boere*'s lies,' the young man said, 'we don't,' saying it with such conviction that for a moment Alex thought this stranger might be right and that Dirk Hendricks really had been lying while he, Alex Mpondo MP, had never broken under torture. In that moment, Alex felt his burden lightening. It crossed his mind that he was hungry, that he should go and grab himself something to eat. But then the young man jived on down the stairs and the moment passed and Alex was left standing, weighed down by truth.

The truth or half of it. The less damning half. Dirk Hendricks had told the world about the weapons but, ever the sadist, he was saving the more serious charge for later. Alex must now wait for that to fall – for Dirk Hendricks to lay bare Alex's betrayal of Steve.

No. He didn't want to think of it. He raced up the stairs and, coming to a dark green door, went slamming through.

The long thick-linked toilet chain licked at his shoulder. He took no notice of it. He shifted position until his back was wedged more securely against the cistern and then sat perfectly still. It was very peaceful. He could hear a dripping tap making jagged counterpoint with the gushing of a line of urinals outside. He fixed his absent gaze on the dirty white paint flaking off the cubicle door.

His thoughts came slowly. He thought: the irony of it that he should end up hiding here in this place, which, with its dirty floors, its sulphurous urine stink and its endlessly dripping taps, would once have been the exclusive preserve of the town hall's black staff. Old habits die hard, he thought: despite the abolition of segregated facilities he had made his way unerringly to this remnant of the past, to this, he smiled as he named it as of old, this *kaffir* toilet.

The smile stretched out across his face and froze. Dirk Hendricks did this to me, he thought. Hendricks who, even cast down, had the power to summon up the *kaffir* in Alex and send him scuttling to the servants' quarters. Hendricks who had this power even though it was Hendricks who was the prisoner and who, when the recess was called, was led away by guards.

Hendricks was the penitent: not Alex. Alex had other options. Free will. Free choice.

And yet? Having found Steve's tin box in the dried-up river bed, Alex was no longer sure of anything. The nightmare from which he had been running ever since his release had caught up with him. The terror of the answer to a single question: had he, by his cowardice, been responsible for Steve's death?

He didn't want to think about it. Not now, ever. Concentrating his gaze on the cracked mosaic tiles, he traced the pattern that ran anarchically along the stall floor and under the door. He followed the line of grouting that was flavescent with age and neglect. An encrusted brew, he thought, just like the past.

He thought back to those times. It was an age away. They had all been so young and high on hope. The things they said to each other: phrases so easily pronounced like: *Silence at all costs; A luta continua; Death rather than betrayal.* Death just like that young comrade's death whose corpse the Truth

Commission investigators had dug up the other day. When they had gentled her out of her makeshift grave she was naked save for the plastic bag she had used to cover herself. She was curled in on herself, foetus-like, with one arm above her head as if she were even now shielding herself from the blows that rained down until she was dead. And there, watching the exhumation, was the man who had put her there and who had led the Commission to her impromptu resting place and who had looked down and who had said, with an admiring shake of his head, 'She was a brave one, that one: she wouldn't tell us anything.'

Hers was the path that Alex should have taken. That he would have taken. That sentence should have been his epitaph. That sentence instead of Dirk Hendricks's gloating: '*You told me where the weaponry was stored.*'

When Dirk Hendricks had said those words Alex had felt the shock waves of the audience's disbelief. He knew that they, like the young man he had met on the stairs, didn't want to believe Hendricks, but he also knew they couldn't hold out for ever. It would take them time but inevitably they would each, in their own ways, come to terms with the fact that their hero Alex had broken.

Remember? Dirk Hendricks had said, and Alex did remember. Not with his mind but with his senses. What his mind had once rejected, his body retained: the tearing of a jaw wrenched open, his flailing skin, the paralysis of fear. And Alex remembered something else as well, more terrible than all that agony. Something else. That moment of stillness and of clarity replaced by rage when he saw Steve standing by the door and Steve's pointing finger. At that moment all the ideals that had underlain Alex's commitment – his preparedness to lay down his life, his faith in the collective not the individual, his certainty that for each one that fell, another ten would rise up – all of them had fallen away. At that moment he had been ready to do to Steve as Steve had done to him: he was ready to betray his friend.

He shook his head. He didn't want to think about it. He wouldn't. Instead, he thought: if only I'd had more control.

If only he'd had more control he could have discharged his hero's duty. He could have chosen death. That's what he'd always assumed he'd do: they all had. But when it finally came down to it, death was not so easy. It wasn't an option he could tick off in a multiple choice when the need arose.

He had been too weak for death. They were all-powerful: only they could grant it to him. And that they had refused. They had kept him no longer a man, just a vessel they had filled and then they had let him out, suddenly and without warning, out into a country rocked by the state of emergency, by army occupation, arrests, disappearances and unending funerals refashioned into mass rallies. They could have killed him but they had chosen to kill Steve instead.

Why Steve? Why Steve and not Alex?

Was it because Steve was braver than Alex? Was that the truth? That Alex was not brave enough to die? And not brave enough either when he was finally let out, to tell the truth: to tell his comrades that he had talked.

And now, after all the time that had elapsed, when those days were gone, when it shouldn't even matter any more, they knew the truth. Not from his own mouth, but from his enemy's. Now, when next they thought of him, what they would hear was not his version but his torturer's. He could try telling them what had really happened, but how was he to give them a different version? There was too much he couldn't remember, and didn't know. The crucial questions, like: had his naming of Steve, his telling of Steve's involvement, led to Steve's death?

So much he did not want to remember.

Sitting on the toilet seat he heard someone groaning.

Steve?

No. Steve was dead. They were his own groans. He had survived his ordeal by finding reasons to live in his country's future. And now? He didn't know whether he could ever live this down. He groaned again. In the now. He should have kept his resolve. He should have kept away. There was nothing for him here.

A sound. The door opening. Silence and then the clip of high heels, coming closer. A voice: 'Alex?' Sarah Barcant's voice.

Alex held his tongue. He did not want to speak to her. He didn't want to speak to anyone.

'Alex? The judges will be down soon.'

30

STRIDING DOWN THE alleyway that led to his office, Pieter saw Sizwe on his hands and knees in front of the building. With his back to Pieter, Sizwe was moving his right arm rhythmically to and fro over the paving stones.

'Sizwe,' Pieter said angrily. 'What are you playing at?'

Sizwe didn't need to answer. When, still on his hands and knees, he turned, Pieter could see exactly what he was doing. He had a bucket of steaming hot soapy water and a scrubbing brush and he'd been using them to try and annihilate a set of painted words. When Pieter said, softly, 'Move away please,' Sizwe got up grabbing the bucket so roughly that water slopped over the edge.

A slogan. In red. Naturally: red paint always had a special

attraction for such spoilers. Not so much a slogan as a question, a rhetorical question, or at least a question without a question mark. Eight words badly scrawled in uneven capital letters: 'WHY PAY A MURDERER TO KEEP YOU SAFE.'

Pieter read it slowly: once and then once again, and then he said, 'Try bleach and if that doesn't work, you'll have to paint over,' and went into the building.

He punched in the security code and when the door swung open he walked in, tossing a 'Môre,' in Kristal's direction as he went over to the coffee table. He took a clean mug and stretched out for the percolator.

It was empty. Taken aback by that – the flask was never empty – he turned to look at Kristal. She was already halfway out of her seat and saying, flustered, 'Ag. I'm sorry, Pieter. I didn't think . . . I . . . I'll make some coffee now, now.'

'You didn't think what?'

'That you were coming in.' On each of Kristal's pale cheeks a pink blotch had appeared. 'I rang your wife to tell you about . . . about . . . you know, outside, and she said you were probably at the town hall. I didn't think you were coming in today.' Her hands were busy sliding, one over the other, and in the flash of their passing, Pieter caught a glimpse of a broken red nail. Shame. Kristal was continually trying to prolong the perfection of her weekly manicures by buffing and polishing and smoothing out her nails, always fighting against the temptation to bite them back, but now she had succumbed. 'Is something wrong?' he said.

Kristal gulped. 'Three of the men failed to turn up for the early shift.'

That was too much a normal irritation to have provoked this outbreak of nervousness: although Pieter only ever employed men he trusted, even he hadn't been able to wean most of them off their sense of African time. 'Did you use the emergency rota to replace them?'

'I managed to fill two,' Kristal's full lips turned down. 'The others insisted they wanted to stick to their days off.'

Which was more surprising – money was so tight in Smitsrivier these days that most of the men were only too eager to take on any amount of time and a half that Pieter could throw them. 'Don't worry,' he said. 'We can operate safely with one man under par.' And then, looking more carefully at Kristal, added, 'Anything else?'

She nodded. She'd been biting her lips as well: her pale pink lipstick was smeared over the light red line she always drew to keep it in and there was a shred of skin hanging off her bottom lip. 'With the first of the month coming soon,' she said, 'I followed up on the renewal letters.'

He could guess, now, what had disturbed her so.

'Three people said they weren't going to renew,' she said quickly. 'Gert was one of them. I asked him what was wrong, but he got so angry he hung up on me.' Her lower lip trembled.

So that was the way it was going to be. Pieter nodded again and, saying gruffly, 'Don't worry. I'll deal with it later,' he turned on his heels and left the office.

It's started, Pieter thought, as he drove homewards. The graffiti was only the first shot in a war that would intensify. Rumours of an impending boycott must have flashed through Smitsrivier like a veld fire and the frightened white community had decided to ditch him rather than be tarred by his brush. He was now the target. Without allies. He wasn't entirely surprised. He'd seen it coming: people who had once crossed the road to greet him scurried away these days when he came into sight. Those who had relied on him to keep them safe had turned their backs on him.

It wouldn't stop either, not with a painted slogan: he knew

enough about the boycott campaigns of the past to know that for sure. It had happened as he had always known, somewhere, that it might. He was now alone.

Alone with Marie, he thought, driving through the gates of the farm. Except that, as he was steering slowly up the driveway, he saw through the gaps in the row of pine trees that served as a windbreak, that there were three parked cars at the turning circle. Marie had visitors.

The Mullers had never been like those outlandish couples who kept their friendships partitioned between 'his' and 'hers'. Marie's friends were Pieter's as well – the people from their community and their church – and it was certain that whoever was visiting was equally well known to them both. Even so, Pieter found himself hesitating.

He never knew these days how people would react to the sight of him and the last thing he wanted to do was embarrass Marie. Since that night when he had found her sewing his suit they had behaved as normal. They had not discussed either the law case or the way that the town had turned against him. And yet someone was updating her with the current state of events. She never said so, but every now and then, looking up, he would find her anxious eyes on him.

He slowed down and turned his thoughts to Dirk. Dirk had mentioned the farm: well, so be it, it could not be helped. Dirk must do what he thought right, what he needed to do for his release. Let Dirk buy his freedom with that useless piece of information: Pieter didn't care. Pieter knew Dirk and he knew that mention of the farm was as far as his friend would ever go. Dirk would get his amnesty and the circus would move on and there'd be another freak at which the fingers of another group of sanctimonious citizens could point. In the meantime, all Pieter wanted to do was keep Marie as free as he could of worry.

So he did not drive his car up the approach. He tucked it

near the trees and got out, making his way up to the house on foot. It was nearing midday and the sun was high in the sky, burning its way through his thick khaki shirt. He breathed in deeply, absorbing that strong, aromatic scent of the veld which was only this sharp when it was very hot. Hearing his heavy boots crunching against the gravel, he kept going, shushing the dogs with a quick wave of his hand when they came bounding towards him.

They were good dogs. Only the youngest let out a sharp bark of excitement and even she soon quietened down. He patted her silky head and then moved away, heading towards the garden, planning to go round the back of the house and into his study to get out some papers that were only crowding up the place and that needed burning.

He hadn't meant to spy on Marie. This was not his intention, even though the route he had chosen took him straight past the lounge where Marie always entertained her visitors. But he wasn't thinking about Marie then. He was thinking about the way Dirk had turned his head when Mpondo had asked the question that meant that Dirk must either lie or mention the farm. In that gesture of Dirk's, Pieter saw a plea for understanding and for forgiveness.

Dirk should not have bothered, Pieter thought. Everything was understood and there was nothing to forgive. Pieter knew Dirk could not lie: he had to answer. Things had changed. Dirk must do what was best for him. They all must do that.

He heard the soft murmuring of voices. Coming to, he realised he had inadvertently stepped into line with the lounge's casement window. He stopped abruptly, thinking to go back.

But why should he? This was his house. His best plan was to keep on walking. That way he would soon have passed by the window. Even if they spotted him before he had moved away, all he had to do was greet them and then decide whether to get on with his day as planned or change his mind and go sit with them a while.

He didn't keep on walking. Against his better judgement he found his gaze drawn inside. He had already identified the dominee's car, and Dora's as well, but he hadn't recognised the third of the line-up. Now, peering in, he could just make out the form of Mrs de Vries. Odd that she had come to visit – Marie rarely mentioned her – but no odder than the feeling that it gave Pieter to stand and look in on this intimate grouping.

Sombre, that was his first thought. In contrast to the day outside, the room seemed to be in shadow and, to add to the impression, its occupants were dressed either in dark colours or in black. But it wasn't only their wardrobe that disturbed Pieter. It was something else. Something in the way they sat, so close together and so close to Marie, and in the way they were murmuring discreet, hushed, considerate words, and in the gesture of the dominee, who, as Pieter watched, leaned forward and patted Marie on the knee as if consoling her. Consoling or condoling with her? Pieter realised why this scene seemed familiar. It reminded him of a funeral. His father's funeral to be exact. Then the room had also been in darkness and there had been many women present dressed in the high bonnet of their Voortrekker ancestors just like Mrs de Vries was, and all of them had sat close to his mother and leaned forward to pat her, to murmur to her that she was not alone.

But Marie was not his mother, he thought: she was his wife and he her husband and he was very much alive. At that moment the door to the hallway opened and Bessy appeared carrying a tray of tea things. Her entrance transformed the whole scenario. She brought colour into the room – she was wearing her usual pink uniform, her unruly mop of hair bundled up in a matching pink doek. Standing, framed by the door, Bessy looked across the room and, although she made no sign of it, he knew she'd seen him.

That's all it took. Pieter no longer felt like a ghost. Knowing he had imagined the gloom in the lounge and the pitying gesture of the dominee, he watched as the dominee leaned back, laughing now, and he saw that Marie was also laughing and that the others had moved apart, Dora smacking her lips in anticipation of tea while Mrs de Vries said something to Bessy. A normal tea party: a normal midday. Pieter got going, walking past the lounge and round the house.

31

WHEN THE CLERK came on stage saying: 'Please rise,' Sarah got up. Beside her she could feel Alex following suit, both of them sitting simultaneously once the committee of judges was safely ensconced. But, when the grey-haired judge said, 'You may proceed, Mr Mpondo,' Alex remained perfectly still as he had warned her he would do.

It was for her to speak. She didn't, not at first. Instead, she continued to sit, rapt by the way Alex's immobility had suddenly transfixed the stage. Then Alex raised his head and looked across the stage until his eyes had locked on his opponent's, the two staring, both deathly still, until Alex broke the deadlock by snarling in Sarah's ear: 'Go ahead. Do what's necessary to find out where Steve is.'

Galvanised, she leaned forward as she should have done before, switching on her microphone to say: 'I trust there will be no objections if I take over the cross-examination of this witness?'

Her voice changed the quiescence into feverish movement, the fluttering of hands and shuffling of papers by the three-man panel of judges, while the interpreters bent to their task, exaggeratedly eager to translate the lawyer's words, and out of the centre of the audience there issued a hissed release of breath.

And Dirk Hendricks? Was that a smile or a grimace across his face? Victory or disappointment?

It was hard to tell because Sarah had thought she caught some slight motion accompanying Dirk Hendricks's expression. She thought he almost stretched forward and reached out to Alex as if to touch him, to reassure him. But she must have imagined the gesture because Dirk Hendricks's chunky fists were wadded together on the table and when the judge said, 'No, Miss Barcant, we don't have any objections to your taking over,' Dirk Hendricks continued to look on impassively, as if it made no difference to him which of the two sitting opposite chose to ask the questions.

'Miss Barcant. Please begin.'

She cleared her throat and began, as she and Alex had planned she should. 'Is it correct, Mr Hendricks, that before you laid hands on Mr Mpondo, before you put the wet bag over his head, you made sure his clothes were removed?'

Dirk Hendricks blinked. He looked startled as if he had been far away and was only reluctantly returning. 'I,' he said, stuttering out the pronoun and repeating it, 'I . . . don't remember.'

'You don't remember ordering Mr Mpondo's trousers be pulled down?'

A shake of the head. 'No, Mr Chairman.' Tearing his eyes

away, Dirk Hendricks turned and addressed his answer to the judge. 'Not specifically. I don't remember that, Mr Chairman.'

'In previous hearings other security branch policemen have testified that when they used the wet bag method of torture, their victims were naked. Was this the normal procedure?'

His eyes still focused centre stage, Dirk Hendricks said, deadpan, 'It is possible, Mr Chairman. I cannot comment on what other officers did.' His confidence flooding back. 'We never talked about these things, you see.'

'Mr Hendricks. I am asking the questions.' Sarah said briskly. 'If you wouldn't mind, I would prefer it if you addressed your answers directly to me.'

He turned back. Slowly and deliberately. Disdainfully? 'No, Miss Barcant,' he said. 'I don't mind,' his composure now complete, giving Sarah a glimpse of the control he must have once possessed.

She raised her voice. 'I assume that your lapses in memory mean that you are in no position to refute Mr Mpondo's allegation that you always made sure he was naked before you began to suffocate him?'

Dirk Hendricks seemed to swallow. 'I do not . . .' but he was saved from finishing his sentence by his lawyer. Hannie Bester, having already leaned forward, now used his broad shoulders to muscle his client out of the way. 'Mr Chairman, I have been paying careful attention and I have not heard Mr Mpondo make any such allegation.'

'May I remind my colleague that Mr Mpondo has not yet given evidence,' she said, wondering as she said it, whether Alex ever would.

Hannie Bester raised an eyebrow. 'Can I take it then that my learned friend plans to lead Mr Mpondo on the question of the state of his undress during interrogation?'

The arrogance of it, Sarah thought, and the contempt: prisoner and lawyer alike – masters of the universe. But all she

said was 'If necessary', mentally crossing her fingers because
Bester was right: despite the fact that he had briefed her in the
toilet, she still had no way of knowing how far Alex was prepared to go. Putting as much conviction into her voice as she
could muster, she said, 'Yes, he will give evidence on this
matter,' taking care not to catch his eye by adding as a distraction: 'Mr Chairman.'

'I thank you for that elucidation.' Hannie Bester twanged
his braces extravagantly, signalling with a dismissive wave
that he was handing over his client.

'Mr Hendricks? Did you remove Mr Mpondo's clothes?'

His lawyer's interruption had bought Dirk Hendricks the
time he needed. 'I'm sorry, Mr Chairman.' He shook his head.
'In all honesty, the state of Mr Mpondo's undress is not something I can remember.'

'I see.' She glanced down at the statement she had put,
open, on the table. 'Well, then tell me this, Mr Hendricks: do
you know a Mr Jackson Thulo?'

Dirk Hendricks hesitated, fractionally, before: 'I can't be
sure. The name seems to ring a bell.'

'Well.' She looked up. 'Let me see if I can be of assistance.
Mr Thulo was a junior policeman stationed at Smitsrivier in
1985. A warrant officer under your command. Does that help
you remember him?'

'As I said,' a pursing of Dirk Hendricks's lips, 'I think I can
recall the name.'

'Mr Thulo's memory seems to be in better order than
yours,' she said. 'He will give testimony that he worked
directly under you in 1985 and that you gave him specific
orders in that year. Would you disagree with that?'

'No, Mr Chairman.' A shake of that large head. 'I would not
disagree. If this gentleman was in service at that time, it is
very possible I would have asked for his assistance.'

'And would you also not disagree if Mr Thulo testifies that

he helped with Mr Mpondo?' She glanced at the judge. 'And to obviate the need for a further interjection from Mr Bester, yes, Mr Chairman, I will be calling Mr Thulo.' She refocused on Dirk Hendricks. 'Mr Hendricks, Mr Thulo will say that he was ordered by you to pull down Mr Mpondo's trousers on several occasions. Is this something you would deny?'

'I can't remember.' Dirk Hendricks narrowed his eyes, almost as if he was really trying to remember.

'Would you deny it?'

Through the slits of his vision, Dirk Hendricks's eyes had changed again, bleached to grey, and the voice, equally cold, carried a warning as he said, 'It is possible,' before reopening his eyes.

'And can you remember urinating on Mr Mpondo and laughing as you did so and telling him that if he didn't co-operate the next time it would be shit?'

'Does Mr Thulo say I did that?'

'Could you answer the question please?'

'Because,' Dirk Hendricks leaned forward, suddenly eager to unburden himself of a thought that had only just occurred, 'even if I did give Mr Thulo certain orders, he would not have been in the room with me when I was interrogating the prisoner. We had problems with infiltration then: we couldn't trust our black policemen. If he says he was in the room . . .'

'Just answer the question, Mr Hendricks.'

The voice dropped. 'No.' Dirk Hendricks sat back, deflated. 'I don't recall doing what you said . . .'

'You don't recall it. Do you then deny it?'

A moment's hesitation before Dirk Hendricks's face cleared. He had made up his mind. 'Yes, Mr Chairman,' he said. 'I do deny that. I do not believe it can be correct. Mr Mpondo was my prisoner. My job was to get information from him but in truth I never bore him any hard feelings. I even felt sorry for the man. When he cooperated, I treated him as decently as circumstances allowed. I took him out, fed him, bought him cigarettes. He favoured menthol and I had a hellova job locating his brand out there in the sticks in Smitsrivier but I managed.' He smiled at the memory, his face lighting up, the blue of his eyes deepening. Sarah saw the man she had interviewed returning, that polite, engaging, powerful man, his considerable charm muted only by his bewilderment at the way his job had brought him down.

And yet: was Alex right? Was everything that man said a lie?

'Don't you find it odd, Mr Hendricks, that you have complete recall of trivialities such as the specific brands of cigarettes you purchased and yet your mind goes blank when it comes to answering questions pertinent to your application?'

Dirk Hendricks separated his hands, turning them over, flattened palms up, the gesture simultaneously graceful and also helpless. 'I'm sorry, Mr Chairman. I know it must seem strange. But there are many things I don't remember.'

'So you keep saying.'

'The doctor who tested me in jail told me that this was to be expected.'

'Ah, yes.' Her voice hardened. 'You are referring of course to your diagnosis as a PTSD sufferer. Did you know, incidentally, that PTSD is statistically much more likely to be visited on victims of torture rather than on the perpetrators?'

'No, Mr Chairman. I am a policeman. Not a psychologist. I did not know that.'

'Unless, of course, you also consider yourself a victim?'

A pause, long drawn-out. Dirk Hendricks frowned as if he was thinking out something complicated. He opened and closed his mouth. Watching this unspoken internal battle, Sarah thought Alex was right: when it came down to it, Dirk Hendricks's high opinion of himself would make it difficult for him to consent to being written down in history as a villain.

She pushed the point. 'Are you a victim, Mr Hendricks?'

He made up his mind. 'Yes, Mr Chairman. In my own way I believe I am a victim.'

'Oh. I see.' She snorted in derision. 'You mean Mr Mpondo should be applying for amnesty for his part in making you torture him?' She swivelled round, playing the line out to the crowd, which responded with a belly laugh that probably had more to do with a collective wish to break the tension than with her wit, because the laughter went on longer than it merited, snaking its way around the hall, one person's amusement feeding that of his neighbours, while the judge looked on, benignly, not doing anything to staunch the noise as if he, too, could do with some light relief, letting the ripple die down as it gradually did and while all this was happening she glanced down, looking at the front row.

The Sizelas were not laughing. Steve's mother was sitting, quietly as she always did during the hearing, her gaze concentrated on her lap. Beside her, her husband was much more erect and beaming the full force of his attention on the stage. His thin face seemed possessed by anger, drawn tight into a furious frown that was directed, Sarah saw, not at Dirk Hendricks but at Alex. She didn't understand it.

'I don't speak so fine like you,' she heard.

Looking up, she was in time to see Dirk Hendricks leaning forward into his microphone. His broad face flushed crimson as he shrugged off his lawyer's cautionary hand. 'My English is not so fluent,' he said loudly, his accent thickened by his anger, his sentences blundering out. 'I speak English now because I thought that this would make Mr Mpondo more comfortable. But I am a victim, if you like, of my own ignorance and the things I thought were true . . .'

He paused to take a breath and, watching him, Sarah found

herself caught up in what he had to say, willing him to spit out the words that were obviously so painful, listening as he continued.

'I am a patriot. It was told to me through my whole life that if we were not vigilant we would be overrun by the communistic menace. I was protecting my country from a takeover by communist-oriented organisations. I was doing only what I thought best.'

He leaned away then, exhausted by the passion of his delivery, the colour bleeding slowly from his face. But when his lawyer patted him lightly – in consolation? in congratulation? – he shrugged him off again.

'I see,' she said, adding, casually: 'How did you get Mr Mpondo into the boot?'

'I beg your pardon?' Dirk Hendricks said, and there moved over his broad face that same faraway look which had been there at the beginning of the session, as if he had been revisiting that same inner place and was struggling to return to the present.

Well, she needed him back. She said slowly, emphasising each one of her separate words, 'You said you took Mr Mpondo to the farm in the boot of your Peugeot. How did he get into the boot?'

'I must have put him there.' Dirk Hendricks's voice was listless.

'On your own?'

'Perhaps I had help.' He sounded very tired. 'I can't recall.'

'Mr Mpondo did not resist?'

'Not,' his head moved sideways, 'not to my recollection.'

'Why not?'

An uncertain shrug. 'He may have been drugged.'

'May have been? Or was?'

'He was drugged. We crushed some sleeping pills into his food and moved him when he was unconscious.'

'We?'

'Me and a warrant officer. I disremember his name. Maybe it was your Thulo.'

'And did "we" – you and this unknown warrant officer – do the same thing to Steve Sizela?'

All through this section of her cross-examination, Dirk Hendricks's lawyer had sat on the edge of his chair. Now, at the mention of Steve he reacted with a loud: 'Objection, Mr Chairman. Miss Barcant knows full well that you disallowed questions concerning Mr Sizela.'

'Indeed I did, Miss Barcant.' The judge directed his scowl downstage.

'Your Honour,' she said, 'your ruling concerned any cross-examination by me on behalf of the Sizela family. I am not at present acting for that family, but rather for Mr Mpondo. And as I understand your judgement, it was aimed at stopping endless cross-pollination between different hearings. My questions, however, do not concern another case: they are directly relevant to the application in hand. My client will testify that he saw Mr Sizela in the place that he thought was the Smitsrivier police station but which now appears to have been a farm. My questions go to the heart of whether the applicant is making full disclosure.'

A beat while the judge bent his head to hear what one of the members of his committee had to say before straightening up and clicking on his microphone. 'I will allow you some latitude, Miss Barcant, but don't stray too far.'

'Thank you, Mr Chairman.' She looked at Dirk Hendricks. 'Did you also drug Steve Sizela so you could transport him to the farm?'

Dirk Hendricks shook his head. 'Mr Sizela was not my prisoner.'

'Which means you did not drug him?'

'Ja.' A nod. 'That is correct, Mr Chairman. I did not do it.'

'Well, whose prisoner was Mr Sizela?'

'I can't remember.'

'Was Mr Sizela Pieter Muller's prisoner?'

It came again. Dully. 'I can't remember.'

'Did Mr Muller drive Mr Sizela to the farm?'

'I'm sorry, Mr Chairman, I do not know.'

'Mr Mpondo will testify that he saw Mr Sizela at the farm. Can you deny this?'

'I cannot say what Mr Mpondo did or didn't see.'

'Which means you can't deny that Mr Sizela was at the farm?'

'No, Mr Chairman, I cannot deny it.'

'Let us take it as a given then.' She had him. 'So are we to believe that there were two cars, yours and Mr Muller's or some other unnamed policeman, ferrying unconscious prisoners out of Smitsrivier and to a farm? Or perhaps there were also other prisoners taken there – a whole convoy of policemen who did not know each other . . .'

She never got to finish the sentence. Hannie Bester was already on his feet, shouting: 'Your Honour, Miss Barcant is involved in a fishing expedition, trying to make a fool of my client. I must . . .'

'No, Mr Bester.' The judge scowled. 'You must not do anything. Please sit down.' Then, turning his head: 'I have been generous with you, Miss Barcant, but if the witness makes it clear that he can't remember you will gain nothing by harrying him.'

She nodded. 'Yes, Your Honour.' And then, to Dirk Hendricks: 'You were at a farmhouse, Mr Hendricks, not a thick-walled police station. How could you have failed to notice that Steve Sizela was also there?'

'Objection.'

'How could you not have heard his cries as he was being tortured?'

'Objection.'

'His appeals for mercy . . .'

'Objection.'

'As he was being killed?'

'Objection.' Hannie Bester launched himself forward, stabbing at his microphone and speaking into it. 'Please, Mr Chairman, I really must object most strongly. We are here to find out the truth, not to batter our respective clients into submission. The questions that Miss Barcant is asking are founded on mere conjecture. As far as I understand it there is no proof even that Mr Sizela is dead, never mind that he was killed by the police.'

The judge nodded. 'Yes, Miss Barcant. I think you have gone far enough with this line of questioning.'

'But Mr Chairman . . .'

'I'm sorry, Miss Barcant,' the judge said. 'Unless you have some different avenue to pursue as to Mr Sizela's whereabouts, you must move on. Do you have a different line?'

'No, Mr Chairman, but I cannot argue strongly enough that the issue of Mr Hendricks's full disclosure is . . .'

'Miss Barcant,' the judge snapped, 'I have made my ruling. And since your cross-examination will now be proceeding in a different direction and since it is already gone one o'clock we will adjourn until two.' And with that he clicked off his microphone and immediately stood up.

32

SARAH AND ALEX went to lunch in a venue so out of the way that no one would have thought to find them there. Because they were the overdecorated café's only customers the waitress insisted on hovering close. Doing her best to ignore this anxious blur, Sarah looked over the white tablecloth, past the ornamented doilies and the plastic daffodils, and said, 'This is as far as I can push it on Steve's disappearance.'

Alex took no notice. He was shifting tinned beetroot and diluted salad cream from one section of his plate to another and he continued to do so and it was only when he happened to glance up, almost by accident, and caught her looking at him that he nodded, a gesture so lacklustre that she thought he would have nodded no matter what she'd said because he hadn't really been listening. Come to think of it, could he even hear above the jangling muzak?

She raised her voice. 'What next?'

He shrugged impassively. She had no idea what that signified. He's such a mystery, she thought. After she found him in the toilet and they'd talked, she'd thought they'd finally reached an understanding. But no: once again he had cut himself off from her.

She pressed on. 'There's no way I can get round the judge's ruling about Steve, so I think we should concentrate on Hendricks's actual application for amnesty. I think I know our way in: I spent last night reading through previous Commission hearings and judgements and I was struck by the aversion most judges feel for torture. They've amnestied all kinds of dubious murderers – especially in cases where there were no witnesses – but they've given torturers a much rougher ride. I think we should tackle the issue of Hendricks's sadism head-on.'

Alex laid down his fork, carefully, across his uneaten food.

'If we can prove that Hendricks continued to torture you regardless . . .' she said.

He didn't let her finish. 'I want it to end,' he said.

'It?' In the sudden flaring of her irritation, she flung the word out louder than she'd intended.

'Your cross-examination of Hendricks.'

Why was he doing this? Pulling her off just when she was getting somewhere? 'I can't stop now. Didn't you see what happened? It's no longer going his way. He's losing his cockiness.'

It didn't seem to matter what she said because Alex just repeated that same stubborn sentence: 'I want it to end.'

Frustrated she threw down her fork. 'Is that an order?'

'Yes.' An emphatic nod. 'It's an order.'

'May I know why?'

When he looked at her she found she couldn't continue being angry. He looks so sad, she thought, so tired and so vulnerable.

'You know I never wanted to come to this hearing?' he said.

'Yes, so I gathered.'

'If I hadn't been pressurised by James's need and also by my own need to lay Steve to rest, I wouldn't have come.' He leaned across the table, suddenly, and reached out for her hand.

She gave it to him, feeling his skin touching hers, and also conscious of a sudden movement nearby. The waitress seemed almost to jump away. In that moment Sarah saw herself through this stranger's eyes. She saw her own loose-fitting trousers, light blue to match her long-line shirt, and she saw her high, dusty sling-back shoes and those manicured nails of hers resting in the callused hand of this man with his crumpled clothes and his crumpled look. Black against white. In Smitsrivier.

If Alex noticed the waitress's shock, he didn't acknowledge it. But he did let go of Sarah's hand. 'I can't do this any more,' he said. 'I can't sit and listen to Dirk Hendricks. I know him too well. I know that the more you pressure him, the more he'll turn the screws on me.'

'He'll try to, you mean. But don't let it get to you – by the time I've finished nobody will believe what Dirk Hendricks says.'

'How do you know that?'

'Because I do. Because I'm good at this.'

He shook his head. 'No,' he said. 'This is different. It isn't New York where everybody plays by the same rules. I can't risk Dirk Hendricks's narrative, his version of history, becoming mine. And he's bound to get his amnesty, so why should I put myself through this? I can't sleep. I can't eat. I can't go on. I'm sorry.' He blinked.

'You want me to withdraw completely?' she said, quietly.

'No. Call Thulo if you want – you might as well. But please. Don't press Hendricks any longer.' He got up quickly, pulled money from his pocket and tossed it down. 'I'll see you in the town hall,' he said, walking off, past the waitress who skipped out of his way, and past the sea of doilies, the dried flowers and the shell ashtrays for sale, making straight for the exit.

She didn't try to call him back. There was no point: he meant what he said. When the lace-covered glass door finally swung shut behind him, she glanced at her watch. One fifty: time to go. She got up. He'd left fifty rand – more than enough to pay for a myriad of limp-leafed salads. She followed him out.

When the judge said 'Miss Barcant?', she clicked on her microphone and said, 'No further questions,' folding her arms, a metaphorical washing of the hands while beside her Alex sat. Unmoving. Unmovable.

Blinking back his surprise, the judge addressed himself to the other side of the stage. 'Mr Bester?'

Also taken aback by Sarah's abrupt withdrawal, Dirk Hendricks's lawyer came up with a number of displacement activities. He yanked his braces, straightened his tie, opened and closed a file and only then, having bunched his hand up and held it to his lips and coughed, did he turn on his microphone. 'A few more clarifying questions, Mr Hendricks?' he said, his voice lilting up, checking the state of his client's preparedness.

He needn't have worried. With Alex out of the way, Hendricks reverted to his role as perfect witness, well bred and well behaved and calmer than any of the rest of them on stage. 'Yes, Mr Chairman,' he said.

His lawyer smiled. 'You heard Mr Mpondo testify that after

the initial period of intensive interrogation, you then interrogated him every four days for a long period of time?'

Listening to the prisoner's bloodless answer, 'That is correct, Mr Chairman,' Sarah thought: Bester understands that Hendricks's sadism could be his Achilles heel.

'And is what Mr Mpondo said right?' the lawyer asked. 'Did you in fact interrogate him regularly every four days?'

With Alex out of the way, Dirk Hendricks could now safely say no to this. In fact, without Alex to challenge him, Dirk Hendricks could say anything he wanted. And he could take his time about it. His answer, delivered with a shake of the head, came after a long pause. 'I'm sorry, Mr Chairman.' His voice wavering slightly, as if he really were sorry, before he steadied it. 'I disremember the exact number of times I saw Mr Mpondo but if he is meaning I interrogated him strictly every four days, then he is surely exaggerating.'

'How can you be sure of this?'

'Because that time was the start of the total onslaught. The ANC had told its people to render the country ungovernable and we in the security branch were stretched almost beyond breaking point. I had many other duties and some took me far from Smitsrivier. I couldn't have interrogated Mr Mpondo so regularly like he says.'

'But you did continue to interrogate him sporadically throughout his imprisonment?'

'That is correct.'

'We heard from you that during the first three days of any interrogation you needed to extract all possible information before the enemy had time to regroup. What were your reasons for continuing to interrogate your prisoner after that initial period?'

'To get information from him, Mr Chairman.'

'Surely you already had that?'

'Not entirely, Mr Chairman. I had learned the location of

some weapons but there were other things Mr Mpondo had kept from me – arms-smuggling routes, names of other terrorists, future plans – that were necessary for us to know. For this reason I continued to interrogate him.'

'In other words, any suggestion that you may have laid hands on Mr Mpondo out of hatred or vindictiveness, or even because it gave you pleasure, would be untrue?'

'Mr Chairman,' Dirk Hendricks said, 'it couldn't be further from the truth. What I did to Mr Mpondo I did in good faith,' repeating it, 'in good faith,' absently, as if his mind was elsewhere, as if he were thinking something out which he must have resolved because, when he spoke again, he spoke louder.

'I believed in what I was taught,' he said. 'I was taught that if we did not hold firm we would be overrun by the communistic forces,' echoing the excuse that so many other policemen and former policemen had brought to the Truth Commission, their prejudices reinforced by the things that they had witnessed, by, as Dirk Hendricks was saying, 'terrible things that were happening in our country. People necklaced, policemen gunned down, houses burning, townships turned into no-go areas.'

Listening, Sarah felt the frustration of having been pulled off him. There were questions she wanted to ask him: like how many necklacings had he actually witnessed? How many in contrast to the deaths in jail or the shootings on the street? And yet, without Alex's consent, she knew she couldn't ask them.

'. . . All these things,' Dirk Hendricks was saying, 'made me think our whole way of life was endangered.'

He paused then. So many facets to this man, Sarah thought, just like Alex. Hendricks had started the hearing as a cowed prisoner and had offered them a glimpse of the torturer inside, but now he was neither of these. He was leaning forward, delivering what he had to say with almost messianic sincerity.

'It's easy to look back now and say that I was wrong.' He lurched forward as if planning to get up. 'We have a new government and there is still law and order in our land. I can see that with my own eyes. But in those days I honestly had many fears about what could happen.'

He *was* planning to get up. He leaned his hands down and pushed back, apparently unaware that his guards had shot to their feet.

'I honestly . . .' he continued.

He was given no time to complete the sentence. His lawyer put a stop to it, reaching up and pulling down his client.

Dirk Hendricks landed heavily. He turned angrily to his lawyer. It was as if he were about to lash out. His chest heaved, his throat pulsated and he was breathing noisily enough to be heard right across the stage. It was like watching a wild thing, Sarah thought, an animal bound by a past that had brought it to this place; and she found herself feeling sorry for Dirk, realising at the same time that it was also the first time she had thought of him as Dirk. As his lawyer said soothingly, 'Thank you, Mr Hendricks. I think you've made your point,' it occurred to Sarah that Hendricks's repeated acts of torture might have been a result not of dispassion, as she'd previously assumed, but of a welling-up of passion so fierce he could not subdue it and a pent-up determination that was consuming him, even now, as he turned his head and looked to the panel of judges.

'Your Honour. There is something I must say. Can I not please stand?'

The judge seemed to hesitate and then said, 'Yes, Mr Hendricks, you may stand. But first,' – he looked over the prisoner's head at the hovering guards – 'officers, resume your seats.' He held up a hand until they had done so before he said, 'Go ahead, Mr Hendricks.'

Dirk Hendricks got up. He stood, silent, gawky, towering

above his lawyer. Then he took in a deep breath and on the out-breath raised his head so that he was taller still.

'There is something I must say, Mr Chairman,' he said, addressing his words not at the panel of judges but at the motionless Alex Mpondo. 'It is not easy to talk about what happened. You can even feel a bit ashamed. But to you, Mr Mpondo, I want to say that in all honesty I didn't know who you were then. I never saw you as you sit there today – an MP, a man with education, a fellow human being. I can understand it if you hate me – I went on too long – but if you could find it in your heart, I would like to talk to you. Not here, like monkeys in a zoo, but in private, face to face. If you agree, I will try and explain to you why I did what I did, to show you that I also am human.'

33

ALEX ENDED UP in a white bar. He didn't particularly go looking for one, he just wandered in accidentally and stayed there. It was a white bar but not city-slick, new South African white. There were none of the requisites for that – no polished waiters or portly businessmen; no cashews, coasters or crooning air-conditioning. This dive was much more basic. It was rural white, poor white, cheap white, clannishly white.

From *kaffir* toilet to white-trash bar, Alex thought, looking round him. While those other smart metropolitan bars competed these days to draw in Africans, this one had probably never served a black customer before. Why should it have? No self-respecting African would ever frequent such a place.

And yet when Alex had pushed open the door and walked over the threshold (was that sawdust on the floor or had somebody just neglected to sweep the place?), no one protested. The other customers, three lone men of indeterminate ages, their heads drooping in successive stages of alcoholic decline, were probably all too far gone to care, but the *tannie* behind the bar nodded acknowledgement of Alex's appearance and then gestured languidly as if to say that if he was really intending to come in, he must pull the door to and reseal them all in the gloomy dankness of the place.

She didn't ask him what he wanted. She merely waited until he had sat down at a rickety table and then she came out from behind the bar bearing a tin mug. As she shuffled over, her scruffy slippers slid against the textured floor. When she reached him, she shifted a dusty bouquet of bright blue plastic magnolias on to another wobbly table before putting down the tankard.

A sour smell issued from it. Alex thought he could guess what it was but he looked in, over the battered metal rim, anyway, to check. He was right: she had brought him that familiar soupy, fermented yellow liquid that was unmistakably maize beer. *Kaffir* beer, he thought, because I'm black? But no . . . looking around he saw that the other customers were drinking the same thing from identically warped tin mugs. Maybe they can't afford commercial beer, he thought, or maybe they no longer have the taste for it. He smiled at the woman. '*Dankie.*'

She nodded and shambled off.

Alex hadn't really felt like beer of any type, but now it had come to him he might as well get on and drink it. Lifting up the tankard he held it for a moment as if making a toast. A silent toast to Dirk Hendricks.

You had to admire the bastard: he was so slick. And his timing was perfect. The way he'd finely gauged the moment to come knocking on humanity's door! Clever Dirk. He must have felt – Alex certainly had – how the audience had been drawn almost against their will into giving their old enemy a sympathetic hearing and he must also have seen the responsive nodding of the judges' heads. Not as the good Archbishop Tutu kept insisting that begging forgiveness was a prerequisite for amnesty, but let's face it, it helped, especially if the plea seemed as unpremeditated and heartfelt as Dirk Hendricks's. Good touch that, his lawyer trying to pull him down. The spectators had fallen for it hook, line and sinker. Alex could see it in their answering smiles – not only the judges' but entire sections of the audience's as well.

In fact, Alex thought it was possible that he was the only person who hadn't been fooled. Only he had noted how the ground for this manoeuvre had been prepared long before it was actually launched.

That was the worst of it. How thoroughly Alex knew the bastard. Not in the sense that you can know someone close to you, your child, for example, or your brother or your lover. It was even more intimate than that. Deeper. The truth was that Alex knew Dirk Hendricks from the inside. Not only the physicality of the man, the smell of his aftershave, for example, crushed pine mixed with lard which soured on his slippery skin when he began to sweat, or the soft grunt of his exertion, or the rough edge of his palm – not any of that alone. It was more and it was worse. It was the way Dirk Hendricks's mind worked. That's what Alex knew. That's what had made the whole experience doubly unbearable, that he had sat opposite his torturer and he had known what he was thinking and known also what he was planning to say next.

In any other situation this might have been considered useful. He knew conventional political wisdom, business consultants, modern warfare tacticians would all probably agree that this kind of forewarning could be vital: they subscribed to the same theory that to know your enemy is the first step to defeating him. But not for Alex. Not in this case. In this case, to know Dirk Hendricks, to know what poison he might next generate, was to fear him the more.

Fear. Alex was an expert in it. It was sited not only in his mind but in his body. He knew its secrets. He had sat there in the hearing and he had felt it coming on. He knew how it would start, flickering in his chest, before climbing up through his throat, crackling at his nerve ends, setting his eyelids quivering. Fear and its anticipation. Dirk Hendricks had taught him all about that. This was his speciality. He had understood the power of Alex's imagination. That was what those torture sessions, spaced out regularly every four days, were all about and that is why Dirk Hendricks felt he had to deny them publicly. The narrative that Dirk Hendricks had chosen for himself was of an honest policeman duped by his government's propaganda, not the story of the sadist that he undoubtedly was. Because what Hendricks had done to Alex was not only inflict pain but also describe its moment in the future. He had made Alex wait for it.

If Sarah Barcant had caught a glimpse of this she had done so only in that competent, lawyer's way of hers. That's why Alex had to rein her in. In the final analysis, all of this was just courtroom strategy to her: her preoccupation was not what Hendricks might say about Alex but rather the best way in which to cross-examine him and thus lay the ground for a refusal of amnesty. As acute as her intellect was, she could never have understood, as Alex did, that Dirk Hendricks hadn't changed at all, that what he wanted now was the same thing he had always wanted – to obliterate Alex.

A hand moved into vision. The barkeeper's hand, depositing another tankard on the table. Had he said something which she'd misinterpreted as an order, or did she just always dictate the speed at which her customers consumed her wares? It didn't appear to matter. She slopped away.

He looked down at the table. Two tankards. Both full. One for Alex. One for Dirk. What a waste, Alex thought. They didn't need two. They were two men made one.

Not that Dirk Hendricks knew this. That was Alex's only consolation, that Hendricks would never guess at the depth of damage he had inflicted on his prisoner. The old ways of thinking still existed too much inside Hendricks's head. He thought he was in prison because his government had lost, because he was white and Alex, his accuser, black. He was so clever and at the same time so stupid. He didn't understand that colour no longer divided them, that, because of what Hendricks had done to Alex, they were the same.

Because what Dirk Hendricks did not know – and what he must never know – was that he had turned Alex white. Bleached white, lily white. White with fear. No wonder Alex's feet had led him into a white bar. He was no longer black.

The *tannie* who ran the bar was a genius. Alex did need another drink. More than one. He picked up the closest of the tin mugs and throwing back his head, let the sour mash flow down his throat until the end, until he had drained the tankard. There, that was better. Brilliant of her to predict how soon he'd need another. He picked up the next as well.

He was in the process of raising it to his mouth when the door opened. A river of dusty light came shafting into the gloom. Turning to look at its source, Alex saw the outline of a figure framed against the light. Not just a figure but a woman's figure. First a black and now a woman, he thought: if the *dronkies* in this place weren't already so far out of it they'd milk enough conversation from these two events to last them at least until their livers packed up.

The woman stepped inside and the door closed. That fashionable get-up and those ridiculously high shoes could only belong to one person: Sarah Barcant. What the hell was she doing here, not just here in this bar, but in this town? She didn't look like Smitsrivier and she didn't act like it. Alex knew her history: she was the optician's daughter who got away. And yet here she was, back again, chasing phantoms.

By the sombre look on her face, he thought, it wasn't doing her any good. Well, that was predictable: she'd made the same mistake as Alex. She should have known, they both should, that Smitsrivier was the kind of *dorpie* the world had passed by, a black hole for phantoms, a place where ghosts were sent for purgatory.

She didn't seem surprised to find him here. She walked towards him, taking her time. He had to hand it to her: she'd changed after the hearing and now she looked great in an ele gant red shift, wisps of her shining black hair straying across her face, softening her features. If she would only stop frowning.

She stopped by his table. 'I thought you'd be here.'

'Here?'

'In a bar. Getting drunk.'

Oh. Right. She'd seen him drunk the other night. 'Miss White Smitsrivier, 1985. Ever tasted *kaffir* beer?' he said.

She grinned at him, not bothering to reply. He liked her for that. In fact, he thought, despite her touchiness and the uptight way she behaved most of the time, he liked her altogether. He said, 'Sit down and tell me what you think of South Africa's very own Band-Aid.'

She frowned.

'The Truth Commission as social antiseptic,' he explained. 'That's what one of the Commissioners called it the other day. Bit like counting your chickens after the horse has bolted, if you ask me . . . or some such mixed metaphor. Aren't you going to sit?'

She shook her head. 'No. I've come to get you.'

'What? To Hendricks? So he can pull his innocent act in front of a private audience? Forget it.'

'No,' she said, 'not to Hendricks. To the farm. I asked him where it was. I've come to take you there.'

That's what he liked about her. There was no bullshitting her. He grinned.

There was no deflecting her either. 'Come on. Let's get it over,' she said.

He inclined his head in the direction of the table. 'I haven't finished my drink.'

She took him by surprise. Her hand swooped down on to the table and before he could work out what she was planning, she'd picked up the tin mug and, standing with those elegant high heels of hers planted in the sawdust, she drank the whole thing down. Then she put the empty tankard on the table along with a ten-rand note and said, 'There. It's finished. Come on. Let's go while it's still light.'

34

How long was it since Alex had last driven down this road? Three days? Four days? He couldn't remember.

He glanced quickly in Sarah's direction. She was concentrating on the road ahead, driving fast and with the same unwavering intensity she brought to everything she did. That suited him. He settled back. It felt peaceful to sit and watch the endless backward-rushing of the tarmac, a slate-grey strip slicing through the ochres and mustards and sage greens of the landscape's passing blur. A moment suspended. A moment of calm. He felt his eyelids closing.

The sound of Sarah sighing shook him alert. He glanced left. Had he imagined the sound? She was still staring straight ahead, apparently oblivious either to the fact that she had sighed or that he was watching her. Taking in the fierce determination of her profile, he saw the strength in her. The strength of an escapee, he thought, an outsider determined to live life on her own terms.

She looked at him then, meeting his eyes casually as if she'd known all along that he was looking, and said, 'The turn-off should be round here somewhere.'

The turn-off to the farm. He felt suddenly quite sober. And thirsty. He licked his lips. They were dry and cracked: he was dying of thirst. Why hadn't he thought to bring water?

'There it is.' She was already lifting her foot off the accelerator.

'There' was an unmarked dirt track that cut away sharply from the road. The sight revolted him. When Sarah turned the steering wheel, it was all he could do to stop himself from reaching across and wrenching the controls from her and turning the car in the other direction, any other direction, as long as they didn't go down that track.

'Hendricks said it was a couple of kilometres off the tar.' Speeding up, she steered the car forward.

It was too bright. Too sharp. The glare was burning his eyes. He shut them, shutting out the sun. Big mistake. In the darkness he was even more terrified.

He opened his eyes hoping that this way he would succeed in driving off the images that had assailed him. Without success. They'd already burned their way into his consciousness: the sight of the track, not now but in the past, flickering back and forth, light and dark, as he lay trussed up in a jolting metallic container, those flashed images mixing with a foul smell, that noxious burning of diesel fumes and the sound of panting he couldn't quite place.

He thought: the drug they gave me didn't work. I was awake. Or at least half awake.

Fear. It came on him again. Burning like the charred surface of the earth.

He caught that thought and, frowning, wondered: why charred?

The fire. Of course. The fire. The week before his arrest a fire had taken hold on the land surrounding, sweeping its fringes of rust flame across the wilderness, swallowing trees as it moved inexorably towards town. He remembered the sounds that accompanied it, the crack of dried wood and the rhythmic beating by the line of men, black and white together, trying unsuccessfully to beat out the fire, until it proved itself easily the stronger and they had no choice but to flee its savagery, skirting round and changing tactics, fanning the flames forward now, pushing them towards the road in the hope that once they hit the long stretch of tarmac, they would burn themselves out. He remembered all that. And Steve as well.

The fire was burned in Alex's memory because of Steve, because he and Steve had fought it side by side. The thought produced a once forgotten image – Steve grinning triumphantly as the fierce flames had flared out across the road and then begun to die away. Alex remembered how Steve's hand had moved up to his close cropped head then, staining his mahogany forehead with the burned black residue of ash before Steve had thrown back his head and begun to laugh.

Steve, laughing. It was Alex's last sight of his friend – of his friend alive – save for that one time when Steve's beaten hulk had been dragged into Alex's cell.

A thought came to Alex. Despite the fact that Dirk Hendricks had denied it, had Steve been in the boot with Alex? Was that his uneven breathing that Alex had heard above the sound of tyres scraping over stone? Or was that later – was that the sound of Steve's dying?

He heard his name. 'Alex?'

Sarah's voice: he had no idea how long she'd been calling to him. Quite a while, he thought, by the look of her.

He said. 'I'm sorry, I was miles away.'

She smiled. 'I asked what James Sizela has against you.'

'James?' He shrugged. 'Simple. He holds me responsible for his son's death.'

Her eyelids flickered and he read in that involuntary movement a question. That's what the future holds, he thought: people wanting to know without asking whether my betrayal ended in Steve's death. A question, the only question. One he could not answer because he genuinely did not know.

Only Dirk Hendricks knew. The irony of it. Dirk Hendricks as repository of his past.

Sarah's voice – thank God for the dogged persistence of a prosecutor – intruded. 'Why does James blame you?'

How to answer that? He said: 'Ever been in his office at school?'

She nodded. 'Yes. The other day.'

'Did you notice the photograph on the wall – James with another man?'

'I did, yes. They were shaking hands.'

'The other man is Barend du Plessis – apartheid's one-time minister of education. The fact that James still displays the picture must tell you something about him.'

Her eyebrows rose. 'Are you saying James supported apartheid?'

'Not supported, no. But tolerated. James takes his Bible literally: he believes in rendering unto Caesar what is Caesar's. Upholding the law and obeying authority is his *sine qua non*. He tried to drum this into all his pupils, me included, and so when Steve joined the comrades, James had no way of understanding the move. He couldn't accept his son might have made the decision on his own so he looked for somebody else to blame. He chose me. He decided I was the one who had led

Steve astray. And I guess he was right in a way: Steve and I were always talking politics.'

'But even so . . . to blame you for his death!'

She sounded so incredulous. Of course. She'd never come up against the anger that simmered beneath James's strict, unbending exterior. The anger of a proud man, a brilliant teacher, who'd been forced by the old government to abase himself, travelling to Pretoria to beg for more money and, even then, when he had done everything they'd asked of him, he would usually return empty-handed save for a black-and-white photograph of a white minister graciously shaking his black man's hand.

And besides, Alex thought, maybe James is right in this as well: maybe I was responsible for Steve's death.

He looked up. Her eyes were still on him. Quizzical, expectant eyes that had nothing to do with James. The car, he thought, it's not moving.

She put the car into neutral and switched off the engine. 'This is it.'

No wonder she'd been looking at him so curiously. They'd arrived. He looked through the windscreen. There was a building there. Close by. A farmhouse in its final stages of dereliction. Surely he had never seen this place before?

Looking more closely, he took in the sight of the boxlike house. Two identical square structures with green tin gabled roofs were joined by a flat-roofed box in the middle of which stood a front door. The place was so neglected: nature was busy reclaiming it. The withered brown leaves of a dusty willow tree dropped down on to one of the gables, while orange water stains, running raggedly from broken roof to ground, took up the ragged theme. An ugly house. A refuge that had been turned into a torture chamber. He tore his eyes away from it. He saw a tumbled-down brick barn standing to one side, the whole plot ringed by a net of wire which, once a continuous fence, was now holed and leering drunkenly from its posts, and beyond it a huge stretch of uncultivated land.

When he looked back, the house was no longer unfamiliar. Of course he knew it. He'd always known it, he'd just placed that knowledge somewhere distant in his memory. Somewhere anonymous. He opened the car door and stepped out, stood and breathed in that faint odour of animal dung that had once followed him into sleep. He took another step.

Behind him he could hear Sarah's door closing. 'If you wouldn't mind, I'd like to go in alone,' he said, and went forward.

Two large square metallic windows, each divided into about thirty small panes, were planted symmetrically, one on each side of the house. As he got closer, Alex saw that the windows were no longer glazed and that shattered glass lay scattered on the ground. It was as if someone had stood close by and stoned the house, or shot it up. That was more likely: the kind of thing Dirk Hendricks would easily have done for fun.

He didn't hesitate. He went up three stone steps that led to the front door and turned the handle. To his surprise it opened easily. He stepped in.

Dark. That was his first impression. The hallway where he was standing was very dark. He stood still, waiting for his eyes to acclimatise. When they did, he saw the house was divided into two, with the hall where he was standing acting as the bridge between each separate part. To the right, the living quarters. To the left, the jail. Someone had hung a huge, heavy steel door to the left. The police.

Alex knew that door.

He pushed at it. It opened, scraping against the stone floor – he knew that sound as well – to reveal a second, barred gate. He pushed the gate as well and it too opened. He stepped in. Sludge-green walls, just as at the police station. Flagstones on the floor – just as there too. Rooms like cells, leading off a corridor, each with its own impenetrable door.

He was amazed at his sense of calm. All that fear for nothing. He knew this place. He knew it intimately. He knew the feel of it and the sound, and the room where they had kept him – second on the left. He didn't go inside to check it out. There was no need. He remembered it precisely as it had been. It wasn't like a sudden clearing of the head but rather as if this scene, this place, had been there in the back of his mind all this time – just waiting to be reclaimed. Now that he saw it again, it was as if he had never forgotten it.

He heard footsteps. Turning he found that Sarah was standing in the hallway.

'This is the place,' he said. 'They kept me here. Me. And Steve as well. And there,' pointing to the corridor's end where another steel door was sited, 'that's where they carried him out.'

35

THE EVENINGS, AFTER they locked him in at five o'clock, were always the most difficult times for Dirk. Then the night stretched out before him and there was nothing he could do to hurry it along. He tried to keep himself awake as long as he could but his problem was how to fill the time. He could read but then he'd never been much of a reader. He could also exercise – but there was a limit to how many sit-ups, press-ups or runnings-on-the-spot any man could reasonably do in such a confined space. Which left him with his thoughts.

That was the worst of it. No matter how hard he tried to avoid doing so, he always ended up thinking about the children. He would think of Jannie in a foreign country starting school without a father to guide him, or diving for his first rugby try without Dirk there to clap him on the back afterwards. Or else he'd think of his sweet Elsie. Who was going to throw her high in the air until she squealed in delight? And who was going to play her favourite magic trick, pulling liquorice strings out of her hair?

When he thought of them like that their faces would come to him – but distantly. That suited him. He didn't want to remember too clearly how they had once looked: he knew they would already have changed, that while he sat incarcerated, counting time, the world moved passed him in a blur.

He thought: what would it be like to come out and no longer recognise your children?

Not that he would have put up with their visiting him in jail, even if it had been allowed. He had sat in on too many prison visits for that: he knew how awkward they were and how, increasingly with time, the parties on either side of the wire mesh found less and less to say to one another. No child of his would ever be subjected to that void or to the torment of wanting to be anywhere but opposite their father. No child of his would ever pity him like that.

But if only they weren't so far away, he thought. If only they were closer. Then he could send somebody, his mother, his aunt, to find out what they needed. Much better that than being at Katie's mercy, reliant on her posting him fresh photographs or else cajoling Jannie into sitting down and writing him a few, wobbly words.

Not that Dirk blamed Katie. The truth was that he felt no anger towards his wife – his soon-to-be ex-wife. He knew how hard it had been for her when things started going wrong. First the rages and then the trial.

Maybe if he'd been a better husband before, he thought, she would have stood by him.

Or maybe not. She had always so looked up to him. And what a turnaround it must have been to see him accused and convicted of murder. Add to that the manner in which their neighbours had turned against them both (and talked about her loud enough for her to overhear) and any woman might have had second thoughts. No: he couldn't, he didn't think too badly of Katie. He understood her decision to separate herself from him.

He felt less tolerant, though, towards the behaviour of their former neighbours. The bloody cheek of them, giving Katie such a hard time. Couldn't they see that she was no different from them? If the charge against her was that she'd gloried in his status then they were equally guilty. He'd seen their faces lighting up the day the Police Commissioner pitched up unexpectedly at his braai and he'd heard them talking about it for months afterwards. See there, he'd heard them boasting to strangers, over there, that's Dirk Hendricks, my neighbour, my husband, my friend: he's in the security branch, you know, he's going places.

Going places! And he'd ended up in C-Max, sentenced to twenty years!

If he thought he was really going to have to serve that time, if he contemplated sitting uselessly on his arse until his strength had all drained out of him, he'd do something drastic. But he didn't believe it. Not any more. The amnesty hearing hadn't turned out to be the ANC-inspired pretence at justice he'd originally assumed it would be. These judges were real, decent people, willing to give him a fair hearing. And he wasn't in such a bad position: unlike many of his former colleagues, he had only one more amnesty hearing after this one. He'd be able to explain why he'd done what he did that day, why that poor man had ended up dead and he'd get amnesty for it. He must get amnesty for it.

And when he did, he thought, he might even emerge from prison strengthened by the experience. An odd thing for him to think, perhaps, but freedom was a different ball game once you'd been in jail. It wasn't just a question of appreciating those things he'd taken for granted before, but also the opportunity to start again. In jail you learned things about yourself and what Dirk had learned was how unquestioning a youngster he had been. Without considering other possibilities, he'd just assumed that he'd go to police college after matric, exactly as his father had before him.

Now it was different. Without his father, God rest his soul, to placate, Dirk could maybe do something for himself. He might even try for a qualification or start up a sports business like he'd always dreamed of doing.

He looked at his watch. Six o'clock. Hours and hours to go. Never mind. He didn't feel too bad tonight. The relief that he'd experienced during the hearing had stayed with him. Then, for the first time, he had understood, really understood, what Archbishop Tutu had meant when he said on television that the truth could set you free. Dirk had felt that strength which the archbishop talked about flowing inside him as he sat there on the stage. Far better that he had told the truth: far better for all concerned. Lying down on his bunk, he rested his head on his upstretched arms.

Not for long though. He heard footsteps in the corridor outside. That wasn't normal. He sat up. He knew this place so well: he could visualise the progress of the custody sergeant along the flagstoned corridor, most likely on his way to check on a new arrival. So much better to be here in Smitsrivier, he thought, rather than in C-Max where every sound was either magnified beyond bearing or frustratingly muffled. But it was also eerie, sitting here, listening to those footsteps, knowing that they, and their mission, might easily once have been his.

Wait a minute. The footsteps had stopped, out there, outside his cell. He got off his bunk. Hearing the grating of the grill, he looked up and a pair of brown eyes looked back. Then the grill dropped and the door opened.

'*Kom.*' That's all the uniformed officer said.

'Where to?'

That one word again: '*Kom.*'

He didn't need to ask where to again. There was only one reason why they would come and get him – he must have a visitor. Walking down the corridor, feeling his jailer's sour breath on his neck, he wondered who it could be. Not his lawyer: Hannie had left in a tearing hurry, intent on catching the next plane from Port Elizabeth to Pretoria so that he could spend the weekend at his beloved game farm.

Alex Mpondo then?

No. He seriously doubted that. He'd been looking at Alex when he suggested that the two of them meet up, and he'd seen Alex's face closing down, shutting him out. If it had been any other person, Dirk might have thought that he'd misread the other's expression, but not Alex. He knew Alex too well – he could not have been mistaken.

So who? Waiting for the jailer on the other side to open the steel gate, he thought: not Pieter surely?

'*Regs,*' the jailer said.

He went right as instructed, going up to the door to the interview room.

'*Maak gou,*' the guard said, gesturing him in.

In he went, into the sparsely furnished room where he had once interviewed suspects or the victims of crime. As he heard the sound of the door closing behind him, he saw who his visitor was. Sarah Barcant. She was sitting at the table reading, dressed in a *lekker* red shift that glowed in the light from the setting sun through the high tiny barred window. Hearing him enter, she looked up and smiled. The lift he felt at the sight of her brought home to him how he missed those ordinary things – a hint of lipstick, a spontaneous human exchange, a pretty girl's welcome.

'Ms Barcant,' he said. 'This is an unexpected pleasure.'

A voice – not hers – grated out: 'Do you know who I am as well?'

He turned in the direction of the voice and saw that there was a frail old man standing by the door. Of course he knew who it was. Ben Hoffman. 'Everyone in Smitsrivier knows you, Mr Hoffman,' he said, registering at the same time how aged and thin Hoffman looked, suppressing his shock to add: 'You're famous.'

Ben Hoffman did not return his smile. 'Infamous, you mean?'

'No, sir.' Dirk shook his head to emphasise his disagreement. 'I know we were on different sides but I always respected your professionalism. When things were slack, I used to come watch you at work. I learned more from you about cross-examination than from any other single person.'

'Given what we've been hearing of your interrogation techniques,' Ben said drily, 'I'm not sure I take that as a compliment.'

The old man always had a ready wit, Dirk thought. A wit that could cut. That had cut. 'You once had me on the witness stand,' he said. 'It was a minor case – you probably don't even remember it. I was the arresting officer of a woman accused of theft. God, you tied me in such knots that by the time you'd finished with me I was ready to agree to anything, even alien abduction.'

Dirk had been talking in jest, but when Ben Hoffman answered: 'I remember the case well,' his expression was in deadly earnest.

The sight brought back the fact that there never had been any getting to know Ben Hoffman – at least for the likes of Dirk. Most advocates had control of their emotions, but Hoffman carried this principle further than the rest of them. It really used to get to Dirk, in fact, the way Hoffman, who had something of a reputation as a performer out of court as well as in (Dirk had often come across him holding an audience of admirers spellbound), would never smile, never laugh, never make the slightest friendly gesture in Dirk's direction. Not that he was rude. On the contrary. He had always been rigorously polite. But so distant, as if Dirk just wasn't worth knowing. But look at him now: an old man.

'There was no hard evidence against my client,' the old man was saying, 'but the magistrate decided to trust the word of a white policeman above the denials of a poor black woman. She got five years.'

What was Dirk supposed to say to that? That he was sorry? Words simple enough to pronounce, except they would be lies. The honest truth was that, save for Ben Hoffman's performance, Dirk hardly remembered the case. It wasn't a political, but just one amongst many in which Dirk had been called upon to do his duty as a police officer. If justice had been skewed – and he wasn't denying that it might have been – he could not be held responsible. It was the way things operated then. Wrong maybe, but Dirk was damned if he was going to shoulder the blame for everything that had gone wrong in the past.

'Why don't you sit down?' he heard.

He was still standing by the door. Sarah Barcant had risen and was looking at him and when he followed the direction of her gaze he saw that his fists were clenched. 'I'm sorry. It's too easy to lose your manners in jail,' he said quickly, unclenching the fists and going over to the table, waiting for her to reseat herself before he also sat down.

Ben Hoffman moved then, limping slowly up to the head of the table to sit beside Sarah. Watching him, Dirk remembered again how this sick old man had once been in court – careful in his preparation, flamboyant in his delivery. He was a real character, a whole world removed from the new generation of legal slicksters with their Gucci suits and their Nokia phones.

Silence. Dirk wondered what they wanted.

Sarah Barcant broke the silence. 'We went to the farm.'

So that was it. 'You found it all right?'

'Yes. Your directions were perfect.'

'Good.'

'I took Alex Mpondo with me.'

He nodded. He didn't speak. What was there for him to say?

'He recognised the place.'

'So he knows I was telling the truth.'

'He remembered the room in which he was kept,' she said.

Dirk nodded. 'He would. He was there for some time.'

'He also remembers seeing Steve Sizela there.'

'He does?'

'Mr Hendricks. You told me something once and I believed you. You told me that you were so involved in the interrogation of Alex Mpondo that you didn't know anything about Steve Sizela.'

He nodded.

'But now that I've seen how small the farmhouse is, I no longer find that credible.'

'Well, I can't be held responsible for what you find or what you think,' he said, watching her, seeing how she was scowling, no longer thinking of her as a pretty girl. She was a lawyer. Pure and simple. Trained, he remembered, by Ben Hoffman.

She said: 'Alex says Steve was taken to the farm at the same time as him – in the trunk of your car.'

He shook his head. 'Then Alex is mistaken.'

She was good, he thought, she didn't waste time flogging a dead horse. Or a wrong one. She moved on. 'Mr Hendricks, I'm sure you know that we have set in motion a civil case for damages against Pieter Muller. In pursuance of our claim, we will subpoena every policeman and ex-policeman that ever worked in Smitsrivier. One of them will crack. You know they will. And when they do, they are as likely to tell us things about your behaviour as about Pieter Muller's.'

'Are you trying to threaten me?'

'No,' she said. 'I'm not threatening you, Mr Hendricks. I'm merely pointing out that anything you did as a policeman and haven't admitted to doing might come out in court. And if it does, it might end up jeopardising your chances of getting amnesty – if not in this case then in the next.'

He narrowed his eyes.

'It would be a pity to spend twenty years in jail for something somebody else did.'

He shrugged. 'I'm sorry. I can't help you.'

She must have realised, finally, that he wasn't to be bullied. She softened her tone. 'Please, Mr Hendricks. All Mr and Mrs Sizela want is to lay their son to rest.' Playing him for a sucker; icing the cake with: 'Please, Mr Hendricks. Help them.'

He said it again. 'I'm sorry. Because they lost their son, my heart goes out to them. But there's nothing I can do to help.'

'Nothing you can do.' Her voice was hard now. 'Or nothing you will do?'

He felt himself stiffen. Fuck her. At least with Ben Hoffman you knew where you stood. Not so with this one: she was like all the rest of them, nice as pie when they wanted something, hard as nails when you wouldn't deliver. He said, 'Miss Barcant. I am to spend twenty years in C-Max. It doesn't take a genius to work out how much I'd like to get out. But I can't just buy my freedom because I want to. If I did that, I would no longer be a man.'

He saw her looking straight at him and he could tell by her frown that she had no idea what he was talking about. Well, fuck her, he thought again. He didn't owe her anything. He'd already taken his punishment: he didn't have to stay for more. He stood up. 'I can't help you,' he said, knowing that if he stayed, voices would be raised and there was no point in that.

He left the table and walked over to the door, banging against it with the palm of his hand to alert the guard. When the door opened, he took a step out.

He heard his name called out.

If it had been Sarah Barcant calling him he would have just walked on. But the voice that called out did not belong to her: it belonged to Ben Hoffman. Dirk turned back.

Hoffman's eyes were locked on him. 'Mr Hendricks,' Hoffman said, and then, in a matter-of-fact voice, as if he was about to tell Dirk that he was moving house or changing cars, he said, 'I'm dying.'

Christ! Dirk didn't know where to put himself.

'Not now, immediately,' Ben Hoffman continued, 'but soon. I tell you this not to get your sympathy or your pity but rather to share with you the way that, when you know that life will soon end, this knowledge helps focus the mind. And if there is one thing I have realised, Mr Hendricks, it is that loyalty is an overrated virtue.'

But all I have is my loyalty, Dirk thought; and my memories.

'You want to protect your friend,' the old man said, 'that's commendable. But in holding your tongue you will at best condemn that ageing couple to sit in court, day after day, listening to lawyers and judges speculating about what happened to their son: at worst you are sentencing them to a life of torment, far worse than C-Max.'

But if I don't protect my friend, Dirk thought, then it makes nonsense of everything we did.

Had Ben Hoffman read his thoughts? He couldn't have. And yet he said, 'This is not about sides, Mr Hendricks.'

How could it not be? South Africa had always been about sides, from even before the *Engelse oorlog*.

'It's about humanity,' Ben Hoffman said.

Looking across the table, Dirk could see the old man's thin chest moving slowly, as if even the effort of breathing was too much for him. He really is on his way out, Dirk thought, and he would have liked to have been able to help. But how, in all conscience, could he?

But then, as he continued to look at Ben, he saw past an old man's frailty to his censorious expression and he was alert, finally. And thinking properly as well. He was no longer taken in by Hoffman's dribblings on the subject of loyalty and humanity. What right had the old man? Did he think that there should be one law for his side and one for Dirk's? No, of course he didn't – or at least if Dirk were to ask him he would say he didn't. But that would be a lie. Ben Hoffman and his kind were hypocrites. All that sympathy they wasted on the likes of Mpondo because he was crucified by his betrayal of his friend, and yet now the two of them were sitting there, opposite, and practically ordering him to betray Pieter. Well, he wouldn't. Just because they'd won, because the law was on their side, that didn't make them right.

He said, 'I'm sorry, Mr Hoffman, there is nothing I can tell you,' and with that he left the room.

Had they known that he would come back? They couldn't have – he didn't know it himself. With his jailer following close on his heels, he walked all the way down the corridor, thinking he had made the right decision. Hoffman was dying – that was sad for him – but Dirk had the living to think of. The present and the future, that's what mattered and not the past. What was gone was gone: it could not be changed. And besides, why should he do anything for Ben Hoffman: a man who up to this moment had never even deigned to speak to him?

All this he told himself up to the iron gate. All this he believed. And yet, standing there, waiting to be led through, he realised that it didn't matter what he believed. Ben Hoffman's appeal to him was unimportant: Sarah Barcant's threats weren't.

He knew their type and he knew that if he didn't tell them about Sizela, they would never leave him alone. They would dig and dig and in the end it would be his grave, not Pieter's, nor anybody else's, that would be dug.

It was no good. He had no choice. He must go back. His guard tried to stop him, but Dirk's urgency transmitted itself eventually and the two of them retraced their steps down the corridor. Not long now, he thought, reaching for the door handle.

When he opened the door, they were still sitting there exactly as he had left them, as if they were expecting him. He almost turned away. How could he be doing this? How could he?

But he didn't turn. He said, instead, 'I had nothing to do with the death of Steve Sizela. Do you understand that?'

Ben nodded. Which suited Dirk. He was talking only to Ben.

'But if he did die in custody,' Dirk said, 'someone would have buried him.'

'They wouldn't burn the body?' Sarah said.

'Someone would have buried him,' Dirk repeated, directing his gaze at Ben. 'Try the field nearest to the farm: directly behind the barn.' And having said that, he left.

36

'I DID IT as a favour,' the farmer said.

He had latched on to Sarah as soon as she got to the field behind the barn and he continued to treat her to the string of self-justification that issued from his lips.

'I did it as a favour.'

and:

'I was only trying to help.'

and:

'I had no need for the old farmhouse.'

and finally:

'I didn't think to ask what was going on in there.'

That last one took her aback. Why did he have to ask? Surely a man, so deeply rooted in this community who knew about the existence of not one, but two police stations, would have understood precisely why some security branch men might want his deserted farmhouse?

'I didn't ever think that they were killing people,' he said.

She looked at him. He was standing close, too close, as if the proximity would give him protection, a man whose body bulk and strong forearms belied those wide eyes and that beseeching face. He didn't have the look of a dishonest man, she thought. Knowing white South Africa, she thought, perhaps he was telling the truth: perhaps he really hadn't known.

Her gaze called forth more words.

'Blacks feel strongly about the bones of their relatives – they never leave them unclaimed.'

'Excuse me,' she said, and moved away, separating herself from him.

It was Sunday and they were in a flat, brown field that lay behind the ramshackle barn. Quite a crowd had gathered. Another farmer, a neighbour, was standing by the fence, the pent-up anger on his leathery face saying plainly that if he could have found a way of getting rid of the lot of them and their search warrants, he would have done so hours ago. Almost all the rest of the crowd were Africans: a crowd from the township – the men in suits, the women in the dark red, white-bibbed frock uniform of their church; workmen dressed in the bright orange uniforms of a road gang and holding picks and spades; policemen in serge blue, one of their number holding back an eagerly straining dog; young, smart officials of the Truth Commission; local politicians with their bulging stomachs and benevolent expressions; a white pathologist carrying his doctor's bag and a black-frocked priest; and all of them here to witness the digging up of Steve Sizela.

There was something strangely festive about the gathering. Strange. As a cloud moved away from the sun, Sarah looked across the field and saw the crowd as a collection of one-dimensional stick figures planted in a low, flat landscape that stretched out towards the mountains, their bodies silhouetted by the searing brightness of the day.

She looked away, directing her gaze to a separate group. Here were no festivities. The foursome – Steve's parents and the Hoffmans – were bunched together in silence. Mr and Mrs Sizela were on their feet, as unmoving as they had been since they'd first arrived, while Ben was seated with Anna behind him holding aloft a red-and-yellow-striped umbrella, shielding her husband from the raging sun.

'Ja. That's about right,' she heard the farmer mutter.

Looking back, she saw that two of the workmen and a number of the besuited members of the Truth Commission had separated themselves from the crowd and were standing over an empty section of ground. At a nod from one of the officials, one of the workmen lifted his pick above his head.

A beat, a moment of silence, and then the pick bit down into a ground softened by a recent rainstorm. At that moment, as the second workman shovelled the earth away, the crowd began to sing. Up went the pick and down again, and the lilting voices swelled, those words sung out, that incessant questioning: *senzeni*, why is this happening?, joined to praises to their God, the sound rising up like an endless flocking of downy birds, driving on the workmen, as one carved his pick into the ground, the sound followed almost immediately by the soft thumping of a spade, pick and spade, pick and spade . . . and . . .

A pause. The singing was abruptly cut off. The workmen stood away from the shallow hole they had dug. The dog moved in. A lean brown hunter's dog leading its handler as it sniffed its way along the ground, going up to the hole, standing there a moment and . . . ?

Even afterwards Sarah couldn't figure out what it was exactly that the dog had done. Had it barked, short and sharply, a message of what it had found? No: she was almost positive that no sound had issued from that dog. Had it planted its feet in the ground then, resisting the efforts of its handlers to pull it away? No, she couldn't remember that either. All she knew was that, somehow, something the dog did was communicated to its handler and passed without verbal exchange through the crowd. The crowd responded as one by moving over to the Sizelas, grouping itself round the motionless couple, the soft hum of their melodious lament rising up to enfold them, as the workmen edged in again, digging more slowly and more carefully, digging out a hole big enough to house a body, looking up occasionally for reference at the pathologist, whose feet were gumbooted, his hands enfolded in rubber gloves, and who nodded encouragingly at the workmen, at least until the moment when he shook his head. Just once.

The workmen climbed out.

There was so much Sarah hadn't noticed before. The stark blueness of the sky, cloudless now, or the gemsbok skittering away in the far distance, or the hearse parked at the other side of the field, or the coffin, plain and white, that had already been carried on to the field, or Alex, standing alone. Were those tears she could see on his face, or was she just seeing him through the mist that hers had created?

There was no way of knowing: the time for questions had long since passed. The gloved man had already climbed into the crater and was transferring handfuls of dirt to the workmen, who laid them on top of the pile of soil they had already made, gently, as if they were precious, and who then went back for more, a slow, graceful chain gang until the moment when they stopped and waited. And then it was no longer soil that was being muscled out of the makeshift grave but a body.

It had to be a body and yet, if it was, it was almost completely disintegrated, a long thin, angular, unwieldy shape that was wrapped in thick polythene and covered by dirt, passed up and carried, wordlessly, to be laid down in the open coffin. The singing that had started up as the polythene emerged died away, the sound replaced by the muttered incantation of a priest who moved over to stand beside the coffin.

It wasn't over. Not yet. The pathologist did not climb out. He said something quietly to the men above him and then he reached up and took two plastic bags that were handed down to him and bent again. For a moment, all Sarah could see was the top of his balding head and then he was climbing out of the grave holding the bags, both of them now no longer empty.

But wait a minute: those weren't two bags in his hands, there were three. She was positive that only two had been handed down. Which meant that the pathologist must have found one buried with the body. As if to confirm this, he called a policeman over and, separating one of the bags from the rest, he handed it over before taking the other two with him, walking them slowly over to the centre of the crowd where the Sizelas were standing.

The crowd parted, giving the pathologist room.

He stood for a moment looking at Mrs Sizela and then he said something, so quietly that only she and her husband could have heard what it was, before he held out the bags.

Mrs Sizela didn't move. She didn't reach out. The bags hovered in mid-air – long enough for Sarah to see that one of them contained a watch and the other a pair of sneakers. And then she couldn't see anything any longer because Mrs Sizela crumpled and would have fallen if one of the women behind her hadn't caught her, and the two stood there balanced for a moment, staggering under each other's weight, as Mrs Sizela opened her mouth and began to wail.

37

WHEN ANNA STOPPED the car opposite the Sizelas' house, she saw why it was that her husband had been so quiet for the last half of their journey. Ben was asleep. Looking across she saw his head flung back and his mouth open, his scrawny Adam's apple moving with the rise and fall of his irregular breathing. He's so terribly thin, she thought, looking down at her own plump forearms and the rounded swelling of her belly and thinking that together they must look like that couple from the nursery rhyme. How did it go? Oh yes . . . *Jack Sprat could eat no fat, And his wife could eat no lean* . . . She couldn't remember the line that followed but she knew the whole thing somehow ended with them licking the plate clean.

Her smile faded. There hadn't been much licking of plates recently. Not even hers. She'd completely lost her appetite. This didn't mean that she had stopped cooking. On the contrary. Take yesterday, for example – she'd spent hours on an elaborate beef stew and a many-layered apple strudel, only to find herself throwing most of the food away. She knew that it was absurd to even contemplate recreating the food of Ben's early childhood in this country with its blistering summers, yet somehow she had found herself compelled to it.

Not that it mattered. In fact, she thought, it was probably a good idea. In conjuring up such elaborate meals, she had kept herself busy and doing that had also stretched out time. And she needed time: as much of it as she could get. Time in the now and not in the future when there would be no Ben.

Or maybe she was fooling herself; maybe this furious animation of hers was only a way of ignoring the reality that Ben was in many ways already lost to her. What little energy he had left he concentrated first on Sarah and then on the Sizelas. For them he had performed miracles, getting out of his sickbed to interview Dirk Hendricks, going to witness the digging up of Steve's body and now insisting on coming here to their house – all of these accomplishments in defiance of the best predictions medical science could make.

Even today, when the doctor had dropped in he pronounced himself stunned by Ben's capacity to keep going. But then, of course, they both agreed that there was no reason to be so surprised. Medical probability applied to average patients and Ben was hardly average. He was Ben. Resolute, stubborn, stalwart.

She swallowed. What she had thought before was erroneous: she hadn't lost him. Not yet. He was the same man she had always loved, the man she had married and with whom she'd lived, the man to whose death she must now bear witness. This Ben whose refusal to be beaten had been his trade mark.

Strange, she thought, how Ben's eyes had always been so firmly fixed on the future. He had never looked back and he had never gone back. Not once: not even on a visit. In fact, her suggestion, made some years ago, that they take a trip to Germany in pilgrimage to his childhood, provoked one of the rare occasions when he had raised his voice to her. 'South Africa is my country,' he'd shouted. 'I will live and I will die here.'

He was right in that as well, she thought.

This afternoon, she had thought for a moment that his time had come. After Steve's body had been carried away, Ben was so tired he had agreed to go to bed on condition that she wake him within two hours. She'd tried to keep her word – she'd tried to wake him. But she had found she couldn't. Ben, who'd always been such a light sleeper, didn't stir when she called his name. She tried again, saying 'Ben' much more loudly. Again with no result. She gave up. She sat down heavily on the chair beside his bed and listened to his breathing, so shallow and with long drawn-out interludes between each breath. Had the end come as the doctor had predicted it would? Was Ben sinking into a coma? She had put her hand on an emaciated shoulder and shook it gently. To no avail.

She didn't try again. Suddenly she didn't want to wake him. This was all she wanted: to sit, alone, beside her husband, sitting in the silence and drinking in the sight of him while he still at least had some breath left. Yes, she wanted this, but it was a bitter gift. This was no longer really Ben, this diminished shell in front of her. How unfair – that death should not only take him from her but also from her memories.

Except, she thought, listening to the hard-won wheezing of his chest, was it really so unfair? She at least had been allowed to say goodbye. Not like the Sizelas, whose last sight was of their son being beaten as he was loaded into the police van. Compared to them, Anna was lucky – she'd been given the chance to bear witness to the ending of Ben's life.

I'm lucky, she had told herself, wondering why she didn't feel lucky as she stretched out to stroke Ben's cheek.

His eyes blinked open. She saw them bleary, white, unfocused, as if a gossamer film had overcoated his pupils, and then he blinked again and he was Ben, returned to himself, smiling at her and reaching out for her to help him up.

She heard his voice. 'Anna?' It startled her.

She shook herself. Of course. She was no longer by his bed but in the car, with Ben demanding fiercely: 'Why didn't you wake me?'

What could she say? That she hadn't woken him because she didn't want to, because she wanted him for herself? No. She couldn't say that. 'You were tired,' she said. 'You needed sleep.'

'I have more than enough time in which to sleep,' he said, and opened the door.

As Anna and Ben moved into the house, murmured words of welcome accompanied their halting advance. Ben had little strength. He walked only a few steps before slumping against her, so suddenly that she might have fallen if she'd had to bear his weight alone, but eager hands stretched out to help her, to support not only Ben but her as well, and when they reached the living room a large African woman rose regally from the sofa to guide the now heavily breathing Ben into the place she had vacated.

The room was packed with people seated on every available surface or standing up or drifting through the room handing out cakes and cold drinks and cups of tea. In the midst of all this activity, however, there was a part of the room, over there by the wall, that was utterly becalmed. There sat Mrs Sizela, a line of women beside her, all of them on the floor, blankets round their shoulders, sitting silent, staring ahead but with unseeing eyes. When Anna went up to her and knelt down and took Mrs Sizela's hands in hers, Mrs Sizela did not even seem to see her. Anna sat a moment, holding on to the other woman, imbibing with her touch this grief that would never end.

She was not a woman who easily cried: nevertheless, there were tears in her eyes when she got up. She went back to the sofa, back to her husband.

James Sizela was next to Ben.

'The document the pathologist found with Steve's body was a page from the detention book that had been torn out at the time and wrapped in plastic to preserve it,' Ben was telling James. 'Sarah is overseeing its authentication. A necessary step for the courts although it is almost certainly a genuine document.'

'But why?' This from James. 'Why would Muller bury evidence with my son?'

Ben shrugged. 'Maybe he didn't. Maybe he got someone else to bury Steve and they, for their own reasons, included the paper. This we'll probably never understand.'

James looked across to where his wife was sitting.

'It's not important,' Ben said. 'What matters is that Muller is exposed. Really exposed. If you still want us to proceed, that is?'

James nodded. 'Of course. You must proceed.' He glanced quickly again at his wife, who sat, unmoving, and then looked just as quickly away. 'We both want you to.'

'Muller has chosen the same lawyer as Hendricks,' Ben said, 'which might have delayed matters, so I asked Sarah to speak with the amnesty panel. She has done this and they have agreed that given today's discovery, tomorrow morning's hearing will be suspended so that we can attend court.'

'Only the morning?'

'It will more than likely be enough,' Ben said. 'The judge anticipates, as do I, that Muller's lawyer will argue for more time to prepare his case. We must expect an early adjournment.'

Another nod. 'We are patient. We can wait. We have waited. All we ever wanted is to be able to bury our son. And to find out how he died.'

38

THEY CAME FOR him in the early morning.

It was what he would have done and so he was expecting them.

He was in the hatchery when he heard their car backfiring in the moment before they switched off the engine. He heard the shunt of car doors opening and, by the synchronised crunch of their hard shoes on the gravel, he knew they were policemen. He put the chick he was holding back into the incubator, shushed an inquisitive silkie out of the way, and went outside.

There were only the two of them, both uniformed – one a warrant officer and one a captain. They had turned off the gravel path and were about to make their way round to the front of the house. Both Africans. Of course. He should have known they'd send Africans for him.

'Can I help you?' he said.

They stopped – abruptly – and turned to face him. 'Mr Muller?' the captain said. 'Mr Pieter Muller?'

'The same.'

'We have some questions we would like to put to you.'

Pieter nodded, and saying 'This way', wheeled round.

Even with his back to them, he could feel their hesitation. He took no notice but, rather, continued to put distance between himself and them. If they chose not to follow, he thought, well, then, that was their business.

He was almost by the kitchen before he heard them setting off after him. He opened the door and held it open as they came round the corner, indicating with a shake of his head that they should go through. By the antipathy on their faces he knew they thought he was bringing them this way through the house because of the colour of their skins. Not that he cared: if they were too green to know that every visitor to the Muller household (including old PW himself, if he had ever chosen to come calling) entered via the kitchen, then that was their problem.

'This way,' he said again, leading them through the kitchen.

He was almost by the study door when something, some slight sound, prompted him to look down to the corridor's end. He saw Marie standing there: she must have just come out of the bedroom. He could see her quite clearly, so he knew she must also have been able to see him, but she did nothing to acknowledge the dipping of his head: rather she continued to stand, apparently unsurprised at the sight of two uniformed policemen in her house.

He thought: had she also been expecting them?

It certainly looked that way. Not for the first time, he wondered who her informant was and what their motives could

be for giving his wife a blow-by-blow account of everything
that occurred. He set the thought aside. It was for later.

And for now?

'Go in,' he said, following them when they complied and
closing the door behind him as he said: 'Please. Take a seat.'

Like the well-trained policemen that they were, they waited
for him first to seat himself. When that was done, the captain
drew up a chair opposite while the warrant officer placed
himself at an angle, pulling his notebook from his top pocket.

'How can I help you?' he said.

'You must have heard that Mr Steve Sizela's body was found
at Ryder's yesterday?' the captain said.

'I heard that a body was exhumed. I didn't know it was
Sizela's.'

'His parents have identified him by his effects,' the captain
said. 'We are awaiting confirmatory dental records, but there's
not much doubt it's him.'

'I see.'

'We have therefore opened a murder docket. We will, of
course, await the results of the autopsy before we proceed further, but this interview constitutes part of our preliminary
investigation.'

'I see,' Pieter said again, looking at his watch. They had
timed their visit nicely. It was only one hour to go before he
was due in court.

'What do you know about Mr Sizela's death, Mr Muller?'
The captain said.

'Nothing.' Pieter listened to the warrant officer's pen
scratching against the paper, ponderously inscribing that one
word: *nothing*.

'You were not his interrogating officer?'

'You asked me about his death,' Pieter said.

The captain looked up, sharply. So sharply that Pieter wondered whether there could be something he didn't know. But

no – the captain just said mildly, 'Did you know that the police station records for that time have gone missing?'

Pieter nodded. 'Yes. I knew that.'

'I see,' the captain said, and then, quickly changing tack, 'Tell me this, Mr Muller. Mr Sizela's family searched for him after he disappeared. How it is possible then that he was buried as unclaimed?'

'I am neither the coroner nor the investigating officer,' Pieter said. 'Surely it is for them to decide what happened.'

They were taking down what he said, word for word, the captain making sure that Pieter knew this by waiting until his warrant officer had finished his transcription and only then continuing. 'We are grateful for your cooperation, Mr Muller,' he said, 'but I have another question. In May 1985, when Mr Sizela's parents asked about the whereabouts of their son, they were told he had been released from custody and had left the country. Why was that?'

'I can't tell you. I never spoke to the Sizelas. I never told them any such thing.'

'But you were Mr Sizela's arresting officer?'

'I was present at his arrest.'

'And you were also his interrogator,' the captain said, in such a way that Pieter heard immediately that this was no longer a question, but rather a statement.

Danger. He was immediately alert. 'I'm sorry? What did you say?'

The captain repeated it. 'You were his interrogator,' he said. 'We know this for sure, Mr Muller, because buried with Steve Sizela's body was a page, now authenticated, which had been torn out from the police records of that time. It states, quite plainly, that interrogation of Steve Sizela was assigned to you.'

A page. From the police records.

So that's how it was. He'd been betrayed.

He didn't panic. He sat quite still. A page. His betrayer had

buried it with Sizela, wrapping it so that the years would not
wipe out what had been done. His betrayer: he knew exactly
who. He had not thought of this and yet he wasn't surprised.
Had he always known, somewhere, that it would come to
this?

'I'll ask you again, Mr Muller,' the captain was saying. 'Were
you Mr Sizela's interrogating officer?'

'Yes.' See how easy it was finally to say it. 'I had a hand in
his interrogation.'

'But you know nothing about his death?'

Shaking his head, Pieter sighed.

'We'll come back to that,' the captain said. 'In the meantime, Mr Muller, are you saying that you know nothing about
the burial of Mr Sizela?'

'It stands to reason, man. If I'd been the one to bury him, I
would hardly have included a document that implicated me,
would I?'

'I cannot say what you would or wouldn't have done,' the
captain said, 'but I'm now going to repeat the question I asked
at the beginning of this interview. Tell me if it is unclear, Mr
Muller.' He stopped and paused a moment, waiting for his
warrant officer to catch up before saying, loudly, 'Mr Muller,
do you know anything about Mr Steve Sizela's death?'

'I'm sorry, Captain. I can't help you.'

'I see.' The captain looked at the warrant officer who, reading the look correctly, shut his notebook. 'Thank you for your
cooperation, Mr Muller,' the captain said, at the same time as
he got up from his chair and walked towards the door. 'We'll
let you get on with your morning.'

Standing in the driveway Pieter watched their car reversing.
As it slowed down by the gate, he smiled at the memory of
that parting sentence: 'We'll let you get on with your morning.' Since the captain knew full well what everybody, even

Marie knew, that Pieter was due in court that morning, the message was clear. They had been given their instructions and they were now serving him notice: they were going after him. Not that Pieter held this against the captain. The man was only doing his job – and he had done it competently enough. He'd been professional, dispassionate and not too heavy-handed – just the way Pieter would once have prided himself on interviewing a suspect.

He stood and looked some more, watching as the car turned and moved through the gates and down the path, disappearing from sight. For a moment it felt to him as if he were watching a part of himself disappear. He thought: there only ever was one job for me – their job.

It had been like that almost as far back as he could remember. Other men joined up for many reasons – Dirk, for example, because it was expected of him – but not Pieter. For him the police service had always been his passion. Whenever he was asked what he wanted to be when he grew up his answer, that he was going to be a policeman, had never changed. As soon as it was feasible, soon after matric, he'd carried his resolution through.

All his expectations could so easily have been disappointed, but they weren't. He liked the job almost until the last. He liked most things about it – the hours, the variety, the mystery, the feeling of being at one with your fellow-policeman, that sense of making order out of chaos. In fact, the only other place he felt as much at home as he had in the police station was when he was alone with his bantams, but even they could not compete with that satisfaction he used to get of a job well done.

If only . . . he thought.

The thought triggered a memory.

How old had he been? Five? Six? He couldn't have been much bigger. He was too small, even, to manage the last stretch of the steep climb. His father had to get hold of him and carry him up that teetering rock face, placing him down eventually on its outcrop.

When his father let go, Pieter had looked down to find himself poised at the very edge of a rock that fell away steeply, far down into a deep gorge. At first all he felt was fear. But then his father had got hold of him again and Pieter had stopped worrying and concentrated instead on following the direction of his father's pointing finger, looking towards those sparse-leafed trees that had sprouted out at a seemingly impossible forty-five degrees, or at an eagle sweeping suddenly and then soaring up on a current of hot air, or there, further down the gully, at the density of foliage watered even in the driest months from a source nobody had ever been able to trace. It was so quiet that he could clearly hear the rise and fall of his father's voice conjuring up an image of what their country must have been like when all this was uninhabited: a mammoth landscape before it was scarred by man, the way their forefathers must once have seen it. And then there had been silence and they both had sat, drinking in the sight, until his father had sighed and said, 'If only . . .'

There was something in his father's inflection that had made Pieter ask a question he would normally have suppressed. He could hear it now again, issuing from the past, his own clear boy's voice, echoing his father's words and hearing them echoed by the rock face and returning back to him: 'If only what?' he had asked.

But the moment of intimacy had already passed. His father's face had closed down. 'Come.' His father had pulled him back up the rock. 'We must leave before it gets too dark.'

And now, Pieter thought, it was also growing dark. Metaphorically dark. Standing in the driveway, the adult Pieter realised why he had remembered that incident so clearly. It was because it had been the last carefree moment of his childhood. After that, his father's accumulating debts had forced them off the land, dragging his father deeper into silence. And now, poised on the brink of another precipice and remembering back, the grown-up Pieter thought that his father had been right: there was no point and never time in life for games of 'if only'.

There was no time for anything, Pieter thought, except the endgame.

No, that wasn't quite true. Not quite yet.

39

SMITSRIVIER NO LONGER needed any tutorial in court procedure. When the clerk said, 'Silence in court,' the silence was immediate: when he added; 'Please rise,' he was wasting his breath because the occupants of the overflowing courthouse got to their feet the moment the door to the judge's chambers opened.

The small courtroom, sited in one corner of the police station, was a space made pompous by a centrepiece of ornately carved mahogany that delineated its three official sections – the prisoner's dock, the judge's lectern and the witness stand. In comparison to such grandeur, everything else looked somewhat tawdry – the plain tables to the left and right behind which the defence and prosecution sat, the frayed green rope that separated the actors from their audience, and the narrow benches that ran along the back, overcrowded now with as many spectators as could be safely squeezed in.

Sarah was on the left next to the Sizelas. To their right, Dirk Hendricks's advocate Hannie Bester had placed himself at an angle so that he was blocking the view of his new client, Pieter Muller. Not that anyone could possibly have missed Muller's entrance. He had left it to the last minute and then he had come in by choice through the public entrance, a wide, confident figure, who strode bullishly down the aisle that separated the two halves of the audience before unhooking the rope and using those huge hands to replace it lazily and finally going to sit down beside his lawyer. By the silence that greeted his arrival, Sarah guessed he had no friends among the audience.

She had been so caught up thinking about Muller that she lost concentration. Now, at the sound of the mallet hitting rubber and the clearing of the judge's throat, she got up quickly. 'I'm sorry, Your Honour,' she said. 'I wasn't aware you were waiting. My name is Sarah Barcant. I am acting as junior for my principal, Advocate Ben Hoffman, who is currently indisposed. Our clients, Mr and Mrs Sizela, are suing Mr Pieter Muller for damages incurred by the disappearance and death of their son, Steve Sizela, in 1985.'

The judge nodded. Sarah sat down. In perfect synchronicity with Hannie Bester, who, rising slowly, straightened his bow tie and said, 'Your Honour, I am Hannie Bester appearing for Mr Pieter Muller, who is seated here on my right.' He turned, gracefully, indicating his client, a solid, determined figure of a man with his ginger hair neat against his broad, reddened face.

'Thank you, Mr Bester,' the judge said, expecting Bester to copy Sarah's movement and also sit down.

But Hannie Bester did not comply. He said, 'May I remind Your Honour that this case has been put forward with very little warning. My client in fact was only served with notice less than one week ago. For this reason, we have been unable to put in writing our application that this case be . . .'

Adjourned, Sarah thought, completing Bester's sentence for him. Ben had guessed right. She began gathering up her papers.

But Hannie Bester didn't say adjourned. He said, '. . . that this case be suspended.'

Suspended? What was that supposed to mean?

'This application for immediate suspension of this private prosecution,' Hannie Bester said, 'is made in accordance with Act number 34 of 1995 – the Promotion of National Unity and Reconciliation Act . . .' the act that had set up the Truth Commission, '. . . section 19, subsection 6 . . .'

It was a short Act and Sarah found the relevant section easily enough. Reading through, she also kept half an ear out, listening to Hannie Bester.

'If I may summarise this clause,' she heard him saying, 'it was written to cover a case such as ours when an act or omission, which is the subject of an amnesty application, becomes the ground of any claim in civil proceedings. The clause stipulates that in such a case the court may choose to suspend those proceedings pending the consideration and disposal of the application.'

Setting her papers aside, Sarah began to rise.

But Bester wasn't yet finished. 'I'm sure I do not have to remind Your Honour that the constitutionality of this clause has already been considered in case number 17 of 1996 by the Constitutional Court in the case of the Azanian People's Organisation and others versus the President of the Republic of South Africa. The court's finding was to uphold the constitutionality of this section on the grounds that the epilogue of the new constitution sanctioned the limitation on the rights of access to court.'

She waited this time until Bester had reseated himself and then she said, 'Your Honour. If I may?'

'Carry on, Miss Barcant.'

She got up. 'I'm sure that Mr Bester knows that section 19 is only relevant if the accused has applied for amnesty under section 18. Since Mr Muller has refused to submit such an application, I cannot see the point of Mr Bester's submission for suspension.'

Almost before she was back down, Hannie Bester was on his feet. 'I must apologise to my learned friend for not having kept her fully informed, but pressure of time . . .' he said – letting the sentence hang before completing it – 'I would like to inform her now that Mr Muller has in fact made such an application . . .'

The words flashed across Sarah's consciousness. That Pieter Muller, who had held out so long, should now apply for amnesty! She let her gaze flick across the courtroom, seeing her incredulity reflected in the expressions of the audience. Only very few in the courthouse succeeded in hiding their response – the judge, professionally trained to do so; Pieter Muller sitting erect, face forward and set in neutral as if he were on a parade ground; and James Sizela who, in contrast to his wife openly displaying a dissolving mixture of grief and relief, sat as erect as Pieter Muller, his whole demeanour the mirror of the other man's impassivity.

'I submitted Mr Muller's application for amnesty this early morning,' she heard Hannie Bester saying. 'Once again, I apologise to my learned friend for not having informed her, but in the light of the speed at which this court case followed the injunction served on my client, I had no other choice.'

James Sizela suddenly leaned forward. 'He cannot do this,' he said, in a clear, loud voice. 'He cannot.'

'I've taken the precaution of making copies of my client's application,' Hannie Bester continued, as if James's outburst had never happened, 'which, with my client's permission, I now put forward in evidence,' holding up a set of papers, which the clerk of the court took first to the judge, who looked briefly at it, and then carried over to Sarah.

Application for amnesty in terms of section 18 of the Promotion of National Unity and Reconciliation Act, 1995, she read. She glanced down the page. The details were all neatly typed in:

> *Surname: Muller*
> *First names in full: Pieter*

followed by the other fragments of information that are used to describe a man's life – his address, identity number, date and place of birth, his employment history and then, over the page under the section headed, *Particulars of the Act*:

> *Act: Death of Steve Sizela.*
> *Date: May 1985.*
> *Place: Ryder's Farm.*

40

As THE FORMALITY of the courtroom dissolved, James continued to sit. His eyes were focused on the document that Sarah had put down on the table. *Act*, he read, *Death of Steve Sizela*.

Act? Is this all the killing of his son signified? Just an act in the continuing play of Muller's life? Is that all it meant to Muller?

Muller, this man who was sitting there across the aisle, proud of himself and the way he'd pulled the rug from underneath them. Muller – whom James wasn't yet ready to face. He looked down again, looking at the next category: *Date*.

Date: May 1985, as bland as that. A month, *May*, a year,

1985. No time, no day, as if the act and the place were knowledge enough, as if it made no difference what day, what hour,
what second after they had arrested Steve they had killed
him.

James blinked. The words kept dancing down there on the
paper as he tried to focus on the final line of the trinity of this
amateur detective's report. *Place*, he read. *Place: Ryder's Farm.*
Not so much a farm, more an abandoned farmhouse deliberately remote so that there would be no witnesses to Steve's
death.

The text had blurred completely. Lifting his head, James
looked to his left. It was very crowded. As soon as the judge
had left the courtroom, the dividing line between protagonist
and spectator had been breached. The aisle was now packed
with women come to lend support, lawyers exchanging
schedules, members of the community celebrating the fact
that Muller had been forced to apply to the Commission; and
over there, across the aisle, detached from all that clamour as
if it had nothing to do with him, Muller, alone at his table, as
was James, but much, much calmer, as if this – his coming to
court to do what he had sworn he would never do and apply
for amnesty for the murder of James's son – was an everyday
occurrence.

Except, of course, as far as Muller was concerned, it wasn't
a murder that he'd committed. James looked down again at the
application, looking to that first page. *Section 1.a.iv: Nature and
Particulars*. He stared at the words that he knew must have
been typed in there. They made no sense to him. No matter
how hard he continued to stare at them, they kept on dancing
and blurring, the story about the way Steve had launched himself at the wall in front of Muller, hitting his head so hard that
he had never recovered. It was another version of those lies
about young men all over the country who were supposed to
have thrown themselves out of fifth-floor windows or at stone

walls, those men who had fought so hard for a new life and yet, when it came down to it, had chosen death.

'They're starting the hearing.'

What? Tearing his gaze from Muller's application, James looked up to find Sarah Barcant standing by the table and saying, gently, when she caught his eyes, 'Since we're all in town, the amnesty committee has decided to continue with the hearing. I have to go.'

James was silent.

'Your wife wants to come,' Sarah said. 'Is that what you would also like to do?'

'No.' James shook his head.

'Are you sure?'

'Yes, Miss Barcant, I am sure,' James said. 'I have work to do.'

She stood a moment, frowning as if she couldn't believe that he had work, but she didn't contradict him. She just said, 'I'll come and see you later to discuss our next move,' and walked away.

James concentrated on the sight of Pieter Muller, rising from his seat, putting away his papers into the black plastic folder that he anchored down under one arm, then turning and moving through the courtroom, slowly and deliberately and without a pause, because the few onlookers that remained parted silently to let through this thickset, strong, bullish man and in his wake they let pass James as well, the two of them walking, one after the other through the exit and into the light.

On Main Street, a dog-owner shouted an instruction at his schnauzer to leave off barking at a terrified street sweeper, while a kombi took off in a cloud of dust and a drunk tottered crookedly off the pavement, oblivious to the furious burst of car horns. None of this mattered to James, following twenty metres behind Pieter Muller, both of them walking through the dust and the grime, deliberately, as if they were on their way to the hearing.

But the hearing was for neither man.

While James watched, Muller stood silent in front of the town hall, watching as Dirk Hendricks was unloaded from the back of a police van, before walking away, around the corner and to his Mercedes, getting in and driving off. James remained rooted to the ground in the middle of the road, staring at the car's retreating back as it moved slowly down the long straight road, gaining speed as it left the town's perimeter behind, until it was at first a blur and then a speck and then a vanishing speck.

It's over, James thought, but he knew it wasn't over. He retraced his steps to the police station where the school's battered van had been parked. It had been full when they arrived. Now James got into it alone and drove away, out of town and back to school.

The phone was ringing when he reached the school. He could hear its distant pealing as he crossed the courtyard. He knew that all the teachers would be busy in class, that there would be no one to answer but he didn't hurry. Whoever was ringing could wait.

James pushed open the iron door and then walked slowly down the corridor. The sound of the phone was much louder as James stopped by the office door and took out his keys from his jacket pocket, pulling them out carefully so as not to strain the jacket's tweed. Choosing the right one from the bunch, he inserted it into the lock, turned and pushed open the door and went in, and all that time the phone kept ringing.

Even now he didn't hurry. He walked behind his desk, pulled out his chair, sat down in it, laid the keys in front of him and only then picked up the phone. 'Sizela,' he said, just as he always did, as he always had.

He heard a voice pronouncing his name. 'Mr Sizela.' He knew that voice, just as he had known he would. It was Pieter Muller's voice – his son's murderer's voice – saying calmly in that guttural way: 'I think you must come and see me at the farm, Mr Sizela.'

41

SARAH MOVED APPARENTLY effortlessly from court case to Commission hearing. She clicked on the microphone. 'Your name please?'

The plump man opposite anchored one of his fleshy hands around the other in a vain attempt to stop both shaking and said: 'Jackson Mbulelo Thulo, sir.'

'You were a police officer, based in Smitsrivier in 1985?'

'That's right, sir, madam.' Thulo was so nervous that, watching him, Alex thought he could even hear Thulo's teeth chattering.

'What was your rank?'

'I was a warrant officer, madam. Until 1990.' Thulo glanced anxiously across at Alex.

Alex met the look. He felt nothing – no onrush of the unexpected, no memory suppressed, no anger. It was difficult for him even to concentrate on what the ex-policeman was saying. Instead, he sat there trying to figure out the meaning of the encounter that he had witnessed in front of the town hall between Pieter Muller and Dirk Hendricks.

'And your current profession?' Sarah said.

Was it possible, Alex thought, that Muller had somehow set up the rendezvous?

'I am presently unemployed, sir,' he heard Jackson Thulo's distant voice saying.

No, Alex shook his head: Muller couldn't have arranged it. Dirk Hendricks was a prisoner and Muller a man without friends or influence left in town: there was no way either of them could have persuaded anybody to let Dirk Hendricks out of the police van at the exact moment when Muller happened to be passing by.

'I have not been able to work since I left the police force.' Jackson Thulo's tongue flicked anxiously over fleshy lips.

Alex looked on, listening vaguely to what Thulo had to say, but at the same time, caught up in re-enacting in his mind that encounter between those two old friends.

'I suffer from stress,' Thulo said.

One detail continued to gnaw at Alex – the reason why Pieter Muller had chosen to park his car in the vicinity of the town hall. It made no sense. Muller knew that the courtroom was blocks away on Main Street and he had also known what Alex could never have predicted – that the court case would be so rapidly suspended. It would therefore have been much better for him to have arranged himself a speedy getaway by parking his car behind the police station, for example, or down one of the many, empty side streets nearby.

'I have a doctor's letter that says this is true.'

But Muller had done the opposite, Alex thought: he'd left his Mercedes far away so that to reach it he had to pass by the town hall. Having done that, he didn't bother hurrying from the court. When the judge suspended the case, it was Muller's lawyer who rushed away, not Muller. He'd stayed to scan some documents that Alex could not believe were relevant, and then, only after a good ten minutes, had he lazily joined the crowd trooping down the road, transferring itself from one hearing to the next. He was easy to spot – his ginger hair standing out in that mass of black – as he walked down a crowded pavement, utterly alone as if there was some invisible force around him keeping everyone at bay.

'Mr Thulo,' Sarah was saying, 'did you at any time in 1985 have anything to do with my client, Mr Mpondo?'

Alex thought: of course. It was the lawyer – Bester – representing both men who must have organised that roadside meeting. Mystery solved. Shaking himself into the present, Alex tried to concentrate on what was happening on stage.

'Yes, sir.' Although Thulo now had his hands under control, one of his legs was jittering uncontrollably. 'I did. I attended the prisoner, Mr Hendricks.' He looked round bewildered as a wave of laughter greeted that statement, frowned and tried to get himself back on track. 'The prisoner,' and then, at last realising what he'd done wrong, he corrected himself quickly, 'I'm sorry, sir, I mean the prisoner, Mr Mpondo.'

'You attended Mr Mpondo?' Sarah said. 'What exactly does that mean?'

'I removed his trousers.' His voice was quaking, in sync with legs and, catching Alex's eyes, he looked away.

But Alex had no recollection of this man, no images of his cracked lips or his quivering hands. Nothing.

'Who ordered you to remove his trousers?'

'Dirk Hendricks, sir.'

Alex had to hand it to Hannie Bester: the encounter had certainly been elegantly choreographed. For just as Muller reached the town-hall steps the doors had opened and Dirk Hendricks had stepped out.

'And why did you obey this order?'

'I had to, sir. I was a warrant officer. He was my superior.'

Superior, Alex heard and realised suddenly that it wasn't only the coincidence of the meeting that had disturbed him but the nature of the exchange. But why? He couldn't quite put his finger on it.

He thought back to the look. That's all it was: a look. No words, just that one, lingering look. Standing to one side Alex had watched in fascination at the sight of Dirk Hendricks towering over the squat strong Pieter Muller, eyes only for each other as something, some emotion he could not quite decipher, had passed between them. Was it anger? No. He shook his head. It wasn't anger. Pity? From Pieter to Dirk or the other way round? No again: it wasn't pity either. A look of comprehension then?

'If I hadn't did what he ordered, sir, I would have been in great trouble,' Jackson Thulo said.

Yes, possibly, comprehension. But of what?

'Did you know why Mr Hendricks ordered this?'

Looking up, Alex looked over at Dirk Hendricks. Dirk was sitting motionless: he didn't appear to be listening either. He was staring straight ahead as distracted as Alex, staring unfocused into the far distance, unaware of Alex's scrutiny, his features set . . . in pain? In sorrow?

Sorrow. That was it.

The look the two men had exchanged had been full of sorrow. Alex turned abruptly, staring down at the line-up in the front row, seeing Steve's mother in her usual place at the front row and next to her . . .

No James.

No James. Shit. Grabbing a pen, Alex wrote on a scrap of paper: 'I'm sorry. I have to go,' and then, shoving the paper in front of Sarah, he didn't give her time to react but got up, quickly, to his feet and left.

42

W<small>HEN</small> J<small>AMES</small> <small>TURNED</small> into the driveway he saw that Pieter Muller was waiting at the other end. At first, Muller was only a distant figure, but as the kombi got closer to him, he enlarged, his details etching in, his heavy work boots planted wide apart on the gravel, his muscled arms folded over his barrel chest, his stout neck supporting his harsh, expressionless face.

'I'm glad you could make it,' he said as James drew up.

Strange, James thought, as he climbed stiffly from the kombi, how the conventions of ordinary life persevere no matter what the circumstances: that Muller, whose face displayed neither pleasure nor any emotion at all, should, of all the options available to him, have decided to choose 'glad'.

'Come into the house.' Muller walked away, over to a side door.

A kitchen. That's the sight that greeted James. A normal, everyday, farmhouse kitchen. Muller kept going, out of the kitchen and down a corridor. James followed, his gaze fixed on those fine ginger hairs that sprouted like moss from that corrugated skin.

The room into which Muller led him was a study. A shaded, manly, comfortable place plainly furnished with framed pictures lined up on the wall and with an unobtrusive Milner safe. Everything in its proper place, the way James also liked it.

'Since this is business,' Muller said, 'let us talk at the desk.'

As he went to the desk, it occurred to James that he and Muller had much in common. They were both men of the old school, bound together by the deed that the one had committed against the other: both men whose lives had led them along a trajectory that could not now be changed and had now brought them to this place, this study to sit opposite each other, looking across the polished surface of Muller's desk, with Muller's gun lying there between them.

The gun. James had spotted it as soon as he crossed the threshold. It was unmissable, lying in plain view on the desk as if it had been placed there precisely so that James would see it. Lying as if in preparation.

In preparation for what?

'It's a .22,' Muller said, sitting down and reaching out to caress the gun's barrel. 'The best. Other arms manufacturers may have copied its polymer frame, but I still stand by the Glock. Try it.' He nudged it with his hands, pushing it a fraction nearer to James. 'See how right it feels.'

No, James thought: Muller and I are not alike. Not at all.

Lifting his eyes off the gun he looked across the desk, straight into Muller's eyes and said: 'What do you want from me?'

'What do you want from me?' Marie heard.

She was standing in the garden outside her husband's study, against the wall and slightly to the left of the window so that if, for any reason, one of the men decided to get up and look out, she would still be hidden.

What do you want from me? she heard, and thought: but what am I doing here?

She'd never eavesdropped on her husband, had never even thought of doing so. Pieter was a private man who guarded his secrets well. She had always respected that in him: throughout the many years they'd shared, she had never pried. Just as her mother had ruled over the household, leaving her husband free to negotiate the world, so Marie had done. She had liked it that way; she and Pieter had both liked it.

'Why ask me to come out here?' she heard James Sizela saying.

Waiting out her husband's reply, Marie thought about those times when Pieter had needed something different from her. She would see it in the set of his brow when he came home, in his distraction over the dining-room table, in the increasingly long hours he spent in the hen house. And although she was not a boastful woman, Marie got quiet satisfaction from knowing that she had always found a way of giving to him the comfort that he required. Not through words, which had never been their custom, but in other ways – by making him comfortable perhaps, or cooking him something extra special, or just sitting with him, she in her rocking chair, he at his desk, keeping him company during his time of trouble.

'Me?' she heard her husband saying. 'Why would I want something from you?'

Now Marie leaned heavily on her stick, thinking how stupid she had been.

'Why would I want something from you?' Pieter Muller said, and then he smiled.

It wasn't quite a smile, more a calculated tweaking of those grim lips. The sight made James wonder: did Muller smile like this with Steve? Was this my son's last sight on earth?

'I want nothing,' Muller was deadly calm, the gun lying casually within his grasp. He looked down at it, deliberately, and then up again at James, looking almost kindly as if James was a colleague or a friend. 'I want nothing,' he repeated. 'But I will give you what you want. I will tell you about Steve.'

That's all it took – that naming of James's son as if Muller and Steve had once been intimates. It came on James then, a rage so intense that his impulse was to reach out, pick up the gun and fire it, straight at the heart of his son's murderer, and watch the recognition of what he had done show itself in Muller's eyes, and see Muller's body twitch and slump forward as his lifeblood drained away.

The image was so powerful that it took all James's concentration to say: 'Why tell me now?'

Had Muller guessed what James was thinking? And if he hadn't guessed, how come he looked down at the gun again, and up again, and how come he smiled that way, challenging James, daring him to take the risk, to go for the gun and try it?

Has Muller brought me here to kill me too? James thought. Surely not? James blinked. 'I'll be there when you apply for amnesty,' he said. 'I will hear what you have to say then.'

Muller smiled. Briefly, this time, and almost sadly. 'But we both know, don't we, Mr Sizela, that the last thing spoken at the Truth Commission is the truth?'

'. . . the truth,' Marie heard and hearing the menace in her husband's voice thought surely not? Surely Pieter would not have picked up the phone to summon James Sizela to their house, their home, in order to kill him?

She registered the thought quite simply: without surprise. The fact that it would even cross her mind was a mark of how far she had travelled in the past few days. She thought: what is it I know now that I didn't know before?

That her husband was capable of killing perhaps? Yes, that was part of it. By his application for amnesty he had admitted that he had killed a man, not in self-defence but in cold blood, a man who was most likely shackled and who was certainly in his power. That she had so quickly accepted and absorbed this knowledge, showed how wanton had been her ignorance before. She, Pieter Muller's wife, along with all their friends and their numerous acquaintances, had played that selfsame, blindfolded game, deluding herself into thinking that nothing was amiss, or, if it was, it had nothing to do with her. She'd gone on with her life, leaving Pieter to do the dirty work.

How foolish of me she thought, although foolish wasn't the right word. Not foolish then, but something else. Culpable? Yes. That was better. Culpable and stupid beyond measure.

Well, no longer. That time had gone. She stood, backed up against her house.

'The Truth Commission is like a ritual cleansing,' she heard her husband saying, 'with all the pomp and ceremony rituals demand – and all the simplifications. You and I: we're alike, we're not interested in make-believe.'

'Then break the mould,' the headmaster said. 'Go to the hearing. Speak the truth.'

'Oh I will,' Pieter said. 'Don't worry. But let me tell you first. In private.'

She didn't want to listen any more: she wanted to walk away. And yet her past blindness meant she now wouldn't, couldn't, allow herself this one indulgence. Turning away was what she had always done before.

James sat, unmoving.

'Let me tell you about your son,' he heard.

He felt himself strangely detached, hearing not only Muller's voice but another's running counterpoint, that secret, silent voice urging James to get up, turn his back, leave. He didn't listen to that inner voice: he wouldn't. He continued to sit quite still.

'Your son was a coward,' Pieter Muller said.

'A coward?' Was that his own voice, saying that?

'A weakling. Who begged for mercy before I'd even touched him.'

It came again. A stranger's question. 'Why did you kill him then?'

There, across the desk, Pieter Muller reached out for his gun. 'You don't think I did it on purpose, do you?' stroking the plasticated snout. 'Why would I bother?' He spun the gun, suddenly, and it whirled round, inscribing a rapid circle, only gradually slowing down until it came to a stop, its barrel facing James. 'Steve wasn't worth that effort,' he said, letting go of the gun.

Had James imagined it, or was the weapon closer than it had been before?

'He wasn't the brightest of boys, was he?' Pieter Muller said. 'I found that out when I interrogated him. I soon realised he knew very little.'

The voice seemed disembodied from that hand lying on the desktop, its index finger twitching. Its trigger finger.

'My job was to find out what he didn't think he knew,' the voice said, 'that small detail that would pin down the bigger fish, Alex Mpondo.'

James's own hand was on the table now as well. Pieter Muller's wry lifting of his lips – that smile again, devoid of humour – drew James's attention to this. Take the hand away, the internal voice said, he's provoking you to draw.

He left the hand lying where it was . . . inches from the gun

'Steve's death was an oversight,' Pieter said. 'I did it by mistake. It was my hand that knocked his head against the wall, that knocked his brains out. He was, as they say, soft in the head.'

That pile of bones, that's all James could remember of his son – Muller was wiping all the other images away.

'But let's face it,' Pieter Muller said, 'I did it for you.'

For me? James thought, his thought echoing round the room as his tongue spoke out his thoughts: 'For me?'

'For you,' Pieter Muller confirmed, 'and for every father who ever produced such a worthless son. He talked about you, you know. At the last. He babbled, on and on, *jirra*, it was enough to send me to sleep, his endless complaints about his unforgiving father. He kept telling me, as if I would care, about the day you turned your back on him because he chose to go to a meeting rather than to church. He said you wouldn't speak to him – not for the two weeks that followed. He couldn't get over that. He called you the father who preached but would not listened. *Jirra*, he wouldn't stop snivelling. He kept on saying that if only you'd listened to him, if only you'd talked to him, he would never have got into this mess. His whining voice played hell with my nerves. I hit him extra hard for that.'

Muller's hand had moved again. Almost imperceptibly, but James saw the movement clearly.

'And now,' Pieter Muller said, 'I'm going to do what you asked of me and break the trend. I'm going to tell the truth to the Truth Commission.'

The gun, James thought.

'I'll tell them everything just as I have told you but with more detail. I'll describe your son and the pain he underwent. I'll tell them what he told me about you as well. I'll make you listen, not only you, but his mother as well . . .'

In that moment, James did not stop to think. When Muller's hand moved, so did his. Launching himself forward, he lunged for the gun.

43

ALEX HEARD A shot. A single shot rupturing the stillness of the day, followed by an outburst of panicked barking. He was at the bottom of the drive, by the gate. He pressed his foot down, hard down on the accelerator, and raced the car to the house, switching off the engine and getting out almost before its wheels had stopped spinning on the gravel, running for the mesh door, wrenching it open and going inside.

And stopped. He was standing in an ordinary, deserted kitchen and the dogs were no longer barking. The sound that now rent the air was a kind of keening, an eerie high-pitched sound. He stirred himself into action, going through the kitchen, down a hallway and to a doorway.

And stopped again. He could see three people: James

Sizela, slumped in a chair, Pieter Muller sprawled across a desk and a woman standing by Muller.

He said, making sure that not a muscle moved: 'Put the gun down.'

The woman – she must be Muller's wife – started, and for a beat she did nothing but look at him. He kept his eyes fixed on her and slowly raised his arms, palms facing, in a gesture both of surrender and at the same time of reassurance. She had been holding the gun loosely in her right hand but now, seeing his arms moving up, she lifted it and pointed it at his heart, her expression hard, determined. Had she killed the two men and was now going for him? He took an involuntary step back.

The thing he least expected happened. The woman dropped her hand, her fingers slackening, so that the gun fell on to the threadbare carpet. The sound acted as his trigger. He was upon her in a moment, kicking the weapon away. She dropped her head, doing nothing. Just standing – so mute, so despairing, that he knew she no longer posed any threat.

He turned to the men. Maybe he could help them. He saw immediately that Muller was the one in trouble: not James. James didn't move but James was breathing. Alex put two fingers flat down on Muller's neck feeling for a pulse.

There was nothing. Alex pulled at Muller, straining against the other's weight, that dead weight, to pull him back, turning him sufficiently to see a gaping bloody wound in the centre of his chest.

Stretching across the desk to pick up the phone, Alex said, to no one in particular: 'What happened?'

For the first time since Alex had arrived, James Sizela raised his head. Although he looked at Alex it wasn't clear that he knew who Alex was. He opened his mouth.

'My husband killed himself,' the woman said.

'No.' James shook his head.

'My husband killed himself,' the woman said loudly. 'He was a crack shot and a strong man – nobody else could have done this to him.'

'Please. Mrs Muller,' James said.

But the woman's voice was much louder and much more resolute than James's. For the third time she insisted, 'My husband killed himself,' her fierce eyes locked on James Sizela. 'I saw it with my own eyes, and if anybody says differently, I will brand them a liar. I will not rest. I will tell what it is I saw. My husband locked up his dogs so they would not be here, brought in Mr Sizela to witness his end, and then he shot himself through the heart.'

There was no need for any siren – Pieter Muller was indubitably dead – and yet as they moved away, the men in the ambulance chose to turn one on.

Standing at the top of the driveway, watching the high-topped vehicle jolting down the dirt track, Alex knew its wailing would soon be heard not only in Smitsrivier but throughout the surrounding countryside. An appropriately dramatic gesture, he thought, that the ambulance should choose to broadcast the final passage of Pieter Muller's body into the town that had abandoned him.

Perhaps that's why Marie Muller had chosen to accompany the body – in defiance of the town. Or perhaps she had just wanted to keep out of the way until the police had gone. Alex could understand that. From what he'd witnessed of it, the police investigation bordered on farce. Why else would they have let James Sizela's monosyllabic answers pass without comment before letting him go home? And why else would they have put the gun away without fingerprinting it?

But then, Alex thought, compared to all the other many acts of violence the police encountered, this one must seem a very simple death. An obvious death: boxed into a corner by

the Truth Commission, Pieter Muller had decided to take his
own life and then, to make absolutely sure, had arranged to
do so with his wife and James Sizela for witnesses.

Had Pieter Muller guessed it would come to this? That
apart from his wife and maybe James, no one else would
really care?

'You can go,' he heard.

Startled, he turned to find a policeman standing by the
door and saying: 'There's no need to stay. Their domestic
worker is already busy washing away the blood.'

44

JAMES TOOK ONLY what was his, packing it into the box he had carried into school specifically for the purpose. It amounted to very little – some photographs, a handful of personal letters and a few precious books – all of them together barely filling half the box. To a stranger's eye it might seem a meagre testimonial to a lifetime's dedication. To James, though, the endorsement of his work resided not in the objects attached to it, but how his pupils chose to live out their lives. That's all that mattered, that they should become good citizens.

And that's why he had to go. He could no longer foster those principles of probity, morality, integrity that were essential for the proper development of any individual. Not after what he had done.

It was time for somebody else to take over. And James was in no doubt that, however difficult the search, the right person would eventually be found. In the meantime, he would keep a vigilant, if slightly distant eye, on the process, ensuring that it was correctly carried through. It was time for him to move over.

His drawers were empty now save for those items that were standard school issue. He placed the chair at the centre of the desk and left it there for whoever was going to take his place.

It was so small, this office, that had once been the centre of his life. He stood looking round, thinking that, for all the mistakes he had inevitably made, he had also done some good. An epitaph to the end of a working life: no man could ask for more than that. He left the room then, shutting the door behind him without a backward glance, walking down the empty corridor, locking and unlocking each of the succession of metal doors, walking with a measured pace, his back as straight as it had ever been.

The last door clanged shut behind him. He locked it and then went to the gate and, walking through, locked that as well, dropping the keys into his jacket pocket and thinking that he would hand them to his deputy on his way home.

Home. It was time. Home to his wife where, together, they would begin to mourn their son.

For the second time in as many days, Alex turned off the tar and began driving along the dirt turn-off that led to Muller's farm. This time, in contrast to the last, he was driving slowly when he reached the gateway to see a cortège of cars parked, nose to tail, on the turning circle by the house. Marie Muller has visitors, he thought: I shouldn't go on, I won't be welcome.

Nevertheless, after only a moment's hesitation, the same unfinished business that had brought him to the gateway now propelled him up the length of the drive. Reaching its end, he parked his car behind the others and got out.

He stood on the gravel driveway wondering what to do next. He knew that one way in was through the kitchen, the same route he had used the day before. It was the way he, and every other black man, would always have gone in the past and, for all he knew, also the way that the Mullers themselves would enter. And yet now, to go in that way without ceremony and to walk past the domestic staff who were in there clinking plates and cups, felt suddenly both too subordinate and, at the same time, too intimate.

He turned away from the kitchen and walked round to the front of the house, heading for the main entrance.

He walked slowly, dragging his feet, trying to get a feel for the place before he entered it. He passed what looked like a games room and then an empty bedroom and then, just after that, he came abreast of a room in which Marie Muller's visitors had gathered. It was a small room overlooking the garden, a room in sombre shade, packed with people. Standing in the harsh desert light, he looked in.

He saw a dominee, leaning down to talk to Marie, who was sitting quietly, dressed in black. She wasn't the only one. Although the post-mortem was still to come and the funeral accordingly delayed, the occupants of the room were all soberly dressed and oddly old-fashioned. As Marie Muller got up and walked out of vision, he saw other high-necked black frocks, black bonnets, sharp black suits, almost like a throwback to another era, like something from the Great Trek, he thought, listening to the low murmuring of voices, the hushed exchange of condolence, the intake of understanding breath – the intimacy telling him what he already knew, that he was an intruder and that he must go, before anyone spotted him.

He turned away.

And heard a voice he instantly recognised calling his name: 'Mr Mpondo.'

He turned back and saw that Marie Muller had left the room and come to stand in the open front doorway. She was using a carved walking stick for support and when she saw him looking, she took one hesitant step forward before stopping and leaning on it.

'It is difficult for me to come to you,' she said. 'If you wouldn't mind . . .'

He hurried over until he was standing opposite her.

'Thank you.'

Now that he was so close to her, Alex thought that his only other sighting of Pieter Muller's wife had not revealed who she really was. What he'd seen before, on the day Pieter died, was someone galvanised by shock and by her own strange determination. Now, standing at the bottom of the porch, he saw a different woman, a woman whose pale green eyes protruded from a face that was deathly pale and lined by melancholy. This is crazy, Alex thought, what am I doing here? This is not the time.

'You came to ask me something?' It was more a statement than a question and her eyes latched on to him, commanding him to answer.

'Why did you tell me that your husband killed himself?'

She drew herself straighter. 'He did,' she said. 'Pieter shot himself.'

Her voice was loud, brash, defiant, but this made no difference. She could talk as loudly, and as long, as she wanted, and still Alex, who knew enough about weapons and wounds, would know that she was lying. Pieter Muller could not have killed himself.

And yet: what did it matter? Pieter Muller was dead. If his wife wanted to falsify his end, if she had picked up the gun so that her fingerprints would obscure James Sizela's, if she stopped James from speaking out the truth, then that was her business. All Alex needed to do was say: 'I'm sorry for intruding on your grief, Mrs Muller,' and turn away.

Which is just what he did.

Once again, Marie Muller's voice tugged at him. 'Pieter may not have fired that gun himself,' she said.

Reluctantly, he half-twisted round.

'But he killed himself as surely as if it was his hand on the trigger.'

Half-turned towards the woman, half-turning away, Alex stood. Quite still.

'I was outside the study,' Marie Muller said. 'I heard exactly what was going on and I knew what my husband was doing. He was deliberately enraging the headmaster to the point that Mr Sizela would try and shoot him. Pieter's job did that to him, you see. It gave him a dim view of human beings: it made him believe that any man, if sufficiently provoked, would be gripped by an impulse to kill.'

'You mean he was planning to grab the gun himself when James Sizela went for it?'

Marie Muller shook her head. 'No,' she said, shaking it again. 'Not that.'

'Then what?'

'There's two things you must know about my husband,' she said. 'One: he would never have gone to the Truth Commission, and two: he would never have gone to jail.'

It made sense. It was the kind of thing people in the townships also said of Muller.

'But he was a good man,' Marie continued. 'He was worried about me. He was worried I wouldn't be able to manage without him. His wish was to see me provided for. He wanted me to be free to cash in his life insurance.'

Which, of course, she couldn't do if he had killed himself.

'But you insisted that it was suicide. You chose to deny

him the chance to see you were provided for. Why? For a black man? For James Sizela?'

'I did not deny him anything,' Marie Muller said. 'Not really. What I did, I did for him.'

'For James?'

'No.' Marie Muller smiled, but sadly. 'Sizela means nothing to me. What I did, I did for Pieter. For his memory.' She wasn't looking at Alex any more: she was looking straight through him. 'When Pieter provoked Mr Sizela into shooting him, he was angry,' she said. 'I know what he was thinking. He was thinking that if he was going to die as he had to, he was also going to take revenge. He wanted to take James Sizela down with him and at the same time make sure I was provided for. I couldn't let that Pieter win.'

'That Pieter?'

Marie Muller blinked, refocusing her gaze on Alex. 'I know you, and your people.'

Your people, Alex heard.

'I know you think we are all the same. I don't blame you for that. But it isn't true. Of us. Or of Pieter. We are not all the same.' She blinked again. 'Probably you don't understand what I'm talking about. How can you? You never knew him as I did. You never knew what a good man he was.'

A good man, Alex thought, who killed Steve and then lied about it, who tried to lay his own death at Steve's father's door.

'The lie I told was in memory of that good man,' Marie said. 'The man Pieter had been. The man he might have been.'

Alex drove away down the dirt road and on to the asphalt. He was driving very fast but then he lifted his pressure off the accelerator. As the car slowed down, the image that came to rest with him was of Marie's pale, drawn face and her strained smile. There was something about the way she had looked at him that continued to grate. What was it, he thought, that he'd seen written there in Marie's expression? Was it malevolence? Vengefulness? Triumph?

Triumph – that was it. But why?

Could it be, he thought, that Marie had told him only half of the truth? The more he thought about it, the more the idea made sense. That was it, he thought: what had pleased her about what she'd done was not that she'd saved her husband's reputation by cutting the loop and preventing James Sizela from being charged with manslaughter, but because she'd pulled it tighter. First Pieter Muller, by involving James in his final act, had taken the choice out of James's hand, and then his wife had gone further. She'd stood by and watched, without interrupting, as James had twisted in the agony of what Pieter had told him and then she had taken up the gun, and stopped James from being James, from telling the truth. She had kept James as her sort had always tried to keep him: securely in his place.

Is that, in the final analysis, what this was all about? Alex thought: image and control? A war of races, a war of supremacy had led them all to this place. But now the war was over and the Truth Commission was there to arbitrate the peace. And yet had Pieter Muller and now his wife refused to accept the terms of the settlement?

45

BEN WAS LYING in the dappled shade of his garden, stretched out on a mauve and white padded lounger. He was wrapped so thoroughly in a plaid blanket that the only part of him that was visible was his face, his eyes on Alex who was sitting close by, the two so concentrated on each other that Sarah might not have been there at all. 'Did you believe Mrs Muller?' Ben asked.

'Did I believe that Pieter Muller manipulated James into murdering him so she could claim the insurance?' Alex shrugged. 'Sure. But I could equally believe that he was trying to take James down with him or at least to show James that, given the right circumstances, anyone can turn killer. One thing I do know: his wife's version of Pieter Muller as a good man who strayed by accident on to the wrong side of morality is peculiar to her. Ask anybody in the township and they'll tell you what a monster Muller was. And so in the end,' Alex shrugged again, 'I don't think it matters why he did it.'

'Although Marie Muller's version does let James off the hook.'

'Yes. They've closed the case.' Alex lapsed into silence, his stillness matching Ben's.

Until that moment the sun had been partly obscured by a branch, but as it moved a fraction lower, its light blared. When that happened, Ben stretched out for a pair of sunglasses that were lying on the wicker table and quickly put them on. The glasses must surely have belonged to Anna. They were winged, emerald green and studded with fake diamonds – Anna had probably bought them from Sarah's father some time in the late fifties – and, with their flying edges that poked out sharply, they nudged up Ben's already bushy eyebrows, making him look utterly ridiculous. To stop herself from laughing, Sarah looked away.

The hot, still afternoon settled heavily around them. The two men kept their silence as Sarah's smile faded. She sat quietly, listening to the harsh cry of a distant hadeda and watching aimlessly as beads of condensation dripped down glasses filled with Anna's home-made iced lemonade until, eventually, Alex's voice summoned her back.

'If James had been tried for murder, he would never have been convicted.'

'Most probably.' Ben nodded. 'But he'd have hated being in the dock.'

'And worse than that, as far as James is concerned,' Alex grinned, 'he would have ended up a township hero – the man who rid them of Pieter Muller.'

Once again, silence. This time Sarah's gaze wandered

around the garden, past the roses wilting in the heat and the climbing jasmine, brilliant with its dainty white flowers and its overpowering scent – sweet and at the same time carrying a hint of corruption and decay – and coming full circle in time for Ben to say to Alex: 'What are you going to do?'

That's better, she thought. That's why she had brought Alex to Ben, so that Ben would talk some sense into him.

'I won't stay for the rest of the hearing,' Alex said, repeating what he'd already told her.

Well, if anybody could change his mind, it would be Ben.

'It was such a struggle to free myself from that man's clutches,' Alex continued. 'I won't be his victim again.'

One of Ben's eyebrows rose up above the diamanté rim. 'Do you think victimhood is a matter of choice?'

'In this case, yes.'

'But not always?'

'I don't know about always,' Alex said, 'but it is now. When I go to the hearing, I sit in the victim's seat. My lawyer,' he gestured at Sarah, 'is known as the victim's lawyer. If I want to go somewhere private during the hearing, to get away from the crowd, I must go to a place reserved for Truth Commission officials and for victims.' With each hit of that one word – victim – his voice rose. 'And when the Commission publishes its report, my name will be among the names of other victims.' As his voice rang out, he started, suddenly, as if he had only just registered how loud it was and when he spoke again, it was much more softly. 'I am not and I will not be, their victim,' he said. 'Steve is. I cannot fill his place.' He looked across at Ben. 'Don't you understand?'

In the moment suspended before Ben's reply Sarah thought that Alex, even if he didn't know it, was asking not for Ben's understanding but for his approval. Good, she thought: Ben was sure to withhold that.

'Yes,' Ben said. 'I understand.'

She started and leaned forward. What was he playing at? He never took the easy way out. Never.

Getting up, Alex offered Ben his hand. 'Thank you.'

Ben pulled a hand from under the blanket. Alex took hold of it and stood quietly holding on for what seemed like an age before he said: 'Goodbye, Chief.' In that frozen moment, seeing Ben's white hand contained in Alex's black one, Sarah thought that she hadn't brought Alex here. He had brought himself. He had come for the benediction that he had known the old man would give him.

Alex let go of Ben's hand. Without another word, with only a nod in Sarah's direction, he turned and walked away.

She didn't move to follow him: she sat listening to his footfalls recede.

'You don't approve?'

Startled, she turned to find Ben staring at her from behind the mask of those absurd sunglasses. He seemed to be frowning as he repeated the question. 'You don't approve?'

'No.' She moved her chair closer. 'I don't approve. We've gone so far: it's crazy to throw it all away.'

'And what exactly are we throwing away?'

'The gains we've made,' she said. 'Look what it took to get Dirk Hendricks to tell us where Steve's body was. You don't think he did that because you appealed to his sense of humanity, do you?' She gave a definitive shake of her head. 'I'm sure what you said had some impact, but in the final analysis what Hendricks wants is out of jail. He told us what we wanted to know because he knew we had him on the run.'

'On the run?' Ben smiled. 'To where exactly?'

Why was his smile so sad? 'To a kind of justice,' she said.

'But the Truth Commission is not about justice,' Ben said. 'It was never meant to be.'

'Well, then, what is it about?' All the frustration that had been building up in her seemed suddenly to surface and instead of waiting out Ben's reply, she furnished her own: 'Is it about truth?' She laughed out loud. 'Hardly. If the new rulers of South Africa think justice is complicated, well, they should know that the truth is even more elusive. So what else is there? Reconciliation? That's what the churchmen preach. Good for them, somebody has to. But I defy you to find reconciliation between the individuals either in this case or in a score of others. Oh, sure – there've been the usual heart-warming sentiments from the mouths of those wonderful old mamas, the ones who always bear the cost of this country. They're South Africa's speciality – they make the world feel good about its own humanity.'

'You've got it all wrong,' Ben said. 'The reconciliation the Commission talks about is not between individuals.'

'You're talking about a society-wide reconciliation then. Yes, well, perhaps the weight of hearings will help change perceptions but you only have to look at the crime statistics, or even what has happened in Smitsrivier since the hearing began, to know how long it's going to take.' Her voice rang out.

Ben waited for the sound of her anger to die away before saying, calmly, 'It is what it is.'

It is what it is? She could hardly believe her ears. *It is what it is* from Ben? He couldn't have chosen a more apt sentence to illustrate how fundamentally he had been changed. He would never have used words like that before. That's what had made him different – the fact that, unlike her father, or her mother, or scores of other ordinary white Smitsriviers, he had refused to accept *what is* but had instead argued and worked for what should be. And now? He was dying and that was his message to her: *It is what it is.*

'It could be so much more,' she said. 'We've found Steve's body. That's a start. But with Muller dead, the only way of finding out what actually happened to Steve is to continue pressurising Dirk Hendricks.'

Ben frowned. 'This is no longer about Steve. It's about Alex. He's man enough to know that.'

Man enough! That enraged her. How dare he? Didn't he understand that he owed her something more than this? Didn't he feel his responsibility for his pre-emptory summons or gratitude for the way she had dropped everything and come at his command? And she knew exactly why he'd called on her. He had wanted her, not only because he had wanted to see her again, but because he needed the kind of lawyer she was. He knew how carefully she prepared, how seriously she took her job. And now? Halfway through, just when she'd got the case in order, he was acting out on whim. The game had been played to his satisfaction: he was ready to discard it. Furious, she shot out: 'Is that all this was about? Men and what they know?'

'That's beneath you, Sarah.'

'Maybe,' she conceded, but then the rebelliousness rose up in her again. 'But don't you see? If we give up now, Dirk Hendricks will go scot-free.'

'No, he won't. He has lost his wife and his children: to lose the hope of such intimacy is a far greater punishment than any jail sentence.'

A greater punishment? Something in his tone told her that he wasn't only talking about Hendricks. About who else then? Her? Was he making a judgement about her and her lack of either husband or children? 'Ben?' she said.

But Ben kept going as if she hadn't spoken. 'Alex is scared that by naming Steve while he was in detention, he delivered a death sentence.'

'That's exactly why we should go on,' she protested, 'because we haven't established the timing. It's just as plausible that Steve was dead long before Alex talked.'

'Alex must be allowed to come to terms with his own sense of responsibility,' Ben said.

His responsibility, she thought: for Steve's death? Or for what he imagined was his part in Steve's death? 'Come on, Ben,' she said. 'This isn't like you. You can't take the case on in their terms. Whatever the timing. Alex did not kill Steve Sizela. Pieter Muller did. Which leaves Alex only with the reality that he broke under torture. How can there be any shame in that? Men like Hendricks were experts: they were trained to break their victims.'

Ben nodded. 'That, of course, is the rational truth,' and then he lapsed for a moment into silence as he lay there, the lens of his glasses so dark that she didn't even know whether his eyes were still open until he spoke again. 'The hearing will soon be over,' he said.

Conversation over, that what's the tone said clearly.

'Will you go back to New York?'

She knew how stubborn he was. There was no point in pressing him. She answered his question as honestly as she could: 'I don't know.'

He nodded again, his face quite serious as he turned, took off the glasses and held them as he looked at her. Waiting.

She couldn't read his expression. 'Why do I keep feeling that I've failed you?' she said.

'You haven't failed me, Sarah.' His gaze turned fierce. 'You've done wonderfully. You've fulfilled all of your brilliant potential and more. And you are so sure of yourself.'

Then he lapsed back into silence, smiling at her, still sadly but with so much love that she saw beyond this old man back to the Ben Hoffman she had first met: that vigorous, determined, passionate man who was also oh so wise, that man who had given her the world.

He put on Anna's glasses, suddenly, breaking the spell. 'And now you have one more duty. You must go and tell Dirk Hendricks's lawyer that we will drop the case, and then, if you are leaving, you must come and say goodbye.'

46

SARAH SAT AT one end of a table in the police station's airless interview room and looked across to where, opposite sat three of them lined up in a row. From left to right: Bester's slim, slight attorney, his glasses glinting as his hand moved across his notebook; Bester, with his starched white shirt, red braces, black bow tie and aroma of Old Spice; and, slightly separated from Bester and looking down in that way that made it impossible to tell whether he was even listening, the shadow of Dirk Hendricks.

'If you don't mind, Miss Barcant,' Bester said, 'so as to prevent any misunderstanding, my attorney will minute the meeting.'

'No,' Sarah said. 'I don't mind. Should I begin?'

Bester nodded.

She cleared her throat. 'My client, Alex Mpondo, will no longer participate in the hearing. We will not therefore be calling any further witnesses to the stand.'

'I see.' This from Bester.

'I won't be making a closing statement either,' Sarah said. 'I've informed the amnesty committee.'

He said it again. 'I see.'

'I have also suggested to them that the proceedings should be suspended. They say it's up to you – do you want to subject Jackson Thulo to cross?'

'I see no reason for that,' Bester shrugged. 'He said nothing of any import.'

Ignoring this point scoring, she continued. 'My feeling when I spoke to the committee was that, given the general state of unease in Smitsrivier, they will most likely agree to our suggestions that they suspend the hearing. I also believe that, given our side will no longer be arguing against amnesty, they will ask you and the Truth Commission lawyer to submit written closing arguments.'

'I'm sure the committee will be contacting me directly,' Bester said, and then, leaning forward, 'But tell me, Ms Barcant, why are you here?'

She frowned initially at the aggression underlining his words, but then modulated her response to say, mildly, 'Perhaps I didn't make it clear that I will no longer be opposing your client's application for amnesty?'

'You made it perfectly clear,' Bester said, 'but since we never needed the presence of either Alex Mpondo or your good self in order to proceed with our application, I don't see the relevance of this meeting.'

What could she say except the truth? 'I want to talk to Dirk,' she said.

To Dirk, who sat there, head bowed.

'As I'm sure you know,' she said, 'I already requested such a meeting this morning. My understanding is that it was refused by Mr Hendricks rather than the police. I wanted to ask him again – in your presence – to see if I could persuade him to change his mind. I'd be happy to talk in front of you.'

'In that case,' Bester said, 'and since you have involved me, I'd like to get the implications of your proposal absolutely clear. Is it conceivable that your client's decision to withdraw from the Commission proceedings would change if my client were to refuse this conversation with you?'

'No,' she said, thinking that if Alex had known she was coming here, he would have done everything he could to stop her. 'That is not the case.'

'I see.' Bester sighed. 'But I still fail to see the point.'

'All I'm asking for,' she said, quietly, warmly, trying to use the pitch of her voice to get Dirk Hendricks's attention, 'is a conversation.'

She had spoken out in vain: Hendricks continued to look down, while his lawyer said: 'Whether Dirk decides to meet with you or not,' – pushing back his chair – 'is entirely up to him,' – standing, looking down on her, smiling as he pulled his red braces into a gentle stretch. 'And now, if you don't mind, I'd like to talk to my client alone.'

She waited in the police station's garish ante-room for two hours. Two hours of watching the occasional drunk booked in, or a robbery reported, or a man speaking nervously as he paid his speeding fine. Ordinary Smitsrivier going about its ordinary business. Two hours to think about what Ben had said to her and what this place would be for her once Ben was gone.

And then, at last, she was shown into the same interview room where Dirk Hendricks was waiting there for her. Alone. Walking in, she wondered whether it was he who had caused the long delay. And if he had: was this because he genuinely could not make up his mind?

He was already seated and, hearing her come in, he looked up, briefly but without much interest. He looked small: disarmed, decharmed, no longer a man of force but just a prisoner with a prisoner's concerns, so that this time when she put down a pack of cigarettes, he took one out and lit it up immediately.

'Thank you for agreeing to talk to me,' she said.

He shrugged. Carelessly – her thanks meant nothing to him.

'There's something I would like to ask you.'

He shrugged again and, drawing in hard on the cigarette, blew out the smoke in one long stream.

'I want to know about the timing of Steve Sizela's death.'

'Why ask me,' he said, a question without a question mark – a monotone – a reluctant duty – followed by a dulled 'I didn't kill Sizela.'

'Because you know the answer,' she said.

His head drooped down.

She raised her voice. 'Come on, Dirk, this is important. Not for you or the outcome of your case, but still important. When did Steve die?'

He looked up suddenly, meeting her gaze. 'What kind of question is that?' He narrowed his eyes. 'You know when. In May. Like Pieter said in his application.'

There was a time, not so distant, when she had felt sorry for this man, and a time also when she had thought she detected his warmth. Not any longer. Now she saw him as Alex must have done, his hard, unfeeling interior, those eyes, no longer blue but grey. Cold grey. Ice grey. Death grey.

She shivered, but pressed on. 'I'm not interested in the day or the hour so much as in the sequence of events. I want to know whether Steve died before or after Alex Mpondo named him.'

'Why?' He was no longer the penitent: he was the aggressor. He said it again. 'Why?' defiant, in control, staring.

What could she tell him? That she wanted to know for Alex's sake? No – she certainly couldn't tell him that. 'I just want to know. For my own satisfaction.'

He smiled – blankly, not at her, but to himself – and looked away. She followed the direction of his gaze over to the unadorned cream wall. There was nothing special there, but he continued staring at it for a long time and in that time she thought that his expression no longer contained either the indifference or the hostility that had been previously evident, but something other, something deeper. Sadness? she thought. Grief?

He turned, abruptly, and caught her looking. He smiled again. 'You want to know? OK. I'll tell you. Alex Mpondo broke first. He pointed the finger at Sizela. He exposed his friend.' His voice was low, almost seductive as he went on. 'What Mpondo said made all the difference. It sealed Sizela's fate. Because, you see, when Mpondo told me about Sizela and I told Pieter, Pieter was enraged. Up till then Sizela had so convincingly protested his innocence that Pieter had even begun to believe that we might have picked up the wrong man. But now Mpondo had helped expose how far Sizela had taken Pieter in. Sizela had never mentioned Mpondo, you see – he protected his friend to the last. But now it was obvious they knew each other well. That infuriated Pieter. He was determined to crack Sizela. And . . .' Dirk shrugged, as if what happened next was obvious and then he put it into words: 'Pieter went too far and Sizela died.' He was smiling now. 'Your friend Mpondo,' he said, 'was responsible for Steve Sizela's death,' leaning back, relaxed, casual, 'and that's the truth of it.'

47

'KEEP GOING,' ALEX said.

It was the third time he'd said this and she was beginning to wonder whether he actually had a destination in mind or whether this was just his way of maintaining silence. She glanced at him but he, his eyes focused on the road ahead, didn't seem to notice her.

So she kept on driving down that one relentless road. It was one of Smitsrivier's perfect bright ringed, still summer days. Through her rear-view mirror she could see the empty road bleached white in the harsh glare of the sun: ahead it looked darker, this same tar road that stretched out all the way to those distant, shimmering blue mountains. Minutes passed and she kept driving until: 'It's left up there,' Alex said.

He was pointing to a narrow asphalt path that led off the main road and then wound its way up the mountain flank. She turned into it, slowing down as the asphalt petered out to dirt. This close up the mountainside was no longer blue but a sepia combination of caramel-brown earth and dusty ash-grey stones, broken up by a scattering of sparse green scrub and withered purple bushes. The track – which was all it really was – was so steep that she was driving in first and even so could hear the engine straining.

'It's somewhere round here.' Alex was peering out through the window. 'There,' he said, much louder, at the same time pointing at a patch of flat earth just big enough to contain the car. 'Pull in there.'

She nudged the car into the space and, switching off the engine, got out.

He was already on the move, climbing over a wire fence to head away from the track and up the last steep stretch of the mountain flank. Following, she found the going rough, the hard earth dry and littered with boulders while she, unsteady in her high heels, struggled to keep pace.

Hearing her stumbling, he turned to offer her a hand.

She kicked off her shoes and took the hand. She felt the solidity of his grasp and, as he pulled her up, a memory of their first touch returned to her. It had happened at the Sizela house when they shook hands. Then she'd felt a charge passing between them, a mixture of suspicion and attraction. And after that, there was the moment in her hotel when he had wanted to come in and she had used humour to turn him away. Without even noticing it, her feelings towards him had been changed. She felt a tenderness for him: a kind of longing.

She was blushing. And he, she thought, has he also changed?

He pulled again and, trusting herself to his grip, she thought instead about his enemies.

About Dirk Hendricks. The way Hendricks had looked at her. His complacency. *That's the truth of it*, he'd said, over and over again, three or four times, each time more assuredly than the last, as if her discomfort was helping fuel his sadistic glee. She had stood there, trying to meet his stare, thinking that the whole procedure – his initial refusal to see her, his lawyer, the wait she'd had to endure – were all part of a power play that he had organised. Now he was assured of amnesty, he'd become himself, a cruel man, who although he seemed to have shrugged off the impact of his friend Pieter's death, still could find the energy to be cruel to her.

'Not far now,' Alex said.

She kept going, thinking how odd it was that the distance she had travelled could almost be measured by the changes in her attitude to Hendricks and Muller. Initially, Hendricks had seemed the more reasonable of the two, prepared as he was to obey the rules of the new South Africa and therefore to embrace it. Not so his old friend Pieter Muller. On the contrary, Muller's stance had been absolute and uncompromising. He had chosen self-annihilation over reconciliation, and death in preference to any freedom bestowed upon him by his former enemies. A wicked choice, on the face of it, especially in the way he'd entangled James Sizela and yet, there was at least a kind of consistency and honesty in what he'd done. And who knows, Sarah thought, perhaps James will come out of this better?

'This is the place.'

Alex half-led, half-pulled her, to the top of the hill where the land suddenly fell away. It was stunning. An almost unearthly sight – a breathtaking vista spreading out to a range of grey-rimmed mountains far, far away, and in between a valley in which nestled the town of Smitsrivier, reduced by distance and the shimmering heat haze to a few indistinct rectangles.

'Come.'

Seeing Alex already sitting at the edge of a large rock out-crop, she went to join him. He moved to give her room. She settled down and for a while they sat, side by side, in silence. It was a silence the like of which could never penetrate the bustle of her New York life, where one case followed another, one person's tragedy acted out in court soon superseded by the next and she always at its centre, juggling their different needs, and always, always pressing on. She'd forgotten what it was like to do this: to just sit and think. Or to sit and not think.

'Steve brought me here,' Alex said. 'He loved it. He was a real country boy. Not like me – all I ever wanted was out.'

Just as I did, she thought.

'I'm sorry you never met Steve,' Alex said. 'He was so alive. So full of life. He loved the details: the feel of sand running through his toes, his body diving through cold water, this place, this view. He was a part of me: like a brother; a younger, daredevil, innocent, optimistic part.' He was talking softly. 'When Steve died that part of me died with him. James never understood that. He'll never know how I mourn his son.'

Mourn, she noted, not mourned.

'But then, of course,' Alex said, 'James can't understand because he's too busy blaming me for leading his son astray.' A hollow laugh. 'If only he knew the truth.'

She glanced at him, thinking she knew what was coming next, but impelled to ask it anyway: 'What truth?'

'That I was, that I am, responsible for Steve's death.'

'No,' she shook her head. Violently. 'How could you possibly be responsible?'

He shrugged. 'There's more than one way to bear responsibility. I might not have struck the blow, but what I said was as deadly as if I had. Through my words I sentenced Steve to death.'

'No.' She wouldn't have it. 'It's not true.'

He looked at her. Calmly. Without rancour. 'How can you say that?'

Had she known that it would come to this? Not consciously. But now it all seemed very clear. She had rarely ever felt so sure of anything. She said, without hesitation, looking straight at Alex: 'I know, because I went to see Dirk Hendricks. I asked him what happened.'

She couldn't read the expression on Alex's face, but she could feel his tension.

'Hendricks told me,' she continued. 'He told me that Steve was dead long before you ever named him.' She spoke confidently, her life sounded out into that vast landscape as she thought that this reassuring of Alex was much more important than the truth could ever be.

Alex looked away, out to the distance and towards the town.

She lifted her hand up to his cheek and held it there, against his stubble, against the softness of his skin. When he turned towards her, she didn't move away. For a long time, he continued to look at her and then finally he bent his head. She smiled, and then her hands went up, embracing him, pulling him down.

48

'Kом,' the policeman said. Just that one word, and nothing else. No goodbye. No regrets.

Well, no matter. That was the way Dirk would also have played it if their positions had been reversed and Dirk was the guard processing out one more in the long line of sinners that came and went, day in, day out, with the kind of monotonous regularity that could turn the most humane of men into a sceptic.

And the policeman was right. It was time to go. Dirk signed the register where indicated and walked out into the harsh daylight.

His Pretoria guards, in their jeans and their short-sleeved shirts stretched tight over their puffed-up biceps, were standing by the kombi, ready to effect the transfer. But Dirk wasn't ready to climb in – not yet. Although it was now almost certain that he would get amnesty for his Mpondo application, his other outstanding hearing meant that it might still be some time before he was out in the open again. He stopped and stood, breathing in the clean, dry air, drinking in the sight of the wilderness and beyond it, those stern enduring mountains.

'Come on. We have a plane to catch.'

Reluctantly he summoned back his gaze, back to earth and back, eventually to town, and when they opened the kombi door he moved towards it. But then he stopped for one last look.

It would be more than a long time before he came this way again. In fact, he thought, gazing down Main Street, it would be for ever. Smitsrivier no longer had any meaning for him. The truth was, it had never meant much apart from Pieter, and Pieter was gone.

Pieter Muller: a brave man who had engineered his own death rather than go to the Truth Commission. Pieter Muller: A fool.

Dirk had known it would end like this. Not from the beginning – never say that, never even think it – but from that moment when, standing by the town hall, he had looked into his old friend's eyes and seen death.

Death. It had started with Pieter – always with him – this Dirk had only just begun to understand. Back then, when he had resentfully dug the hole as Pieter had ordered him to and when he laid inside the remains of Steve Sizela, how could he have known that what he did would stretch far into the future to be ended only by Pieter's death? And if he could have known, did that mean that his betrayal had killed Pieter?

No. Dirk refused that option. He could not have known. Never say that. It wasn't his fault. His had been an impossible choice: either to tell them where Sizela was buried or else to allow himself to be buried in prison. How could anybody, even Pieter, have expected him to do anything other than he did?

And anyway. It was Pieter's fault. If Pieter had taken the trouble to dispose of his own bloody problems, all this would have turned out different. How could Pieter have let it happen in the first place? Why had he, usually so meticulous, suddenly been so careless? Foolish Pieter: killing a suspect by mistake.

What excuse had Pieter given for not burying the body himself? He couldn't quite remember. He knew it must have been something ordinary, something to do with Marie or a church function. That was always Pieter's way, pillar of the community, mainstay of the church, he had so much to keep him occupied back then. And he had rarely put a foot wrong. Never, in fact, except for that one time when he had made a mistake that had such terrible consequences. Not only killing Sizela but also dumping Dirk in the shit like that.

It was Pieter's fault that Dirk had ended up burying a piece of the custody record with the body. He had been angry with Pieter. Understandably so. And he had to take precautions. I mean, Christ, Pieter was so worried that somebody should find out what he'd done that he wouldn't even give Dirk a lookout. As a result, Pieter had left Dirk completely exposed. What if somebody had come upon him, there in the middle of the night, burying a corpse? Dirk had been in such a hurry that he couldn't be careful. The dirt had got everywhere, in his skin and in his clothes; he remembered how much Katie had complained about the way the red dust had clogged up the washing machine.

So Pieter shouldn't have done that and Dirk had been angry, yes. But he had got over it. He had never meant it to end like this. How could he have foreseen that, fourteen years down the line, just because he had torn a page out of the interrogation book and buried it with the body, Pieter would die?

He couldn't have. What happened afterwards was not his fault.

Pieter's death. It had started with Alex Mpondo. If Mpondo hadn't held out so long none of this would have happened. But Mpondo was obstinate.

What a terrible combination: Mpondo's ridiculous heroism (Dirk knew he'd break him in the end) and Pieter's ribbing of Dirk, during a drunken evening, about Dirk's failure to extract anything useful from the bastard. How was Dirk to know, when he proposed the bet that he and Pieter should compete to see which of them would be the first to break their prisoners, that it would end that way? It wasn't Dirk's fault. Pieter should have known better. He'd not had the same training or practice as Dirk had: he should never have accepted the wager.

But he had, and as a result things went out of control. Pieter went too far and Steve Sizela died. And in the end, Pieter had as well. Dirk was sorry for that. Pieter had been his friend. But it wasn't Dirk's fault.

The only consolation for this whole calamity was the look that had passed over Sarah Barcant's face when Dirk planted the seeds of his lie in her. What a fool she was. To have asked him, of all people, when exactly Sizela had died! What had she expected – that he would tell the truth? The truth that Mpondo only broke after Sizela's death? That Pieter was just clumsy? That it was an accident? How could Dirk have said any of that? Of course he couldn't. Not if he cared about Pieter.

But in a way Dirk was glad that Ms Barcant, as she liked to be called, had been stupid enough to tempt him with that question. You didn't get much pleasure in jail and it was great to see her confidence so dented. She was so certain of herself, that one, so sure that his answer would let her and her beloved Alex Mpondo off the hook. And when Dirk had dashed her expectations he had read it in her face – it was the first time that she, so cocksure in her own rightness and her own ability, had looked uncertain.

Let her now float on this unease. Let her pass it to Mpondo in his new life with his MP's salary and his friends in high places. Let him live with the knowledge that he had killed his friend. That would be his cross to bear, not Dirk's.

Because Dirk was not responsible. He had done what he had to, that was all. It was over now. It had to be. If he dwelt on it, it would drive him mad and that was an option he refused. He would no longer live in memory. It had happened – in the past – and there was nothing to be gained by harping on at it. The past was just that – the past: it could not be changed.

Pieter was gone. That was reality.

Now what Dirk had to do was to ensure that he kept on living, to hang on until he was free.

The vast brown landscape scrolled past as Alex put distance between himself and Smitsrivier. It was over. That's what he kept telling himself: over.

But not entirely.

He understood what Sarah had tried to do on the mountain before they had made love. She'd been trying to let him off the hook. He appreciated the effort and he liked her the more for her sudden naiveté: that she could think that, by a simple lie, she could so easily let him off the hook! He smiled at the memory of it. The fact that she'd assumed Alex would believe what she'd told him, showed just how long she'd been away. She'd forgotten what this place was like. She'd forgotten that the story with a beginning, a middle and its own neat ending, which was what she'd tried to give him, was something New York might offer, but not South Africa. There was too much history here, too much bad history, for that kind of completion: all that South Africa could aspire to was a general moving-on.

She was so smart and yet the one thing she didn't seem to get was the extent of the feeling that lay between Alex and his torturer. That's what coming back had taught Alex: how well he knew Dirk Hendricks, perhaps as well, better than he knew or would ever know any other human being.

He knew the man's twisted mind and how it worked. He knew what gave him pleasure. And in knowing Dirk Hendricks he also knew that even if the sequence of events had been exactly as Sarah had described them, if Steve had died before Alex named him, Hendricks would never admit to it. No matter the truth of what happened, Hendricks would have lied, most certainly said anything, to keep Alex on the hook.

So much for the Commission's packaged slogan: *The truth will set you free.*

The truth was never so easy to come by. With Muller dead, Alex would never know whether the things he had said, not only in pain but also in the anger of his conviction that Steve had betrayed him, had led to Steve's annihilation. But then, he thought, even with Muller alive he would most likely never have known anyway.

And yet, he thought, as he steered away from Smitsrivier, he didn't regret coming back. He had looked Dirk Hendricks in the eye. Perhaps that was a start.

Settling himself into his seat, he looked ahead. The long, straight road stretched out into the far distance. He pressed down on the accelerator and the landscape accelerated, its muted colours joining into one vast sage blur, passing him by.

He let it go. Keeping his foot on the gas, he thought of nothing in particular: he just drove.

'Sarah.' Opening his eyes, Ben raised himself up.

She took his hand. 'Yes.'

He rested back against his pillows. 'You're staying then?'

She nodded and then confirmed her nod in words: 'Yes. I'm staying. For a while at least.'

He breathed out.

As he relaxed, she felt his hand soften. Letting go of it, she settled herself back in her chair. She sat, quietly, thinking that although what she'd just told Ben wasn't a lie, it was also only half the truth. She would stay. A while. Longer than she'd first intended. But she knew she wouldn't be staying as long as he wanted her to.

He was so rarely wrong and yet he was this time. That she had run away from this place, and kept away so long, revealed to her what she had previously refused to acknowledge – that, try as she might to escape it, this country defined her. It would be with her no matter where she was. South Africa in its extravagance. She thought back on her arrival in Smitsrivier, remembering how alien the town had seemed then and how unreal. No longer. Now, looking through one window, she took in all the old familiarities, the brilliant light, the harsh, dry scent, the distant, lilting interchanges. The feeling of home.

It had once been home to her and yet now New York beckoned. She had a different life there, an ordinary life unmarked by the contours of heroism, sacrifice and guilt that were so much a piece of everything South African. Soon she would be going back. Of that she had no doubt.

Acknowledgements

Although Smitsrivier and its inhabitants are a fiction that exist only amongst these pages, the South African Truth and Reconciliation is a real event. Its amnesty hearings began in 1996 and continue to this day. But by bringing the Commission into Smitsrivier, I have taken liberties with certain of its rules, particularly with the cut-off-date for amnesty applications.

In researching the book, I was reliant on the kindness of strangers. Many thanks to Sandra Antrobus, Mike Antrobus, Brenda Goldblatt, Mike Loewe, Hilary Meyer, Ian Meyer, Brenmar Minnaar, Denise Minnaar, Ken Ross, Rose Ross and Alison Shultz for letting me into their lives and answering every question I threw their way. Thanks also to Frances

Bassom for her beginner's guide to the breeding of bantam hens and to John Carter of the New York District Attorney's office.

I am also indebted to Clare Alexander, Richard Beswick, Victoria Brittain, Andy Hine and Harvey Mollotch for their invaluable feedback and to Gavin Williams and Erica Platter for their attention to the language in the book. Many, many thanks to Robyn Slovo and to Sam North for their acute perceptions and enduring patience between drafts, and to Ronald Segal for his help that went way beyond the cause of friendship.

My enduring gratitude to Caradoc King for helping me, one memorable day on the beach, to find this book. For almost twenty years he has been an invaluable guide and friend. And thanks also, more than I can say, to my editor, Lennie Goodings, for her persistence, patience, keen eye and mind, and her continuing good humour in the face of excessive barracking.

Finally: thank you to Cassie for her good natured tolerance as Smitsrivier took over her dinner table and, as always, to Andy Metcalf for his sharp understanding, his invaluable contributions and his faith that one day it would have been worth it.

Other titles by Gillian Slovo

THE BETRAYAL

In the secret underworld of ANC activists, fierce loyalty is the code by which one lives – or dies. When the security forces discover an arms stash and kill a legendary freedom fighter, the whispers of betrayal begin.

This is the story of Alan, a white ANC member, who is suspected by his comrades of the unthinkable; of Rebecca, a black woman the ANC chose to judge him, whose own past holds a sad secret; and of Sarah, an English woman whose political curiosity and love for Alan throw her up against the secret police.

An unputdownable novel about power and passion, set in South Africa, the land from which Gillian Slovo and her family were exiled in 1964, *The Betrayal* is a remarkable achievement.

CATNAP

Who knows that Kate Baeier is back in London?

Who wants her gone – badly?

What is everyone – even her former sleuthing partner – hiding from her?

Still raw with grief over the death of Sam, her lover, Kate finds herself the target of inexplicable threats and then violence. Has her last abandoned case – its tendrils of corruption reaching from Hackney to Chelsea – come back to haunt her? Witty, dark and classy, this fast-moving thriller doesn't finish until the devastating truth is hounded down by the unstoppable Kate.

'Appealing and headstrong, Kate Baeier has a
nice line in self-deprecating wit' *The Times*

CLOSE CALL

WPC Janet Morris is in trouble – in her own police station – and even Kate Baeier is unable to help her.

Is it because WPC Morris can't call for help?

Or is it something even more sinister?

After five years abroad as a war reporter, interviewing Chief Superintendent Ellis for a personality piece should be straightforward for Kate Baeier. And it is. Until she hears of WPC Morris' alleged ape – in Ellis' station – and begins to ask questions. Evasions and silence quickly turn to threats as Kate, tenacious and sometimes reckless – pursues an increasingly terrifying collision course with the truth.

'Slovo combines adroit plotting with visceral thrills. Eminently satisfying' *Literary Review*

THE CURE FOR DEATH BY LIGHTNING

Gail Anderson-Dargatz

'I loved it from the first page, she's fluent and graceful and there's passion and tension, in fact all I want from a novel. The writing is so powerful and yet shows a restraint that tightens the whole atmosphere. An excellent read – I was gripped' Margaret Forster

The remote Turtle Valley in British Columbia is home to fifteen-year-old Beth Weeks and a community of eccentric but familiar characters. There, amidst a stunning landscape of purple swallows and green skies, strange and unsettling events occur: children go missing, a girl is mauled by a crazy bear and Beth too is being pursued. . .

The Cure for Death by Lightning is a rich and thrilling novel, as filled with strange deeds and dark fears as with beauty and magic.

Now you can order superb titles directly from Virago

☐ The Betrayal   Gillian Slovo   £6.99
☐ Catnap   Gillian Slovo   £6.99
☐ Close Call   Gillian Slovo   £5.99
☐ The Cure for Death by Lightning   Gail Anderson-Dargatz   £6.99

Please allow for postage and packing: **Free UK delivery.**
Europe: add 25% of retail price; Rest of World: 45% of retail price.

To order any of the above or any other Virago titles, please call our
credit card orderline or fill in this coupon and send/fax it to:

Virago, P.O. Box 121, Kettering, Northants NN14 4ZQ
Fax 01832 733076   Telephone 01832 737526
Email aspenhouse@FSBDial.co.uk

☐ I enclose a UK bank cheque made payable to Virago for £ . . . .
☐ Please charge £ . . . . . . to my Access, Visa, Delta, Switch Card No.

Expiry Date   ☐☐☐☐   Switch Issue No.   ☐☐

NAME (Block letters please) . . . .

ADDRESS . . . .

Postcode . . . . Telephone . . . .

Signature . . . .

Please allow 28 days for delivery within the UK. Offer subject to price and availability.

Please do not send any further mailings from companies carefully selected by Virago   ☐